WHERE
DARK
THINGS
GROW

WHERE DARK THINGS GROW

A NOVEL

ANDREW K. CLARK

COWBOY JAMBOREE PRESS
GOOD GRIT LIT.

Categories: Southern Literature / Southern Gothic / North Carolina Literature / Dark Literature / Magical Realism / Horror

Cover Design: Marcus Amaker
Interior Design: Adam Van Winkle
Author Photo: Parker J. Pfister

Cowboy Jamboree Press
good grit lit

www.cowboyjamboreemagazine.com/books

Praise for Andrew K. Clark and *Where Dark Things Grow*

In *Where Dark Things Grow*, Andrew Clark leads us, with a keen eye and an evocative voice, into the Appalachian Mountains during the Depression, and there we find the poverty we expect to see as it's experienced by the novel's central character, Leo, a teenage boy who soon discovers what we don't expect, a world filled with dark magic and powerful shadow creatures Leo thinks he can control in an effort to alleviate the hardships he and his family suffer. His naivety sets the stage for a battle between good and evil that's ultimately more ancient even than the mountains surrounding him. Clark's voice is as authentic as his imagination is vivid, and the mountains he writes about are uniquely his own.

–Marlin Barton, author of *Children of Dust*

If you're a fan of magical realism and Appalachian Gothic, Andrew K. Clark's *Where Dark Things Grow* is a must-read -- a high and haunting tale of highland lore that burns with forces both dark and light, rendered with a poet's eye for detail and wild sparks of wonder.

–Taylor Brown, author of *Rednecks* and *Gods of Howl Mountain*

Earthy, primal horror full of backwoods magic and poetry, *Where Dark Things Grow* is a terrific first showing by a lyrical new voice. Andrew K. Clark is one to watch!

–Andy Davidson, author of *The Hollow Kind*

This is Southern Gothic that blows the rockers right off that big Appalachian front porch. Andrew K. Clark has written a fierce narrative rife with an evil foreboding in the 1930s, North Carolina, Blue Ridge mountains. Prose that shimmers with the atmosphere of the darkest midnight hue. All Hail *Where Dark Things Grow*— a novel that burns with frozen blue horrors.

–Daren Dean, author of *Roads*, *This Vale of Tears*, and *The Black Harvest: A Novel of the American South*

Where Dark Things Grow is so richly colored it pulls you into the depths of Appalachia, and every shadow and sun ray will swing you through the spectrum of emotions right along with the characters that feel like our friends and family. Man, this book is so fuckin' good it made me plan a trip home to West Virginia so I could sit in a forest clearing and hope for some magic.

–Steven Dunn, author of *Potted Meat* and *Tannery Bay*

Andrew Clark's *Where Dark Things Grow*, is a page-turning epic of gothic adventure, full of wildly imagined creatures and black magic, propulsive, deeply felt, and wonderful. A marvel of a book.

–Tessa Fontaine, author of *The Red Grove* and *The Electric Woman*

Andrew K. Clark's *Where Dark Things Grow* shimmers in the atmospheric penumbra cast in this beautifully rendered and imaginative debut set against the tattered backdrop of 1930's rural Appalachia. Leo, the young protagonist battles family dysfunction, a landscape fraught with tormentors, folkloric beasts, and the dazzle of light and shadow.

–Robert Gwaltney, author of *The Cicada Tree* and Georgia Author of the Year

Where Dark Things Grow is alive, haunted, magical. All of that is so grounded in place, not just through the details that accrue, but in the particularity of the language that shapes the country and the characters. Leo and his harmed people, the surprises, the mysteries his actions uncover, are born up by Clark's masterful control of the word. Something absolutely alchemical happens in the telling.

–Geoff Herbach, author of *Cracking the Bell* and winner of the Minnesota Book Prize

With roots as deep and tangled as the Blue Man's trees, *Where Dark Things Grow* is a mesmerizing tale of magic and monsters, of family and fate, but also a reflection on the problem of power and the weight of abuses the most vulnerable carry, and how maybe we should be looking to the children to save us. A bold debut from a natural storyteller.

–Meagan Lucas, author of *Songbirds and Stray Dogs* and *Here in the Dark*

As haunting as all fireside stories should be. *Where Dark Things Grow* will make you sleep with the lights on.

–Jason Mott, winner of the National Book Award, and author of *Hell of a Book*

Where Dark Things Grow is a sweeping tale set in a fully realized world of faith, belief, myth, folklore and violence in the not so distant mountains of North Carolina, a world of rippling shadows and late-night journeys wrapped in darkness and the young and old who must survive and save each other at any cost. Andrew K. Clark boldly puts a name to the evil.

–Robert Olmstead author of *Coal Black Horse*

Stephen King meets Appalachia meets Flannery O'Connor's the Misfit.

–Leslie Pietrzyk, author of *Admit this to No One*

Where Dark Things Grow is a chilling, poetic debut. With gorgeous language and gothic ghosts, Andrew K. Clark will break your heart on one page and make your skin crawl on the next.

–Ivy Pochoda, author of *Sing Her Down*

Let me be plain – *Where Dark Things Grow* is full of magic, in the deepest, oldest sense of the word. At times endearing, at times brutal, but at all times haunting, Andrew K. Clark's debut novel is a spiraling tale in the greatest tradition of the Southern Gothic. Creeping out of the mythic and the monsters, the Old Testament revenge lines and the old world occult, is a tale of men and women, boys and girls, each at their most fallible, each being tempted and tested. This is not the sort of praise I throw around lightly, but it must be said- with *Where Dark Things Grow* Clark has made his mark in Appalachian literature.

–Steph Post, author of *Miraculum*

With a poet's tongue and fireside storyteller's spare style, Andrew Clark infuses his novel *Where Dark Things Grow* with a good, strong dose of timeless Carolina twilight. Like a combination of Ray Bradbury and William Faulkner, he tells an adventure tale of young people facing terrifying forces both real and unreal, of mountain magic and violence and man's evil, and a sense of menace older than the woods. *Where Dark Things Grow* is a book to read aloud, to savor, to ponder. It's not about haunted things, it is itself haunted.

–Polly Schattel, author of *Shadowdays* and Bram Stoker nominee

For Elijah, Abbey, Andrew, Nat, & River – The answers are in the trees.

Part I

Wherever there is light,
look for the shadow.
The shadow is me.
—Anais Nin

Andrew K. Clark

Prologue

Spring 1927

The big man walked the two women up the mountain through the woods, black sack hoods over their faces. His large hands gripped each by the shoulder as they came on. They knew not where they were going, but they knew who took them there. The last face they saw before the darkness: a broad fleshy skull with deep set green eyes, a face so wrinkled and drawn it resembled that of a troll from a child's fairytale book.

In the distance, a cluster of old trees, their dark trunks thick, their limbs full of vibrant black leaves. Beyond the trees, men rolled large rocks in place to finish the walls of an enormous structure at the edge of the mountain. The sound of hammers striking steel echoed through the woods, and in the ears of the women in sack cloth.

The big man stopped them in front of another wearing a dark blue suit, black tie, and many rings on each hand. The big man bore heavily down on the women's shoulders, forcing them to their knees. One of the women whimpered quietly; the other was silent.

The man in blue was shorter, but still quite tall, perhaps six feet. He had broad shoulders and wore a gray top hat. Dark eyes, almost black. He took off the hat and set it carefully on the forest floor. He straightened his tie and ran his fingers through his thick black hair, pushing it back out of his eyes.

"Let me to see them," he said, his deep voice a strange accent unknown to the women.

The big man pulled off the sacks. The women blinked their eyes against the bright spring sun.

The man in blue looked at each in turn. He held their faces in his black gloved hand, examined their hair, short and brown on one, long and blonde on the other. He forced their mouths open and looked at their teeth. Pulled at their tongues and ran his fingertips slowly over their pale bare necks.

"Quite hardy," he said, nodding to the big man, who grunted a response.

He took a knee in front of the women. "Fret not, my dearest beauties," he said. He opened his hands and a blue flame formed there in his palms. The girl with short hair gasped. The blue flame became a lovely painted butterfly before their eyes. It fluttered its wings, and the blonde girl smiled briefly before remembering her circumstance.

He stood the blonde girl up and slowly undressed her. Some of the men stopped their work to gaze upon her before he cut his dark eyes at them, and they quickly turned away. Harsh purple bruises marred her back and ribs and he traced them with his fingers as she winced. He slid a cotton yellow dress over her and cinched it in the front. He carefully painted her lips red.

When she was ready, he took both of her hands in his own.

He said, "It will hurt for a moment only."

He spun in circles with her, the way an adult might swing a child. Her feet left the ground, and they moved together for a moment before he released her into the air. The woman screamed and flew, back first, toward one of the large trees behind her.

The immense tree cracked violently open, curving its limbs as if to offer her a lover's embrace. The bark itself spread open, the grain of the tree as pink flesh inside. She disappeared into the trunk, and the bark closed around her body, her muffled cries audible only briefly, before silence.

The girl with short hair screamed and found her feet to run. The man in blue caught her quickly. He spun her body against his chest and released her toward a second tree. It spread open and quickly received her, then closed.

The man in blue walked over to his hat on the ground, retrieved it, returned it again to his head.

To the big man he said, "I am well pleased, but many will be needed. The trees are full of hunger."

Chapter 1

Late October 1931

She looked at him but did not see him. Her eyes through him somehow, to something beyond him, beyond everything.

She'd come out of the woods, just a flash of white in the trees. He'd tried to stay it but stopping an ax in mid-swing ain't easy. His body had twisted, and the ax head came down into the cool earth beside his boot. He'd looked up to see the widow, glowing in the low dusk light, waving a hand above her head. She wore a white shirt, dungarees, and her dead husband's cowboy hat.

The widow stood in front of him now, looking at him but not seeing him, leaning on her twisted wood cane.

"You got to knock off for the night, Leo, you done lost the light."

In the forming twilight, Leo had strained to see the logs he was splitting into kindling, whittling them down until they were small enough for the widow to carry in from her back porch to the stove inside. Several of his last swings had failed to strike the center of the grain, glancing off and pulling him to the side.

"Yes, ma'am," he said.

Leo stood with the handle in his calloused hands, the ax head resting on his boot. His muscles ached from the work, but in a good way. At fifteen, most folks said Leo was practically grown, ought to know the weight of a maul in his hands or that of a scythe for clearing fields. Indeed, Leo had long sinewy limbs formed for labor, though nothing felt better in his hand than a book. He was tall for his age, with copper eyes and hair the color of river sand. His hair grew darker each year, gradually washing away the white blond locks he'd had as a child, the tide raking the shells. He had tan skin, slightly darker than his siblings.

Leo stole a quick glance toward the woodshed. He heard Old Possum's feet shuffling in the dirt, thought he made out a face there in the shadows. Sometimes when Leo came to the widow's, the animal would curl around his feet like a cat. He and Missus Possum had babies back around the time the heat of summer broke. Old Possum would let Leo pet the baby possums, as the missus looked on, her face offering something akin to a grin. Leo could get near animals in a way other folks couldn't, pet on animals that normally hissed or growled. It had been this way as long as he could remember.

"Nobody ought keep working past dark," the widow said, looking into the trees for a long time as if expecting to find something there in the gathering gloom. "You ought to have stopped a while ago, looks like." The widow spit and wiped her mouth with the back of her hand.

The widow used to chop her own wood till she fell. She often recounted the story of how she broke her hip, how she had slipped off her back porch on a frosty morning, flailing like an insect on her back for what seemed like hours.

"I prayed to Christ Jesus," she'd said, "prayed he'd come down and show an old woman mercy. Help me get up off my back."

The idea that one could break a hip perplexed Leo. Breaking an arm or leg made sense; he knew a kid who broke his leg when he fell off a rope swing out over a creek and hit a big rock, but hips looked too stout to break, especially on the widow.

Leo loaded up the kindling in a wheelbarrow. He left the unfinished logs in a pile to tend to in the next day or so, depending on what chores Mama had around the house.

The widow's eyes fixed on the trees above them.

"Reckon you heard what happened to that Davis boy?"

"Yes, ma'am, I did," Leo answered.

"He was cutting a tree down near on dark, just over that ridge yonder. He was driving a wedge, but when he hit it with his maul, it flipped. It went plumb through his thigh."

16

Andrew K. Clark

Leo remembered the funeral, remembered how in life the boy's cheeks were always flushed, giving him the perpetual look of just having come in from the cold. How old had he been? He might have been a year ahead of Leo in school.

The widow spat again, her cheek poked full of snuff. "He bled out, right there in the woods."

A breeze stirred the leaves on the ground around them.

"Anybody heard tell from your daddy?" she asked.

"No, ma'am," Leo said. He looked at the ground.

"How long has he been gone this time?" she asked.

"Just a week," he said.

Leo himself went back and forth on whether Daddy was really missing or if he meant to be gone. How many times had he disappeared for days on end, only to show up with a sack full of groceries one morning, smiling like a Baptist preacher, as if nothing had happened?

"How's your mama?" the widow asked.

"She's all right, I reckon, she don't seem too worried about it."

Daddy disappearing wasn't anything special. He'd just fail to show up home from work one day and then a few days later word would get back to the holler that someone had seen him laid up in town somewhere, drunk. Town meant Altamont, which was the closest city to where the family lived, in the mountains of North Carolina. But seven days was a long time, even for Daddy.

"You best be getting home, boy," she said. "I got your money in my change purse. You come on up to the house now and bring me a load of that kindling. You might could make it a good ways home 'fore dark takes over."

"You ain't got to pay me."

The widow squinted. "I hired you to split wood, course I'll pay you your wage."

Leo had heard church folk say Christians should take care of widows, sick folk, and babies with no parents. He'd taken money from her plenty of times for chores, but he'd

17

meant to split the wood on charity. The widow had more money than most, everybody knew, but it was still the right thing to do. At least he should offer.

Leo stacked a load of kindling on the porch, and she pressed three quarters into his palm. He rolled them over in his fingers, feeling the weight of them.

"But I ain't even finished the cord yet. You don't need to pay me till I done all the work. Besides, this is too much." Leo looked at Lady Liberty holding a shield in one hand and what looked like flowers in the other.

The widow didn't answer. While he felt a bit guilty, Leo liked the way the coins felt in his pocket, thought of how the money would make Mama happy, especially if she could keep it hidden from Daddy. If Daddy ever came home.

"You takin' the road home or the trail up Dog Leg?" asked the widow.

Leo caught chill at the thought of taking Dog Leg Gap after dark. "I don't know," he said, "I ain't thought on it."

Taking Dog Leg Gap would mean being in the woods the whole way home, with no light except what the moon gave after dark. The dirt road home would be twice as long, but there would be the comfort of farmhouse lights along the way.

The widow rubbed her chin. "Whichever way you go, wherever you go in this world, Leo, don't ever forget that you got the good Lord Jesus to watch over you."

Leo nodded. His mouth formed a half-smile. Out at the tree line sunlight pushed through in its last stand.

"If you take Dog Leg, watch out for them wild boar hogs."

"Boar hogs?"

"Some of them got in my October beans the other night. Dug in my root cellar before that. I fired my shotgun to run them off, but I missed. Still, they came back. They're stubborn creatures, and you got to watch out for their tusks."

Leo had heard about the sounder of boars that had been making themselves a nuisance around the valley, but this was the closest they'd come to his neck of the woods. Somebody said they read in the paper that some rich Yankee son of a bitch bastard had brought them down south for hunting.

"They ain't like them domestic hogs that make for good eating," the widow said. "They're wiry and the meat is tough. Nothing like them farmer pigs that will roll over and let you rub their bellies when they're little baby pigs. They'd as soon gut you as look at you."

"Yes, ma'am," Leo said.

"You see them, just shimmy up a tree and let them pass," the widow said.

"I will," Leo said, his hands clammy.

The widow lowered her voice. "Some say it was them wild boar hogs what got a hold of that Davis boy."

"What now?"

"Something gnawed the meat off his bones after he died."

Leo tried to swallow, cotton mouthed.

"But people that's close to the Lord," the widow said, straightening her back, "they need not fear such things. If you got Jesus, son, ain't nothing to be scared of. The Bible says we ain't to be afraid. Fear is of the devil. Maybe that Davis boy wasn't right with God."

Leo nodded, looked down the dirt road.

"Old Warne," the widow said, "he said he seen a wolf around the time that Davis boy died."

Warne was the mailman. He delivered to folks around the valley, and the widow got more mail than most.

"Said he seen it running in the woods behind the trees," the widow said. "Swears it. I told him wolves ain't been seen around these mountains for many years. Told him it had to be a dog or a black bear."

The widow got a glint in her eye every time she talked about Old Warne. Sometimes she'd mumble to herself, "That Warne is a damn good-looking man" when she didn't think Leo could hear.

19

Leo looked at the widow, then to the trees. All this talk about wolves and wild boars was unnerving, but Leo was more worried about Mama's wrath if he lingered much longer.

She went on: "My daddy talked about them old gray wolves that would come down and get people's chickens, sometimes feeding on a baby goat or killing calves. Said he shot a few of them when he was a boy."

"We learned about them at the day school," Leo said. "There ain't none around here anymore. Just out west. We killed all ours off."

The widow took off her hat, turned it in her hands. Her hair was almost as white as her shirt. She returned the hat to her head and looked up into the mountains. "My mama always said there was things in the woods no man had ever seen. In the deepest darkest places, she said there was creatures people hadn't ever even heard tell of. Something about Old Warne seeing that wolf reminded me of the wulvers."

"Wulvers?"

The widow met Leo's eyes, her face animated.

"They roamed the old country, kept always to the highlands. These aren't like the wolves you seen in books, Leo, these were the ancient wulvers. They stand as high as a horse, and some say they can walk on two legs, just like a man, they take a notion."

Leo tried to brush off the image of huge wolves, walking on two legs. He reminded himself the widow often told tall tales when she wasn't talking about Jesus. Daddy always complained about the widow's *damned fool superstitions*. But then, Leo had seen things that weren't supposed to be real. Things that other people didn't seem to see, things worse than giant wolves.

"Some say they followed us here."

"Who?"

"The wulvers, Leo," the widow said. She was smiling as if on the verge of dropping the punchline to some joke. "Some

20

say wulvers crossed over from the old country to the mountains right here in North Carolina."

Leo shook his head. This was a bit much, even for the widow. "People say a lot of things."

"My mama said two wulvers used to wander these mountains." She looked up at the sky, raising her eyebrows. "Oh lord, it's almost dark! You better be on your way. And you still ain't decided which path to take."

Leo didn't want to leave. He didn't want to leave because he loved a good story, and also he dreaded the walk home.

"What else did your mama say about them wulvers?"

The widow looked around. She held her cane long ways in her hands, putting her weight on her good hip. She wobbled a bit, and Leo started, thinking to grab her if she began to fall.

"One so bright you can hardly bear to look at him straight on, some said, the Silver Wulver. He's as bright as a winter moon. The other is a ripple of shadows wrapped in darkness. They called him the Shadow Wulver." She took the cane and held it above her head, arching her back like a stiff old barn cat. "These were the tales that was told. Yet sometimes I wonder."

She pushed her cane into the dirt. "You got to go, your mama will skin you alive. Some other time." She shooed Leo with her hands as if he were a mutt dog perched on her favorite chair. She smiled, the creases at the corners of her mouth bearing deep brown tobacco lines. Her face grew serious. The smile disappeared.

"Leo, you watch out for them wild boar hogs."

Chapter 2

The sun cast orange on the horizon, daylight nearly gone. The light from the widow's house grew distant. Leo paused in the middle of the dirt road that wound between the mountains. He stared at the trail that veered up over the ridge and into the woods: Dog Leg Gap. He remembered something Daddy once said.

If you ever seen a monster, boy, best thing you can do is walk right up to it and look it in the eye. It don't do no good to run.

Daddy had held him by the shoulders, his thick fingers pressed so hard into Leo's skin they burned like hot pokers pulled from the fire. He shook Leo and asked:

If you seen a monster, what'll you do?

Leo hesitated, and Daddy slapped his face hard. Daddy had shaken him again, the whites of his wide-set eyes streaked with blood, the way they got when he'd been drinking.

Now I asked you a question. If you seen a monster, boy, what'll you do, goddamnit?

The taste of iron washed over Leo's tongue, Daddy's hot breath smelling of onions. Leo had wanted to grab the fire poker from the stove and shove it into Daddy's belly. Pictured it. Thought about how deep it would go before it struck bone.

"If I seen a monster, Daddy, I'll walk right up to him and look the son of a bitch dead in the eye," Leo said through his teeth.

That's good boy, that's good. I'll make a man out of you yet. I'll beat the soft right out of you.

To take the trail was to march right up to the monster, to look it in the eye, to say *I ain't afraid*. But Leo was afraid. He imagined wild animals along the trail. He pictured boars, the widow's giant wulvers running around on two legs. He thought about walking up on a she-bear with her cubs. People said a she-bear with cubs was the most dangerous animal in all the world. Leo wondered if a bear would lean into him, sense what was special about Leo, the way he had with

22

animals, the way Old Possum would. Maybe even the wild boars would stand pat and let Leo rub the whiskers on their faces.

Hearing the widow talk about boars made Leo think of Pastor Harmon's sermon about when Jesus cast demons out of an evil man into swine. Leo pictured the Biblical boars with white tusks and thick black whiskers, devil horns sprouting from their wide skulls, as Jesus ran them headlong into the water to drown.

For a moment, he was sure he would take the road, stay close to the light. But when the moon burst through a series of clouds, the world was bright and the trees lit, his courage returned. He sprinted up the bank onto the trail through Dog Leg Gap.

Once he was in the woods, he felt a chill at the base of his neck; a sense of being watched. In the tree limbs above, shadows stretched like dancing ghosts with long bony fingers, as clouds veiled the moon.

Leo held out his hands to pet the trees. They were old friends, and he loved the way the ridges of their bark felt under his fingertips. Sometimes Leo would put his forehead against the trunk of a tree as if he could feel the earth's heartbeat within. Many a night the trees had kept him on the right path when he could not see, and now they helped him keep his footing as his toes tested root and rock.

In his head, Mama grumbled about him being so late. But coming home late meant a good wage from the widow. He imagined Mama being pleased when he gave her the coins, if only she were the Mama she used to be. She'd pat him on the cheek, and give him a big hug, looking over her shoulder with disdain at his lazy brothers: Hank, a year older, and James, a year younger. They laid by the wood stove, as if the wood to feed it would chop itself. They didn't worry themselves, because they knew Leo would never let the wood pile get too low.

The fall moon looked warm, but cold air worked its way through his green coat. There was a place where the fabric was torn at the ribs, where the chill bit down most. Leo froze in place when clouds eclipsed the moonlight, painting the world around him an inky black. That's when he heard a sound off to his right: something moving through the leaves. When the moon peered back out again and the world was awash in cold light, Leo craned his neck, but heard nothing. He walked on, quickening his pace.

The noise came again. Something creeping slowly over the dry leaves, something big. Leo held steady, his heart lurching in his chest. He pictured the widow's wild demon swine with sharp tusks, working their noses, picking up his scent. They whispered to him as they did to Jesus:

I am Legion.

Leo imagined a pack of the beasts, maybe a dozen, shuffling along the slope toward him. He thought about running but froze and held his breath instead. He reached in his pocket to grip his pocketknife. He ran his thumb over the wood grain on one side of the handle, and where the wood was missing on the other side, the metal was cold and slick as glass.

Whatever it was, it was silent now. He retraced his steps in his head. How far had he come? Could he go back now and take the dirt road home? Going back to the road would put him home so late he'd catch the switch. He pressed ahead on the trail, walking on the tips of his toes.

The earth sloped downward, the trees opening up ahead. Thin slivers of moonlight lit up a holler where the trail snaked along the edge of a clearing. The shuffle of the leaves came again, closer now.

Daddy said if a man didn't face what scared him, he'd lose his mind. Leo pulled out his thin pocketknife and held it in front of him. Tried to keep from shaking.

Up ahead, in the trees, haloed in soft blue light, there formed the silhouette of a boy. Leo thought of his dead brother

Jacob. Jacob had come to Leo many times since his death, floating up to whisper in Leo's ear in an unknown tongue.

"Jacob?" Leo whispered.

The outline of the boy stretched and twisted into shadow between two trees, and Leo's stomach curled. There was something familiar in the way the darkness flickered and danced like smoke, stretching taller, as if a reflection cast from some imaginary fire. Leo had tried hard to forget all this. This ghost wasn't Jacob.

"I told you to go away," Leo said. His voice trembled.

What was it he'd said before? To make the apparition disappear.

"Get thee behind me," Leo said.

Pastor Harmon said if the devil tempted you, all you had to do is say those magic words and the devil had to leave. Even the devil has to follow the rules. But there was more to it, Leo thought, more you had to say. What was it? Leo closed his eyes. He whispered: "Get thee behind me Satan, in the name of the one we call the Christ." Yes, that was it. One had to invoke His very name.

Leo opened his eyes. The shadow was gone, the outline of Jacob too. Leo straightened his back, stuck out his chest. The world looked less frightening when you simply took charge.

But ahead of him the animals shuffled along. He crept along toward the clearing, the beasts' heavy feet in the leaves.

"Get thee behind me," he whispered again.

Whatever was ahead in the woods didn't stop moving. Maybe the magic words worked on devils, but not on wild animals. Just on the other side of the thicket. What awaited him? The wild boar hogs? A she-bear? The widow's wulvers?

The sounds rose all around him. He pushed through, his knife out in front. Then he saw them.

Rabbits. There were a dozen rabbits shuffling around a patch of grass that was deep and green, despite the brown of the surrounding forest. The rabbits had a funny look about them, and for a moment they seemed out of focus, as if they were behind a pane of stained church glass. Hunger stirred within Leo, and he thought about how well he could feed his family if he caught a few for a stew. But these rabbits didn't look good for eating.

They didn't run from Leo. Several of them bounded over to where he stood, sniffing his boots. He folded the pocketknife and reached down to one that leaned against his leg. He got on his knees to pet them. Their fur was soft but cold, reminding him of frosted grass. The rabbits were see-through in places and although their fur was brown, a silver light haloed their bodies. When he looked again to the clearing, more crystal rabbits had emerged and now hundreds milled about, all with brown fur and white sock feet. The clouds fled, and moonlight lit the clearing, while the rest of the woods remained dark. Somehow Leo wasn't cold anymore and the air around him grew as warm as a spring morning. One of the rabbits nuzzled the palm of Leo's hand, just like Old Possum.

Leo wondered if the magical rabbits came out every night, or just with a full moon. He was determined to remember how to get back to this clearing, determined to bring his baby sister, whom Leo called Goldfish, to pet the glowing rabbits under the moon.

After a while, Leo stood to leave when a light flickered at the corner of the field. At the edge of the woods, behind the first line of trees there was a bright silver light. For a moment the light was hazy, but then the shape of a tall man formed. Was it a man? Where the face should be there was something that appeared as lightning to Leo's eyes. The spirit walked through the woods, and the rabbits followed him. Leo wanted to call to it but couldn't speak.

The man – or spirit – moved quickly, its robe shimmering like the surface of a lake, its body flattening as if it were flying before touching down to the earth, moving on all fours. When it rounded a large tree, it turned in Leo's direction. It was a large wolf-beast, with silver tipped fur that glowed like delicate stars. Leo thought of the widow and the tale of the two wulvers that roamed the mountains. This would be the Silver Wulver. It nuzzled the rabbits around it, and Leo recalled the Bible story that talked about how wolves will lay down with lambs at the end of times. When the beast raised its head, Leo realized it was as tall as a horse. Seeing it here in the woods was a sign. Maybe there was good in the world.

When the Silver Wulver began to run, disappearing in the trees, Leo followed. He was drawn to the glowing silver trail it left in its wake. Was he supposed to follow? Did the Silver Wulver want to show him something? The rabbits bounded after the wulver now, as if he were some kind of angelic pied piper calling them away.

"Wait!" Leo yelled. He ran through the woods until the silver light faded and he realized he'd lost the trail. He bent over, panting, trying to catch his breath. Reluctantly, he turned away and ran for home.

Chapter 3 - Vey

The Blue Man gonna get you! *A taunt for kids that got out of line. Something mamas would say, like talking about the boogie man.* Better be good, he comin'! *Little girls would squeal and run around. The boys laughed and the men just brushed their shoulders off.*

I don't know when it started, who made it up. But they said he'd snatch you up on the road. In the field. Outside your mama's house. But only if you was pretty. People looked at the pretty ones and grinned like it was a joke. A way to get the pretty ones back. It was something me and my friends started saying to each other around the fire. The Blue Man gonna get you! *Like telling a ghost story. If you wanted to be real mean, if the girl was ugly, you say:* Even the Blue Man don't want you.

In church, the preacher said it wasn't true, but girls did go missing from time to time on the mountain, so I began to wonder.

Some said he rode in a big black car, the weather was nice. Girl named Cassie, she said he offered her money to get in his big car. Showed her gold coins, leaning out the back window, wooden booger mask on his face. Ugly giant man in the front jumped out and tried to grab her when she said no. Said she barely got away.

What'd he say to you? *People asked Cassie.* That I was pretty and I should have all the bread and honey I want if I'd just get in his car, *she said.* Only he was hard to understand. He talk funny, *she said.*

When the weather turned and the road got muddy, they said the Blue Man would ride a black horse up and down the mountain. Just grab a girl and throw her over the back like there wasn't nothing to it.

Cassie looked like me. Dark skin, curly hair. People said the Blue Man, he liked black girls and white girls. Indians too. Wanted us all. But wherever he took them, not a one come back. By the time the leaves turned, I knew three girls that was missing. All pretty. All from right here on the mountain. Two black girls like me and Cassie, and one white girl. The men said they were runaways but deep down I knew better.

I became scared to look pretty. There's a danger in it, my mama said, in a girl looking too pretty out in the wild. You wanna look pretty, *she'd say,* you do that in church. Out in the Sunday sunshine. Rest of the time, better for you to look like a boy.

After church one day, I heard kids talking. They said the Blue Man drug the girls to the top of the mountain. Way up, far as you could go, where the clouds was lower than the trees. Where the dirt turned black. That's where they disappeared. That's where they went forever. It was just some crazy story, I kept telling myself. Like any other fairy tale. Ain't no more true than the Three Little Pigs or Little Red Riding Hood. But then, if it weren't true, where did them girls go?

Chapter 4

Mama hadn't spoken when Leo came home. There was no anger, no switch. The next morning she'd taken the quarters from him without smiling, offering him only the slightest dip of her head. She hadn't made eye contact, never did since Daddy had gone missing. Leo felt the heat of his brothers' stares on the back of his head. Hank seemed especially angry, and James sulked like always. This delighted Leo. He lifted his chin as far as he could, looked over his shoulder to be sure Hank and James saw.

Mama had Leo and his brothers split and stack wood all morning, and Leo started to get a broad blister at the center of his palm. It stung but he pushed past it. There was no time for pain, given all that had to be done around the house and what he still owed the widow. Mama supervised the work, urged Leo to split more, to stack more wood in the lean-to under the trees at the edge of the yard, and though Leo carried two loads to that of his older brother, Hank, and probably four to what James could be bothered with, Mama said nothing to them. Hank sniggered each time he passed Leo, as if he were in on some inside joke. Mama paced while the boys worked, stepping in at times to help, then staring up at the mountains, going on about how fast winter was coming, how this one was going to be cold as hell, the almanac had it right.

Leo scanned the woods as he worked, thought constantly of the Silver Wulver and of the crystal rabbits, the way they'd sparkled in the clearing. Back at home, in the ugly daylight of the world, he wished he'd pushed harder, run faster to follow the Silver Wulver. There had to be more to life than what his ragged family knew.

Leo dropped a load of wood under the lean-to, re-stacking the pieces dropped by his brothers. He had to go behind them because they just threw their pieces wherever, never paying attention to how it was stacked. If the pile fell, the wood would get wet. Wet wood was about as bad as having no wood at all.

Mama came up behind him. "I'm just fixing the stack is all, Mama. I'll get after it, I get this straight."

"Never you mind about that right now," Mama said. "Come on up to the porch, I need a word."

"Sure, Mama, let me run down to the creek for a minute." Leo had felt nature's call for at least a half hour, but he'd put it off, knowing Mama was watching, knowing how frantic she seemed to see more wood stored up.

"Just go piss in them trees" she said.

"It ain't – I mean, I got to go."

"Okay, go do your business, then meet me at the porch." Mama walked briskly up the hill toward the house, cutting her eyes at Hank and James as she passed.

The day was cool, but Leo felt sweat dripping down his back. When he reached the creek, he walked the shaky bridge boards to the outhouse suspended over the moving water; he was almost relieved when he pulled his britches down and the cold air hit his bare ass. In the winter, the freeze of the outhouse could be brutal, but today it felt good. Daddy and Leo had built the little outhouse over the creek when they'd first moved into the one-room house. Before Jacob died and Daddy lost his good job, back when the family'd had a nice white house with three rooms, a picket fence, and a big, pretty whitewashed outhouse.

When Leo got back, Mama stood on the porch. She lit a cigarette, her eyes on Hank and James, who trudged slowly along as if the labor might kill them. She closed the door to keep the smoke from going in.

"What is it, Mama?" Leo asked. He leaned against the rickety porch rail, thought better of putting his weight on it.

"You'll have to do it," Mama said. She studied the tip of her cigarette, straightened the shaft a bit with her fingers. It was hand rolled, but Mama couldn't roll one like Daddy.

Mama always said hers weren't pretty, but they tasted sweeter.

"Do what, Mama?"

"You got to find your Daddy. If I sent the others, they'd never come back."

"How's that?"

"Hank would be laid up somewhere, just like your daddy. Drunk as a skunk, maybe find him a whore and foller her to Tennessee."

Leo studied the lines of her face. Gone was the gentle mother he'd once had. He remembered nights she would snuggle him close before bed or pull him against her warmth on the church pew when he was a small boy. When Daddy was gone, she'd tell him to come *scrooch up* on her bed, which meant he should nestle against her, be the little spoon. Leo would push back into her, disappear within her.

"James would never find his way to town," she went on. "He'd get lost and starve to death or wander in front of a moving train."

Mama's voice dropped. She looked Leo in the eye. "You'll have to go."

Leo still doubted whether Daddy really was missing.

She coughed. "You know where to look?"

Leo knew where he'd start. He'd been to Altamont many times with Daddy, usually because Mama made Daddy take him, assuming Leo would somehow regulate the old man's behavior.

"But Mama," Leo said. "He goes off like this all the time. Done this at least a dozen times before."

Mama took a deep drag on the cigarette, its long red ash extending like a bony finger. "But usually when he goes off, it's like he's got it planned out. He leaves me money."

"Oh," Leo said.

"He even had a boy run me cash one time," she said. "Reckon he was too drunk to bring it himself." She snuffed her cigarette out on the porch rail. "Or maybe he was having too big a time to bother. Didn't want to lose his place in line. Devil's got his hooks deep in that man," she said. "Always had hooks in him, since before me, probably since before he entered this world. But after your brother died, Devil got a hold of him real good."

Mama's face caught the midmorning sun. She'd started changing after Jacob died. Her warmth had dissipated like a morning fog caught in the sun. Now Mama was a collection of sharp angles, pivoting from place to place on long straight legs that lacked form. Her face was pointy and protracted with an air of harshness in her eyes that Leo did not recognize. Her chin so angular it looked like a weapon. Still, Mama was a pretty woman, and Leo had seen the way men looked at her at church or when they went to the trading post. He loathed their eyes on her.

"God can save Daddy," Leo said.

"Can he?" she asked, eyebrows raised, forehead lines deepening. "Can God save what don't want saving?"

"Yes," Leo said, but he knew it was horse shit. Besides, Leo wasn't sure he wanted the son of a bitch to come home.

He walked over to her, put his hand on her arm, thought to hug her. She twisted away as if Leo's touch burned her skin.

She stared up into the mountains. Her eyes darted back and forth, and she took on a wild look. Leo knew he had to find Daddy soon. Her descent was coming faster now. If Daddy stayed gone much longer, she'd disappear.

"I had a dream, Leo," she said. "I burnt this house to the ground. And everything in it."

Leo looked at her, had to look away.

"I throwed all the animals I could catch on the fire. All the dogs, and all the cats. I caught them all. I throwed them all on the fire. Watched them burn, them screaming."

Leo looked over at one of the family's cats, laid out on the dirt just off the porch. It was the one he called Snowflake on account of the fact she'd been born on the first snow one year. She snuggled with Leo every night, keeping his feet warm.

She'd been Jacob's cat before he died. Snowflake wanted to sleep with Goldfish, but Mama shared her bed with Goldfish and always kicked the cat out when she came to bed. Snowflake would then make his way over to Leo's straw mattress on the floor between his two brothers. Leo pictured Snowflake squirming on the fire, legs kicking.

"Watched them all burn," Mama said.

Leo took a step back.

"Mama?"

"Took the shotgun and a knapsack and set out for the highest peak. The highest mountain around. That's where I went. Light as a feather, I was."

She looked at him now, held his gaze too hard.

"I become a mountain witch in my dream," she said.

"Mama," Leo said.

"Living off the land, nothing to hold me down. Eating fish raw, right out of the streams, way nature gives them to us. I lived in a cave. Slept beside a she-bear."

"But Mama, we need you," Leo said.

"Do you?" Mama said. Her eyes softened. She looked at her feet. "Find your daddy, son. I can't hold out."

"I'll go today," Leo said. "After I finish my chores."

After the boys had stacked the wood under the lean-to, Leo filled the kindling box beside the wood stove in the house. On his last trip, he saw Mama bent over a small chest in the corner. She clutched something in her hands, her back mostly turned, as if she wished to hide some precious relic from the world. When she dropped her shoulder, he saw what she held: it was a child's jumper, dingy white with a round collar and buttons down the front. The bottom half tapered into short pants, and Leo recognized the yellow stain. Mama turned away, stuffing the cloth back in the chest as if Leo might leap across the room and steal her treasure. The jumper had been Jacob's.

"You don't miss him," Mama said. She looked at Leo, bit into her cheek.

"Mama, what?"

"You boys. You don't miss Jacob one bit. Not a one of you."

Leo's eyes stung.

Mama squatted down in the corner, her long legs bent, knees up to her neck, her skirts dragging the floor. Her voice dropped. "You don't know," she said.

Goldfish coughed from her place on Mama's bed. Her voice was hoarse and deep, as if she had grit caught in her throat.

Leo walked over. Goldfish was asleep, her eyeballs dancing beneath her eyelids as if she were having a nightmare. Her breathing was labored. He kissed her forehead, and she was flushed, her whole body radiating a feverish heat. Leo felt around her long blonde hair and neck. There was no sweat. He picked her socks up off the floor and folded them together. Goldfish had the habit of tearing off her one pair of socks as soon as she got into bed, no matter the weather.

"She's on fire," he said to Mama.

"You think I don't know that?" Her tone dared him to say something else about it. "We're all on fire," she said, her voice a razor. "Ever last one of us."

Leo ran to the creek to dip a rag in the water and took it back to put on Goldfish's forehead. She awoke briefly to offer Leo a broad smile before slipping back under.

Chapter 5

In mid-afternoon, Leo left for Altamont to find Daddy. It was a three hour walk from the valley, but he could make it in one if he caught the bus up near Wilson's Trading Post. But Leo had given Mama all his coins. If he took them for the bus, they'd have less to eat. He'd have to walk. He'd gotten on the road when he saw a man lumbering along, near the creek. Leo headed off the road toward the man.

It was Reverend Wormley. He was a tall man, but so fat it obscured his height. He had hands as big as baseball gloves. He wore a fine gray suit that was too small, the button at his belly threatening to pop. At his belt, the gold chain of a pocket watch gleamed in the afternoon sun. He tipped a tan brimmed hat as Leo approached.

"Young man," Reverend Wormley said.

"Reverend," Leo said, lifting his chin.

"Your daddy made it home yet?"

Leo looked back toward the house. Mama was smoking on the front porch. "He ain't, but I expect he'll turn up any minute now."

Leo knew Reverend Wormley didn't like his daddy, and Daddy didn't like that fat son of a bitch neither. Daddy wouldn't be pleased if he were home. Wormley preached at a different church from where the family went, which was headed by Pastor Harmon. Leo loved Pastor Harmon, but, although he could never quite put his finger on it, there was something about Reverend Wormley that just didn't sit right.

The preacher looked around, and Leo wondered why he'd come along the creek instead of down the road like everyone else did. Like he didn't want to be seen.

"I come to pray over your sick sister, may God have mercy on her soul."

"Yes, sir," Leo said.

"And to counsel your poor lost mother," Wormley said, looking up at the house, spotting Leo's mama on the porch.

The preacher rubbed his lips with an enormous fingertip. "In her time of need."

"He ain't dead," Leo said. "Daddy's just gone off for a while is all. He does that. This ain't a *time of need* for nobody."

Wormley narrowed his eyes and offered a half smile. "Nevertheless," he said. He dipped his head, dismissing Leo. There was something about the way Wormley touched the brim of his hat, something Leo had seen before, this gesture. But he couldn't quite remember when.

Wormley made his way along the creek, up the hill toward the house. At the porch, he and Mama exchanged words and the preacher went inside. Mama closed the door behind them. Hank and James dropped the loads of wood they had in their arms and made for the woods.

Thinking about Mama in the house with Reverend Wormley made Leo sick to his stomach. He thought about running home and barging inside. He could make up something about how he wanted to learn to pray for Goldfish the way preachers do. Leo looked up at the position of the sun in the sky. If he lingered much longer, he wouldn't make it to Altamont and back by nightfall. He looked at the road and back to the house. He was nauseous, picturing Wormley's face when he'd seen Mama on the porch.

Leo made his way toward the widow's. He planned to stop there on his way out of town. He was hungry and hoped she might have something to eat. He'd also let her know he wouldn't be coming today to split the remaining wood. That debt would have to remain unpaid for the moment. He ran through the woods, stopping at the clearing where he'd seen the rabbits the night before, somehow knowing they wouldn't be there. There was grass in the clearing, sure enough, but it wasn't as lush as it had looked in the moonlight. It was green, but a dull green that bordered on brown.

On the walk, fall clouds stirred, concealing the sun. The air had held the gaze of summer when he was back home, but now it bore the kiss of fall. The skies darkened unnaturally, as if late afternoon had suddenly taken hold, though it couldn't have been later than one o'clock.

He thought about what Mama said, about the devil's hooks in Daddy. He pictured them, fishhooks as big as his hand, stuck in Daddy's back and chest.

Jacob had been seven, a year younger than Goldfish was now, when he'd died. He'd been a boy full of joy, bouncing around the world with a quick smile. He always had a joke or made a funny face that made people forget the things that weighed on them. He'd died from an infection, one of the old churchwomen had said, caused by a blood blister on his heel. Leo's daddy had cursed the boy's hard shoe, throwing it against the wall the night Jacob died, cursed Leo's mama for not telling him about the wound, cursed himself for the boy having to wear shoes a size too small. Leo remembered looking at the round ugly wound on Jacob's heel that was so mean and yet he'd never heard Jacob complain. It seemed like such a small thing that could fester and spoil all the blood in a body, snuff a boy out like a candle.

Leo was thinking about Jacob when he noticed a group of shadows stretch tall in the forest, just off the road. Behind the trees, something skulked there. Something familiar, like black smoke from a campfire.

But hadn't he told the ghost to go away? He shuddered when the pillar of smoke began to form in the trees. He'd been on a trip with Daddy to Altamont the first time he'd seen it and it had stalked him ever since.

Get thee behind me, Leo said. *In the name of Jesus.*

The shadow dissipated like ink streaking in clear water.

Just then he heard someone on the dirt road. It was a girl from school. Lilyfax, whom everyone called a tomboy.

Leo took one last peek at the trees, looked for any shape in the shadows, looked for the outline of his dead baby brother, Jacob. He saw only dry, brown leaves shaking on the wind. They made a sound like a baby rattle.

The girl was coming closer now.

She spoke but Leo couldn't concentrate on her words, couldn't process them. His head felt as heavy as a bale of cotton.

"You just never know who you're gonna run into on an old country road," Lilyfax said.

They met at the widow's mailbox.

"Cat got your tongue?" she said.

Leo stared at the girl. She was the same height as Leo. She had a skinny body with arms and legs that were wiry and defined, and pitch-black hair that fell midway down her neck. She had curt eyes the color of seawater. Her default expression was one of mischief, one eyebrow always just slightly higher than the other, unless she gave a big smile, which wiped away the mischief and revealed two deep dimples on her cheeks. The first time Lilyfax had smiled at Leo, those dimples had hit him like sparks from a campfire. Mostly, however, Lilyfax smirked, rarely doling out dimpled smiles, as if they were precious commodities. They'd changed the way Leo thought of Lilyfax, changed Leo himself, though he hadn't known it at the time.

"Leo?" Lilyfax said. She was wearing a blue dress that broke at the knee, the kind of dress girls wore if they were headed to church. It looked mostly new, with only a slight fray at the hemline. Lilyfax never, ever wore a dress.

"I reckon," Leo said.

"Reckon what?" Lilyfax said.

"Reckon the cat's got my tongue, is all."

Lilyfax followed Leo's eyes to the blue dress. "I know, I hate it."

"It's pretty," Leo said, his face warming.

"Looks like something they'd bury an old lady in." She rolled her eyes. "Daddy's home, if you can't tell."

"And Daddy likes you to wear church dresses?" Leo asked.

"Daddy says he wants his daughters to look like girls." She motioned over her shoulders to her knapsack. "I got me a change of clothes. I'll be back to normal before you see me next." Lilyfax had one older sister who looked more woman than girl, and a younger brother that was known for kicking people in the shins and then sprinting away, chuckling. His laugh sounded like a yodel.

"You headed to the widow's?" she asked.

"I got to check in on her."

The widow was standing on her porch, but her house was far enough from the road that Leo could not make out the details of her face.

"What're you doing after?"

"I'm headed to town." Leo could study the girl's dimpled cheeks for days, if he could figure out how to keep her smiling. He was staring too long, afraid he might start sweating. He looked away.

"A bunch of us will be over at Farmer Rex's barn." She looked off in the woods, near the place Leo had seen the moving shadows. She turned back to Leo. "You should come."

Leo nodded and was about to speak when Lilyfax took off in a sprint down the road, her long legs smooth under the flutter of the dress. She looked back over her shoulder.

"Smile, Leo," she said. "Don't be such a stick in the mud."

He wanted to smile. It was as if the muscles in his face had forgotten the shape, the movement to make it happen. He was happy to see Lilyfax. But he couldn't stop thinking about the shadow that wouldn't stop stalking him, the pillar of smoke. He thought about the Silver Wulver. Maybe it was the answer? If only he'd followed it deeper into the woods. If only he'd been fast enough to keep up. Then he remembered Mama's dream of becoming a mountain witch, of how she'd talked about burning the house down. He pictured Snowflake on the fire. Heard the animals screaming.

It was time to go find Daddy. But first, maybe the widow would have something he could eat.

Chapter 6

"The first time I caught the spirit, I was about your age," the widow said, sitting back in her chair. She held a hand to her cheek and chuckled. Today her white hair was pulled up on top of her head in a bun that bounced when she spoke. Leo studied the container of snuff on the kitchen table between them. Just minutes before, she'd tucked two pinches in her cheek. She could drink coffee and talk for hours all while holding her snuff. She rarely needed her spit jar. When Leo took a plug of tobacco, his saliva glands went to working overtime, requiring him to spit every time he turned around. The bitter smell of the widow's brand turned his stomach.

"The spirit run all through me, and Mama said I went to whooping and hollering and just running up and down all over that little church, praising glory!" The widow stared at the ceiling, her head tilted back. Her eyes were glassy, wistful, as if she were looking into the heavens themselves. "The Bible tells us to sing and make a joyful noise unto the Lord."

Leo had seen all kind of folks catch the spirit. The first time it happened, he'd jumped out of his skin when a short old man in the pew behind him let out a blood curdling scream right in his ear. The man then proceeded to run the aisles of the church, a prominent vein poking out at the center of his forehead that resembled a small snake. It seemed like the best place to get the spirit was at the big tent revivals held down by the French Broad River in the summertime. There was something about being outside, under that big tent, that really brought it out in folks. At the revivals, people sometimes spoke in tongues or wallowed in the sawdust on the ground. The sawdust kept the mud down if it rained, and there was something about the smell of that sawdust in the heat that Leo loved, though he disliked almost everything else about camp meetings.

Leo remembered Mama going down to the altar many a night at tent revivals to pray for Daddy. Preachers and elders would gather around her, laying their hands on her, praying loudly about how Daddy needed the Lord Jesus to help him let go of the Devil's liquor and for him to stop running around like he was wont to do. Leo himself had cried at the altar a couple of times for Daddy, but sometimes he hadn't wanted to pray for Daddy at all. Sometimes he'd pretended to pray, squeezing his eyes shut tight, and balling up his fists with feigned enthusiasm. Once, he'd prayed that Daddy would get lost and never come home again. Now Leo worried that maybe his prayer had come true. People always said to be careful what you pray for.

"You ever catch the spirit?" the widow asked.

Leo thought on it. "I don't reckon."

The widow smiled. "Now don't you go trying to catch it. It don't work like that. You can't just up and decide you want to get the spirit. God has to move in you, son, you can't just go to hollering and expect it's God."

"No, ma'am," Leo said.

The air in the room was heavy with spice and the smell of fatback. The widow had a stew going on her wood stove, and Leo felt a pang of hunger deep in his gut, a fist jabbing at his belt line.

"Remember you were talking about them tall wulvers?" Leo said.

The widow's face was scrunched up. She did this when she was deep in thought, and every time she did, the wrinkles on her face deepened, which seemed to age her by a hundred years.

"People do peculiar things when they catch the spirit," she said, rubbing her chin.

"Yes, ma'am," Leo said, "but the other night, you started telling me the story of the wulvers. I was hoping to hear more about them."

"Have you ever seen old man Madison catch the spirit?" the widow asked.

Everybody within three counties had seen old man Madison catch the spirit. He was so prolific that preachers begged him to come to their revivals or camp meetings so he could stir up the faithful.

She went on. "Why, he's as lithe as a squirrel, he gets going," she said. "I seen him run along the backs of the pews one hot summer, and him seventy-five! Beats all I ever seen." She stood up, grabbing for the twisted cane she had propped against the wall. She made her way over to the stove and stirred the pot with a big wooden spoon.

"Remember the other night, we were talking about them wulvers you said come over from the old country?" Leo asked.

"Come get you some of this stew," she said.

He tried not to run to the pot. "Thank you, ma'am," he said.

The widow ladled out three big scoops into his bowl. He felt woozy walking back to his seat, as if he were in a rickety boat. The smell of the food was overwhelming. The widow was nothing if not a good cook. He had a spoonful of the stew in his mouth before his ass hit the chair. He devoured it, turning up the bowl to finish the juice at the bottom. When he set the bowl on the table, he noticed the widow staring with raised eyebrows. She scooped him a second bowl bigger than the first.

He almost asked again about the wulvers, frustrated she'd been ignoring him, but he didn't want to seem disrespectful. Clearly, she didn't want to talk about it, and Leo couldn't think why as she'd brought them up so freely before.

Leo started working on the second bowl and the widow stood with her hand on her hip, a look of pride on her face.

"Did you finish those books I give you last time?"

"Yes, ma'am," Leo said. "They're in my pack on the porch. I'll put them up after I finish eating."

"That's good," said the widow, "you pick you out two more. A man needs to read all he can."

Leo looked through the dining room toward the bookshelf in the widow's living room. It seemed like she must have a thousand, brilliantly bound in reds, browns, and greens. When he'd struggled to learn to read, the widow had taken the time to sit down and help him along. She'd told him books were powerful, and people ought to read so they wouldn't be ignorant. Leo loved to read each night by candlelight, as everyone else was drifting off to sleep. While Mama never said much about it, Daddy complained about how it was a waste of a good candle. More than once, Daddy had grabbed a book from Leo's hands and tossed it across the room. But Daddy left Leo alone if he was reading to Goldfish, who loved a good story more than anything. She loved stories the way Jacob had. Before Jacob died, he'd always crawled onto Leo's straw mattress and asked him for a story. He was more particular than Goldfish, only wanting stories about dogs or other animals. If Leo'd started a story about cowboys and Indians, or Army men, Jacob would just shake his head. In Leo's pack outside, there was a book about Tarzan and a copy of *Black Beauty*. Jacob would have approved.

"Your daddy come home yet?" the widow asked.

"Not yet," Leo answered.

"I'm sure he'll turn up," she said. "Even the wildest tomcats come back home, they get hungry enough."

"I'm gonna go find him," Leo said, pushing back from the table. "Drag him back by his toenails if I have to."

The widow thought about this, her hand to her chin as if she were weighing her words. "Him gone, you know you'll have to be the man of the house, Leo."

The widow always talked this way, going on about how Leo was special.

"Daddy'll turn up. He always does. I'm headed to Altamont directly."

"And where will you go look for him?" she asked.

"I got some ideas."

The widow was silent for a moment. Then, "and little Goldfish, she getting any better?"

Leo remembered the girl's hoarse coughing, and how fevered she'd been when he left the house. "No, ma'am, she had a high fever today."

"We got that sweet angel on our prayer list," the widow said. "Bible says to pray without ceasing, and that's just what I try to do."

The widow sat back down at the table as Leo turned up the bowl to finish what was left in the bottom.

"Your friend at the mailbox," she said. "Who was that girl? I don't know her."

"That's Lilyfax," Leo said. "Everbody at school calls her a tomboy."

"They do, do they? What do you say?"

"She's pretty funny for a girl, I reckon."

"Something peculiar about her, I noticed right off."

"How's that?" Leo asked.

"Something about her hair, that point at the center."

"Yes, ma'am?" Leo pictured Lilyfax's hair, the widow's peak.

"Old folks said it was bad luck," the widow said.

"Bad luck? That seems silly."

"Silly?" The widow's face grew stern. She frowned. "You can think your elders are silly all you want to, but they know things you can't possibly know. Best pay attention."

"Yes, ma'am," Leo said, "I didn't mean no harm."

"You be careful around that girl."

"Yes, ma'am, but she's really—"

"And you tell her to be careful."

"Okay," Leo said. "What do you mean?"

"They's rumors around about girls going missing. Not just town girls, neither."

"Missing?"

"Missing, like kidnapped, like taken." The widow shook her head. "I don't know what this world is coming to. And that ain't no gossip, neither. That's the truth."

The widow loved to tell a quick story of gossip but she disliked this about herself. She'd often tell Leo something about one of her neighbors, or someone at church, but she always followed it up with a quick prayer under her breath, something like *Forgive me Lord Jesus for telling tales on people.*

"I'll tell her."

"Some men," the widow said, "take what they can't get the right way, steal what can't be got the right way, I mean God's way."

"Yes, ma'am," Leo said.

"Never be like those men."

"No, ma'am."

The widow covered her eyes with her hands. She inhaled sharply and jerked in her chair.

"Are you all right?" Leo asked.

"After I heard about them girls, Leo, it come to me."

"What did?"

"I seen a vision. The whole world gone dark. The sun marked out by the clouds."

"What did you see?"

"It was some great beast dragging a girl up the mountain by her ponytail, way up high like, up where it's hard to breathe."

Leo said nothing. The widow worked her jaw.

"That ugly, rough beast! Face like a raisin. He took the girl and tied her up to a tree."

"To a tree?"

"Yes, but only he used the vines of the earth to hold her there. Not rope."

The widow shook her head. She stared at Leo. There was something like fear in her eyes, a kind of panic. It was as if she might get up and run.

"Was it a wulver?" Leo asked.

46

She looked out the window. "No, something much worse." She shuddered, her narrow shoulders drawn. "You keep an eye on that girl, Leo, on your mama and sister too. Keep a watch out for all the young womenfolk."

Chapter 7

It was after three o'clock when Leo left the widow's. He stood in the road for a moment, considering the trip to Altamont. It would be near dark by the time he'd get there, and then how many places would he have to go look for Daddy? The son of a bitch wanted to be home, he'd be home. He also couldn't shake off Lilyfax's invitation. He turned away from the road to Altamont, toward Farmer Rex's barn.

He'd been in that barn just this past summer, working, hanging tobacco leaves up in the rafter beams where the temperatures in early August flirted with a hundred. After all the leaves were hung, Miss Rex poured all the boys iced tea and they stood looking up at the leaves that would soon dry and take on a warm golden color, their smell sweet and tangy. Farmer Rex had stood in the middle of the barn after the harvest, stretching his arms out. "Take in that smell, boys," he'd said. "That there's the smell of money."

This late in October, the tobacco was gone, having been taken off to market, only the smell of its curing left in the air. Leo ducked under the half door entrance and walked through the livestock stalls to the open floor, where he found a group of kids hanging out in the rafters and in the loft. Some of the kids were walking the round beams in the second story, where the tobacco would hang next summer. Leo saw his cousin Declan on the first beam. Declan was easy to spot because he was tow-headed with bright white skin. Further up in the rafters, he saw Lilyfax. She'd lost the dress and was back in her faded overalls. In the loft, a group of kids chattered, their feet dangling off the ledge. Among them was Ezra, a kid from school who was forever dressed in black, save for his bright white shirts, which he buttoned all the way up. People at school called him the *Little Priest*. He had harsh black eyes that reminded Leo of a crow's. His hair was equally dark.

The kids laughed and dared each other along. The beams stretched the length of the barn and were spaced four to five feet apart, set at different heights so tobacco leaves could be hung with ample room for curing. The tobacco would be spread on the beams using wooden stakes, long sticks with pointed ends for impaling the leaves. Lilyfax had climbed to one of the highest beams in the barn. She walked along, arms folded in front of her, without the hesitation other kids showed. Leo couldn't tell if she saw him, but even at this distance he could see the familiar look of impishness spread over her face.

Declan crept on his beam, much slower, balancing himself with his hands out to his sides. "Look at this, boys," he said to his friends in the loft, "pretty as you please."

He looked away from his feet, as if to make sure his friends were watching. When he did so, he lost his footing. He tried to grab the closest beam, and for a moment it looked like he'd catch himself, but his fingers slipped on the slick wood, and he fell to the barn floor below. Dust swirled for a moment, and all the kids stopped talking to stare at Declan, who lay on his back, not moving. He was as still as a corpse for several seconds. Then he sat up slowly, inhaling deeply, the fall having knocked the wind from his body.

Declan looked around like a caged animal who'd just been set free and couldn't come up with a direction in which to run. He was up on one knee when the kids, now realizing that he wasn't hurt too badly, began to laugh. Leo laughed too, as he approached his cousin, holding out his hand.

Declan slapped Leo's hand away and found his feet. He looked up at the kids in the rafters, then to Leo. "Oh, y'all think that's funny, do you?"

Leo stopped laughing. "No, man, I just—".

Declan paced in a circle, his arms held out like a gorilla. His ears were as bright as a red onion. Finally, he stood toe to toe with Leo, his chin up. Though the boy was shorter, he was broad shouldered. He was thick, the kind of boy people would call corn fed. He held Leo's gaze for a moment, then turned to the kids in the rafters. He held out his arms, palms up.

"Well if it ain't my old cousin Leo, come to grace us with his presence," he said.

Declan's skin was so sheer Leo couldn't stop staring at the bright blue veins that wound up his skull. His head looked as delicate as an egg membrane.

"If you think you can do better," Declan said, turning to Leo, "let's see you get up and run the beam like I done, see if you can stay on, since you think it's so easy."

"You weren't really running," Leo said.

Declan's face hardened.

One of the kids in the rafters yelled out, "Look how high Lilyfax is! Ain't nobody ever goes up that high."

Everyone looked up to Lilyfax on the top beam. She was standing still, watching Leo and Declan. She had her hands in her pockets, while everyone else on a beam had their hands held out straight and trembling, for balance.

Declan turned back to Leo. "I bet you're too scared to go up on them beams, *Leonard*."

"Declan," Leo said, "I didn't mean no harm."

"That girl," Declan said, "maybe she ain't a' scared, but Leo is." He pointed up at Lilyfax, keeping his eyes on Leo. "That girl can climb like a boy, seen her hit a baseball like a boy. What kinda name is Lilyfax anyway?" Declan's friends in the loft laughed.

"Declan, this ain't no big deal." Leo said. He held his hands up, palms out in apology. Declan was always a blowhard, but one that could usually be reasoned with.

"Why, just look at her!" Declan said half to Leo and half to his friends. "She practically looks like a boy with that cow lick across her head." Some of the kids laughed uncomfortably. Leo locked eyes with Ezra, the Little Priest, who did not laugh. "Matter of fact, every time I turn around, I see Leo with her. Maybe she's his girlfriend."

Lilyfax looked down on the proceedings, sitting on the tobacco beam, easily balancing herself. She crossed her arms, and Leo thought he could detect a trace of amusement about her.

"Declan," Leo started.

"Leo done got him a girlfriend," Declan said, "only one that looks like a boy. Maybe Leo got him a boyfriend."

One of the kids up in the loft began to chant:

Leo got a boyfriend, Leo got a boyfriend!

Soon the whole barn chanted in unison. In the group of kids near Ezra, stood Hank, Leo's older brother. Hank's voice was louder than the others.

Leo got a boyfriend, Leo got a boyfriend!

Leo stared at Declan, felt his skin warm. He hated the boy's smug face, the way he carried himself, arms out wide from his body like he wanted to take up all the space, leave none for anybody else.

Declan seemed to read Leo's thoughts. He smelled blood. He looked Leo in the eye, squared his shoulders. Leo glared at the egg-sac forehead. Thought about how it might feel to strike it with his fists.

"Does your girlfriend know," Declan started, "that your daddy's run off?"

Leo shook his head, as if to say *don't you dare.*

"Does she know he lays up drunk all over town, that he left you and your mama and all his damned kids to starve? Wonder what your daddy would think if he seen you laid up with your little tomboy hussy?"

Leo balled his fists and clenched his jaw. Stared at the spot on Declan's head he'd strike first.

Declan turned to the other kids. "Old Leo will grow up just like his daddy, houseful of young'uns he hates so much he can't stand to stay home." He turned back to Leo. "A drunk and a waste, just like his daddy."

Leo leaned in, swung hard. He struck Declan on the side of the head. Declan fell back on a bale of hay. Leo jumped over the bale, kept swinging, but only a couple met their mark. Declan rolled and found his feet. He stood and charged Leo, his face as red as his ears. He caught Leo on the chin and Leo fell to the barn floor. As he struggled to stand, Declan kicked him in the stomach, and all the air escaped his lungs. As he scrambled, someone moved into his field of vision. It was Ezra.

"Declan, that's enough, leave him alone," Ezra said, stepping between Leo and his cousin.

"Move back, *Little Priest, Little Prick,*" Declan said. He pushed Ezra so hard the boy fell on his back. "I'll beat your ass next."

Leo had almost caught his breath when Declan dropped an elbow on top of his head. He kicked Leo again in the stomach, and Leo balled up. He didn't think he'd ever catch his breath again.

In the corner of the barn, shadows contorted in the familiar way. The same twisting, the same shape he'd recognized in the woods on the way home from the widow's. The inky shadows twisted around a pitchfork propped against the wall.

A voice echoed in Leo's head. A deep mechanical voice that reminded Leo of grinding tractor gears. He'd heard it before, a voice he'd tried hard to forget.

Stick the boy, stick him good.

Leo pictured it. He could grab the pitchfork, break open Declan's egg sac with the tines. He stood. The pillar of smoke leaned the pitchfork from the wall toward Leo. Only a few short steps and it would be in his grasp.

Stick him Leo, you know you could!

Leo turned just in time to see Declan running toward him. Leo took a step back and tripped over something. Over someone. As his back hit the floor, he saw Hank standing over him. Hank had stuck his foot out.

"Have a nice trip, see ya next fall," Hank said.

Then Declan was on him, punching his head and ears. Leo flipped to his stomach, and Declan forced his head down into the dirt floor. His arms trapped beneath him, he wriggled, unable to move. When finally he worked his hands free, he positioned them around his head to block the blows. Declan kept pounding and Leo grew dizzy.

Declan dragged Leo across the barn floor, under the half door, and out toward the creek outside. When he struggled for a moment with Leo's weight, Leo felt another set of hands on him. He knew without looking. It was Hank.

Outside the barn, Declan pushed Leo down the bank, where he rolled into the cold creek mud. Declan was on him again, pushing his head under. Leo breathed in the creek water, mud filling his nostrils. He coughed and choked.

"Just like your old man," Declan said. "Wallering down with the pigs."

Declan pushed Leo's head below the surface. Held him there. Leo bucked, his lungs filling. He felt like he might drown.

Suddenly the attack stopped. The kids, who had been whooping and chanting *Fight! Fight! Fight!* fell silent. There was a loud thud and Declan cried out in pain. He felt Declan ease off his back now, and Leo rolled over, clearing the silt from his eyes and nose. He coughed mud up into his hands. There was another loud THWACK, another cry from his cousin.

When he pried his eyes open, Lilyfax was circling Declan, a tobacco stake over her head like a sword. Declan was on his knees. Lilyfax stepped in, swung the stake hard against his head, catching him at the ear. Declan howled. Lilyfax took a step toward Hank, who stood up on the creek bank. She swung, and he ducked, the weapon whirring above his head. He turned and ran into the gathering dusk.

Lilyfax stepped down, holding a hand out to Leo. She held the stake in her other hand as a warning.

"She even fights like a boy," Declan said to no one in particular. He climbed the creek bank slowly, sliding down a few times.

At the top of the bank, Ezra held out his hand to help Declan take the last few steps. Declan pushed the boy out of the way. The other kids backed up, some of them sniggering about what had just happened. Some pointed at Lilyfax, who stood with her head high, the tobacco stake at her side like a sorcerer's staff.

Leo wanted to say something but had too much grit in his throat to speak. For a moment Lilyfax had one eyebrow raised, her face full of mischief, but then she let a smile break and there were those illusive dimples. Ezra walked up, as all the other kids left, the ones in Declan's gang following him up the hill toward his house.

"You okay, Leo?" Ezra asked.

Leo nodded.

"You were really something," Ezra said to Lilyfax.

She nodded at Ezra, turned to wink at Leo. She smiled, the kind of smile where she wasn't holding back. He studied her face, the smolder of her dimples, the widow's peak, her black hair, the green haze of her eyes. He thought of the widow's words of warning, about how the girl could be bad luck. The widow had been wrong, Leo decided. She was maybe the best kind of luck in the whole wide world.

Chapter 8

Two days after taking a beating in Farmer Rex's barn, Leo stood in the doorway of the family's home, watching church elders pray over Goldfish. It was a sunny morning, which tasted bitter on his tongue. Lately, he had taken more to the days of gray, the days when clouds hid the sun, the world falling under. Today, the sun was oppressive – too bright, though the air was brisk and cold.

There were not one, but two goddamned preachers in the house, several deacons, and a flock of chattering church women in black, flapping around like a murder of crows. They'd come in pairs, mostly, down the dirt road, starting at sunrise, the word having gotten out that Goldfish was getting sicker. One of the preachers Leo liked. The other he positively loathed.

Pastor Harmon had smiled at Leo when he arrived, patting him on the shoulder. He carried a big brown Bible, as always, and shook every hand, keeping eye contact with every adult and child. His smile was warm, and Leo longed to be back on his church pews, nestled next to Mama, listening to Pastor Harmon's sermons, which were somehow never as boring as other preachers'.

"We'll see you on Sunday, won't we Leo?" he'd said. "You'll come and bring your brothers?"

"Yes, sir, I can't speak for my brothers," Leo answered. "But I'll be there, Lord willing and the creek don't rise."

Leo had shared a few cross stares with his brother Hank, since Hank had tripped him in the barn, taking Declan's side. The last thing Leo would be apt to do is concern himself over Hank's heavenly salvation and where he chose to spend his time Sunday mornings. It didn't seem possible that Hank's face could appear even more smug, but somehow, it did. Leo tracked his older brother, saying nothing, biding his time.

Reverend Wormley came too, unable to miss an opportunity to show off his ability to pray louder than another preacher. Around eleven he'd strolled up into the yard, passing Leo and his brothers without acknowledging them, not shaking their hands, or patting them on the head as Pastor Harmon had done. He'd stood on the porch, a look of disgust on his face as he used the edge of the boards to wipe dogshit from the bottom of his wingtips. Leo suppressed a smirk.

Once inside, Wormley took charge, shaking hands with the adults and body-hugging Leo's mama up close. He took off his suit jacket and hung it over a chair at the family's small kitchen table. He laid his hands on Goldfish the way the other elders had done and began to pray.

"Dear Christ Jesus, in your name, we call on you to heal this precious child. Bring your spirit around her, Oh Lord, take this cough from her, take this fever, in the name of the Nazarene."

He took off his tie and threw it over his shoulder, as if it were a hindrance to getting down to the seriousness of God's business.

"And to the evil one we say, we rebuke you! You'll not harm this little girl, and she shall not be punished for the sins of her father. We call for your mercy, and your grace."

Leo watched from the doorway, fuming. *The sins of her father*? What did Daddy have to do with Goldfish being sick? He watched the fat red-faced preacher as sweat formed on his forehead and upper lip. Leo hated the man, hated the way he looked at his mama, the way he had his hands on his sister now. He wanted to scoop Goldfish up, carry her off somewhere quiet, tell them all to go to hell.

Goldfish took to coughing for a spell, sitting up and hacking phlegm on Wormley's white shirt. She then laid gently back, as if her work was done. The preacher never took his hand off her leg, using his other to fish a handkerchief from his pocket. He tried to wipe the expulsion from his shirt, but it simply smeared, leaving a delightful green splotch as big as an apple. Wormley could barely conceal his contempt, lip snarled, yet he continued to pray, ever aware of his audience.

Wormley squeezed Goldfish's leg a bit harder as he prayed, and the girl winced.

Leo wanted to throw them out of the house the way Jesus had done the money changers in the temple. Leo loved the story of Jesus throwing dishonest preachers out of his house, and he felt sure if one of those evil bastards had jumped up and smacked Jesus across his face, the Lord wouldn't have turned the other cheek. Not on that day. It might be good advice in general, to turn the other cheek, but sometimes, Leo thought, a man ought to get good and mad. Break shit that needed breaking.

Goldfish's breathing became more labored, the prayers more solemn.

That morning, she'd squeezed Leo's finger as he sat with her before everyone else woke. She'd strained to smile, to sit up, but he'd encouraged her to lay back, to try not to speak. He wanted her to get out of that bed, to come outside, to play the way she'd done back in the spring. She loved to run with Leo along the creekbank, her long gold hair falling over her narrow shoulders, calling for Leo to chase her through the trees, to play hide and seek. She did cartwheels until she lay exhausted in the grass, where she made pretend snow angels. He wanted Goldfish to crawl in bed with him, to read to her from her favorite books, for her to *scrooch up* the way she did when she was well, to push her back into him, to be the little spoon.

Leo wondered what Daddy would think of this spectacle. A spectacle at least partly caused by him. Would all these elders be here if Daddy were home? Definitely not Wormley. That morning, when Leo sat with Goldfish, Mama had whispered quietly, her face fanned with frustration: "You got to keep looking for your daddy." Leo hadn't looked her in the eyes. "I'll go again," he'd lied.

The truth was, Leo didn't want to find Daddy. Didn't want him to come home. He didn't want to think this way, felt mean about it, but they'd just have to find the son of a bitch again next month, wouldn't they? Wouldn't Daddy take the quarters Leo made from the widow and pitch a drunk someplace? If Daddy were here, he'd keep the church folk away all right; but maybe that'd be bad for Goldfish. What if she needed these prayers, at least from the good Christians? And if Daddy were here would he repent and beg mercy for Goldfish, get down on his knees and pray like the faithful?

As hard as he was on his boys, threatening always to beat the soft out of them, Daddy absolutely melted for Goldfish. With her, Daddy could be real tender, setting her on his lap, petting her cheeks as if she were the most amazing creature he'd ever seen. He would whisper to Goldfish gently, and she'd giggle at whatever silly things he said. Daddy had been like this with Mama too, once upon a time. Leo remembered Mama on Daddy's lap, her long legs draped over the arm of the chair, him running his fingers through her hair. They'd sit like that for hours, then sometimes Daddy would send the kids outside. Leo and his brothers would sit by the door and listen to Mama giggle and carry on. Mama hadn't giggled like that in so long, Leo had forgotten how it sounded.

After Jacob died, all that was over. Daddy's tenderness fled like a barn rat. He drank every night, and Mama nagged him along. The more she talked, the more he drank. He lost one job after another, stayed gone a night or two here and there, sometimes for two or three days. Mama took to cutting the liquor in his bottles with water. Daddy would sometimes figure it out, become enraged, hurl the iron skillet off the stove.

One hot summer day, Mama had emptied all of Daddy's liquor bottles while he was gone. She didn't cut the liquor with water, just poured them out in the creek, and set them back on the shelf, pretty as you please. Leo had panicked, picturing the blistering fight that would crescendo when Daddy got home. When Mama wasn't looking, he took all the bottles down to the creek, upstream of the outhouse, and filled them with creek water and silt. He had held the bottles up to the sun to make sure the color was the shade of brown Daddy would expect. When Daddy came home, he'd yelled at Leo's brothers about the chores they hadn't done. He'd sat down at the kitchen table with a bottle, pulled out the cork, took a big swig. His face pinched and he spit creek water across the floor. Daddy yelled at everyone in the house, especially Mama, throwing the bottle against the wood stove, raining glass over everything, including his children, who stood staring at their feet.

The procession of visitors to pray over Goldfish continued all day and into the afternoon. Leo's aunt and cousin Declan came. While Leo's aunt prayed, her hands on Goldfish, Declan lurked in the corner. Each time he met Leo's eyes Declan ran an index finger menacingly across his throat. Leo scowled back. The pale bastard wouldn't get the drop on him next time.

When the widow arrived in a small horse cart driven by Old Warne because the road was too rough for his car, she took over the proceedings. She smiled at all the churchwomen and Wormley as she gently elbowed him out of the way. Over the wood stove she prepared all manner of poultices to put on the girl's chest, and herb concoctions for her to drink. She chopped onions, and squeezed lemons, and held bottles of honey up to the light to pick the right ones. She talked cheerfully about the old ways and pecked Goldfish's forehead with kisses when she saw the girl was awake.

Leo heard his brothers yelling in the front yard.

"James," Hank was saying, "Look! He's back."

For a moment, Leo's heart dropped, as he thought Hank had spotted Daddy coming. Leo followed their eyes out to the tree line. It wasn't the old man. There behind a big maple, peeked the head of a red fox.

"Go get your slingshot," Hank said. "I'm gonna go 'a hunting."

"Why?" James asked. "I think he's pretty."

"What in the hell are you babbling about?" Hank said. "Get the slingshot."

James dropped his shoulders. Without another word, he went around the house and came back with the slingshot. Hank grabbed it from him and pulled a couple of stones from his pocket.

"We ain't close enough," James said. "You won't hit shit this far out."

Leo snuck up behind the boys and grabbed the slingshot out of Hank's hand. Hank dropped the stones and showed his teeth.

"You clod," he said. "Give me that back."

"It's bad luck to kill a fox," Leo said. "You're a terrible shot anyhow."

Hank stomped off around the house. Out past the field, the red fox darted from one tree to another, his eyes ever on the little house. Leo watched him for a long time, still holding the slingshot to keep it from his brothers. The fox was beautiful, with bright red and black fur and a thick tail that bounced when he sprinted from one hiding place to the next. His eyes reflected the sun, a copper twinkle even though the day was bright.

"I seen him too," the widow said. She stood on the porch behind Leo, one hand on her good hip, the other on her twisted cane. "He's been watching over this place all afternoon. Watching over Goldfish and praying with the elders. It's a sign."

In the late afternoon, the sun began losing its strength, its rays stretching out on the horizon in slow surrender. People had come and gone all day, praying and gossiping over Goldfish. A woman brought some vegetable soup that Hank and James would have devoured completely if Leo hadn't intervened and saved bowls for Mama and Goldfish. Leo tracked the movements of the red fox, which seemed to patrol a wide perimeter, when he heard a commotion at the front of the house. Leo came around the corner to find a group of folks crowded around a man on the front porch.

"I have come to see about the child and to see if I might render any service which may be helpful in her speedy recovery." When the man made an S sound, it came as a Z. Leo started to laugh at the man's weird voice, but everyone else seemed serious so he pushed it down.

The man was quite tall and thin with sharp cheekbones and deep eye sockets. His eyes were creek stone gray and he was bald, save for a shock of silver at the edges of his temples. He was dressed in black from head to toe, wearing church pants that fell into a wide cuff around his dull cowboy boots. He had on a leather belt with a golden buckle and wore several gold rings on each hand. He carried a brown leather bag that clinked against his leg.

"Perhaps there are z-*cientific* means by which to treat this precious girl," the man said.

The widow came out onto the porch, hobbling on her twisted cane. Her eyes narrowed when she saw the man, her nose scrunched up like she'd caught a whiff of something foul.

When the man noticed her, his face lit up. "I do declare, my good sister," he said.

"My Lord," the widow hissed.

The man approached; his hands outstretched as if he might embrace her. "I am so pleazed to zee you." The man stretched out his words so long they hung in the air. He didn't sound like local folk, but more like an old lady Leo knew from church. She was from down east, where the mountains disappeared, and the earth stretched out flat to the sea. Mountain folk said flatlanders couldn't help but stretch their words out long on their tongues like the land around them. The man talked like that, but with a dark coarseness in his throat.

The widow puffed out her chest like a bullfrog, resting both hands on the cane in front of her body to block the hug.

"We don't need your potions, Alchemist."

"They are not potions, my dear sister in Christ. These are the great elixirs of science, of medicine. Of the most advanced

61

thinking. There are many things in my bag what might cure her within a fortnight. You must know that I can help her, as I have helped so many." He showed the widow his open palms.

"You ain't needed here," the widow said, her lips pursed. "We've the power of the Lord to call upon in these dark times."

"Can you help my sister?" Leo asked, stepping up onto the porch.

The Alchemist turned to Leo. He bent down and opened his bag to reveal dozens of bottles of liquid, some full of powder. When he bent, it was with only his waist; his legs remained straight, as if his body had one large hinge in the middle. When he straightened, he looked from Leo to the widow, then back.

"Ahhh," the man said, clasping his long fingers together in a bony bouquet. "I can help your sister. God works through man, you see, God gives us industry, knowledge, science. We mustn't fear these things. Science is of God. For God used the laws of science and physics to craft the very earth on which we stand. He made it from the elements and of the firmament, the rudiments and chemicals we now harness in the cure of disease for those who suffer needlessly in the world, ignorant of the power of all He has provided."

Leo studied the man. Maybe he could help little Goldfish.

To Leo, the Alchemist said, "Might you know if there is any coffee in this house? I should like a cup before I examine the girl to make recommendations regarding her care and the selection from my apothecarist bag."

The family had run out of coffee weeks ago, but the smell of coffee had wafted through the house all day, a pot kept full on the wood stove, undoubtedly brewed by one of the church women that took up residency inside.

While Leo was embarrassed to bring the well-dressed man coffee in a bent tin cup, the Alchemist took the drink with both hands, as if it were made of fine China. He brought the cup to his lips with an expression of such overwhelming joy, one would have thought he'd been presented with a magical elixir from the Garden of Eden itself. Leo noticed the man's eyebrows were not flat like most. Instead, the lines of his eyebrows slanted up at the outer edges into wrinkles that extended up and over his bare skull. These lines were perfectly symmetrical, and Leo shuddered when he imagined them extending up from his forehead to form perfect horns.

The widow watched the Alchemist with distaste as he set his empty coffee cup on the porch banister and went inside. Passing Mama, he dipped his head, whispering "Ma'am." Bedside, he listened to Goldfish's breathing, his head to her chest. He then put his forehead to hers, once more bending only at the waist, knees straight, his body a perfect right angle. He picked up each of her hands and let them drop again to the bed, doing the same with each foot. He shook each foot gently. He stood then, for a long time, his hand on his chin. The churchwomen and elders watched him closely, leaning in when he spoke.

"I do not discount the power of prayer," the Alchemist said. "For what is more powerful than our God? Yet God has provided chemistry and alchemy to form a magnificent bond for man's health and wellness."

The Alchemist gestured to the faithful.

"I do not discount God's hand in all our fates. But I most assuredly can help this young lady. I only ask for a small, hmmm, let's call it a donation. I only seek to replace the stock of medicines I use so that I may go forward and help the next soul in need. Certainly, this is reasonable and to be expected."

"And there it is," the widow said, stepping into the room. "A *donation*, indeed. Man of science? You may use long words full of fancy to move people out on the town square to open up their pocketbooks, but God says be thou not deceived. We are not deceived."

"Sister," the man said, clearly frustrated. He turned to the folks gathered around Goldfish's bed. He looked from person to person, as if trying to locate a friendly face. "Ahh, brother," he said at last, to someone in the back of the room.

From the corner, Wormley emerged. He strode across the room and held out a hand to the Alchemist. When he did so, his shirt sleeve slid up. Leo saw a small blue tattoo of a snowflake, just at the wrist.

"It's true," Wormley said to the room, lifting his arms to the heavens. "I have seen this man cure many a body, right on their deathbed. I propose we take up a collection to help this girl, and of course, we continue to pray for her, without ceasing." Reverend Wormley nodded so slightly to the Alchemist, it could have been easily missed. Leo marveled at how the preacher had deferred so quickly to the Alchemist in front of so many people.

A collection was taken up, and Mama fetched the quarters Leo had made from the widow to put on the table with the other money. The Alchemist quickly slipped the coins and bills into a black change purse which he slid even more quickly into his pants pocket. He then bent over the kitchen table, mixing liquids and powders into a small bottle. After the Alchemist had administered his concoction to Goldfish by dropper, he slipped outside as the faithful prayed over the girl once more. Wormley stood at the head of the bed, his garishly plump fingers splayed over the girl's forehead. He prayed even more loudly than before.

When Leo had enough, he went out into the fall night. The Alchemist was in the field near the creek, leaning against a weeping willow tree.

"Kind sir," the Alchemist said, dipping his head. He now wore a black cowboy hat, and smoked a cigarette, holding it between his thumb and middle finger. The cigarette was a perfect cylinder, clearly machine rolled. Leo noticed a snowflake tattoo on the Alchemist's wrist, just below his black cufflink. The ink was dark blue, the color of the sky before a storm. It was identical to the one he'd seen on Reverend Wormley.

"What is your name?" the Alchemist asked.

"Leo."

The man repeated the name, somehow adding a syllable: ELL-EE-OH. "What a bold name, as strong as a lion, your name is."

"Thank you," Leo said.

"Thank you for the most excellent coffee," the man said.

"Welcome," Leo said. "Thank you for helping my sister."

"I only come to do my humble part. The good Christian sister," he said, "distrusts things she doesn't understand. Things of chemistry and of the study of science."

"Yes, sir," Leo said.

"We mustn't fear things we don't understand, Leo."

"I like what you said inside," Leo said. "How God give us the laws of science, like gravity, and physics. I read about them in books."

The Alchemist dipped his head. "That's good Leo. Nothing is more powerful than science."

The two of them stood for a long time, not speaking.

"Well," the Alchemist started, "there is one thing more powerful."

"God?" Leo asked.

"Maybe so," the Alchemist said, lighting another cigarette from the first. "But that's not what I mean."

"What then?" Leo asked.

The man turned to look Leo in the eyes. "*Words.*"

"Words?"

"Words start wars, Leo. Men can be incited to absolute violence with a clever turn of phrase. One can stir a crowd into a frenzy with a simple slogan."

Leo looked at the grooved wrinkle lines that spread up the man's face until they reached the the Alchemist's cowboy hat. He wondered what they would feel like.

"Words can overthrow kingdoms. Take poetry, Leo. I can write a poem, right here tonight, and make the biggest, strongest man lose his mind."

Leo pictured a man brought low by the words of a poem, the man weakening like Samson after Delilah cut off his long locks.

The Alchemist took a drag on his cigarette, the tip pulsing orange. He reached down to pick up his bag. The liquid in the bottles jostled.

"Are you a man of industry, Leo?" the Alchemist asked.

"Sir?"

"Work, Leo, are you a man who likes to work, to make coin, to provide for those whom he loves? I seek collaborators in my endeavors. In town, I mean."

"In Altamont?" Leo asked.

"Yes," said the Alchemist.

Leo looked at the house, saw Mama on the front porch, talking to the widow. He was torn about trusting this new stranger. But he thought of his hunger, of Goldfish's illness.

"We could use the money," Leo said.

"Most excellent, Master Leo," the Alchemist said. "We'll meet soon again, for I've foreseen it in the very stars."

Chapter 9

Leo woke sick to his stomach, a deep ache that worked through his middle till it reached his backbone. He'd felt it before. He hadn't named it, hadn't said anything about it to Mama, though he'd had it all week, every night before falling asleep, every morning when he woke. But there it was: hunger. He held his tongue, but his younger brother couldn't. Before everyone had their eyes open good, James went to grousing. "Mama, what've we got that's good to eat? I'm starved."

Without looking at his brother, Leo pictured James's face, the way he tended to draw his mouth when he was whining, like he'd just taken in a mouthful of kyarn. He thought of lecturing him about how he was old enough to fix his own damned breakfast and to help work for the food they needed, that every task didn't need to be laid at Mama's feet. Instead, he frogged his brother in the leg.

"Owww," James whined.

"Eat you a potato," Mama said. Her voice was flat, her tone distant, as if she answered from far away.

"Will you fry us up some?" James asked, face puckered tighter, by the sound of it.

"Eat it raw like I done for my dinner last night," Mama said. "Nature give it to us raw." She rose to empty the ashes of the wood stove to build a fire for the day. When Leo's feet hit the floor, it was like stepping into a frozen lake. A shiver took hold in his body that worked its way up the back of his legs and into his spine. It made the hunger worse, somehow.

One thing made Leo feel better. Goldfish had been taken to the widow's a few nights before, on account of how sick she was getting, and how drafty the family's shack was. It had been about a week since the elders came to pray, and so far, prayer had failed, along with the remedies left by the Alchemist. Goldfish would get three solid meals a day at the widow's, and all the bread she wanted, if she was strong enough to sit up and eat it. Leo thought of the widow's stew, and his stomach twisted.

He tried to take the shovel and bucket from Mama, to take care of the fire for her. Mama cut her eyes at him. "You got more important things to tend to, and I'm tired of asking you to do what's yours to do."

Daddy had been gone for two and a half weeks now. Leo started to throw up the excuse of the wood that needed chopping at the widow's, but Mama's face told him all he needed to know about that way of thinking.

After he was dressed and at the door, Mama met him on the porch with a potato wrapped in a blue washrag. It wasn't peeled, but it was good-sized, about as big as his palm.

"Go now," she whispered, looking up into the sky, as if Daddy were up there, floating in the clouds.

Leo made his way down the dirt road that snaked through the holler. He thought of going to get Lilyfax, who'd offered a few days before to join him on the trip. Because her people had moved from Tennessee a year before, she had only been to town once or twice. Her daddy had taken her along the river to a feed and seed but refused to take her downtown to see the tall buildings she'd heard so much about.

Leo was still on the fence about going round to fetch her when a peculiar feeling took hold in him, his vision narrowing, as if the world grew smaller around him. Though the sun was mostly obscured by clouds, Leo's shadow stretched out in front of him on the dirt road, bouncing with each step. Now it expanded, and he lost the outline of his body, as if it had been swallowed entirely. It was as if something behind him towered over him. Leo jerked around. Nothing but empty road.

Turning back, he saw only the shape of his body outlined in shadow for a few moments before, once more, an enormous profile formed on the ground out in front of him. This time the hulking silhouette was more defined, as if it were a painting on the ground. Leo stopped walking. The shadow poured out in front of him, till limbs emerged, a huge head in the pitch. A large mouth, jagged canine teeth. Leo spun again toward the sun. There was nothing behind him but an open road and the vast blue mountains that stretched toward the horizon.

Leo thought of the widow's wulvers. The one he'd seen in the woods with the rabbits, wrapped in bright light, the Silver Wulver. He thought then of the one ever bathed in shadow, the Shadow Wulver. He tried to push them from his mind, the idea of them, the silliness of it all.

He tried to focus on the task at hand: getting to Altamont. Finding Daddy. Talking the drunk bastard into coming home. Pleasing Mama. Keeping her from floating over the edge, from burning their animals to death, from becoming a mountain witch like in her dream.

He kept his eyes way out in front of him, ignoring his shadow, pretending not to see the inky specter there, sweeping the dirt road in front of him. Finally, he couldn't help but look. The long neck extending over Leo's own head, the profile of its jaw opening wide.

He knew if he turned around there would be nothing, the beast toying with him somehow. Then his eye caught something in the trees off to his left. Just inside the wood line, the shape of a boy. Jacob in the trees. His skin emerging from the shadows, pale in the garish sunlight.

Get thee behind me, Leo whispered. But Jacob did not go away, instead leaning from the trees, a grin on his face, his lips stretched unnaturally wide across his face.

Leo thought to run as he had so many times, each time Jacob had come to him. Each time he had come and whispered in Leo's head. But Leo decided not to run. He stopped walking and looked at the boy, studied his face, the thin long lips. The bowl haircut, the dingy jumper with the yellow stain. Jacob stopped smiling. He spoke to Leo in the horrible unknown tongue, as if in death, the dead forgot English, spoke only the language of angels and devils, a language foreign and forbidden.

Leo had tried everything to keep his distance from the ghost, to stay away from the dead boy. Today, Leo decided, *I ain't running.*

Only Leo did run. Toward Jacob. Toward the trees, toward the shadows, Leo sprinted into all the darkness the woods held. Jacob saw Leo coming, a slight tint of blue haloing his body. Jacob's eyes offered a hint of contempt as he turned away. Jacob descended and ran through the trees deep into the woods. Leo gave chase as Jacob darted between huge maples and elms. The forest floor was covered with a deep blanket of dry leaves that swirled around their feet.

Ahead, Jacob drew up suddenly. Between two trees, the outline of the boy extended up to tower over Leo, who slid on the leaves, trying to stop. Between the trees, the pillar of smoke formed, the familiar kaleidoscoping of dark pitch cloud and smoke. Then came the deep grinding voice in his head, unnaturally low, octaves below that of a man. A voice Leo had tried to forget.

I am darkness, and I am night –
I'll eat your dreams and steal the light –

Leo froze, as if in the midst of some hellish nightmare, an unseen weight of fear burdening his body, forbidding movement, forbidding escape. He thought of the beast's words, and how the Alchemist had talked of the power of words. Of what they could do to a man.

A long hand with slender fingers extended from the pillar of smoke. The shadows formed a body, the head deep black and blue ash. Leo was drawn to the emptiness there, as if his eyes might be pulled from their sockets. He'd felt this horrible pull before, but he had tried to forget it. Leo tried to speak, but words wouldn't come at first, his mouth dry and his head empty.

Then, the words came: "Get thee behind me."

The shadow cut him off, its words banging around Leo's head like rocks in a barrel.

Behind thee, I should get?

70

Behind thee, I should go?

The pillar laughed; a hollow bellowing cackle that echoed across the valley and scaled the mountains. Leo stared into the darkness. For a moment, he was sure he saw black teeth. Fangs.

The shadows twisted, with a crowing howl. It jerked violently and contorted, collapsing in on itself, the darkness folding. Soon it was a great beast, at first appearing in outline much like a giant black bear. The darkness continued to mix, until before Leo, between the trees, stood the Shadow Wulver. The wulver was on all fours, and it growled so loud the earth vibrated. Bottomless cobalt blue eyes formed in the skull, and, while parts of the specter appeared leathery and tangible, its other surfaces were see-through, bearing a blurred translucence. The Shadow Wulver lowered its head and showed its teeth.

Pushing the weight off his chest, Leo ran.

The wulver was behind him, he could tell, but not on his heels. Instead, it stalked slowly along, while Leo frantically ran, banging hard into trees and brush, his arms and face cut and burning. Leo didn't look back, tried to tell himself he'd make it to the road and the Shadow Wulver would fade into the darkness, just as the pillar had always done.

Leo made it to the road, stopped to catch his breath. He turned to see the Shadow Wulver coming with an abrupt staccato march, up on its hind legs, its head high in the trees, the limbs of the forest cracking as if under the weight of some bitter ice storm. When the beast reached the road, it returned again to all fours and bounded toward him. The earth shook with the thunderous sound of its paws striking the ground.

Leo sprinted until his lungs smoldered, the cold morning air taking up in his chest. He scoured the ground for a weapon. Looked for a large rock or stick, seeing nothing.

Up ahead on the ground, just at the edge of the road, something caught the light. In his frenzy, Leo scooped it up, only to realize it was a book. It wasn't much of a weapon, but it would have to do. Leo turned, holding the book in his hand as if to throw it at the wulver.

The Shadow Wulver drew its body suddenly up, as if it wanted to stop, but had too much momentum. It stretched its paws out in front of its body, using them to brake its forward motion. The creature's paws dug deep trenches in the earth as it came on. It stopped just feet from Leo's face. It growled, head low, and paced back and forth on the road, as if there were an imaginary line it dare not cross.

A bright light shone behind Leo, creating a new shadow from his body out on the road. This was impossible, as the sun was in front of him now, but still his shadow was there, stretching out near the long legs of the Shadow Wulver. The Shadow Wulver looked past Leo and snarled at the light. Leo turned to see a bright light coming through the trees, highlighting a path off the road, a path that snaked into the woods. The Shadow Wulver stirred the earth with its paws, as if frustrated. Leo turned the book over in his hand. *Hymns of the Psalter* was printed in gold lettering on the cover of the red book. Leo opened it to find lines of music and words printed above them.

A few feet ahead of him, there was another book in the dirt. Another hymnal. Following the path in the woods, Leo found hymn books every ten feet or so, some quite dirty, some covered in mud. He picked up each hymnal as he went, wiping them off on his shirt. Leo followed the bright light along the path off the road. When he looked back, the Shadow Wulver was gone.

At a certain point, the path was just tamped down vegetation. Leo turned a corner, trying to balance eight songbooks in his hands when he saw the frame of a building ahead in a clearing. Beside it, sat a truck with a wooden bed. A man came across the field, carrying an ax.

"What in the world! Let me help you with those," the man said.

The man had bright red hair and a full beard. He wore brown pants with suspenders over a white shirt. He blotted his freckled forehead with a handkerchief as he approached.

They met near the truck and the man threw his ax in the bed.

"You saved my bacon, sure as the world," the man said.

He took the hymnals and stacked them in a crate. There was a dozen more hymnals in the large wooden box, all with the same gold lettering. In the bed beside some freshly planed boards there was a cross made of iron. The man followed Leo's eyes.

"Yep, that's a cross," he said. He looked toward the small building. "I'm building a church."

Leo examined the man's face. "You some kind of preacher man?"

"No," the man laughed, "Just a humble church builder."

The frame of the church building was quite compact, much smaller than any church Leo had ever seen.

The man stuck out his hand.

"I'm Mr. Goodman." The man's grip was tight, like a deacon's. "Good-Man. Though some folks call me Red." He put his hands on his hips. "What do they call you?"

"Leo."

The man had deep brown eyes with bright gold flecks that caught the light when he spoke.

"Excuse me," Leo said, "but ain't this building a bit small for a church?"

The man nodded, scratching his head. He smiled, his mouth full of bright crooked teeth.

"This here is a different kind of church, Leo."

"How's that?"

"It's a church anyone can call their own."

Leo didn't answer.

"Leo," the man continued, "this is a church anybody can go to. Anytime they like. It will be open twenty four hours a day, seven days a week. It won't have locks on the doors. There won't be any preachers, or choir. You just come in whenever you take a notion and get close to God. Pray, or sing, read your Bible, whatever you feel called to do."

"Why would folks do that, instead of going to a regular church?"

"Why wait till Sunday if you need to get off alone with God today?"

The man walked toward the structure for a moment, before turning back to Leo.

"This is a church everyone is welcomed into. You don't have to be baptized, you don't have to be a member, you don't have to know anybody. It doesn't matter who your daddy is."

Leo nodded.

The man held both his hands up toward the sky. "A church for the sinners and the saints."

"What do you mean?" Leo asked.

"Leo churches are for the sinners. But sometimes the faithful forget that. Look down their noses at folks that have got a past."

"Yes, sir," Leo said.

"This church is for people that're close to God, but the whores and the drunkards, Leo, they can come too. I'll have little candles in the windows, and there are free bibles, and, thanks to you, hymn books if they take a notion to sing."

Leo thought about the last time his family went to church. He'd loved seeing Pastor Harmon, and hearing the good man preach, but when his family sat down in a pew near the back, the people next to them had gotten up and moved away. Leo could still see the woman's hard face as she hooked her hand in her son's arm pit to drag him off. Maybe they'd heard about Leo's daddy going missing. Maybe they didn't like the ragged clothes the kids wore, the way the sole of James's shoes had started to flop when he walked.

"Can I visit this church sometime?" Leo asked.

"Maybe you weren't listening," Mr. Goodman smiled. "This church is for everybody. You are welcome anytime, Leo, day or night. But first I got to finish building it."

Up the mountain something bright caught Leo's eye. This time it was the Silver Wulver. Had it been the source of bright light Leo had seen? The Silver Wulver glided along just beyond the tree line. Maybe that's why the Shadow Wulver hadn't been able to follow? Maybe it was on guard? Maybe churches were sacred ground? Leo recalled the breath of the Shadow Wulver on the back of his neck, and his body caught chill, his shoulders quivering. He thought to leave Goodman's side now, to approach the Silver Wulver in the trees, but he was afraid.

When Leo looked back to Mr. Goodman, he had a look of knowing, as if he'd seen the Silver Wulver as well, knew all about the presence of the wulvers. Leo thought to say something, but when he looked again to the trees, the Silver Wulver was gone.

"Mr. Goodman," Leo said.

"Yes, Leo?"

"What will you name this church?"

The man fell silent for a moment. His broad shoulders flexed, then relaxed.

"Just over that hill yonder," he said. "There's a little creek, Leo. It kind of bubbles down, soft like, peaceful like. I'm thinking of naming the church after that creek. I am thinking to call it *The Brookside Chapel.*"

On his way home, Leo thought of Goodman's little church, of there being a place his mama and sister could come to worship God, away from the gawking of the hard-faced church women back in the valley. He was home before he thought again of the Shadow Wulver, having passed through many miles of dark woods before it occurred to him to once again be afraid. Then he thought of Altamont, of Daddy and his failed mission to retrieve the bastard. Leo felt guilt for a moment but pushed it down.

Chapter 10

The next morning, the air thick with the smell of snow, Leo prepared a small pack and set out for Altamont. When he got up the road a good ways, he looked back at the house. A figure in the front yard. A towering, rotund man, and when the man reached the porch, he looked in Leo's direction. Reverend Wormley. He'd come along the creekbank as he was wont to do, rather than take the road, the way a dog slinks around when it's up to no good. Leo started toward the house when Mama came onto the porch. She yelled something, and his younger brother James came out, disappearing into the woods. Uncharacteristically, Hank had set out before daylight. Wormley and Mama went into the house, Mama slamming the door behind them. Leo drew up, balled his fists.

He turned back to the road and ran until his legs got tired. He would get to Altamont, he'd find Daddy today, if it killed him. If for no other reason than for Daddy to run off that bastard Wormley for good. But first he'd stop to get Lilyfax. He smiled at the thought of hearing her laugh as they traveled along the road, of the way her dimples would conspire to show themselves despite her best efforts to keep them hidden. But thinking of Lilyfax made bile rise in his throat.

His dreams had been full of dark shadows, of a world void of sunlight and loud with the sound of a thousand wailing voices. He caught chill at the image that had come to him over and over during the night: that of Lilyfax tied to a tree. Only she wasn't bound with ropes or chains. Instead, great thick vines snaked along the ground and up her legs, wrapping around her, squeezing her to the tree until she had no air. Till she turned blue. Leo tried to shake his dreams off now, to tell himself they weren't visions of things to come, the way the widow always said of dreams, that they had no meaning.

He took a fork in the rutted road, and it narrowed, a steep bank up the hill on one side, a drop off on the other. Sometimes when Leo walked this piece of road, he caught the slight notion of vertigo, especially if he got too close to the edge.

He heard voices. They were close, but they didn't come from the road, as he could see ahead for at least a mile. He stood still and listened. He heard several boys, on the bank above him. Leo hugged the bank, to avoid being seen. Then he recognized one of the voices. It was his cousin Declan.

"One down, one to go," Declan said.

"The fun one," another voice said. It took Leo a second. It was Hank.

"Ain't it the truth," Declan said.

"She was feisty like I figured," said Hank.

"Now, she said he'd be coming along directly. Where is Leo?" Declan asked.

"He was still in the bed when I left," Hank said.

"He's gonna be madder than hell."

Leo felt his ears warm. He stepped away from the bank to the middle of the road.

"Madder than hell about what?" he said.

Declan startled then sneered, folded his arms over his chest. "Well if it ain't old Leo, out for a morning stroll."

"What're you talking about?" Leo asked.

Declan squatted down, rocking on the balls of his feet. He took out a cigarette and put it to his lips. "Part of me," he said, lighting up, "wants to jump down this bank and beat your ass, since your girlfriend ain't here to protect you." He spit some of the extra tobacco off his pink tongue.

He turned to the other boys. "He don't look so tough now, no tom-bitch to take up for him."

The boys sniggered in agreement. Leo met Hank's eyes.

"She said you'd be coming," Hank said.

"Who?"

"Your girl that looks like a boy," Declan said.

"She was a lot of fun." Hank said.

"What did you do?" Leo asked.

"Fixed her up," Declan said, "fixed her up nice. She's got girl parts under all that tomboy."

"I'll skin you alive," Leo said. He fished for his pocketknife, thought how it would feel plunged in the boy's gut.

To Hank, Declan said, "You know the thing that surprised me most?"

"What's that?" Hank asked, with a smirk.

Declan met Leo's eyes. "How good a kisser she is."

"You son of a bitch!"

"Hell," Declan said, "I didn't think we'd get her off the last boy, that hussy."

Leo looked at Declan, then Hank, and the three other boys with them. He knew the others from school. He marked their faces down in his mind.

"She wanted all of us to kiss her. So, we had to be gentlemen, give her what she wanted."

"I'll kill every last one of you," Leo said.

"Don't be mad at me," Declan said, taking another drag from the pinched cigarette. "It ain't our fault she likes it so much."

Leo ran toward the bank and scaled it, his hands pulling out clumps of weeds and sticks as he tried to scramble up.

He was near the top when a rock struck his shoulder. It sent a wave of pain down his side. He looked up to see Declan holding a larger rock, big enough to take him two hands. He lifted it over his head and took a step toward the bank. Leo let go of the weeds and rolled down to the road. The huge rock struck the earth beside him.

"If you hurry," Declan said, "you can probably catch her."

"Where is she?"

"She's sweeter than she looks," one of the boys said, puckering his lips.

"Where?" Leo said.

"Well, she was down by Sawyer Pond," Declan said. "Reckon she could still be there, if she ain't run off with the first man who come along. Little whore."

Leo pointed at Declan. "I'll come for you." He pointed at each of the boys, ending with Hank. "Every last one of you."

"You do that," Declan said. He flipped his cigarette at Leo. "We'll be waiting."

Leo ran down the road toward Sawyer Pond.

He ran harder than he'd ever run before. Ran until his chest hurt and he was sure he'd throw up. Replayed everything Declan and Hank and the others had said, their ugly faces twisted and proud.

He found her beside the pond, her back against a tree. There was a fresh hole in the knee of her overalls, her white shirt covered in mud.

"Lily!" Leo yelled.

She looked up. She'd been crying, streaks dried down her cheeks. Leo took a knee beside her. He was panting, struggling to catch his breath.

"You okay?"

"Yeah," she said, but she didn't look okay. Her hair was tousled, and a black eye formed thickly beneath one eyelid. Leo reached out to touch her shoulder, but she slapped his hand away.

"I almost got away," Lilyfax said. She brushed loose hair from her eyes. "Till they cornered me at the pond. Didn't feel like going for a swim."

"Who hit you? Who hit your eye?"

"Chased me for a good long while. I was faster, but there was more of them."

"Your eye," Leo said.

Lilyfax grinned. "Will I have a good shiner? Make my old man proud?"

"Who did it?"

She stopped smiling. "Who do you think?"

"Declan," Leo said.

"Of course. The others mostly just held me still for him. Mostly."

"What," Leo started. "What did they do to you?"

"They held me down so he could stick his lizard tongue down my throat. Put his hands all over me."

Leo pictured his cousin on top of Lilyfax, the other boys holding her arms and legs, the way the vines had in his dream.

"I should've hit him harder with that tobacco stake," Lilyfax said.

Leo pictured Declan's egg sac head, the pulsing blue veins under the skin. Pictured pounding it until his fists were bloody – not from his own blood, but Declan's. He remembered one time getting so mad at Daddy he'd gone outside and punched a tree. The pain had surged all through him like a virus taking hold in his blood. Leo remembered the way the wood felt, busting open his knuckles. He wanted to feel that pain again.

"I'm sorry," he said.

Lilyfax started to smile, but the corners of her mouth eased back into a frown. "You should be," she said, "if you'd been about a half hour earlier, instead of lollygagging all morning."

"Lilyfax," he said. He put his forehead against her shoulder.

"Ow!" she said.

Leo pulled back. "It hurts?"

"Everywhere," she said, lip trembling. "They hit me all over. It was the only way they could get me to stop kicking their balls."

"Did Hank—" Leo started.

"He mostly held me down, but he hit me too."

"Did they all—" Leo started.

"Did they all kiss me? They all tried. But I drew blood a couple times. Some of their tongues will be swollen before sundown."

He said nothing.

"I'm a biter," she said.

A knot tightened in his gut.

"I reckon spitting on Declan's face was a bad idea." She cupped her hands together. "That's when he hit my face."

"I promise," Leo said, standing. He looked up into the mountains. "I'll get every last one of them."

"I busted his ear drum – at least that's what he said, said he can't hear out of that ear a lick now," Lilyfax said, "He give me a shiner for it, maybe we just call it even."

"Hell no," Leo said. Blood rushed to his head, through his limbs. He felt alive. He wanted to break everything in the world, tear it all down to size.

Lilyfax reached in her pocket.

"The worst part," she said, pulling out fragments of green glass, "is they smashed my guardian angel."

Leo remembered the angel, something Lilyfax had said her ninny gave her before she'd died of consumption.

"I carried it a long time, years it watched over me." She wiped a tear from her cheek. She looked away, out over the pond. "It fell out of my pocket. One of them stomped it."

One wing was still intact, the other shapes just shards.

It began to snow, an angry gray cloud stretching monstrously in the sky, the undulating shape of some rabid beast, mouth full of foam. Big fluffy snowflakes appeared in the dark sky. Lilyfax opened her mouth to catch one on her tongue, like a child. He thought about what Declan had said, about how Lilyfax loved to kiss, and he pictured Declan's fat tongue against hers and he felt sick again.

"Damn." Lilyfax jumped. She looked down at her hand, where the glass had just cut her. Red lines radiated out filling the grooves at the center of her palm.

Leo remembered the way the shadows had wrapped around the pitchfork in the barn, the day Lilyfax had saved him from Declan. The darkness had tried to show him the way, but he'd resisted. Why had he resisted? Declan should have been impaled on the tines of the pitchfork. All over that fast. He couldn't have hurt Lilyfax if Leo had only taken it up. And Hank. If Hank had seen Leo run the fork through Declan, he'd have learned his place. He'd have learned never to mess with Leo again, or Lilyfax.

"The snow, Leo," Lilyfax said, her eyes wide with wonder. "Even on ugly days, there are beautiful things."

Leo nodded, but thought only of how Declan's blood would look, dripping onto the white snow that would soon cover the earth.

"Leo," Lilyfax said, "Walk me home."

On the walk, she took his hand. This was the first time they'd ever held hands. Leo had put his hand over hers once, and she'd pulled hers away. Her hand was warm, and her heat radiated over him, though his thoughts were far way. On Declan.

After Lilyfax was safely inside, Leo headed for his cousin's. He wouldn't take the road that opened up into vast fields where he could be seen. No, he would take the mountain road and come round from behind.

Chapter 11

The world folds up in wintertime. Leaves fall and curl upon themselves and the vast tree branches hang bare, outlines only, tracing their former splendor. Long gone the vibrant opening green shoots of spring, the drooping petals of flowers baptized by dew on summer mornings, their tranquility broken only by the warm buzz of honeybees at work. In winter, the world slouches, the landscape brown and gray, cold rains come, mud creeping over every road and trail. But something magical happens when the ground hardens, frozen from the deep cold, when snow begins to fall, painting the world a silent blanket of white, all the ugly hidden beneath. At least for a time.

The late afternoon sky slunk grey, the clouds low and heavy. Several inches of snow had fallen by the time Leo found the old mountain path that would allow him to come in behind Declan's house, an approach that would keep him unseen. All the anger in the world boiled within him, and he was impatient, at times running off the trail to cut the angles, before finding it again.

Leo feasted on his anger, wallowed in it. There was so much to draw upon: the missing worthless daddy, Mama slipping into madness, the coy ugliness of Hank's betrayal, the snarling church women. Goldfish on the bed at the widow's, dying, just as Jacob had done. There was Wormley, his fat hands doing God knows what to his mama. There were the other three boys, who, conspiring with Hank and Declan, had held a girl down, taking turns touching her body and kissing her face. Leo held each boy's facial expression in his mind, pictured the way their looks would change, their hideous smugness erased, when he came for them. He thought of rocks that would break bones, sticks that would bruise skin and bring forth blood, of knives and axes and pitchforks that can tear open the flesh. Leo was hot, despite the cold. The snow melted as quick as it met his neck, its cool offspring running down his back.

The widow's words came to him. She warned against letting one's anger take over, about how it could find one's heart and twist it like a gnarled root. Could Leo let go of this anger? Could he stay in the light? Maybe. After Declan was punished. And Hank. And the other boys. And Wormley. And everyone who had ever throw'd off on his people. Only then could he live in the light, leave his anger behind. For now, it must be fed.

Leo stood on a ridge pondering the mountains around him. The trees shook, the heavy snow on their branches sloughing off in thick sheets. Something swayed the branches; they didn't move of their own accord. Then he saw dozens of white butterflies sparkling in the trees. They fluttered their wings in unison, as if they were one creature, taking flight into the twilight sky. There were soon hundreds, then thousands. They swarmed Leo, gleaming like crystals. They landed on his shoulders and arms, and when he held out his hand, several danced on his fingers. Their legs felt like minute strands of ice. They caught the breeze, flying up and over the ridge ahead. Leo raced after them.

In a clearing, there were huge marks in the tree trunks, the bark missing, as if this were a place bears met to sharpen their claws. Ahead of him, the crystal butterflies mounded on the ground. They morphed into various shapes, stretching and elongating. Leo approached slowly.

The mound of butterflies grew larger, and all was silent in the woods, save the soft flutter of their icy wings, which clinked lightly like small bells. The mound took form: legs took shape, then a tail. The body settled, the butterflies flying away one by one up into the trees, the smooth legato rhythm of their wings in perfect accord. Beneath the butterflies was silver fur. When they disappeared, the Silver Wulver remained.

A wave of warmth washed over Leo, and for a moment he was on the pews of the family's church, back in better times, back when Mama snuggled him up close, when the church women walked up to put their hands on Mama's, whispering words of encouragement to Leo and his siblings. Back when Pastor Harmon gave sermons that brought Leo peace, the crackle of the church's fireplace making the world toasty and warm. But there was something different about the Silver Wulver, its eyes bearing a smoky cobalt blue color, unlike the shiny pearl-colored eyes he'd seen before.

Then Leo was on his bed, back before Jacob had died. He and Jacob nestled back-to-back on the straw mattress, slipping under, approaching sleep. Snowflake curled between them, radiating heat against their bare legs. It began to snow, and because the house's wood shingles curled with neglect, there were gaps in the roof where snow fell through. The snow made thin white lines along the floor and over Leo's bed. Jacob stuck his tongue out to catch some of them as they fell. The snowflakes sizzled as they landed on the wood stove.

Then Leo floated up, into the air, the heavy blankets falling away, Jacob calling after him in the unknown tongue. As he reached the ceiling, Leo's body shimmied through the gaps in the roof, to race through the trees, past the creek and into the mountains. He floated above the peaks and when he looked down, he saw his cousin's house, smoke curling from the old rock chimney, cutting a dark swirl in the waxing snowfall. Leo remembered then, his anger. The way Declan had licked his lips when he spoke of Lilyfax's body.

Then Leo was back in the clearing before the Silver Wulver. It raised its eyes to meet his, now bearing a hint of menace. The flapping of a thousand butterfly wings purred in perfect unison, before they slowed, until each butterfly was perfectly still, the whole world held in quiet suspension. All was calm for a moment before the great wulver showed its teeth. It growled, deep and horrible the sound echoing through the trees and over the mountains. Leo wasn't afraid. He was too angry to be afraid.

Behind the wulver, Leo's eyes were drawn to a spark of orange. Within the base of a great tree, in an amber glow, there was an outline: a figure posed with outstretched arms, legs long beneath. Leo walked toward the tree and saw it held a girl. It was Lilyfax, suspended in the great trunk, arms outstretched, wearing the blue dress she'd had on that day at the widow's mailbox. Her legs were straight below her, one bare foot placed elegantly over the other. Her face held an expression of horror, as if she'd been frozen in the middle of some nightmare.

Leo ran to the tree and struck it with his fists.

He called to the wulver.

"Help me!" Leo struck the icy surface, his knuckles cracking open.

He turned to find the wulver creeping toward him, head low.

"Help me free her!" he yelled.

When he turned back to the tree, the amber glow was gone, along with Lilyfax. His hands gripped only the cold bark of the enormous oak, thick snow gathering on its broad limbs.

Behind him the wulver howled, the deep low sound quaking through the earth. In the trees one of the crystal butterflies turned dark. Then there were two dark butterflies, then a dozen, like so many flakes of pepper in a sea of bright salt. Leo stared into the eyes of the wulver. He walked down from the tree to where it stood. The wulver lowered its head, teeth visible. Gray strands of fur stretched out from its eyes. They raced up at an angle, spreading over the colossal cranium of the beast.

Behind the wulver, thousands of dark butterflies flickered like waves, washing away the light. Their wings fluttered in a disjointed rhythm, out of sync, the noise deafening.

The wulver's face darkened. The fur of the animal steamed as if there were some immense source of heat within. Leo realized the wulver had not been silver at all, but had been covered by snow, which now melted, revealing dark fur beneath.

Leo should have been afraid. But he was not afraid.

The Shadow Wulver, its transition complete, took a step toward Leo. It spoke to Leo inside his head, the deep metallic voice echoing low in his gut:

Lean to darkness, lean to night,
Eater of dreams, and stealer of light.

Leo leaned toward the wulver, closed his eyes. He felt the head of the massive beast against his own, its hot breath on his chest. For a moment they stood together, the breathing of the beast finding Leo's rhythm, Leo's heart finding unison with the unnatural thump of the beast's own heart.

To break bones, shall we away?
To break the boy, right where he lay?

When Leo opened his eyes, he no longer viewed the world through his own eyes. Instead, the world was mostly monochrome, bearing a slight shade of cobalt blue throughout, through everything, to include the trees, the earth, the snow, the rising night, and angry moon. He heard the deep growl of the wulver within his own chest, within his own body. Leo saw the world as the Shadow Wulver.

The Shadow Wulver stirred the snowy earth with its paw, howling angrily at the coming night, its jaw set in its purpose. One aim, above all other aims on earth and in the heavens. The one thing that must be done: the unleashing of all its fury upon the boy, upon Declan.

The Shadow Wulver broke through the trees at a furious pace. Its running wasn't smooth, bearing a disjointed stilted rhythm. Yet the Shadow Wulver's movements were efficient and powerful. It slammed into the trees, crashing many to the earth. The woods crackled and moaned, as the wulver scaled the mountain. Leo ran along behind the wulver, though in his mind's eye he was within the beast, leaping over great logs and steep embankments, the deafening sound of its footfalls echoing through his ears.

The Shadow Wulver soon skulked in the trees near the small house Declan shared with his parents and three brothers. Smoke circled above, giving the sky over the home a gray veil of melancholy. Leo knew that he would wait as long as it took; nothing could dissuade his wrath. The wulver panted, hungry for the taste of blood, the satisfying crunch that would come with breach of bone.

There was movement in the house, but no one came outside for a long time, until Leo's aunt emerged to sweep the snow from the porch, setting an oil lamp on the banister to light her work. She disappeared inside, and then it happened. Declan came out onto the porch, stretching his arms above him, using a porch plank to scratch his back, animal against tree. Lazily he bounded off the porch into the front yard, eyes half open. The wulver caught the scent of roasted chicken; the boy had just eaten. Declan would be slower than usual, Leo thought. *Good.*

The Shadow Wulver crept along the edge of the woods toward the outhouse, presupposing Declan's destination. The wulver was so enormous his body curled around three sides of the small building, just peeking around at the door, where Declan would soon appear. Leo's senses roused, all the world opening to him now, a vast awareness he'd never known. He heard the footfalls of the boy in the snow as he lumbered along, heard Declan's heavy breathing, his belly distended with food. Leo raged with all the violence of a summer storm, all the darkness in the world boiling up into this moment. The claws of the wulver dug into the earth as it positioned its body to strike as Declan came around the corner.

Declan stopped in his tracks, at the door of the outhouse, as if he sensed something amiss. The wulver did not pounce, instead extending slowly its massive head around the corner, lips curled. Its bottomless growl shook the structure and the earth around it, the deep guttural sound of the wild things in nightmares. Declan's eyes widened and he took a step back as if to run. Then he froze. When the full frame of the wulver's body came into view, the boy's hands began to shake. The wulver stood, towering over the boy, lowering its head so their eyes could meet. Leo wanted Declan to pay for what he'd done to Lilyfax, to pay for every time he'd poked his chest out at Leo, every time he'd bullied the other kids around the valley. Leo recalled the tears on Lilyfax's cheeks, the bright blood spreading in her palm, the shards of glass from her guardian angel.

The wulver opened its mouth, an enormous fang resting against the blue vein that pulsed frantically on the boy's head. The tender egg sac, ready to break open at last. The beast's breath harsh against Declan's face, and the horrible voice that shook the outhouse at its foundation.

I am the eater of dreams, the light taker.

Declan fell back in the snow, closing his eyes tightly, shaking his head as if to will away the terror before him. The wulver lowered his head to the boy.

Look at me.

Declan kept his eyes closed tightly, bringing his arms up to hold his hands in front of his face.

Look at me! The wulver thundered. Leo came around the corner of the outhouse.

Kiss me like you did the girl. It said.

Declan opened his eyes, seeing Leo beside the wulver. He pissed all over himself now, the pungent smell filling the night air. The wulver cackled at the boy, who shook on the ground, and started to cry. Leo smirked. The wulver took a step away from the boy.

No, Leo thought. *This ain't enough.*

The Shadow Wulver leaned down, growling again, his hot breath rustling Declan's hair. He grabbed the boy's thigh in his teeth and shook violently. Leo heard the snapping of the bones, felt them shatter in his own teeth. Declan screamed in pain.

Leo laughed. The Shadow Wulver cawed with delight, the taste of Declan's blood on its tongue. Declan's parents rustled on the porch, calling the boy's name. The wulver sprinted away into the gloom.

Leo followed the wulver, rubbing his hands together, a broad grin across his face.

Who's next, he thought. *Hank? The other boys? Wormley?*
One by one to make them pay,
One by one to eat the day.

Chapter 12 – Vey

I shouldn't 'a done it. You know how sometimes you know a thing ain't the right thing to do, but you just do it anyway? It was like that.

All day long I'd thought about them chestnuts. The ones past Farmer Hayes's barn, up on the ridge in the forest. A whole cluster of chestnut trees in a clearing. And I love me some chestnuts. Mama does too. All day I thought about finishing up my chores and going up there. Getting me some chestnuts. Then it was dusk, and snow started falling. It didn't make no sense to go then. But all I could think was, if the snow laid on them too long they might not be good no more. They fell late this year, and I'd harvested them a couple times. Me and Mama, we roasted them over the fire. Ain't nothing taste better to my mind. So when I finished my chores, I set out with a little pail. I didn't tell nobody where I was going, 'cause I knew I wouldn't be gone long.

Where you going Miss Vey, a boy yelled at me when I got out of the yard. I know'd him from church. Handsome boy named Mattis. Wide shoulders, skinny legs. Deep mahogany eyes that seemed to see everything.

Just got to get out for a little while, *I said.* Been working all day.

You want me to go with you? *he asked.* No, *I said. I wish I'd said yes. Everything would have been different.*

I went down the road a ways. Snow was still falling. Big heavy flakes, soft as cotton. Peaceful. I looked back, half expecting Mattis to be following me. But he wasn't there. Wasn't nobody around.

I ran for a while, straight up the ridge, past the barn, till I couldn't catch my breath. I looked back down the mountain, and snow was catching in the tops of the trees. It was beautiful. I'll never forget how it looked. I found the trees, and I could see a bunch of them chestnuts, the tops peeking up out of the snow, and I started filling my bucket. I broke open the burrs on the side of the pail so I could carry more. That was my other mistake. I shoulda just piled the burrs in the bucket, cracked them when I got home. But I didn't want no

*bucket of burrs, I wanted a bucket full of chestnuts. Kept thinking
how Mama would smile when she seen them.*

*That's when I heard it. It was a baby crying. I looked around. I
didn't see nobody, but the sound was off deeper in the woods. I looked
at my bucket full of chestnuts. I looked at the light at the edge of the
forest. The way home. But that baby kept crying. Who in the world
would have a baby out there in the snow? What if the baby's mama
was in trouble? I walked deeper in, toward the baby's cries.*

*Finally, I seen it. It was high up in the crook of a twisted birch.
Pink puckered face. I looked around. There wasn't nobody around.
The baby was at least fifteen feet up. I went over to the tree and set
down my bucket. I was about to climb up when he come around from
the other side.*

The Blue Man Gonna Get You! *was all I could think. He was
there, right in front of me. I didn't know fear had a taste until it was
there on my tongue. He wore a blue fur coat, a fur hat on his head.
Black gloves, black boots. Black eyes with almost no white. I didn't
hear the baby no more. I looked up and it was gone. There was only a
big horned owl up in the tree looking down at me.*

Ocean farers on the sea, *he said,* could be tempted by the
siren's call. *His words lay heavy in his mouth, some thick strange
accent.* The temptation, the idea that if they just followed the
sound, they'd find a beautiful woman waiting for them.

I started backing up, and he stepped closer.

A man's call wouldn't bring a woman. No, not in the
same way. But how could a woman be lured? A baby's cry has,
for a woman, the same power. I can lure women for miles.

*I turned and I ran as hard as I could. Right into something that
felt like a tree. But it wasn't no tree. It was a big giant man, nasty
pruned up face frowning down at me. He grabbed me and turned me
around. The Blue Man, he come right up to me. Held my face in his
hand.*

Oh Vey, so long have I wanted you.

How you know my name? *I asked.*

Andrew K. Clark

He didn't answer. Just stared at me hungry-like. They threw a sack over my head. Squeezed my throat. I kicked over the bucket of chestnuts, and everything went dark.

Chapter 13

The next morning when Leo set out, the world looked different. Though the sun was rising, he was keenly aware of the shadows that crept along behind the trees and rocks on the ridge. They coiled with the slightest shade of blue, and Leo's shoulders didn't round in on themselves the way they usually did, and he didn't look down at his feet, the way Mama always did. Leo felt his chest open, his neck sure and strong, his head high. Not in the way his daddy always walked, that ever-haughty look of an ignorant man itching for a fight.

Leo's people had always bore the sense, deep in their bones, that they weren't the kind of folks who could take up space in the world, that they didn't belong anyplace really. Even their children felt it, knew it in the cradle. Their stock was born to tenant, born to pay rent, to give away their labor to the powerful. But now all that was over. Leo determined to look up at the world, to meet the eyes of anyone on the road or anywhere else for that matter, having just as much right to be there as anyone. He had the goddamned right to be anywhere he damn well pleased.

When he'd woken, he'd sensed immediately the bond of the Shadow Wulver. Leo felt it outside where it stirred just beyond the tree line, on the other side of the creek. For a moment, he fantasized about it ripping off the front door where the family slept, the Shadow Wulver towering on two legs over Hank and James's bed, making them both piss all over the way Declan had done. The beast would drag Hank out into the front yard, out in the snow in his yellow-stained long handles. It would pick him up and hurl him into the creek where he could suffocate in the mud, just as Leo had that day at the barn, when Hank had betrayed him. The wulver had taken a few tentative steps from the woods, Leo seeing the world through its ever cobalt gaze, when he remembered Mama. He heard her heavy breathing on the bed. He knew the woman couldn't take it. Bringing the Shadow Wulver out into the light in front of Mama would be to tighten the noose, to hasten her undoing. He decided to bide his time on Hank's reckoning.

For now, he'd fetch Lilyfax, and they'd catch the bus to Altamont near Wilson's Trading Post, and they'd find Daddy and bring the son of a bitch home whether he liked it or not. If Daddy resisted, he'd be drug back along the road, his arm in the massive jaws of the Shadow Wulver. And if any town people got in the way, they'd suffer. There was no more smiling when you didn't want to, no more being polite to people because they were older or had money. All that was dead and gone.

Leo looked up at the gray clouds, listened to the crunch of the snow under his feet. He let his eyes roam over the landscape, the perfect dark morning holding him. That's when he looked down at the creek and saw that son of a bitch Wormley, lumbering along in the snow.

Leo moved off the road, loping toward Wormley, to cut him off. Though it was bitter cold, Wormley was already sweating, and Leo realized he'd never seen the man when he wasn't sweating, hot or cold, day or night.

Wormley's face was all pink jowl. He smiled at Leo, his eyes looking past him to the house.

"Morning," Wormley said, tipping his hat. "What's got you about so early, son?"

"Just doing some hunting, is all," Leo said.

The preacher looked him up and down.

"Reckon it'll be hard to catch much without a rifle. Maybe what you mean is trapping."

"No," Leo said. "I said it right the first time."

The man considered this for a moment, adjusting his tight suit jacket. He pulled on his pocket watch chain, opened the face to see the time. The watch sparkled, even in the low gray morning light.

The man offered a big, toothy smile, his lips curling dryly over his teeth. A practiced smile, forged from years in front of crowds, bent over sick beds, winning over a congregation. Wormley fished out his wallet, thick with dollars and papers. He carefully slipped out a single and offered it to Leo.

"Now see here boy, why don't you head out to Wilson's and get your mama a pack of those clove cigarettes she likes. Heck, while you're at it, get yourself some chaw or candy. Whatever strikes your fancy."

Leo spit near the preacher's shoes, wiped his lips with the back of his hand. He held his chin up, pointing it like a weapon. "Mama said she don't need you to come around here no more."

Wormley's eyes narrowed, the smile thinning. He gave a slight chuckle, tickled.

"That right?" he said.

"That's right," Leo said. "She told me herself. Just yesterday as we had our supper. Maybe you can pray for her and my poor sickly sister, *without ceasing*, at home, or at the church house. Anywhere but here."

Wormley sucked in his fat cheeks. "Last I talked to her," Wormley said, "she told me to come back around real soon. I rather think she has much use for me. In ways I'm sure you can't understand."

Leo's chin was so high he viewed the world through slits. "Why don't you high tail your fat ass home, like you know what's good for you," he said.

Wormley scowled. "I think maybe your daddy has done you a disservice, boy, sparing the rod as he's done, so you don't know how to proper speak to an adult."

Wormley fussed with his trousers, pulling off his belt, doubling it in his hand. "Come here and let me show you your place, like I done your mama when she's needed it."

Leo didn't budge, held his eyes on Wormley.

In the woods behind the preacher, a deep otherworldly growl shook the trees.

Wormley dropped the belt, turned toward the forest.

"What was that?" he asked.

The growl came again, and Wormley twitched as if he'd caught chill.

"You'll never come around my mama again," Leo said.

At the tree line, the Shadow Wulver emerged, stalking down the bank slowly, as if it intended to give the preacher time to run, should he choose.

Leo watched the preacher, through the cobalt gaze of the wulver. The man seemed so small, so insignificant. The Shadow Wulver leapt across the creek and bounded up to where they stood.

"You'll never look at my mama again."

Wormley backed away, the Shadow Wulver up on two legs now, following him.

"Say it!" Leo growled.

Wormley looked at Leo, then back to the wulver.

"Say it."

"Wh-what? Say what?" Wormley asked.

"Say you'll never look at my mama again."

Wormley sat with a thud. "I'll never look at her."

"You'll never touch her again," Leo said.

"What is this?" Wormley said.

Say it! the wulver thundered, the deep voice full of gravel, speaking to them in their minds.

Wormley looked at Leo. "I'll never touch on her again."

"You'll never even come down this road again."

Wormley raised his hands to his neck.

"I won't, I promise."

The Shadow Wulver bent low over the man, to hold his gaze, teeth exposed. Wormley drew back as far as he could, the hot breath of the beast ruffling his hair. Wormley struggled to sit up, flailing on his back like a turtle. "You're the devil," he said to the wulver.

"He ain't," Leo said, "but I'd wager good money you'll meet the devil one day."

"Oh God, don't let him eat me," Wormley said.

"I would, but we'd be here all day, I got places to go, preacher man."

Leo circled Wormley, who sat on the ground like a kid who'd fallen off his swing.

"Stand up," Leo said.

Wormley struggled up, his eyes never leaving the wulver. As he stood, his wallet fell out on the creekbank. Leo scooped it up. He took the wad of bills from the wallet and stuffed them into his own pocket. He threw the empty wallet on the ground. He unclipped the pocket watch chain from the preacher's belt loop. He put the watch in his own pocket.

"Is it real"? Wormley asked.

"Show him you're real," Leo said to the wulver.

The wulver, now on all fours, approached Wormley slowly.

"No!" Wormley said.

The Shadow Wulver opened its massive jaws, mouth agape over the preacher's head. It let its massive fangs rest against Wormley's mammoth cheeks. The wulver's spit dripped down the man's face and neck.

Leo scrunched his nose. "What do you think Reverend? It seem real to ya?"

Wormley wept. A loud, snorting cry of a volume that almost rivaled his praying voice.

"Lay off," Leo said, and the wulver slipped away.

Leo took the bills from his pocket and counted them in front of the preacher. Sixty dollars. A fortune.

"You're a very charitable man, Reverend, so generous to my ragged little family, living in a shack way back in the holler, so far they got to pipe in the sunshine."

Wormley quieted, sizable tears rolling down his red cheeks. Armpit sweat showed through his suit jacket.

Leo took the pocket watch in his hand. He admired the outside of the watch, gold and silver, before clicking open the face to check the time.

"Would you look at that?" he said. "The time just flies when you're having fun." He put the watch in his pocket. Wormley's eyes rested on the pocket for a moment, then he looked back to Leo's face. For a moment Leo felt a pang of guilt about the watch, but when he stared again at the preacher's ugly face, thought of his fat hands on his mama, the guilt dissipated.

"You come back down this way again, and I will command him to eat you whole."

Wormley shuddered.

The preacher's hat was on the ground. Leo fetched it and put it on his own head. It was so large, it slipped down over Leo's eyes. He took it off and threw it in the snow, dirty now from the scuffle. Wormley watched it land near his feet, making no move to retrieve it.

"See here now," Leo said, "You ought to get up and just run as fast as you can back toward home." Leo gestured to the winding creek. "I see you stop, I see you walking, I'll send him to eat both your legs. You can crawl on your belly like a worm the rest of your days."

Wormley sniffled, staring from the path home, to the wulver, to Leo.

"Git," Leo said.

Wormley took off with a lumbering gait, his feet heavy in the snow, it caked over his wingtips.

"Faster!"

The fat preacher fell several times, struggling to his feet, looking back over his shoulder before resuming his slow slog.

Leo smiled, watching Wormley struggle. The good reverend was getting a taste of his own medicine, at last. People all around these parts would soon get a taste.

Leo took the pocket watch out and flipped it over in his hand. He spun the chain, letting it wrap around his finger.

"Come on," he said to the Shadow Wulver, "let's go fetch the girl."

The wulver slunk off into the woods, its body fusing with the shadows at the edge of the trees.

Leo kept his head high, back on the road. He pictured the route to Altamont, of where he would look for Daddy first. The tramp could be in any number of the speakeasies or boarding houses where they served hard liquor, but Leo knew where he would start: Aunt Lila's, Daddy's favorite place, maybe in all the world.

Andrew K. Clark

Part II

Come Fairies, take me out of this dull world,
for I would ride with you upon the wind
and dance upon the mountains like a flame!
--W.B. Yeats

Chapter 14

May 1929

Leo's first visit to Aunt Lila's came about on account of a big fight between Mama and Daddy. They'd stood out in the yard yelling at each other for at least an hour, until finally Mama called Leo up from where he sat with Jacob near the creek.

"If you're 'a going off, you're taking this one with you."

Daddy had grinned. "Like hell."

Mama said, "If you got to wander all over tarnation like a damned old tomcat, you'll take this boy."

Leo looked at the ground, shoulders slumped.

"I ain't babysitting this one, nor that little tow-headed son of a bitch neither," Daddy said, motioning to James. "Since when are you in charge of where I'm a' coming or a' going? A man can't stay around the house all day. I ain't, and I ain't taking this goddamned boy."

"You will take this boy with you, and he will be a witness to all that goes on." Mama leaned in, her finger in Daddy's chest. "You test me, and I'll be gone. Just test me."

"I should be so lucky," Daddy said under his breath.

"Lucky?" Mama said. "You can take your turn at raising these young'uns around the house all the time, stuck here, while I go off gallivanting, you wondering where I am, what man I'm with. We'll see how lucky you feel then."

Daddy's face reddened. He grabbed Leo by the arm and jerked him across the yard like a rag doll.

"You heard your old lady, boy. She's got me babysitting you like a priss."

The two of them were on the road when Mama yelled after them. "Leo, you stay with him, you hear me? You stay with your daddy, or you'll catch the switch."

The generous rain that spring, along with ample sunlight, had cultivated a sea of wildflowers in the fields along the road. Everything awash in bright yellows and oranges and purples.

Daddy and Leo fell into perfect rhythm, Daddy taking one step for every two Leo took. The old man mumbled under his breath.

"I'm the only miserable bastard on God's green earth got to drag a kid over every mountain in this God-forsaken place." Then, "So she thinks she's the man of the house now?"

"Son, you got yourself a girlfriend?" Daddy asked. He fiddled with cigarette paper and a pouch of loose tobacco. He could roll a cigarette pretty as you please while walking. Leo'd even seen him do it on the back of a horse at trot.

"No," Leo said. He had been thirteen at the time, before he'd had an interest in girls and before Lilyfax moved to the valley from over Tennessee way.

"They ain't nothing but trouble, son. Nothing but a world of fuckin' trouble."

Leo didn't answer.

"I ain't got to take you with me, son. Into town I mean. I might leave you in the woods somewhere along the road. You understand?"

Leo nodded.

"A man has got to take care of things. I've got to be in town 'cause I have a lot of business to tend to. Women don't understand about man things."

Daddy licked the edge of the cigarette paper and rolled it up tight.

"Your mama is the stubbornest woman who has ever drawn breath," Daddy said.

He always spoke in extremes. So-and-so was the *dumbest son of a bitch that ever lived,* thus-and-so would be *the ugliest bastard who ever walked the face of the earth.* No one could ever be just plain old *ugly* or just *dumb.*

Daddy stopped walking and grabbed Leo by the shoulders.

"I'm going to take you with me so you don't wander off and get mauled by a she-bear. Where we're going, though, is between me and you, and me and you only. You got that?"

Leo nodded.

"When we get home, you will tell your mama that we went to the hardware store and to see about a job. And that is all you have to say to her, hear?"

"Yes, sir."

"'Cause if you tell her one thing other than we went to the hardware store and to see about a job, I will beat you to within an inch of your life."

Leo swallowed hard.

"I'll give you a beating worse than what any kid has ever gotten since the time of Methuselah."

"Yes, sir."

Daddy took a drag from the cigarette. "Methuselah was the oldest son of a bitch that ever lived. Bet you didn't know that, did you?"

"No, sir."

"My granny took me to Bible school. Don't you go thinking you little bastards know more than your old man. I know things too."

Daddy took Leo's shoulders again. "Pretend I'm your mama." He made his voice high, mocking. "Now Leo, where did you and your low-down son of a bitch daddy get off to today?"

"We went to the hardware store and to see about a job is all."

Daddy gave Leo the side eye, unconvinced. "You better say it like you mean it, like it's the gospel, boy, sober as a judge."

"Yes sir, I will," Leo said.

Daddy grinned and turned back to the road.

To get to Altamont, Daddy took Leo along several roads, taking short cuts through farms and patches of woods. After a while, they came out back on the road, near Wilson's Trading Post. At Wilson's people could get eggs and fresh milk, produce or meat. You could get fresh bacon if you had a lot of money. Mostly Leo's mama bought dried beans if they worked through what they had canned at home, and the occasional piece of fatback. Even outside, at the bus stop, Leo smelled the smoked meat and his mouth watered. Many a time he'd been at Wilson's with Mama, eyeing the salted cuts of meat hanging in the back. Sometimes Leo took measure of the distance between the clerk and the door, figuring on whether he could grab a big ham and make it out without being caught. Leo was sure he was faster than the clerk, and if he ever got the nerve to do it, the family would eat like kings, at least for a week.

At an intersection in town, Daddy yanked Leo off the bus by his ear. On the brick streets outside, people walked in every direction all at once. Cars buzzed by, their tires thumping in the grooves of the street. Leo couldn't understand why everyone was moving so quickly. The men had on handsome hats and crisp jackets with ties. Leo could hear the swish of their pants as they passed. The men nodded to each other, but none nodded at Daddy.

They passed some women who stood on a street corner. The women laughed, throwing their heads back, and Leo was astonished to see their dresses cut higher on the leg than those worn by his mama or the womenfolk back home. He couldn't stop staring at their bare arms, and at the rouge of their cheeks. He thought about how it might feel to touch their faces, to touch their legs. He felt mean for it.

People in Altamont seemed in a hurry all right and had a lot to smile about with bright white teeth, and low belly laughs all around. On a brick building a freshly painted sign read "Hoover: A Chicken in Every Pot." Leo had heard Daddy talk about how Hoover was a dirty pig-faced Republican son of a bitch bastard, whom he hoped would rot in hell.

That day in Altamont, right on the street, was the first time the pillar of smoke had come to Leo.

Across the street a large building took an entire city block. It was the tallest building Leo had ever seen, and as he let his eyes float up the face of the building, he saw a large American flag flapping on top. Big sign letters seemed to float

just at the edge, almost out in space by themselves. They read
LANGREN.

On the roof of the building, Leo saw a small dark cloud.
A cluster of shadows, twisting and swirling in on themselves,
rising and falling like black curtains. In some places, the sky
was visible behind the pillar of smoke. At times, the shadows
seemed to take the shape of a man. Looking into the darkness,
Leo was sure the apparition focused only on him, that it saw
only Leo in the crowd, that it stared directly into his eyes.

Leo was drawn to the darkness where the face should be
in the man's shape, and he felt weightless, his body losing its
grounding to the earth, as if he might float up the face of the
massive hotel, be pulled into the dark eyes of the specter, be
sucked into the gloaming, and disappear forever.

Leo looked at Daddy, whom he'd have expected to have
slapped him on the back of the head by now, chastising him
for stopping to gape. But Daddy stood still too, though he did
not look up to the Langren, did not see what Leo saw there.

The world fell silent; the sounds of the people talking, the
clang of cars and horses, the clinking of spoons in soup bowls
had all disappeared. There was only the terrible sound of the
American flag flapping in the heavy wind, a sound that grew
louder and angrier. Then came the voice in Leo's head, octaves
below that of a man:

Push him.

The words banged together like church bells that held no
harmony.

Push him, Leo, the time is nigh.

Leo stared into the pillar of smoke, thinking about the
words, about what they might mean. He turned toward
Daddy, then to the street where cars buzzed by at great speed.
He pictured it. His hands moving, catching Daddy in the small
of his back, right at the last moment, so he would be struck by
a car. He heard the sound of Daddy's ribs cracking, the thud
of his head splitting open on the cobblestone.

How many times had he thought about doing it? Of taking the ax to the side of Daddy's head, cracking open his skull like a pecan shell with a hammer. How many problems would it solve if he did it, just pushed Daddy right now, so Mama wouldn't have to worry anymore. How if Daddy's arms were broken, he couldn't use them to strike Mama.

Push him Leo. You know you must!

Ashes to ashes, and dust to dust!

Leo stared into the twisting black and blue pillar of smoke, feeling as if his feet would leave the earth, that he would be pulled up into the sky, forever into darkness. He was picturing Daddy's blood on the street when his father smacked him hard on the back of his head.

"Snap out of it," Daddy said, "We got to get moving."

Leo looked back to the roof of the Langren. The pillar was gone.

After they'd gone down a couple of streets, Daddy's attention was drawn to something coming toward them. It was like a bus, but it was attached to cables that ran above the street. Daddy studied it, timed it, his brow set.

"We get on that cable car, we got half as far to walk."

With that, Daddy took off running, grabbing Leo by the arm to pull him across the road. Soon, they were behind the moving car and Daddy jumped up onto the back, holding on to a steel rail. He held out a hand to pull Leo up.

From the cable car, with its bright bells clanging, the town moved by quickly. In the center of a great square, a stone pillar rose from the earth, the top a point stabbing at the sky. Gargoyles peered down from their perches, on the corners of great gray buildings. Myriad smells attacked his senses: of savory meats smoked with heavy spice, of roasted vegetables, of fresh coffee and baked bread, of melting butter. Leo's hunger overwhelmed him and he'd have given anything to have the leftovers taken away by busy waitresses.

This was what it was like to be city folk, Leo decided. To sit outside on a warm spring day sipping soup and drinking coffee, watching pretty women walk by. Black men strolled the streets on a long slope, wearing suits with ties more colorful than their white counterparts. A man at the edge of one street juggled balls high in the air and a group of children pushed their way through the crowd to catch a glimpse. As the cable car took a curve and climbed a steep grade, Daddy signaled it was time for them to jump off.

At first the streets were busy, but they gradually grew quieter. They turned down a lane with large two and three-story houses, with vast yards that stretched out in front of them. Though it was daylight, electric lamps burned in some of the windows. Some of the porches were whitewashed, while others were painted the same color as the rest of the house. Most of the porches had a dog or two lying near the front door.

Daddy turned into the yard of a big yellow house with a white awning. It had an immense wraparound porch. Daddy walked to the back of the house, up onto the porch. Chained up near the back door was a muscular brown dog with a white spot on his chest. He had enormous paws, and long strands of drool hung from his massive jaw. He growled as they approached. Daddy reached into his pocket, fishing out a piece of dried pork. Leo's stomach flipped when he saw the dog getting a piece of meat bigger than he'd had in a couple of weeks.

"Careful, Brutus can smell if you're scared," Daddy said. "He smells it, he'll tear into your hide for sure."

Daddy entered the back door and they rushed across the landing. Daddy closed the door as Brutus finished the pork and pulled the chain taut. The house had fancy wooden floors and plaster painted walls, crown molding at every angle along the floor and ceiling. The ceiling was as high as a church house's, and the floor was put together so tightly there were no cracks between the boards. Daddy led Leo down the hall. Jazz music played nearby; the kind of music Daddy called black folk music. Leo loved the brush over the drums, the radiance of the trumpet, the drive of the piano.

"Lord have mercy!" A large woman with a top-heavy build, adorned in a fancy violet dress, came gliding across the room. She reached for Leo's daddy, kissing his cheek, leaving bright crimson lip marks. Her voice was smooth and rich, like honey and butter on a plate. She backed away, sizing Daddy up.

"I didn't expect you for a few more days. You must've gotten more hours."

Daddy lifted his chin. "Got more work than I know what to do with but finally got off that godawful farm. Figure you wouldn't take stinky old chicken eggs over cash money."

The lady laughed too long at this, before noticing Leo.

"Oh myyy," she said. "You brought us a guest?"

"That's just my boy," Daddy said, pushing past the woman.

"He's a little on the young side, I mean," the woman said.

"Hell no that ain't it. Just stick him in a corner somewhere." He looked at Leo. "You are to be seen and not heard, that clear?"

"Yes, sir," said Leo.

"This here is Miss Lila," Daddy said. "You do as she says, or I'll beat your eyes shut."

"Aunt Lila," the woman corrected. "You can call me Aunt Lila." She smiled at Leo. Her lips were large, her cheeks as pink as a slap. She was like the busty women Leo liked to gawk over in the Sears Roebuck catalogue. Her skin was the color of fresh milk.

"You go on up," Aunt Lila said to Daddy. "Me and the boy will be just fine. We'll have us a big time." The woman shifted her weight from one leg to another, her violet dress rustling as she moved. She examined Leo from the top of his head down to his feet, then back up again, slowly. "Leo, is that your name?"

"Yes, ma'am."

"You're a handsome fella. How old're you?"

Leo told her his age.

"Thirteen and already so tall and handsome." She put a warm hand to Leo's cheek and he blushed. "The girls are gonna just eat you up," she said. She smelled like cinnamon, and that reminded Leo of Christmas.

Aunt Lila took Leo down a long hall that opened into a large room with several couches and tables with lamps. She led Leo to a thick red couch with deep cushions. Across the room, on a blue couch, a young woman sat. She had blond hair, pulled up in a ponytail. Leo had never been in a room like this.

"Tell me, Leo," Aunt Lila said, "have you ever had a cup of hot cocoa?"

"No, ma'am," Leo said, looking over at the girl on the blue couch, who held a magazine.

"Oh myyy," Aunt Lila said, "then you're in for a real treat."

Leo couldn't stop looking at the girl. She flipped the pages, her eyes just visible above the magazine. Her eyes weren't the dark mahogany color of Aunt Lila's. Instead, her eyes were light blue, the color of a spring sky. When she dropped the magazine slightly, he saw her cheeks were painted like Aunt Lila's. She had her long legs tucked under her and wore a peach dress that broke at the knee. Her blond hair reminded him of Goldfish.

When Miss Lila left the room, the girl lowered the magazine to look at Leo, catching him staring. Leo looked away, his face warming.

Just then a petite girl with red curly hair sauntered into the room. Her hair reminded Leo of a wild fox.

"Oh Camille, do you think the parlor is all yours today?"

"I ain't the only one in here," Camille said motioning with her head.

The red-haired girl stared at Leo. She puckered out her lips.

"He's a young one!"

"I think he's just waiting," Camille said, "on his daddy."

"He's cute, though." The red-haired girl walked over to Leo and put a hand on her hip. She smiled. "You mean nobody gets to break in this little pony?"

Camille laughed and went back to her magazine.

The girl stared at Leo, her tongue poking out her cheek. "You come back sometime and ask for Maude."

Leo stared at his feet.

"You hear me speaking to you, boy?"

Leo looked up, then back at his feet.

"Maude. That's the one, hear, that's the ticket."

With that, the girl twirled and left.

In the hallway, a man with a thick Yankee accent whispered with Aunt Lila. Leo tried to make out the words but couldn't. Somewhere in the distance, a woman sobbed quietly. In the corner of the parlor an enormous grandfather clock ticked, its pendulum swinging behind frosted glass.

"Pay Maude no mind," Camille said.

Leo nodded, tried to think of something to say.

Camille stood and walked to a table in the corner of the room. On the table was a phonograph. She cranked the handle for a few moments and dropped the needle on a record. Jazz music came from the horn. Leo had only seen a phonograph once before, at the widow's. The widow only owned gospel records, and many that featured preacher sermons. The widow called jazz the devil's music, but there was something about the way the brass instruments curled their notes that Leo couldn't get enough of.

Leo was watching the girl when Aunt Lila floated into the room. She was carrying a cup on a small plate.

"I've got your hot cocoa, Leo."

She bent, placing the plate and cup on Leo's lap. There was also a small spoon on the plate. Leo tensed, trying to balance the cup and spoon on the tiny plate, terrified it would slide off and shatter on the floor, or stain the extravagant couch.

Aunt Lila looked at him, her face full of anticipation.

"Well, come on, boy. Try it!"

Leo lifted the cup. Immediately the plate tipped and the silver spoon slid off onto his lap before clanging to the floor. Leo was afraid Aunt Lila would be angry.

She bent and retrieved the spoon, wiping it on her dress before setting it on a side table. "Never mind about that. Try the cocoa."

Leo took a sip. The drink was so sweet it made his mouth draw. But it was delicious. He took another sip. Aunt Lila was pleased. She glanced over her shoulder at Camille.

To Leo, Aunt Lila whispered, "If you like it, I'll fix you some more. And if you're nice, Camille might teach you how to dance. It's her favorite thing in all the world." Her dress rustled as she twirled out of the room.

Leo sipped the cocoa, watched Camille, who still stood with her back to him, listening to the music. She changed the record and soon a bouncy piano riff echoed in the room. A woman sang:

Ain't nobody to talk to
I'm just here by myself
I try not to be a bad girl
Just wait on you to come—

Camille crossed the room and stood in front of Leo. He glanced up at her, then down into the cup.

"What's your name?"

"Leo."

"You know how to dance, Leo?"

"I ain't never danced before."

"The Charleston?"

"No, ma'am," Leo answered.

"The Shimmy?"

"No."

"Stand up," Camille said.

Leo didn't think she was serious.

"Come on," she said. She took the cup and plate from him and set them on the side table.

When Leo stood, he realized that, although the girl was older, he was taller. He felt awkward, looking around the room, suddenly feeling hot and sweaty. Camille shook her shoulders and moved her feet. All the blood rushed to Leo's head and he felt faint.

"No? Not your style?" Camille said. She smiled widely, displaying perfect white teeth. "Put your hand on my waist, the other"—she held Leo's left hand in her own, at shoulder height—"in mine. Yeah, that's it."

Camille smelled like honeysuckle. A whole field covered with honeysuckle. She pulled him close and began to move his stiff body. He looked down at her feet, tried to mimic her movements.

She dipped her head. "I'll teach you all these moves, and you'll go use them on some other girl behind my back," she teased.

"No," Leo said. "Ain't nobody dances back in the valley."

"Let me lead," Camille said. "Just relax. You're stiff as a board."

Just then Maude and a couple of other girls came into the room.

"You said he wasn't to play with," Maude said, circling the two of them as they danced—as Camille danced, and Leo tried desperately to follow along.

After the song ended Leo returned to the couch, taking the cup and plate in his lap, though the cup was empty. He didn't know what to do with himself. The girls sat around him laughing, he assumed, at him. They asked a million questions, if he'd ever been to a moving picture show, if he had a girlfriend. They wanted to know if he played football, wore one of those leather helmets boys had, or if he played baseball at his school. Leo glanced from girl to girl, at their painted faces, bare legs and arms. He decided right then and there he would raise his hand to volunteer should Daddy ever need to *go to the hardware store* or to *see about a job.*

Leo had let himself relax, chatting with the girls, a smile on his face, when Aunt Lila called him from the hall. Daddy stood beside her, his face beet red.

"You making a nuisance of yourself, boy?"

"No, sir," Leo said, standing.

"You come back and see us," Camille said. "I got to finish your dance lessons sometime. You'll be a little heartbreaker sure as the world."

"Now girls, shush up now," Aunt Lila said.

When Leo turned to leave, Camille stood and gave him a hug. She squeezed his hand. Behind her Maude offered Leo an exaggerated wink.

"Come on, goddamn it," Daddy said.

Outside, Daddy and Leo made their way past Brutus. Leo fought smiling, the sweet cocoa still on his tongue, Camille's smell in his nose. As they reached the side of the house, they passed a man. Though it was a warm day the round man wore his collar up around his neck, his hat low on his forehead. He kept his face down as he passed.

"Afternoon," Daddy said to the man, Daddy's hand on the bill of his own flat cap. His voice dropped, *"Reverend Wormley."*

Leo returned many times to Aunt Lila's with Daddy, seeing Camille most times. His heart would always sink if he stepped into the parlor to find she wasn't around. A few times he'd seen Maude as well. Each time she would wink and call him *The Little Pony* and offer to break him in any time he was good and ready.

Chapter 15

Late November 1931

The clerk eyed Leo suspiciously as he and Lilyfax perused sweeties in a glass case at Wilson's Trading Post. After their long walk, they made it to the bus stop only to find they had a half hour wait before the next bus to Altamont. Leo had suggested coming into the store to get some candy. Lilyfax refused at first, not knowing about the wad of cash Leo had in his pocket.

"Pick you out something, get a couple of pieces," Leo said.

Lilyfax dipped her head sheepishly.

"You got money?" the clerk finally asked. He was short and bald, with a face as round as a dinner plate.

"I got money," Leo said and glared at the man. He fished a bill from his pocket, careful to leave the wad unseen. The man's eyes widened when he saw the five.

To Lilyfax, Leo said, "Pick you out some. We got money."

The clerk bagged the candy, his eyes never leaving Leo. Leo peered into the back room, which used to be full of curing meat. The room was now empty, and a cobweb hung in the upper corner of the door frame.

"What happened to all the meat you used to have back there?"

"Times is hard," the man said, handing Lilyfax the bag. He eyed Leo's bulging pants pocket. Leo put his hands in his jacket pocket and pulled it around his waist. "People ain't got money like they used to. Got some potted meat is all."

Outside, Lilyfax and Leo sucked the hard candy. Leo took out the shiny pocket watch, aware of Lilyfax's eyes on him. He twirled the chain around his finger, then let the weight of the watch unspool the chain in the opposite direction.

"Where'd you get that?" Lilyfax asked.

"Found it along the road," Leo said. He popped open the face as if to check the time. "You like it?"

"It's awful fancy."

Leo noticed some other folks waiting for the bus nearby. A man in the group kept his eye on Leo and the watch. He had the flat nose of a boxer that had seen too much action.

"They'll steal it, Leo," Lilyfax whispered, following his eyes to the man. "Put it away."

Leo's instinct was to put away the watch, to keep it hidden, but in the shadows that gathered in the trees, in the stretched spreading of their limbs, Leo knew what watched, what awaited his command. "Let them try to come take it from me," he said, twirling the watch in ever wider circles. He met the eyes of the flat nosed man. Leo held his gaze until the man looked away. The flat-nosed man had rolled trousers and he held his cigarette between his thumb and middle finger, the ash long. Half of his index finger was missing.

"There's something different about you," Lilyfax said. "I can't quite put my finger on it."

"I've just had all the shit I plan to eat," Leo said.

"What?" Lilyfax said. "Keep your voice down. Don't cuss in front of strangers."

"To hell with them people," Leo said. "I ain't taking any more from people back in the valley, and I ain't taking any from strangers at no bus stop, neither."

Lilyfax considered this, said nothing. She sat down on a log, staring down the dirt road. It stretched on for maybe a mile, before hooking into the trees.

When the bus reached Altamont, it deposited its passengers on a street near the French Broad River. Lilyfax looked around and up the slope where the tops of the buildings were visible. Leo noticed Flat-nose talking with a companion, a man with a comically long neck. Leo couldn't hear their words but read the intention on their faces. He took Lilyfax by the hand and led her up the bricked street toward downtown, toward the secret bars, boardinghouses, toward Aunt Lila's.

The day was gray, and a blanket of refrozen snow covered the city, except where cars had carved a path, the edges of the streets mounded with mud-swirled drifts.

When they turned down an alley, Lilyfax said, "Leo, I think they're following us."

Leo smiled. "I ain't worried about them."

When they approached the street at the end of the alley, Flat-nose emerged. The man with the long neck approached behind them. They'd been cut off.

"Leo," Lilyfax whispered.

"Hey fella," Flat-nose said. "Lemme hold that watch for a second. I won't do it no harm."

Leo closed his eyes. He tried to feel the shadows curling along the walls of the buildings. He opened his eyes and leered at the man in front.

"Hey, he was talking to you," said Long-neck from behind, now just a few feet away.

"Don't be rude," said Flat-nose. Long-neck was so close Leo could feel his breath.

"Leave us alone," Lilyfax said. She stood with her hands on her hips.

Leo tried to conjure the wulver from the shadows, closed his eyes expecting the world to fan out in cobalt blue. Nothing happened. He felt a million miles from the wulver. He stopped smiling.

"Give 'em the watch," Long-neck said, his hand on Leo's shoulder. "And ain't nobody gets hurt."

Leo held his eyes closed harder, pictured the wulver twisting to life, the shadows becoming animated the way they did in the barn, the pitchfork leaning toward him. Nothing. Had he lost his power to summon it? Had it abandoned him so quickly? Fear took hold in his spine.

Flat-nose took off his jacket and unbuttoned his shirt cuffs.

"After we get the watch, let's take him around the block, teach him some manners," Long-neck said.

Flat-nose's lips were thick, too thick for his face, as if he'd been hit in the mouth with an iron skillet. Or maybe boxing had flattened his whole face. His ears were too fat for his head. He put his hand on Lilyfax's cheek. "And let's buy this one some hooch, get her cheeks warmed up," he said. "Show her a good time." Lilyfax kicked him in the shin and Long-neck grabbed her by the throat, lifting her feet off the ground.

"Let her go!" Leo said.

"Or what?" said Flat-nose. "What'll you do, you little urchin?"

Lilyfax's face reddened, and she made a choking sound.

Leo rushed toward her when Flat-nose swung, a broad fist catching Leo above his eye. He fell back onto the street.

A fire took hold in Leo then. He remembered his cousin's sneer when he'd bragged about kissing Lilyfax. He thought of the church people looking down their long noses at his family, of Wormley holding his mother. He pulled up his anger within his chest. He balled his fists, pictured busting open that old fat nose. He closed his eyes and the world fell immediately into cobalt blue, shadows stretching long against the wall, the wulver forming there.

The otherworldly growl of the Shadow Wulver echoed around them. Long-neck jumped before letting Lilyfax go. She moved close to Leo.

"What was that?" she said.

Let us eat them both, oh let us eat them whole.

The voice as loud as the growl, crashing against the walls of the alley, shaking the stone beneath their feet.

"*Mein Gott im Himmel*, goddamn," said Long-neck. He removed his hand from Leo's shoulder and backed to the opposite side of the alley. The wulver's enormous head pushed through the shadows along the wall, as if held back by a thin black sheet, swelling, and pressing its way out into the world.

Let's eat the ugliest first. Oh let us.

Leo smiled, watching the men, who stood together, their legs shaking, mouths agape, eyes wide with terror. Beside him, Lilyfax shuddered, her cold hands gripping his forearm.

"Don't worry, Lily. All is well."

Lilyfax stared at the massive head of the wulver, stretching forth from the wall in inky blue-black shadow.

"Leo, what is it?" she asked.

"It's with me," Leo said.

Lilyfax looked from the wulver to Leo and back again. She let go of his arm. The wulver's body disappeared, suddenly emerging on the opposite wall behind the men.

But they're both sooo ugly, how to choose, how to choose?

The two men ran down the alley and in opposite directions when they reached the street. Leo laughed and yelled after them, "Wait, didn't you want to hold my watch?"

To the wulver, Leo hissed, "Break their legs and throw them in the river."

The Shadow Wulver stretched forth from the wall now, its body coming into view, its monstrous paws thudding against the cobblestone. It bounded after the men and in the distance, one of them screamed.

Lilyfax backed away, her face pale. "Leo?"

"It's all right," Leo said.

"What is it?" she said.

Leo took a moment to answer. "It's the Shadow Wulver. I can tell it what to do, and it does it. I'm inside it somehow. And somehow, it's inside of me now."

"Where did it come from?" she asked.

"From the old country," he said, "according to the widow. But I don't know if I believe that. It's always been here, I think, maybe since the very beginning of everything."

The normal coolness to her face, the normal mischief of her eyes was gone. "You made it come out of the wall like that, you conjured it?"

119

"Yes," he said. Then he thought on it, his nose scrunched. "Only it didn't come at first. I ain't sure why it took a minute. It should have been here quicker."

He squatted down and traced the outline of the wulver's paw on the stone. Its outline was there in mud as if the wulver had stepped directly from back in the valley into Altamont when Leo had gotten good and mad.

He stood up. "That's it. I had to be mad." He looked at Lilyfax. "I got to get mad for it to work right."

"Mad?" she asked.

"Yes, because that bastard was hurting you." He took a step toward her. He could see the place on her neck where the man had gripped her, her skin red and angry. As he came on, Lilyfax took a step back. She jumped when she bumped into the wall behind her. She looked around, as if expecting the open jaws of the beast to be reaching out for her.

"It does what I say," Leo said. "It wouldn't never hurt you."

"It does what you say," she repeated. "That giant thing does what you say."

"Yes," Leo said holding out his palms toward her. "Don't you see? This changes everything, Lily. I ain't kowtowing to nobody anymore again. Ever. You ain't got to neither. With this thing we can do what we want. We can get what we want."

"And what do we want Leo? What will we do with your big bad wolf?"

Leo rubbed his chin. A smile spread across his face.

"We'll make money, Lily. Lots of it. We'll make money and we'll get back at all the people that's done us wrong."

"My name is *Lilyfax*," she said. "Stop calling me Lily. So, revenge? Revenge and money. That's what you got? You have this big bad wolf and you'll use it to make money and get revenge. That's it?"

"I bet she didn't think we could control them," he said.

"Them?" Lilyfax said.

120

"The wulvers," he said. "The widow is the one that told me about them. I don't think she knew we could control them."

"There's more than one?"

"Yes, but I felt no connection to the other one. The one made of silver."

Lilyfax said nothing.

For a moment the world was quiet. A car passed, its tires spinning in the snow. A man followed after it, yelling something about alms. Lilyfax's forehead creased, her gears spinning.

"Wolves?" Lilyfax asked.

"Wulvers," Leo said, "I seen them both."

"What does the other one look like?"

"It's so bright it hurts your eyes, and its face looks like lightning."

"Did you tell this one what to say? When it said it wanted to eat those men?"

Leo met her eyes. "What to say? No."

"But I thought you controlled it?"

"I do," Leo said. But he did wonder where the words came from.

Lilyfax paced. Finally, her eyes stopped on Leo's bulging pants pocket. He dropped his hands in front of it.

"I seen that big pile of money you're carrying. The clerk at Wilson's seen it. Half the people at the bus stop seen it. Everybody in the whole damned county will have heard about that by now. And the watch. Where did that watch and all that money come from?"

"From a bad man."

"You took it?"

"Not exactly," Leo said.

"Not exactly? What does that mean?"

"I mean, he give them to me. He, he donated it." Leo grinned.

"Did your big bad wolf, he have anything to do with that?"

Leo didn't answer. He looked her up and down. Her shoes were old, her pants and shirt and jacket—they were all hand-me-downs. Like in his, the knees of her pants were almost wore through, the fabric lighter on both legs. It would give way any day, and the cold air would run up her legs, and she'd have to wear those pants for what? Six months? A year? Didn't she understand? That was all over now. Who wanted to live that way? Who wanted to grovel and wallow with the pigs when they could own the pigs? When they could get their way, do what they want? Wasn't she tired of being pushed down in the mud by the world, by the people that thought everyone from the valley was garbage? When Leo took a step toward her, she held up her hand to keep him at bay.

"You know me, Lilyfax. You know who I am. I'm still the same person. Your Leo."

Lilyfax stared down the alley. She no longer had the look of someone on the precipice, someone about to run. Instead, she bore a look of wariness, someone who doesn't know what to think.

Leo pulled out the pocket watch and clicked it open. He did not twirl it by the chain this time, instead carefully slipping it back into his pocket after he saw the time.

"We got to go."

Leo reached out to put a hand on her arm. She pulled away.

"Don't touch me," she said.

"We got to find my daddy," he said.

Lilyfax considered the palms of her hands, turning them over.

"Please," Leo said.

Lilyfax glared so long at him, he had to look away. Finally, she shook her head and bit her lip.

"I'll come," she said at last. "On one condition."

"What?"

"On the rest of this trip. You keep the big bad wolf in your pocket."

"Okay," he said. But he didn't know if it was a promise he could keep.

"I mean it," she said. "No matter what happens, I don't want to see that thing again. You pull it out again, and I'm gone."

Leo nodded.

"I mean it," Lilyfax said. "Say you got it."

"I got it," Leo said.

Chapter 16

Altamont was an abandoned ghost town for the first few blocks up from the river to the city's center. There, signs of life began to emerge: people shuffling by, a few cars moving slowly along, their tires spinning in the slush. The cable cars weren't running, due to the weather, and Leo was disappointed he couldn't take Lilyfax for a ride – not illegally as his father had done, hitching on the back like some hobo, but instead walking right up to the depot and paying with shiny silver coins.

Lilyfax kept her distance as they walked. On the bus ride, she'd sat close to Leo, letting the back of her hand rest against his. Her warmth had vanished when she'd seen the wulver. She didn't understand, but she soon would. He would make money, bring her new dungarees, and clean white shirts. He'd bring her bags of coffee and sweeties and new shoes. No one would ever hurt her again, the way Declan and Hank had done. He would keep her safe. Always. Hank and each of the boys who'd hurt her would soon meet the Shadow Wulver. They'd regret ever touching his Lilyfax. Leo thought also of Mama and Goldfish. He pictured the new house he'd have built for them after he'd used the wulver to make enough money.

Altamont was a different city now. It was wintertime, the world painted entirely in shades of gray. The restaurants were empty, their colorful signs in the windows taken down, boards placed over the windows.

"Leo, what are them people doing over there?" Lilyfax asked.

There was a line of folks in front of a building on the opposite side of the street. It was too cold to stand still for very long, and so the men in line shivered, the twitches of their shoulders passing through the crowd like a wave.

"I don't know. Maybe they're looking for work."

A man passing dipped his head at them. He had on a ratty suit jacket that was two or three sizes too large.

"That ain't no work line," the man said. "Ain't no work to be had, really. But if you're hungry they got hot potato soup and coffee over there. Sometimes toast." His pants slipped off his spare hips and from time to time he reached around to hitch them up. One of his shoes had a large hole in it, and two socked toes extended there, crusted with frost.

"Thank you," Leo said.

"Ma'am," the man said, dipping the bill of his hat to Lilyfax. He turned back to Leo, sizing him up. "Go on over there, if y'all are hungry. Get yourself something to eat. It's free."

"Thank you," Lilyfax said.

"People can't be shy about it no more," the man said. "People dying in their homes, hungry. Cold." The man cupped his hands in front of his mouth and blew. His fingers held the slight tremor of a drunk that's been forced to dry out. "Mama raised me not to take no charity." He looked at Leo's shoes, then up to his pants, to his bulging pocket. "It goes against my religion not to make my own way, but a man can't make his way if he ain't got no way to."

Leo looked from the man to Lilyfax. Her eyes widened, like she wanted him to take some of the money out of his pocket and give it to the man. She said, "But if you had a quarter, reckon you could get some potatoes or rice to feed your family?"

"Reckon I could," the man said. He looked away, his ears red.

Leo met Lilyfax's eyes. She tilted her head slightly, gesturing to the man. She wanted Leo to give the man money. The money Leo had just earned. Just today. Leo shook his head slightly, tried not to let on. He stuffed his hands in his pockets, squeezed the cash tight as if it might up and fly away.

The man tipped his hat again to Lilyfax, as if he'd read the gestures passed between them. "I hope y'all have a good day and be sure to keep warm."

"Yes, sir," Leo said. "You too."

They went on and Lilyfax's face sagged with disappointment. He knew what she'd wanted him to do, and he'd let her down. But who had ever come into the holler to help his people? Who was donating coins to Mama for potatoes for her kids? Nobody. Nobody, except Leo. Why should he give away what he'd earned for his family? Why shouldn't he use his money to take care of Goldfish, of Mama, and Lilyfax? He'd get food but he'd also buy Mama a new Sunday dress. Goldfish too. He'd even make sure Hank and James had enough to eat, after he put Hank in his place.

Leo led Lilyfax down the maze of streets until they approached Aunt Lila's.

"Wait in them woods right there," Leo said, gesturing to an empty lot sprinkled with trees. "The first place I mean to look is just ahead. I'll be right back, unless he's in there, then I'll holler for you."

"You're going to bring me all the way here, and have me wait outside?"

"It's just," Leo said, struggling to find the words, "it's not really a place for womenfolk."

"Why, they sling liquor in there?" she said. "I can handle myself."

"No," Leo said, "That ain't it. It's just a place men go. Women don't really go there."

"I ain't your dog. Or your horse. You want to tie me to that tree over there till you're good and ready to go home?"

"Damnit, Lilyfax, it ain't like that."

"Then let's go."

"Okay," Leo said. "Just stay close."

They went off the street to the back of Aunt Lila's. Leo stepped up onto the porch, reaching into his pocket for a small piece of jerky he'd brought for Brutus, but the dog wasn't there. The dog's empty chain lay across the porch, rusting.

They knocked on the door. There was no answer for a long time. Then the locks released on the other side. When the door opened, Aunt Lila stood before him. She was less put together than he'd ever seen her. She had a single streak of gray, about an inch wide, running through her hair, and the normal blush of her cheeks was gone. Though her cheeks had been round and full, they were now slightly sunken, and her green dress was stained at the breast.

"What you want?" she asked, all the normal bounce and sweetness absent from her voice.

"Aunt Lila," Leo said.

"Do I know you, boy?" the woman said, first eyeing Leo, then shifting her focus to Lilyfax. When she turned her head into the light, there was a patch of yellow around her eye like an old bruise.

"Yes ma'am," he said. "I'm Leo, I been here before."

Aunt Lila stared back to Leo. She squinted her eyes, studying his face.

"I come here a bunch of times with my daddy," Leo said. "You gave me hot chocolate?"

"I remember you, boy. But who's this girl?" She jutted her chin at Lilyfax.

"She's with me."

"There's no work for you here, girl," Aunt Lila said, shaking her head. "I got too many mouths, and I can barely keep them fed as it is."

"Oh no," Leo said. "She's just traveling with me is all."

"Probably for the best," Aunt Lila said. "These are hard times, men get hard up, try to bribe their way with black potatoes and stale eggs."

Aunt Lila opened the door. "You ought better come in."

They followed Aunt Lila down the hall and into the parlor. The woman limped, using a cane to walk, her ambling stride that of a woman twice her age. A single electric lamp bearing a stained glass shade barely lit the room from a table against the wall. Though there were a few coals smoldering in the grand fireplace, the room was only slightly warmer than outdoors. Aunt Lila sat heavily in a chair opposite the red couch. She motioned for them to sit.

Leo sunk into the cushions. He remembered the couch from prior visits, the way it had curved around his body, the way his eyes got immediately heavy when he leaned back into it. Yet the flutter of the painted girls in the parlor would always spring him back to life. Lilyfax looked around the room, at the paintings on the walls, the grandfather clock, and up at the height of the ceiling. Leo wanted to point out the phonograph, perhaps to show her how to dance, a skill that held little currency back in the valley. What would Lilyfax think if he put on the jazz records and twirled her around the room in a way she'd never moved before. Now dust bunnies clumped on the area rugs, and papers were scattered across the floor. Aunt Lila followed Leo's gaze. "Never you mind about that. I gave the maid the day off."

Leo smiled. "I'm here looking for my daddy. He here?"

"Your daddy? No. Hell no."

"You seen him lately?"

Aunt Lila frowned. "I hadn't thought on it, because so many stopped coming when the banks closed up, but I ain't seen him in an age."

"He's missing. About a month."

Aunt Lila placed her hands in his lap. "I reckon it's been at least three months."

"Three months," Leo said. He knew Aunt Lila's was one of Daddy's favorite places. Where had Daddy been going to when he left out, if not to her place?

"About that," Aunt Lila said, straightening her dress. "It's been at least three months, if not longer. I ain't think nothing of it. Men don't have cash money these days. Well, most of them don't. The ones that still do, why, they're meaner than snakes."

"Is this a whorehouse?" Lilyfax asked. She glanced from Leo to Aunt Lila and back again.

Aunt Lila huffed. She took out a handkerchief and coughed into it, her voice raspy and stuttered. "Honey, you come in here with your big doe eyes," she hissed. "Don't know much about the world, I'd wager. Places like this didn't exist, the wheels would fall off this town. They'd fall off every town, everywhere. They'd be blood in the streets. We're holding society together, and just barely."

"I didn't mean no disrespect," Lilyfax said.

"Men don't get work soon, the wheels *will* fall off this machine, and it'll run right into a ditch. It won't be pretty. These people will burn Altamont to the ground, they don't get some relief. And not just the men, neither."

"Ma'am," Lilyfax started. Aunt Lila raised her hand to shush her.

"Young lady, I could take the time to talk about how good I treat my girls, about how we are doing God's work, you get right down to it. I could give you a history lesson, school you on how the Romans and Greeks thought about such things, but I'm tired." Aunt Lila laid her head back on the couch, staring at the ceiling. "I'm just so, so tired."

"You got any idea where my daddy might could be?" Leo asked.

Aunt Lila rested a hand on her cheek. "The man likes to drink. Only one thing in the world he likes more than drinking, and if he's been doing that, he ain't been doing it here."

Some girls laughed out in the hall, their footfalls on the wooden stairs. Leo both hoped and worried that one of them might be Camille. He wanted to see her, thinking of her warm hugs, but felt funny about Lilyfax meeting her. Truth be told, Camille was the main reason he'd wanted Lilyfax to wait outside, though he'd tried to think of it as worrying over her safety, given that a lot of men shuffled in and out of Aunt Lila's, some of them rough and violent. Violent men like Daddy.

"I got to find him," Leo said.

"Would one of you mind lighting those oil lamps either side of the fireplace?" Aunt Lila asked. "It's awful dark in here. Seems like the sun ain't found its way out in days. I don't mind the cold, but when everything's gray it brings me low."

Lilyfax stood and walked to the fireplace. "Where are the matches?"

Aunt Lila sat with her head back, eyes closed. "In the side table, top drawer."

Lilyfax fetched the matches and worked to light the lamps.

"Who give you that shiner?" Leo asked.

Aunt Lila dropped her head, looked at her lap. "Now don't go worrying about things that don't concern you, boy."

Just then, two girls shuffled into the room. Both wore shorter dresses, more flapper style than Aunt Lila's traditional long dress, which was almost Victorian. They had short haircuts, one with brown hair and one with black. Aunt Lila introduced the brown-haired girl as Clara, the black-haired girl as Ginger. Clara had lovely thick eyebrows that rested above her eyes like caterpillars.

"Oh man, that ain't a new girl is it?" Ginger scowled, staring at Lilyfax with sharp eyes.

"No she ain't," Leo said, with a little too much force. He was both relieved and disheartened that neither of the girls was Camille, or the flirty red-headed Maude. Lilyfax seemed amused by the girls, watching Clara stroll to the other side of the room where she plopped down, her bare legs draped up over the arm of the chair.

"Good," Ginger said. "There's too many of us here now, hardly no men coming around."

"And them trying to shut us down," Clara said.

Ginger shook a cigarette out of a pack and lit it with a match. "At least we're still *here* to be shutdown." She smiled, a perfect gleaming gap between her front teeth.

Aunt Lila cleared her throat. "Shush up now. We have guests."

"What do you mean, still here?" Lilyfax asked.

Ginger glanced at Aunt Lila before meeting Lilyfax's gaze. "I mean at least we haven't been taken."

"Yet," said Clara.

"Taken?" Leo asked.

Aunt Lila fussed with the hem of her dress, then running a hand over the stain on the front, as if she could wipe it away by force of will. "Now girls, there's no reason to gossip in front of our guests."

"Who's been taken?" Leo asked.

"They took a bunch of our girls, Aunt Lila said they grabbed the prettiest ones," Clara said.

"Girls!" Aunt Lila said, standing. "That's enough." She was shaky on her feet, sinking immediately back to the couch the back of her hand to her head as if she felt faint.

"What's the big deal?" Ginger said. "Everybody in the whole county knows about it."

"They got Maude," Clara said.

"Tania, Camille, Lana," Ginger said. "Who else? Somebody else."

Leo felt his insides twist up.

"Damn near broke Miss Lila's leg too," Clara said.

"Who did this? Who took the girls?" Leo said, rising to his feet.

"I try to take care of my girls," Aunt Lila said. She sat with her legs spread, her skirts falling between them. She hunched over, looking at the floor, all the normal grace of her posture melting into drooping shoulders. "I do everything for them, try to," she said. "Try to keep them happy, get what they need. I make the men treat them nice. These are good girls. I tried to stop them. Tried to run them off. My pistol jammed or one of them would have met his maker."

Leo took a knee in front of Aunt Lila. "What have they done with Camille?"

"Who's Camille?" Lilyfax asked.

Leo didn't look at her. "A girl I met here. A nice girl. Her and Maude. They were both nice to me."

"I bet," Lilyfax said. She turned her back to Leo, facing the fireplace.

"So you've met Maude? Oh Lord Jesus, she's a handful," Ginger said, laughing.

Leo placed his hands over Aunt Lila's. Without makeup, and in the yellow light of the oil lamps, he saw fine lines spreading over her face. He remembered her laugh, the way she'd swished about like nobility when first he came to visit. The way she'd teased him about dancing with Camille. He thought of Camille, of her warm embrace during their dance. Of the way she'd hugged him close, showing him more kindness than anyone he'd ever met. Until Lilyfax. He remembered Maude and the way she had of winking at him when no one else was watching.

"Where are they?" he asked.

"I think *he* got them," Clara said. "Has to be him."

Leo walked toward the girl. "Who?" Leo would find out who had the girls and where. He'd find them and conjure the wulver from the shadows to set them free. He pictured it, pictured Camille's smile when he rescued her. Then he stared back at Aunt Lila's black eye. If they'd hit a woman like Lila, what might they do to such a fine and delicate girl?

"The Blue Man," Ginger said.

"Girls!" Aunt Lila said.

"Blue Man?" Lilyfax asked.

"They call him that. Everybody calls him that. He was always in that jacket, lined with fur, the edges of it blue," Ginger said. "And the glasses too. He wore blue glasses, the lenses."

"That ain't the only reason they call him that," Clara said.

"How's that?" Leo said.

"He likes to leave bruises."

"I tried to run him off, but he kept coming back," Aunt Lila said. "He has friends in high places, that man. Had the law down on me, the preachers too, even some that were customers. They called me by name from their pulpits. Tried to shut us down. Of course," Aunt Lila chuckled, "that only made business go up, at first. Said we were a den of iniquity, then said we were encouraging race-mixing, 'cause we had a couple black girls. Some Chinese. That brought even more customers."

"He has the girls," Clara said. "I know it. He would've took me, if I'd been here. He knew I hated to be alone with him. He'd have taken me just for spite. I was off with a friend when him and his goons did this."

"And that other one. The huge one that always guards the door. The one with that old raisin face, the one they call Goat," Ginger said. Her shoulders twitched.

Leo returned to Aunt Lila, sitting beside her on the couch. "I'll get them back, all the girls they took. I'll get the Blue Man. Punish him for he did to you."

"Hush up!" Aunt Lila said. "Don't write checks you can't cash, boy. You'll get yourself killed. These ain't schoolyard bullies, the hicks back home you're used to. They've got them girls kept up as slaves someplace. They won't give them up easy. They won't fight fair."

"Neither will I," said Leo.

"We still ain't found your daddy," Lilyfax said. "You might be too busy for a new adventure."

Leo stood and pulled out his pocket watch, checking the time. Ginger crossed the room when she saw it. "That's lovely. Let me see?"

"Sure," Leo said, squaring his shoulders.

The girl held it in her hands, turning it over, clicking the button to make it pop open. She smiled. Leo couldn't stop staring at the gap in her teeth. Somehow it made her more beautiful. He thought of what it would be like to put his tongue in there. Ginger pulled on the chain playfully, making it taut against Leo's belt loop. She tugged, making him take a step toward her. Behind her, Lilyfax rolled her eyes.

"That's a nice watch for such a young man," the girl said.

Leo gently took it from her and placed it back in his pocket. He smiled at her and turned back to Aunt Lila.

"This Blue Man. Tell me everything about him."

Aunt Lila's eyes fell to her lap. She laced her fingers together.

Chapter 17

It was a comfort to be with her, to walk the winter streets of Altamont with Lilyfax, despite the cold, despite the day having grown long now, shadows waxing hungrily along the snowy surfaces of every sidewalk, park, and square. Lilyfax seemed even more distant since Aunt Lila's. Leo had drug her to every speak easy and secret bar he knew and the ones they learned of by asking drunks along the streets. At one bar, a place down a spiraling iron staircase from the street, the keeper slammed the door in Leo's face, likely due to his age. He had to wait outside for a drunk man to stumble out. Leo asked the drunk after his father. "Ain't heard tell nothin' about that son of a bitch," the man said, before bending over to puke on a tree trunk. When he finished, he stood up and squinted at Leo. "I see the resemblance kid," he said, then, "your daddy is the fightingest son of a bitch I ever seen. He'd fight a lamp post he thought it looked at him wrong." Lilyfax chuckled at this and mumbled something about how the apple didn't fall far from the tree.

With each passing minute Leo felt the distance grow between him and Lilyfax and yet he did not regret bringing her here. Now Lilyfax had seen the real Leo. She'd witnessed the power he possessed, his new strength at work, putting the smug clerk at Wilson's in his place, dispatching the would-be robbers. She saw him take charge at Aunt Lila's, the way the girls had treated him like a man. She saw the history he shared with his daddy; deep secrets he'd kept for an age. She saw something of where Leo came from and what he was made from, away from the dull predictability of the world back in the valley. Maybe it hadn't been pretty, but he was happy to finally, at last, be seen.

"One more stop, and we'll head back," he said.

"He won't be there," Lilyfax said. "He's up and vanished."

"This ain't about Daddy. I have to meet the Alchemist. He's got some new medicine for Goldfish, and some work for me."

Leo took a left at the next street, and they went on. She walked ahead of him, so that someone passing might question if they were even together. Leo stepped quicker along, tried to close the distance.

"Aunt Lila's," Lilyfax said.

"What about it?" Leo asked.

"That girl Camille . . ." She stopped herself.

"What about her?"

"Did, did you two. I mean, did y'all ever. . ."

It took Leo a moment. "Oh. No," he said. "It wasn't like that. Daddy took me there when I was younger, first time I saw her. She looked at me like I was a little boy."

"And the other girls?"

"No," he said.

"So. Because of your daddy? That's why?"

Leo didn't know what to say. He'd never considered the question. He didn't know how to answer. Everything he thought to say would sound like a lie. Finally, he settled on, "I ain't ever looked at a girl that way. Until you, I mean." And that was almost the truth.

He thought he could see Lilyfax's cheeks flush, and heat washed over his own face. They were both quiet for a moment, the silence terrible and somehow worse.

"You ever get the idea in your head," Leo said, "that you've always known someone, that even before the world began or back from some ancient time, you've known them?"

"Maybe," Lilyfax said. "I never thought on it."

"I get that feeling sometimes when I look at you. It's like I never felt like I was meeting someone new when I met you, because I already knew you somehow deep down."

"Maybe it was in ancient times," Lilyfax said. "Maybe we did know each other back then. In another life."

"Yeah," Leo said. He was pleased to see her smiling. "Maybe I was a knight, and you were my lady."

"Your lady?" she said. "No way."

Leo pursed his lips. "Really?"

"I wouldn't have been anybody's lady. It's like you don't even know me at all, mister."

"What would you have been then?"

"I'd have been a knight too."

Leo laughed. When he glanced over, her face was serious. "You couldn't have been a knight. They wouldn't let you."

"I wouldn't have asked. They wouldn't know anyways. I'd always have kept my helmet on."

"Okay," Leo said. "So, we were both knights, back in the olden days."

"And I beat so many men, they had to give me a special title. The queen would have to come down and give it to me."

"Wouldn't surprise me a bit," he said. Her smile came back. "I mean it, though."

"Mean what?" she asked.

"I mean I feel like I've always known you. Like when I look at you it feels like we were together before everything."

"I know," she said. "It's the same when I look at you."

Leo smiled.

"But we ain't boyfriend and girlfriend," she said. "Don't go getting things in your head."

"I know."

Lilyfax reached over and took his hand. The cold numbness of his fingers faded straightaway. He looked at her face, hoping for a glimpse of her dimples, but although they were close to showing, she still held something back.

On the porch of the Raven Thicket Boarding House a row of empty rocking chairs see-sawed gently against tired wooden boards. In the summertime, porches like these brimmed full of boarders, smoking pipes and cigars, sharing the tall tales of their travels. Leo and Lilyfax walked past the chairs and into the house, which opened into a great room with couches and chairs and books on the wall. Leo stopped to study the books, turning his head to read the titles printed along their leather spines. A few people milled around the parlor, and a short woman with wide hips waddled up to them.

"Will you be needing a room?" She stared at Lilyfax suspiciously, narrowing her eyes.

"No, ma'am," Leo said. He asked after the Alchemist.

"Wait here," the proprietor said, her voice curt, her heels ticking against the floor in sync with her short strides.

They moved to the far corner of the room, away from the door. Leo continued looking through the books, and Lilyfax took a volume from the shelf. She opened the cover, scanning the first few pages. Leo read its title: *Dark Laughter*. "That's some kind of name for a book," Leo started. He was interrupted by a scuffle across the room.

At the door, a woman yelled in some foreign language. She stuck her finger into a bearded man's chest, her face red, her brown hair tousled, as if she'd just been roused from bed. Her voice rose as she pushed the man across the room, grinding her tall heels into the wood floor as she came on. She took a wild swing at him. He ducked, his top hat falling to the floor. His long black hair fell across his face. He held up his cane, as if he might strike her with it. The woman swung again, and he jumped back. The bearded man reached behind him to swing open the door and it cracked hard against the wall. A rush of cold air fell over the room.

The bearded man motioned to someone outside, hissed, "Goat, come."

The man called Goat appeared, and Leo's stomach dropped. Goat was enormous with broad shoulders and unnaturally long arms. He had deep wrinkles on his face, his cheeks drawn in like a prune. The woman grimaced when she saw him. She scurried toward where Leo and Lilyfax stood. The man leapt over a table and hooked an arm around her midsection. He threw her roughly over his shoulder as if she were a sack of potatoes, knocking all the air from her lungs. Goat's wide set and dull green eyes met Leo's for a moment before he spun toward the door with the woman. She gasped for air, and when she finally found it, she screamed, kicking her legs, and swinging her arms.

Leo took a step forward. Lilyfax placed her hand on his chest. "Wait," she said.

The man called Goat stepped around the proprietress, who rushed into the center of the room. The short woman walked to the bearded man, who scooped his top hat from the floor and placed it on his head.

"You know I got no problems," the proprietress said. Her voice was stern, but Leo thought he heard a tremor within it, a slight hint of fear.

"Of course not, Miss Condon," the bearded man said. His accent was thick and foreign, as if his tongue were too large for his mouth. He took an exaggerated bow. "Please forgive the disturbance, I beg you."

He stepped to the door and opened it again for Goat.

Goat carried the woman across the porch and down the stairs to the street. She was still screaming, her desperation building. Goat lifted her overhead and threw her so hard Lilyfax gasped. She sailed through the air, landing in a deep snowdrift marbled with mud. There she lay still for a long time, as if she were dead. Goat stood pat, hands on hips, as if prepared to squash her possible rally.

The bearded man pinched the sharp creases of his pants, as if to tease them back in shape after the scuffle. He brushed off his shoulders. He had long hair of one length that fell below his white collar, and deep-set eyes beneath an overdeveloped brow line. His beard and hair were shiny and black, catching the light from the electric lamps scattered about the room. He wasn't exactly handsome, instead bearing a kind of primal ruggedness though dressed quite extravagantly.

Leo looked out the window to see Goat still standing guard, his back straight. The woman was gone.

When Leo turned back, the Alchemist had appeared and was whispering to the bearded man. As they spoke, the bearded man craned his neck to look in Leo's direction. The Alchemist half turned, as if to determine what his companion found so compelling and he smiled when he saw Leo and Lilyfax.

The men crossed the room. The bearded man held his cane longways in front of his body. Leo wondered why he carried a cane if it was unnecessary for walking. He wore a coat trimmed in animal fur and the shiny leather shoes of a traveling evangelist. His beard was trimmed to form a point at the base of his chin, and his eyes were so dark the pupils were almost invisible.

"Mr. Wake," the Alchemist said, "meet my good friend and employee, Leo."

Wake dipped his head slightly, extending his hand to Leo. He looked past Leo to Lilyfax.

"How do you do, Leo?" Wake said. His eyes wandered over the girl.

The Alchemist seemed amused. "I am sorry, Leo, but I am afraid I cannot make a proper introduction for your friend here."

"This here is Lilyfax," Leo said, stammering.

Mr. Wake dropped Leo's hand as if it were a dead fish. He took Lilyfax's hand in both of his own, smiling broadly. When he extended his arms, his sleeves rode up his forearms. Leo thought he'd lose his balance. There on the man's wrist, a blue snowflake, identical to those he'd seen on Wormley and the Alchemist.

Wake dipped his head gracefully. "*Lilyfax*, what a curious name, and what a delight to meet you." Leo stared at the man's mouth, trying to ascertain how he formed his words so strangely.

"Hello sir." Lilyfax smiled at Wake, her full dimples on display, cheeks aflame. The sweetness of her voice sickened Leo. He wanted to grab her and pull her out of the boarding house, get her on a bus, get her back home to the valley. Back to the holler where the boys would mock her as a tomboy, a place they did not look at her the way this man did now.

"Tell me," Wake asked her, "is Altamont your hometown?"

"No," she said. "Me and Leo live out in the country. We're just visiting is all."

"How pleasant," Wake said. "Perhaps you could show me around sometime, as my escort? I'm still learning my way, I'm afraid."

Lilyfax's eyes darted to the floor, around the room, then to the man's chest before floating up to meet his. She grinned as if he'd just given her a puppy. The man took it all in, tilting his head slightly and squaring his body with hers. ·

It took the Alchemist to break the spell. "Mr. Wake, if you please, I need to attend to some business with these two. But you and I," he said, placing his hand on Wake's shoulder, "have much to discuss. Perhaps tonight. Our usual place and time?"

The world seemed to shift beneath Leo's feet. He was dizzy, as if he were a sailor lacking sea legs. There were several moments, as he watched Wake with Lilyfax, when he was tempted to reach into the shadows outside the Raven Thicket to call forth the Shadow Wulver. But he remembered Lilyfax's warning to keep the wulver at bay.

Wake's parting was largely lost in this fog, Leo catching only a few of the man's words. Wake described himself as Lilyfax's *humble servant* and said he *desperately hoped* to cross paths with her again *quite soon*. Not once during the entire exchange did the man make eye contact with Leo. Not once did he treat Leo as if he mattered. Leo marked it down in his mind.

Leo was thinking about this slight, when at the door, Wake turned to them, waving, before slipping on a pair of glasses. The frames were large circles, bearing blue lenses. Leo's heart skipped. Blue heavy coat. Blue glasses.

Lilyfax gripped his arm.

"Yes," Leo said. "I seen it too."

Wake was the Blue Man.

In the Alchemist's room there was a tall four-poster bed, with a colorful quilt draped elegantly across the mattress. On another wall sat a leather couch with thick wooden legs. There were only a few cracks and tears in the leather. Lilyfax wandered around the room, letting her hand slide along the gray painted walls. For the Alchemist to have a private room in a boarding house said something about the man's status in the world, and Leo thought about how he too would be as industrious, using the Shadow Wulver to make money, to change his fortunes and those of his kin. It was high time he got himself some new duds too. People like Wake wouldn't dare ignore him then, if he dressed like someone who mattered, someone owed respect. He thought about the Alchemist's connection to Wake and the missing girls. He wanted to grab the man by his collar to get him to tell Leo where the girls were. But perhaps it was too soon to tip his hand.

The Alchemist handed Leo several packets of powder.

"Medicine for your sister," he said.

Leo fished the wad of cash from his pocket. Both the Alchemist and Lilyfax ogled it.

"How much do I owe you?"

"As long as you're in my employ," the Alchemist said, closing Leo's hands around the money, "you won't pay a dime for the medicine your sister needs."

"I got money," Leo said.

"I see that, Master Leo. But it won't spend here."

"And here," the Alchemist said, handing Leo several folded bills, "payment for a quick delivery I need you to make on your way out of town."

"But I ain't done it yet," Leo said.

"But you will," the Alchemist said. Leo hated having cash money before doing the work that earned it. He thought then of the widow, and how he still owed her more wood split. He'd almost forgotten that debt.

"I appreciate the work," Leo said, "more than you know." He turned to Lilyfax. "We've scoured every inch of this town, and it looks like my daddy won't be found anytime soon. Don't want to be found."

"You still haven't tracked him down?" the Alchemist asked.

"No, sir. Nobody's seen hide nor hair of him. Not for months."

The Alchemist pondered this for a moment. "I'll make some inquiries."

"Thank you," Leo said.

"Come over by the bed, Leo," the Alchemist said. "I need to outfit you. Take off your jacket."

Leo followed, glancing at Lilyfax, who seemed bemused by the proceedings. By the bed, the Alchemist put a harness on Leo. He adjusted it snug against Leo's body. From under the bed, he retrieved a trunk and pulled out several metal containers. These were curved, and when the Alchemist put them into the harness, they contoured perfectly to Leo's body after some adjustment of the straps.

The Alchemist affixed eight containers to Leo in this fashion before standing back to survey his work.

"What're those for?" Lilyfax asked.

"Mustn't ask us," the Alchemist said, offering her a wink.

"Everbody knows it's some old hooch you're gonna put in there," Lilyfax said.

The Alchemist tsked her, shaking his head. "Please do not insult me in such a way, young lady. There is nothing I

143

have ever produced for consumption that could even remotely be referred to as *hooch*. I brew no common moonshine or riverbank swill, let me assure you."

Leo and Lilyfax looked at each other.

"Try on your jacket," the Alchemist said.

Leo tried to put it on. There was no way it was going over the bottles and harness.

"As I suspected," the Alchemist said, fishing a long brown coat from his trunk. It was way nicer than anything Leo had ever owned. It fit perfectly. The Alchemist walked over and ran his hand along the coat, pulling the fabric taut.

He turned to Lilyfax, pleased with his work. "Can't see the outline of a single bottle. Doesn't look too bulky, looks natural. Yes?"

"Just looks like a bigger Leo is all," she said. "Maybe one that's had too many biscuits with gravy."

The Alchemist took each bottle to fill in the closet. These he attached to the harness. They felt heavy when they were all in place, but not terribly uncomfortable.

"Hope I don't have to run with all this on," Leo said.

"They won't even notice you," the Alchemist said. "You'll pass for just any old rube walking by."

"Rube?" Leo asked, unfamiliar with the word.

"Bumpkin," Lilyfax said, "he's calling us bumpkins."

"Nothing of the sort. But better to look like a country fellow passing through, than some city rapscallion who may be carrying something of interest to the law."

Leo wasn't worried about being caught. The Shadow Wulver would scare off lawmen as easy as criminals.

"Speaking of which," the Alchemist said. "Anything happens, you get taken in, you just ask for Skinny Boo."

"Skinny Boo?" Leo asked.

"Yes, and don't say another word. Don't let on that you know anything or anybody. Just keep saying Skinny Boo to each officer until they bring him to you."

"Yes, sir," Leo said.

The Alchemist took out a pencil and paper and drew a map. "You see this square here?" he said. "That's Pack Square. You know where that is?"

"It has the big pillar on it, with the point at the top?"

"The obelisk. Yes. That's it." The Alchemist kept sketching. "Three blocks northeast, on the corner of an empty lot, there's a patch of bushes."

"Yes, sir."

"It stands out, because the rest of the lot is mostly cleared off, except the trees."

"Okay."

"In the middle of the bushes, there's a staircase. It goes down to a door. You're going to go to that door and knock three times. Three times Leo. Do you understand?"

"Yes, three times."

"Not two times, not four times. *Three*. And there's a pattern you have to follow." The Alchemist closed the trunk and tapped out the pattern on top. Leo walked over and repeated the pattern.

"Good, good. Now when they open the door you ask for Reeves."

"Yes, sir."

"Say it."

"I knock three times in that pattern, and I ask for Reeves."

The Alchemist was stoic for a moment. Eventually his face relaxed, satisfied.

"And the young lady," he said, gesturing to Lilyfax, "she's to stay out of sight. Understood?"

"Yes, sir," Lilyfax said, "the city is no place for a girl." She shook her head slowly. "I'll just stand off in the trees like I'm his dog."

"These aren't choir boys," the Alchemist said.

"Got it," Leo said.

"One thing," Lilyfax said. "How do you know Mr. Wake?"

Leo shook his head slightly at the girl. He wasn't sure how, but the snowflake tattoos connected the Alchemist to Wake and Wormley. And Wake had kidnapped the girls from Aunt Lila's. Leo did not want to tip his hand to the Alchemist. What if he too were involved?

The Alchemist's face dropped. He cut his eyes at Lilyfax with the expression of a parent scolding a child.

"Wake – that's a name you must forget. Both of you. Forget you've ever heard the name, that you've ever seen his face."

They walked out of the boarding house and through the streets of Altamont toward Pack Square. Lilyfax was mostly silent along the way, both of them wary of drawing attention to themselves. In the metal containers contoured to his body, Leo could hear the jostling liquid.

"I don't hardly know you anymore," Lilyfax said.

"How's that?"

"I just didn't think you were the kind of boy to run shine. Big Bad Wolves. Hooch. You're just different now."

"Wulver," Leo said. "You seen my house, the cracks in the ceiling, my mama losing her mind. Old fellars are gonna drink whether I deliver it or not. Might as well be me that makes the money."

Lilyfax said nothing.

Leo's stomach was pitted when they reached the empty lot. Lilyfax waited across the street, standing in the dark doorway of an abandoned building.

Leo descended the stairs and knocked on the door three times, in the pattern the Alchemist had dictated. A grate slid open, just below Leo's chin. He bent down to meet the eyes of the man on the other side.

"I don't know you," the man said, closing the grate.

Leo knocked the pattern once more. The grate opened.

"Reeves," Leo said.

"What about him?" the man said.

146

"I'm here to see him. He's expecting me."

The grate closed and the door opened. Leo was ushered into a narrow hallway, a man behind him pushed him along, and into a room off to the right. Dim electric lights in metal cages lit the hallway, and a single bulb hung from the ceiling in the center of the room. Two men huddled in the corner.

"Ok, boy, let's see what you got," said one.

"You Reeves?" Leo asked.

The other man stepped forward. "I'm Reeves. Let's go, off with the coat."

Leo took off the coat and the men took each bottle carefully off the harness and set them on a rickety table.

The man who was not Reeves opened one of the bottles and took a swig.

"Jesus Christ," he coughed. "That'll grow hair on your chest."

"You got to cut it," Reeves said. "Don't drink it like that, dumbass. You cut it. Two parts water to one part hard."

"Mother of God," said the man who wasn't Reeves. "Now ya tell me."

"Serve it like that, up in the Portico, there's bound to be a dead Yankee come tomorrow morning. We don't need that shit."

Reeves handed money to Leo. Leo was confused. The Alchemist hadn't mentioned more money. Reeves read his face. "You're the delivery boy, ain't you? It's yours. We paid for the lightning already."

Leo put the bills in his pocket. Both pockets were now full of cash. Leo liked the way the money felt there, the ability to reach in anytime and touch it. He wanted to keep his pockets ever full. To always have this feeling.

When Leo and Lilyfax headed back down the slope toward the bus stop near the river, sleet began to fall. At first, just a smattering here and there, but soon it filled the early night sky. It was almost nine. They'd just make the last bus.

"I'm going to find the girls," Leo said, half to himself. "Soon as I get pointed in the right direction."

"But what about your daddy?"

"Either he's dead someplace, or he don't want to be found. That's the long and short of it."

"I'm coming with you," Lilyfax said. "When you set out."

"The hell you are," Leo said. He shook his head.

"Why not?" she said.

"It ain't safe. Besides, I can't take you anywhere without you being gawked at and batting your eyes over every little ounce of attention you get." Leo felt hot at the collar. He unbuttoned the coat the Alchemist had given him.

"You mean Wake, that old dog?" Lilyfax said.

"I hardly ever seen you smile that big, like he just really tickled your fancy. Thought you were gonna jump in his lap."

Lilyfax laughed. "Are you jealous, mister?"

Leo's face hardened. "Hell no, I ain't jealous. Jealous of what? He's got to be the Blue Man. You seen his glasses."

"I could've taken that creeper down in a flash," Lilyfax said.

"You were eating it up, staring at him," Leo said.

"I was staring," Lilyfax said, "at how high I'd need to kick to get him in the balls."

Leo looked over at her. The old mischief returned to her eyes. She smiled at Leo, her dimples returning.

"I'm coming with you. End of story," she said.

Leo smiled and returned to walking. He knew there would be no dissuading her. He was at peace with her coming, but not because she was tough enough to kick some asshole in the balls. Leo knew that when he set out with her, he'd have the Shadow Wulver to call forth anytime he needed, to protect Lilyfax, and to set the kidnapped girls free.

They were almost to the bus stop when someone called after them. For a moment Leo panicked, patting the front of his coat. He forgot briefly that he'd already delivered the bottles.

"Leo!" called the voice again. It was three syllables. Ell-Eee-Oh. Only one person said his name that way.

From the darkness, the Alchemist emerged. His face was red, and sleet flakes melted quickly on his bald head.

"Master Leo," he said.

Behind them, the bus approached the stop. It was maybe a quarter mile away. They'd have to make it quick.

"What is it?"

"It's your daddy," the Alchemist said, trying to catch his breath.

"What about him?"

"He's not missing. And he's not dead."

"Oh? Then where is the son of a bitch?"

"In jail, Leo. He's in jail."

"Like in the tank you mean? With the rest of the drunks?"

"No, like the penitentiary. He's been sent down east."

"What?" Leo said. "What for?"

"He's killed a man. Been charged with murder."

Chapter 18 - Camille

The one called Goat, he was careful when he hit me. Never on the face, arms, or legs, no place visible. No place that could damage the goods. Always his fists came down on the top of my head, and I knew he left bruises, even if nobody could see them. I felt them for days after. You get hit hard enough, enough times, you stop fighting, I don't care who you are. But then he tried to make his voice soft, gentle-like. It was hard for him. Didn't come natural. He said, Wake's gonna put you on a pedestal, you'll see. Way up high, like you deserve. Nobody'll hurt you. You got me to watch over you. Said I'm to treat you like my own sisters. I won't hurt you none, less I have to, less you need to be hurt. Mama never let me hurt my sisters, less they needed hurting. Then she made me do it.

And his face was almost kind, a face with so many deep wrinkles I wondered what it would be like to put my finger into the creases of them, to see how deep they would go, to see if they were as soft as they looked, like delicate ribbons. I seen him with his shirt off once. He had the chest of a young man, full of muscle and veins that popped like twine. His legs too, when he changed his boots, they don't have wrinkles, or the creases of an old man's legs. But his face. He looked to be a hundred in the face, a thousand deep wrinkles and his hands too, gnarled and bony. I don't know who give him that name: Goat. But it fit. The way he looked at you, side-eyed, like he can't see you straight on. The way a sheep does. I seen the Blue Man kick him. High in the ribs. Used that cane across his back. Ain't that the way of it? Man gets hit by another man higher up, comes home to hit the women. Some men come in Lila's that way. Been put down, beat down by the man that owns the land, wore down by their wives who hen peck at every flaw. They don't want the warmth of a woman. They want to put a woman in her place. Kick the cat across the barn.

But what came next. It was worse. Hog-tied in that horse cart, the narrow road just one switchback after another. Maude threw up on my back. Some other girl kept crying on and carrying on. I stopped looking out, the way the land dropped away to nothing, just straight down, looked like for miles, the wheels sometimes slipping, the horse fighting to keep us from sliding off the side of the mountain. Goat kept kicking the horse. I couldn't see him kick it, but I could hear it. His grunts when he done it. The same way he grunted when he hit me.

And the land changed at the top of the mountain. It was hard to breathe. The trees were black, the earth too. Like everything had been scorched by fire. But it wasn't burnt up. The trees still had their black leaves. There was still plants along. I remember the mushrooms. Red mushrooms. The big building, walls of limestone. The Temple, they called it. They had me in a dog cage for a long time. Then he come to get me. Fur coat, trimmed in blue, the blue sunglasses. Even his boots were blue. Like it's the only color he can see. He dressed me up, like for a night on the town, real fancy-like. Painted my face, put earrings on me, paid attention to every detail. Labored over it. Kept telling me what a work of art I was, how men had fought wars over faces like mine, killed their own brothers for faces like mine. Got me gussied up then took me outside. The trees were so big. Bigger than any I'd seen before. Some as wide as a car. When he rubbed his fingers together, there was sparks between them, like his fingers were made of flint stone.

Then he did it.

Oh god, he did it.

So cold it hurt, hurting me to the bone, hurt all over.

The freezing!

Oh God, the freezing.

Chapter 19

On the day Leo told Mama about Daddy being in prison, she'd continued to scrub the iron pot before her in the wash basin as if she'd just received news about the weather.

"Well now we know," she'd said, offering only the slightest shrug.

Later, she sat on the front porch, warming her face in the midmorning sun, smiling at Leo and his brothers as they went about, as if all the world were a delight, she without care.

And yet, when twilight came, its looming arms creeping up the holler toward the one-room house along the creek bank, Mama changed. Her smile faded and her face fell gray. Her eyes gained a kind of wildness, and just after sundown, Mama put on a Sunday dress along with her one pair of earrings and sprinted from the porch through the muddy field to the creek. There she waded quickly across and ran up the hill, disappearing into the tree line.

"Mama, wait!" Leo yelled after her. He gave chase, eventually finding her deep in the woods, sitting with her back against a huge oak tree, hugging her knees to her chest. Leo had picked her up and carried her out of the woods, down across the creek and back home. There he'd made a fire, turning his back as she changed from her wet clothes, slipping on a pair of Daddy's long-handles in which to sleep.

This ritual repeated itself daily. Leo would leave the house during the day, careful always to come back well before nightfall in order to intervene in whatever the evening's madness might be. One night, Mama climbed atop of the house, stripped off her clothes to huddle near the moonlit sky. Leo climbed up after her, averting his eyes as he walked toward her with a dingy blanket spread wide to cover her nakedness.

She'd been cheerful the morning the ruddy-faced clerk from Wilson's brought groceries, which Leo had paid for using the wad of cash he'd gotten from Wormley. Leo had also bought everyone in the family new clothes and shoes, everyone except Hank. For himself, Leo bought a pair of deep indigo dungarees, some dark brown shoes, and two crisp white shirts. These he wore under the long brown coat given to him by the Alchemist. He also purchased for himself a black hat with the slight pinch of a fedora. This he wore everywhere. He and Lilyfax had ventured into town twice in the weeks after they'd discovered Daddy's fate. Each time, they had called on the Alchemist and Aunt Lila, trying to learn more about the missing girls and where they might be.

Leo had gone to Altamont on his own several times, once browsing pawn shops for hours until he found just the right thing at Finkelstein's: a glass angel music box, which he had gift wrapped for Lilyfax. That afternoon, he'd rushed along the dirt road from the bus stop, eagerly presenting it to the girl on the front porch of her house as a cold rain fell around them. She smiled, hugging him close. It was almost as if, in that moment, she had forgotten the fear she'd had of Leo when she'd witnessed him summon forth the Shadow Wulver. Leo had been careful not to make that mistake again, though this hadn't stopped him when Lilyfax wasn't around.

One by one, Leo stalked the other three boys from Lilyfax's attack, terrifying each to the point of frantic horror, ever viewing the world through the cobalt blue eyes of the Shadow Wulver. Leo particularly enjoyed torturing the first boy, a squat-legged bastard named Earl, who had more freckles on his face than made sense. Leo watched Earl for several days, toying with him by having the Shadow Wulver growl anytime the boy came outside, whether to go to the family's gray barn out back, or to their root cellar to fetch potatoes. Earl quickly became a nervous mess, jerking his head back and forth each time he left the family's cabin, which sat at the mouth of the valley on a large hill surrounded by tall maple trees. As Leo and the wulver stalked through the woods behind Earl's home one night, Leo was delighted to observe the boy's parents and older sister, his only sibling, leave Earl alone. When the boy's family was far enough down the road, perhaps on their way to visit relatives, Leo directed the wulver to creep up to the cabin window. There, through the wulver's eyes, Leo saw Earl eating a piece of cornbread at the family's dinner table. The wulver growled and when Earl looked, he must have seen its blue eyes glaring through the window. Earl nearly choked on the cornbread, falling out of his seat. The wulver then leapt to the top of the cabin and began to pace, the shingles creaking beneath its immense weight. Finally, when Earl had enough, he threw open the front door of the cabin and ran out carrying his daddy's shotgun. Earl could barely hold the long gun straight for shaking, and he pointed it up to the roof of the cabin, where the Shadow Wulver glared at him. It spoke to him in his mind:

Ahh boy, would you to punish me?

I, who raise the wind and stir the sea?

Earl fired wildly into the evening sky, and Leo felt the slugs sting as they passed through the wulver's body. When Earl looked again to the rooftop, the wulver was gone, and he swung the rifle around trying to sight it again. Leo laughed in the woods and the wulver cackled loudly with him, shaking the trees. The Shadow Wulver sprinted from around the side of the cabin, knocking the shotgun from the boy's hands. It lifted Earl from the ground with its teeth, hooked in the straps of the boy's overalls. The wulver climbed the highest maple nearby, hooking the boy by his clothes on the tallest branch. There the boy cried out in terror, his body wobbling in the wind. The branch creaked as if it might break. The wulver descended.

Leo stepped out of the shadows, staring up at Earl. The wulver sat beside him.

"You know me boy?" Leo asked.

"Yes," Earl said.

"You know why I'm here?"

"I don't know," Earl said.

"You touch my girl again, I'll have him drop you from the tree on your head."

Earl said nothing. Leo and the wulver set out.

"Hey!" Earl cried out after them. "You can't leave me up here like this!"

Neither Leo nor the wulver bothered to answer.

The second boy got his when he went out to hang up the wash for his ma. Leo made sure he saw the outline of the wulver through a white sheet he'd hung on the line. The boy fell backward to the ground, spilling wet clothes around him as the Shadow Wulver pushed through the sheet to reveal his enormous open mouth, its jaws snapping closed mere inches from the boy's face, so close the rancid heat from the beast's mouth blew back his hair.

The final boy ran so far and fast from the Shadow Wulver that he got turned around deep in the woods, becoming completely lost. There Leo and the Shadow Wulver left him to the horrors of the forest, to the bitter cold of winter. It would be up to the boy to find his way home. He'd certainly showed Lilyfax no mercy, Leo reasoned, when he'd held her hands above her head to let Declan and Hank have their way. As for Hank, more than once Leo had begun pulling the Shadow Wulver from the darkness to exact revenge. Each time, he'd realized Mama was nearby and this had stayed his hand. There was no way Mama would recover from seeing the enormous beast in the trees. She'd think it the devil coming for sure. So then, Leo let his anger simmer along, just below the surface, biding his time, imagining ways in which to inflict the most damage.

After these delightful moments of revenge, Leo set his mind to new purposes. First, he thought of the other people in the valley that had shown contempt for his family. He thought of how to make them pay, and lay awake at night, his fingers interlaced behind his head, dreaming of the many ways he could use the Shadow Wulver to punish his enemies. So too did his attention turn toward the need to make more money.

The stash he'd taken from Wormley was almost gone, and so he knew he'd soon need to find chores to complete for farmers, the widow, and others in the valley who had cash money.

Leo mowed a field for Farmer Rex, spending hours sharpening and swinging an old scythe. Afterwards, he stood looking sadly at the few coins in his palm. This was not nearly so productive or convenient as the way he'd earned money from Wormley, just taking the man's billfold and fancy watch outright. That had taken, what, twenty minutes? Twenty minutes to earn more cash than Leo could make in six months working for Rex, Johnson, and the widow. Perhaps, then, Leo could find more hypocritical, evil men, who deserved to be parted from their treasures.

In the first few weeks after learning Daddy was in prison, Leo had, on his trips to Altamont, inquired not only about the kidnapped girls, but also about Daddy's status. He'd wondered, fingering the wads of cash in his pocket from his work for the Alchemist, if bail could be paid, or if a lawyer might be secured. Truthfully, Leo was relieved to learn that Daddy had already been sentenced after going before a judge and confessing his guilt. There was no option to pay bail, no option to aid his father. He was beyond Leo's grasp. Leo was relieved because when it came right down to it, he didn't want to throw money away on Daddy. He didn't want Daddy to return home, despite Mama's madness. At the same time, questions clouded Leo's mind. Why had Daddy killed a man? Sure, he could be violent toward his wife and children, but Leo hadn't ever figured him capable of murder. Why would he do it? Did Daddy have a good reason? In the end, Leo kept returning, over and over, to the worthlessness of the man. Daddy'd just gotten drunk and done something stupid, Leo decided. Just like he always did. He thought, *let the man rot right where he lay*.

Leo had also gone to see Goldfish, who seemed in good spirits, perched on her bed at the widow's. The widow said her prognosis was better, and she eyed the powders Leo mixed for the girl with suspicion, knowing they'd come from the Alchemist.

"I tried to get better," Goldfish had said.

"You done good," Leo said, kissing her cheek, and retrieving her balled socks from the floor.

"I don't like wearing them socks," she said.

"I know," Leo said. "You're stubborn."

"I ain't neither."

Goldfish had giggled when Leo gooched her cheek and held on to his finger for the longest time when he told her he had to go outside to finish chopping the remaining wood for the widow. The girl's fever came and went, the widow said, returning as sure as the sun rises.

It was against this backdrop, against days full of chores and the plotting of revenge, of searching for word of Camille and her kidnapped peers, of nights disrupted by bouts of Mama wrestling, of wrangling her indoors against her will so she couldn't disappear or harm herself; it was in the milieu of these moments that Leo was startled on a cool December afternoon by the taunting words of James from the yard:

"It's Leo's girlfriend, come calling. Leo got himself a *girlfriend*. And look! She's brought along the *Little Priest*."

Hank slunk around the side of the house at word of Lilyfax's arrival. In the field, near the weeping willow tree, Lilyfax approached, Ezra by her side. The boy wore black from head to toe, and as he walked along beside her, Leo realized Ezra was slightly shorter than the girl, something he'd never noticed before. He couldn't imagine why the pair of them should be together.

"You never know who's going to come calling," Leo said, crossing the road to the field.

"I picked up a stray along the way," Lilyfax said.

"I see that."

"Leo," Ezra said, tipping his newsboy cap. "Good to see you again." The boy approached, hand extended.

"What brings you out this way?"

157

"Ezra is looking for the Gelders," Lilyfax said.

"Ain't nobody looking for the Gelders," Leo said. He crushed a dirt clod with his heel.

The Gelders were a group of believers who worshiped out in the woods, usually at night; folks who'd been cast out from various charismatic churches around the valley, their practices too outlandish, too fanatical, it seemed, to be confined by four walls.

"I am," said the boy, hands tented in front of him. "People say all kinds of things about them. I'm sure much of it isn't true. But I'd like to find them. I understand they meet around here someplace?"

"They're known to," Leo said. He spat on the ground. "They're a batshit crazy bunch. You sure you want to find them?"

"I do," Ezra said. He grinned, as if he knew something Leo didn't.

"What for?" Leo asked.

"Well Leo, I figure I'm a lot like you. I'm looking for answers. Always seeking."

"That right?"

"That's right. John the Baptist was an outcast too. Maybe these Gelders know something the rest of the churches around here don't?"

"Oh, I don't doubt that," Leo said. "You're too crazy for the Church of God crowd, that's saying something." He pointed across the creek to the rise of the mountain. "They don't stay in the same place long, but they're usually somewhere over that ridge yonder. They got a couple of spots."

"Would you want to show me?"

"Show you?"

"Yeah, maybe help me find them, or at least get me close so I can track them?"

Leo looked at Lilyfax, then back at the house. Mama was walking around the yard, holding James's hand.

Lilyfax seemed keen, eyebrows raised. Leo looked up into the canopy and out over the field. Near the creek there was a committee of black vultures, about a dozen. An albino one sat in the middle. Leo looked up at the clouds. It was early enough to make the trek and be back in time to anticipate Mama's twilight spell.

"All right," Leo said. "Might not get you all the way to them, but I'll at least point you in the right direction."

Leo, Lilyfax, and Ezra made their way across the creek via a narrow bridge about a half mile from the house. Once across, Leo cut up through the trees toward the top of the ridge. The grade was steep, their breath labored as they climbed.

"Where abouts do you live?" Lilyfax asked Ezra.

"I live with my grandma about two miles the other side of Wilson's. You know that area?"

"Passed through it is all," Lilyfax said.

Leo recalled Ezra from school, but he'd never seen the boy at church or anyplace with his grandmother or any other adult. Ezra had only recently taken up with some kids from the valley shortly before Leo's fight with Declan in Farmer Rex's barn. He had stood between Leo and Declan in the barn. Leo had not forgotten.

When they crossed the first ridge, they saw a fence ahead, and the stretch of fields that were part of the Johnson farm. As they reached the fence, they saw that a section had been trampled. Leo figured by cows.

"We cut through the field, make better time," Leo said.

The sky was overcast, the world having fallen into monochrome. A column of smoke billowed from the chimney of the Johnson house along the ridge. The smoke filtered up in a funnel and twisted down to the ground, pooling around the house.

Ahead there was something in the field. At first Leo thought it was a small pile of brown leaves. When they drew closer, he realized it was a chicken. Its head was missing, and blood stained the brown grass around it.

"What did that?" Lilyfax asked.

"Coyote, maybe, or a dog," Leo said. "Don't know exactly."

"I don't think so," Ezra said, pointing to a place over in the field where there were deep ruts, the ground freshly turned.

"What then?" Lilyfax asked.

"Wild boar," Leo said. "There's talk of them all over the county, tearing up fields, killing farm animals."

"Yes, we heard about them at the home," Ezra said.

"The home?" Lilyfax asked.

Ezra shifted his weight from one foot to the other. In the graying day, his black eyes gleamed. "Home, I meant," Ezra said. "Granny and some of the neighbors have been talking about the boars, back home."

Leo imagined what a pack of boars could do. For a moment he forgot about the Shadow Wulver and a streak of fear ran up his spine.

"Over there," Ezra pointed. "Look there. Is that a cow?"

When they crossed the field, they saw a calf. It had several small punctures in its chest, having been gored to death.

"Damn sight, ain't it?" came a voice behind them.

"Sure is," Leo said, turning to see Farmer Johnson coming across the field.

"They're going to put me out of house and home," Johnson said. "I mended the fences a dozen times. Shot several of the bastards—pardon my language, miss. I've set traps. I can't get shed of them. Seems like there must be a thousand."

"I can get rid of them for you," Leo said.

"How'll you do that?" Ezra said.

Lilyfax glared at Leo. He didn't meet her eyes.

"What would it be worth to you, to be rid of these boars?" Leo asked.

Farmer Johnson scratched the side of his bald head. Leo marveled at how the man's eyebrows met exactly at the center of his forehead, giving him, in effect, one thick eyebrow.

"Let's see. All the hours I keep putting in to fixing fences. Plus, wood I got to cut and plane.

Then there's the dead chickens. All the eggs they ate from the roost. It's getting expensive. Reckon I'd pay top dollar to get shed of them, boy, but now, don't go getting yourself killed over this. Them things are dangerous. I don't need that on my conscience."

"I won't," Leo said. "I can do it."

The farmer seemed unconvinced, looking past Leo to the field and the missing section of fence. He tugged on his overall straps. Then he looked Leo in the eye, studying. After a moment, he seemed to let go of his doubt. Or perhaps he was desperate for help from wherever he could find it.

"You do that, and I'll pay you what it's worth. Seven days field wages, how's that?"

"Leo—" Lilyfax started.

Leo held up his hand to the girl. "Maybe give me a week."

The farmer nodded.

"All right. It's a deal."

It was late afternoon by the time Leo, Ezra and Lilyfax passed over the next ridge heading down into the clearing where the Gelders were known to assemble.

Walking along, they heard voices. The sound of gospel hymns.

"That's them," Leo said.

Soon they could make out the words of the singers.

Yes we'll gather at the river,
the beautiful, beautiful river . . .
Gather with the saints at the river,
that flows by the throne of God . . .

Leo had sung the song many times. Was it possible the Gelders, long rumored to be snake handlers and poison drinkers with peculiar ways, weren't that different after all? Here they were, singing the same songs as all the church folk that had cast them out.

The outline of people came into focus, and Ezra jogged along, taking up behind a large tree. Lilyfax and Leo flanked him, craning their necks to catch a glimpse of the worshipers.

When the song ended, a woman spoke in tongues and thrashed her own back with a makeshift whip. The crowd circled around a large bonfire.

"Oh lord," Ezra said, looking over at Leo. "You think they're going to firewalk?" Excitement spread over his cheeks.

"People do all kinds of dumbass shit in the name of God," Leo said.

"I liked the singing," Lilyfax said. She stood on the other side of Ezra. "But I don't want to watch nobody burn themselves."

The woman on the ground grunted. The crowd followed her lead, moaning and harmonizing with the sounds she made. Leo looked up at the clouds. They had over an hour walk back before dusk would settle in and Mama would lose her way.

"Well, I helped you find them, Ezra, but me and Lilyfax got to get back."

"I changed my mind. I want to watch them walk on the fire," Lilyfax said, her eyes meeting Leo's.

"I got to go see after Mama is all," Leo said. Lilyfax nodded.

Ezra looked from Leo to the Gelders and back. "Thank you for bringing me here, brother Leo."

Leo wondered why Ezra called him "brother," the way deacons and preachers did. Maybe his nickname fit. As he was turning to leave, Lilyfax squeezed his arm, her eyes wide. Near the fire, a man walked, leading a goat along beside him, a rope around its neck. The woman who had spoken in tongues earlier stood opposite, waiting for them. She held a long knife in her hand, her expression blank, her eyes far away.

Chapter 20

When Lilyfax and Leo crested the ridge there was a break in the trees where they could make out Leo's family's house down below, across the creek. Leo's shoulders relaxed. There was no sign of Mama nude on top of the house, and nothing seemed to be on fire. Dusk had found its full vigor, the cool winter wind whipping up through the trees to smack their faces bright. Halfway down the ridge it began to snow, thin icy flakes kissing their cheeks. By the time they crossed the creek, there was an inch of snow on the ground.

Leo and Lilyfax stood on the porch, peering inside. James was at the wood stove, ladling some beans out into a bowl. The sweet smell of fatback overwhelmed everything. Since Leo had been buying the family groceries, Mama's cheeks had begun to fill in slightly. She wasn't right in the mind, but her body was gaining some semblance of its former shape. Mama sat at the table, rolling a cigarette, wearing the navy skirt Leo had bought for her, along with a canary yellow top with three large buttons down the chest. As James walked around, his leather shoes creaked from their newness. Quite a sight they cut, Leo thought, the little poor family with fancy clothes, still in this drafty old barn of a house. He'd not made enough money to fix up the house yet, but he'd tend to that next, after rescuing the kidnapped girls. Hank remained hidden. He'd likely seen Lilyfax coming, his shame driving him to draw up like a curling worm exposed to sunlight.

"Let me walk you home," Leo said to Lilyfax. Mama didn't have the wild look about her that foretold her twilight madness. Leo felt safe to leave her for a while. And he really wanted time alone with Lilyfax.

They were moving through the yard when a loud thud crashed behind them. Mama was struggling with the frame of her bed, banging it loudly against the wall. She appeared to be trying to pull her bed outside.

"Mama, what're you doing?" Leo asked.

She flipped the bed up and worked it from side to side, trying to shimmy it through the doorframe. Leo watched the whitewashed wood drag the door as she worked. He remembered the day Daddy had brought the bed frame home on the back of a neighbor's truck. He and Mama had laughed and joked, outside in the spring sunshine, as they'd painted the bed a bright white. Daddy had gone on and on about how the thirsty wood had required three coats.

Lilyfax went up onto the porch, putting her hands on the bottom of the bed, helping Mama pull it free. The two of them worked the bed around, the straw mattress dragging across the porch as they progressed. James stood behind them in the house, eating his beans as if nothing were amiss. When they got to the steps of the porch, they lifted the bed and carried it down.

"Where're you taking it?" Leo asked.

Mama pushed the bed across the front yard. Lilyfax moved around it to help. A leg of the bed snagged on a root. Leo came down off the porch to lift that end. When they got about twenty feet from the house, Mama abruptly stopped, turned, and walked back inside. Lilyfax looked at Leo, shrugging her shoulders. They followed Mama inside.

Mama dug through a chest, pulling out an old flask of lamp oil.

Across the room, James held up a ragged teddy bear, its brown fur faded, one button eye dangling. "Look here. This is Hank's Teddy! He's practically grow'd and still cuddles with it. I seen it under Mama's bed when she drug it out. He told me he throw'd it away, that he didn't need it no more."

Leo remembered the stuffed bear. Hank used to carry it everywhere with him when they were small. Leo remembered Hank's face the day Mama gave him the bear, back when he was wide-eyed and innocent. He couldn't have been more than three or four. He'd named the bear Oscar.

"So, that's Hank's?" Lilyfax asked. "Give it here." James walked over, his leather soles dragging the floor, shoulders slumped. He handed Lilyfax the bear, which she stuffed under her shirt.

By now Mama had a flask of lamp oil in one hand and a lamp in another. She went out the door.

When they got outside, Mama was standing over the bed, disassembling the oil lamp. She turned it up, making a circle with the pour. She opened the flask and did the same.

"Mama?" Leo said.

Mama fished in her skirt pocket, pulled out a wood box of matches. She struggled, striking the head of one after another against the side of the box, the snowfall wetting each before they could catch a spark. She'd gone through four or five matches when finally Lilyfax went over and cupped her hands. Mama did not acknowledge her, but kept striking matches until one lit. She settled her own hand over the lit match, turning slowly to drop it onto the center of the bed. The bed exploded with an orange flame so high the heat rushed over Leo's face. Mama stood too close, so Leo took her by the arm to pull her back. She shrugged him away. She stared into the fire, as snow stuck to her shoulders and hair. She stood so still she didn't appear to breathe.

After a few moments, she reached into her pocket, pulling out a small tobacco tin. She opened it and took out a crooked cigarette. She leaned toward the fire, the cigarette between her lips. When it lit, so too did her hair, crackling as it singed. Lilyfax rushed over to pat her forehead. Mama said nothing, made no motion to put out the fire in her hair herself. She dragged deep on the cigarette, never taking it from her mouth. The night was still, save the crackle of the fire on the front lawn, the sizzle of melting snow as it struck the flames.

Mama stood so dangerously close, Leo imagined her slipping and falling in, or worse: leaping into the flames on purpose. Leo stepped closer, and though her mouth barely moved, she whispered:

We're all on fire
We're all on fire

165

There came a crunch of footsteps in the snow. Hank came around the side of the house, mouth agape. "What in tarnation is going on here?"

No one answered.

"I leave y'all alone and everything goes to hell in a handbasket," he said, feigned palm to forehead.

"Mama burnt her bed," James said from the porch.

"I see that, buddy," Hank said. "Thanks. And y'all," he gestured to Leo and Lilyfax, "just stood and watched her do it?"

"Leo's girlfriend helped her do it," James said. "And she has *Oscar*."

Hank looked at Lilyfax but said nothing. His hands formed fists.

Lilyfax met his eyes. She walked around to the other side of the burning bed. She pulled the dingy teddy bear out from under her shirt. She held it over her head, her eyes never leaving Hank's.

"Is this your Oscar?" she said.

"Mama give him to me when I was little is all."

"Then you won't mind if I drop it on the fire? Being you're grown and all now."

Hank took a step toward her. "Give it back," he said.

"Is it precious to you?" Lilyfax asked.

Hank looked at his feet. "Just give it back."

"Do you remember my angel you smashed?"

Hank said nothing.

"Just grinding it into the dust? Do you remember holding me down, so Declan could put his hands on me?" Her voice held a timbre Leo had never heard. It wasn't shaky, or tentative. Her tone was solid, punchy, each word slashing the air like a blade.

"It weren't my idea," Hank said, eyes down.

"Look at me!" Lilyfax said. "I remember where *your* hands went too."

Hank looked at Leo.

166

"Don't look at him. Look at me," Lilyfax said. "Look. At. Me."

Hank stared again at the ground.

Look at the girl.

The voice of the Shadow Wulver echoed around them. Leo's anger ran through him, and in his anger, he'd forgotten his promise to keep the wulver away. He'd pulled it from the shadows that gathered around the house, welling up in the night, welling up within him. Hank rubbernecked the trees behind him. Leo looked to Lilyfax, afraid of her reaction. Her eyes never left Hank.

Look. At. The. Girl.

The ground swayed with the words of the Shadow Wulver, a throbbing ricochet of clanging bells, just off key, unnaturally deep. Hank's shoulders twisted with fear, but he did as he was told. He looked at Lilyfax, finding her eyes.

"You broke my angel. My ninny give it to me. It was precious to me, like this bear is to you."

Again, Hank took a step toward the fire, toward Lilyfax.

The Shadow Wulver growled. Hank took a step back.

"I am going to burn your bear. Your Oscar," Lilyfax said.

"No," Hank said. "Please, I'm sorry. I'm sorry about the angel, and I'm sorry about what we done to you. We was trying to get back at Leo, is all."

"What does Leo have to do with my angel?" she asked.

Hank said nothing.

"What does Leo have to do with me or my body? Watch."

Lilyfax tossed the bear onto the fire. The flames in the center of the bed licked higher, the button eyes of the bear running black streaks.

"You bitch," Hank said.

"I think," Lilyfax said, looking at Leo, then back to Hank, "that since you put your nasty hands on me, maybe the big bad wolf should put his nasty paws on you."

As she spoke, the growl of the wulver rumbled through the hollow in vast crescendo. James and Hank held their hands over their ears to muffle the enormous sound. James yelped and ran into the house. Mama lit another cigarette from her first, unfazed. Lilyfax did not cover her ears. She looked at Leo. She lifted her chin, giving the okay.

Soon the footfalls of the Shadow Wulver thundered through the trees and Hank ran. Leo saw Hank's back as he ran, through the dark cobalt blue of the wulver's eyes. Hank panted hard, frantically banging into the trees, falling again and again to the snowy ground. The Shadow Wulver toyed with him, leaping from side to side, throwing his voice through the trees. Finally, it swiped at him with a huge paw, catching Hank across the back, rolling him across the earth in the snow, his coat and shirt shredded.

When Leo and Lilyfax made it to where the Shadow Wulver had Hank cornered, they found him balled up in the fetal position. The wulver circled the boy, its tail swishing the tree limbs above.

Lilyfax stood close to Hank, hands on hips. Though Hank shuddered on the ground, she didn't seem satisfied. Leo stared at her face. It was dark with rage.

"Stand him up," she said to the wulver. "Let me get a good look at him."

The wulver lowered its head to take the boy by the collar of his jacket, jerking him upright, his toes dragging the snow from where they peeked out of his old boots. Leo wasn't sure he'd given the wulver the command, or if Lilyfax had. He pushed back into the blue view of the wulver.

"You don't look so tough now," Lilyfax said.

Hank had tears streaming down his face, his breathing jagged and irregular.

Lilyfax kicked the boy hard between his legs. Hank cried out in pain, drawing his body up. There was a hunger in her eyes, and for a moment, Leo was sure she'd demand more damage be done to the boy. Lilyfax audibly ground her teeth, her eyes grey. Leo put a hand on her shoulder, and she twitched as if his touch burnt her skin. Slowly her features returned to normal. She looked ahead, eyes blinking.

Leo was about to call the wulver off when it spoke.

To break his legs, oh can we please?

To crunch the bones and twist the knees?

"No," said Leo. "When we head out for the girls, this weasel will have to watch over Mama."

The wulver growled, squinting its enormous eyes.

"No," said Leo.

The wulver tossed the boy across the ground like a scarecrow. It stirred the earth and dropped its head, taking a step toward Leo. It showed its teeth, offering a gloomy growl of protest. For a moment, fear pricked up Leo's neck.

"You'll get the chance to crack a thousand bones. I promise."

The wulver twisted its nose in disgust, turning to disappear in the trees.

"What was that all about?" Lilyfax asked. The old Lilyfax had returned.

"He needs to draw blood," Leo said.

"How's that?" Lilyfax said.

"It's time to go boar hunting," Leo said.

Just then, Ezra stepped from the shadows opposite from where the wulver had departed.

"What was that?" he asked. Snow caked his pants as if his knees had been drug along the ground. He could barely speak, he was so out of breath.

Leo and Lilyfax looked at each other.

"I was coming back from the Gelders. I heard these roars. Like a lion's. I thought of the Lion of Judah. I ran down as fast as I could." His face was ghostly pale, all the more stark against his black hair.

Lilyfax winked at Leo. She put a hand on his. "No more secrets," she said. "I guess the wolf is out of the bag."

Chapter 21

The hour grew close to midnight, the night starless, a thin silver moon offering only a slash of resistance to the enveloping darkness. Leo crossed the creek and headed up the ridge toward Farmer Johnson's, the Shadow Wulver padding lithely behind him, its tail high, grazing the tallest limbs in the trees. Leo saw both the path spread before him, and the cobalt vision of the wulver, its sight so much more detailed and attuned to the nuanced shadows of the night. Leo was one with the wulver, as if their very hearts beat together, the thought of each shared by the other. Yet, back at the house, when the wulver had pushed to break Hank's bones, it was as if they were miles apart. Leo had not been able to see the wulver's thoughts in those moments, when it curled its nose in disgust, denied the full scope of its desire for violence. Leo thought of this now, of how the wulver had growled at him threateningly, how it had skulked angrily away, as if it were an insolent child, full of scorn because it could not have its way.

Why had the wulver not obeyed him immediately? Why had it questioned his authority, wanted to act on its own? Leo entered the world through the wulver's eyes, detected no divergence between them, no hint of enmity. Though Leo basked in the power of the wulver and what it would do for him and his family, his mind sometimes turned to the enigma of the beast. How had it come to him, and why had it chosen him? Could someone else wield the beast? Could this power be taken from him? He vowed to never lose it, gritting his teeth.

Leo and the wulver crossed through Farmer Johnson's fields, past chicken coops and a large barn. There, at the edge of the woods, the wulver caught scent of the wild boars. Leo tasted them on his tongue.

"Yes," he said to the wulver. "That's what we hunt."

The wulver sneered, dropping its snout to the earth to track the boar herd at the edge of the field and into the forest.

Leo followed, picturing the way the trail ran along toward Nettle Pond. With any luck, they could hem the sounder of boar in at the pond, providing little chance of escape. The wulver huffed in agreement at this thought, which passed easily between them.

Leo's thoughts turned to how he and the wulver would soon track the men who'd kidnapped Camille, Maude, and the other girls. He pictured the men cowering, especially the smug Mr. Wake, the Blue Man, before the wulver, who would stand on two legs, swooping down to exact the kind of justice such men deserved. He thought then of Camille, and his pulse quickened. He was reminded of her soft skin, the warmth of her body, of the way she'd hugged him close at Aunt Lila's, of their dance. There was a danger about the girl, a spark in the way her lips came together. He longed to touch her once more, but he thought then of Lilyfax. While Camille was beautiful, Lilyfax had taken up her place in Leo's imagination. She swooped Camille from his thoughts, as if brushing away so many cobwebs in a barn. Leo no longer saw Camille the way he once had, nor the lusty Maude with her bouncy strawberry locks. Now he tried to think of them as sisters, two people who would forever be special to him, two girls that had showed him kindness when he, the son of a nobody, deserved none. Who would harm such girls? What kind of men would take women against their will?

Deep in the woods, the boars snorted. They were close now. The wulver crept low along the ground, blue eyes keen. Leo jogged from tree to tree. Ahead, the boars took shape in the shadows. There were at least two dozen of them milling about, some of them pushing their noses through the snow to root the earth beneath. Deep trenches weaved along the forest floor, just like the way the earth had been turned in Johnson's fields. With enough time, these beasts would tear the whole world inside out.

Leo perched against a tree, peering around it at the boars, the wulver low in the trees opposite. They were getting close when a baby shoat, no taller than Leo's shin, squealed. The others joined in, a huge chorus of boar cries in the night. They ran headlong through the woods, weaving in and out of the trees with surprising dexterity given their massive size and the thick snow on the ground. They ran toward Nettle Pond. Leo smiled, following the wulver, already giving chase.

The ground leveled near the pond and the animals grew agitated when they realized they were cornered. Leo watched them through the eyes of the wulver, as it stalked them through the tree line. The boars saw it then and ran in mad circles, a few of them leaping into the pond as if to escape. The Shadow Wulver leapt into the middle of the herd, grabbing a large male in its teeth. The wulver lifted its massive head and let it drop, severing the boar's spine. Warmth rushed over the wulver's teeth, and Leo felt its bloodlust wax wild and frenzied. He too tasted the boar's pink flesh. The wulver bit down once more, before hurling the carcass into the pond. It then reached down to grab another by the throat, severing the thick veins at its neck. Four lay dead in a matter of seconds, when two bore down against the Shadow Wulver, their tusks plunging into its leg. The wulver howled in pain, and for a moment Leo felt the sharp pain in his own leg, as if he too had been gored. It took the wulver two quick swipes of its enormous paws to hurl away his attackers, the largest of which struck a large rock head on, dying instantly.

The wulver plunged then back into the herd, killing one boar after another, until it reared back before pausing briefly, in mid-strike. Leo realized the boar on which it focused was the shoat who had squealed. Through the wulver's eyes, Leo sought to turn it away, toward the adults, to leave the baby be. He thought it would do so, that it would follow his lead, when instead the Shadow Wulver howled angrily, bearing down to crush the tender animal in its teeth.

"No!" Leo yelled. But the wulver did not stop its attack, killing several young pigs and swallowing them whole. Seeing this, many ran into the pond and drowned. At the edge of the herd, Leo noticed two peel off and run along the pond's edge around to the woods on the other side. The one in front was a large male, with a single stripe of white hair across his skull, the rest of his body covered in dark brown fur. Before he could think it through, Leo bounded from behind the tree to run after them, leaving the wulver to continue its slaughter.

At first Leo heard the snorts of the boars as they ran through the trees, but soon he could hear only his own heavy breathing. He reached a clearing and circled, listening intently for the sound of their hooves in the snow. In the distance, the dying swine bellowed by the pond. Leo turned back toward the path to the pond when he heard a low snort behind him. The striped boar stood, perhaps twenty feet away, dropping its head, its tusks gleaming darkly in a ray of moonlight. Leo ran in the opposite direction when he saw the second boar, a sow, appear in the shadows. They came on. Leo ran his fingers through the cold snow, fishing for a rock or stick, any kind of weapon with which to defend himself. He came up empty-handed. He fished out his pocketknife and held it out in front of him. It was comical, really, to consider the tiny blade as potential defense against the enormous creatures that easily weighed three hundred pounds.

The sow came at him first, and Leo twisted at just the last moment, barely missing the broad skull which would easily have shattered his ribcage. Stripe snorted and dropped his head, beginning his charge. It was only in the last moment, in the seconds before he would have been gored open, his entrails to spill heavily in the snow, that the treetops shook above them, the limbs cracking. The boar was less than five feet away when the sweep of the Shadow Wulver leapt through Leo's field of vision, its massive jaws seizing the boar's neck, an enormous crunch echoing around them. The wulver picked up the boar by its back, its neck a red fountain, and hurled the pig into the base of a tree where its back cracked, the carcass wrapped around the trunk. The sow was not dissuaded, coming in at the wulver still. He met her with a paw across the face which blinded her and severed her trachea. She lay in the snow, struggling, as the wulver put both paws down to finish her, raising its head toward the moon to howl. The wulver's face was covered in blood, the only part of it truly tangible, the rest a twist of ashen smoke.

Leo had the wulver pile the dead boar carcasses on the Johnson farm near the barn, reasoning that the farmer may be able to cure some of the meat to feed his family, or at least make dog gruel. The Johnson farm would no longer be plagued by these beasts. He and the wulver had tracked down and wiped out over thirty-two wild boars, but Leo winced when he thought about the shoats, hearing again the crack of their tender bones in the wulver's teeth.

Chapter 22 – Maude

The big ugly fella, Goat, he took me into the room, and he drew me up a bath. Kept asking me, me standing there in my robe, kept asking me to put my fingers in to see if it was hot enough. It was still daylight, I remember the light coming through the blue window, it was stain glass, like from a church, but just blue, not all different colors like in church windows. He kept pouring water in from the fire, stirring it with a ladle like he was cooking beans. He got the temperature right, right enough to suit me, then he lit the candles all around and left. There were bubbles, thick on the surface, the basin bigger than any I'd ever been in. I got in the bath, and it was the best feeling. It covered my whole body if I wanted it to. I could stretch all the way out in there. My legs, my arms, everything ached from the cold, from the ride up the mountain, from being balled up in that dog cage. I'm not gonna lie, it was heaven in that water. There was nothing like that bath, but I was scared when he come in, Mr. Wake.

He told me not to be afraid, and he pulled a stool over, to sit by the basin. He looked at me for a long time; not in an ugly way, and not gawking over my body, course I was covered with bubbles, all the places that counted anyways.

He said, Rest your feet up on my knees. *He had that funny way of talking, it's hard to understand till you get used to it, but I done it, I put my feet up, and he took a sponge and begun to wash my feet, real slow like, real tender. He took his time, each toe, between my toes, he scrubbed the heel, my arch, the top of my foot, everything. He was careful when he eased one foot down, before taking up the other. He scrubbed it just as long, just as careful, taking and soaping up the sponge, in between, sopping up the hot water, dripping it over my feet to rinse.*

I knew if I was ever gonna get away, if I was going to keep from being thrown back in the trees with the other girls, I was gonna have to get on his good side, so I asked him questions. I asked him where he got that beautiful accent. What country was he from? I asked him why he brought so many pretty girls to the top of the mountain like he done. I asked him why he always wore blue. He never answered none.

Turn around, *he said,* I shall wash your hair.

I slid around the basin, tried to bring the bubbles with me, keep things covered. He took one big hand and rested it under my neck, he let it drop into the water to wet it good, and then he used the other to put in the hair soap. I kept thinking about his hand on my neck, how strong it felt, how he could snap my neck in two if he wanted, how he could just hold me under the water. Put a quick end to me. Simple as pie.

He was so soft about everything, the only thing I could feel was the tips of his fingernails. They were long for a man, but they didn't hurt. They felt good. I was afraid to let myself relax, to let it feel good. I tried to tell myself it hurt, but it didn't. He washed my hair over and over till it squeaked through his fingers.

Your hair, it's exquisite, *he said,* like bright leaves at autumn tide.

I said thank you, and he went on and on about how men would want me like a dessert, to just eat me up, but I didn't hear him. I couldn't hear him. I just kept thinking about how his fingernails could rip me open, or about him strangling me in the water, making Goat bury me out under some old tree. He was just so gentle, his movements, a kindness. Like the way my daddy was to our pig, getting it all fat and lazy and tender, 'fore he cut its throat and hauled it up by its hind legs to bleed out while it screamed. Tried to scream. Mr. Wake wasn't fattening me up exactly, but I couldn't help thinking he was buttering me up for something, trying to make me feel like this, all relaxed and tingly and then what?

There was a knock at the door. Goat come and whispered in his ear. Goat never looked at me, but I could tell he wanted to.

Let him in. *Wake said.*

But, sir. *Goat gestured to me, to the bath.*

Let him in.

A fat man come in. He sat in a chair maybe six feet away. Wake never stopped rubbing my neck to look at the man. He kept on washing my face, all the while one hand holding my neck, supporting it, making me feel like I was floating. There was still a lot of bubbles and I kept my eyes closed mostly, but when I peeked, I seen the fat man staring into the water, trying to see. When he called the fat man Reverend, *I remembered him. I remembered him from Aunt Lila's. Something about how red his face always was. The way it would get. Like he was always struggling to get enough air.*

Wormley, *Wake said,* pull up that stool.

So the preacher man, he done it. He was at my feet, Wake still holding my head in his hand, still washing my face and neck.

Wake said, Don't look at her.

To me, Wake said, put your feet up on his knees. *I done it, but I hated touching that man.*

Reverend, take that sponge. Take that bar of soap there, that's right. Wash her feet.

The preacher hesitated, but he did as he was told. It didn't feel good. It was like he was doing something he loathed. Like it hurt his hands. Like he was washing an old mangy dog with lye in the back yard.

Your Jesus, *Wake said,* he washed the feet of his disciples.

Yes, *the preacher said,* and Mary Magdalene washed his.

Careful, *Wake said, watching the preacher wash my feet,* take your time, don't rush through it.

The preacher grunted, but he slowed down. He said, But we got important things to discuss. *He looked at me, into the water, then remembered to look away.*

I know you've come to talk to me about the boy, *Wake said.* And his dark wolf.

The preacher stopped washing my feet. He let my foot drop into the water, the splash darkening his pants. He stared at Wake for a long time.

Tsk, tsk, *Wake said.* You're becoming derelict in your duties, preacher. *He nodded to my feet. The preacher reached into the water to find my foot, haltingly, like he was afraid of what he might find under there, under the water.*

How did you know? *the preacher asked.* About the wolf?

177

Wake moved his hand down to wash my shoulders. He used his palms, his long fingernails never touching my skin.

To me, Wake said, Something about you reminds me of my mother.

Did she have red hair too? I asked.

She raised me in a place not unlike your Miss Lila's. A place full always of beautiful girls.

Was it nice? I asked.

She taught me to paint the girl's faces, from the time I was five. She made me dress impeccably, in case any of the men were to see me. If seen, I must look perfect, a tiny gentleman.

Is that when you started wearing all the blue? I asked.

Sometimes I regret her passing. *He said, letting my head drop with a thud against the side of the metal basin. He rubbed his hands together, and blue sparks came up between his fingers, like when Daddy used to rub his knives over a flint stone. There was a blue flame, just dancing on his fingertips. I was scared. I drew up my knees. I saw the preacher staring at Wake's fingers too, we both seen it. It wasn't just in my head.*

So much hatred, *Wake said.* This boy and his wolf. It can take many forms. The *Lystyven.*

The Light Taker, my people called it. Only absolute rage, only one most full of hate can summon it from the shadows. This wolf, *he said, looking at the preacher,* doesn't belong to the boy, no matter what he thinks. His shoes have I worn.

The preacher nodded. Wake went over to the fire, gathered another pot of warm water, and came back to pour it carefully into the basin. The suds were beginning to disappear, and I saw the preacher staring into the water, at my bare skin.

Have all the brothels been shuttered? *Wake asked the preacher.*

All of them. The ones we couldn't get shut by ordinance, we got on race mixing. The law squeezing one side, Klan on the other.

Good, *Wake said.* I own Altamont now. Let them come to me. Let them beg. We'll bring them from the four corners of the earth.

Wake got down on one knee. He held out his hand and for a second I didn't know what he wanted. When finally I offered my own hand, he seemed pleased. He took the sponge and began to slowly wash my fingers, palm and forearm. He dipped his head, a kind of half bow. Smiling, he said, Together, we'll do wonders, my dearest Maude. Won't we?

Will you put her in the trees with the others? *The preacher asked.*

I felt sick when the preacher asked that. And I hate the relief I felt when Wake didn't say one way or the other.

Chapter 23

In the days after the wild boar hunt, the immediate needs of Mama and Goldfish tended to and money in his pocket, Leo turned his attention obsessively to the question of the missing girls. At night his dreams were full of visions of Camille, Maude and the others being held by black creeping vines with the heads of snakes. He thought of Aunt Lila's black eye, of the girls bearing such marks on their faces and legs, and of the men capable of such things. He imagined the Shadow Wulver descending upon them, breaking their bones, and severing veins in the same manner as it had done the wild boars.

Each night after Mama was safely in bed, Leo hurried along the road to Altamont, Hank having given his word that he'd watch over her should she wake. Hank had been considerably more agreeable since the Shadow Wulver, though he now eyed Leo with a sense of wariness and seemed always to believe that he was being followed, craning his neck to peer over his shoulders constantly.

Leo was never afraid on these late-night journeys, always sensing the Shadow Wulver in the darkness, ready to come forth, should it be needed. Leo spied incessantly on the Alchemist, watching his movements, at the Raven Thicket as well as other boarding houses, hotels, and at the underground speakeasies. Business was brisk, and Leo conducted a great many deliveries both to earn money and to get closer to the Alchemist. Leo had his mind ever on the connections between the Alchemist, Mr. Wake, and Wormley, each of the three bearing the deep blue snowflake tattoos, brothers in some wicked conspiracy. Sure enough, on several nights, Leo observed the Alchemist meeting with Mr. Wake, usually with one or two other men Leo did not recognize. Each time Leo saw Mr. Wake, he wore various blue coats and donned the blue lensed glasses he'd had on the day he'd gawked at Lilyfax at the Raven Thicket. How easily, Leo thought, a man can deceive the world, hide his true nature. For when Leo had first met the Alchemist, he'd almost been convinced the man was a benevolent traveler, concerned primarily for the welfare of others. How far from that he must be, trafficking in liquor, his mysterious powders, and aiding Mr. Wake in whatever enterprise involved kidnapping women from the finest brothels in Altamont.

So it was, these thoughts clouding his mind, that Leo stood before the Alchemist one night, in his private room at the Raven Thicket, that Leo truly took measure of the man. He stared at the lines that ran up over the Alchemist's bald head, each ascending from perpetually raised eyebrows; Leo recalled how, when he'd first seen them, he'd imagined painted horns up into the space above the man's head. He considered for a moment, standing there, the bottles being affixed to his body, calling forth the Shadow Wulver, to squeeze the man until he squealed, spilling the beans on where Camille, Maude, and the other girls were imprisoned. At the last moment, as shadows conspired to form in the dark alley behind the boarding house, something stayed his hand. What if this would tip off Wake? What if they, made aware that Leo and the Shadow Wulver were coming, hid the girls? He might never find them. Leo let go, then, of his anger, letting the shadows fade back into the trees and into the crevices of the houses nearby. He would bide his time, keep asking questions at the periphery, keep spying on the Alchemist and Mr. Wake, until he discovered the truth.

It was on one such night, as Leo moved along the dirt road beyond Wilson's Trading Post toward town that he saw a figure coming down the road toward him, on the opposite side. Uncharacteristically, Leo was afraid when he saw the man coming on. He stretched out his hands, ready to pull the shadows together, much as a man puts his hand on a pistol in his pocket. There was a bit of moonlight, but not enough to make out who approached. The figure was a bit shorter than

Leo himself. As the strange man passed, he turned toward Leo at the last moment.

"Leo? Is that you? What are you doing out so late?" It was Ezra.

"Might ask you the same," Leo answered.

"Coming back from a revival," Ezra said.

That night Ezra accompanied Leo to Altamont, where they spied on the Alchemist, watching him convene with a number of men on the porch at the Raven Thicket. Along the trip, Leo told Ezra about Mr. Wake, the Alchemist, and Wormley, about their matching tattoos and potential connection to the kidnapped girls. He told him about Aunt Lila's black eye, of how he and Lilyfax would soon leave the valley to search for the missing girls and to rescue them.

"And you'll use the wulver?" Ezra asked.

"Yes," Leo said. "I can't think of a better thing to do with it than to punish these men, and to free the girls."

"You're a good man," Ezra said. "I knew that from the first moment I met you. You're a seeker, like me."

"You keep saying that," Leo said. "But I'm sure I don't know what you mean."

"People that want answers," Ezra said. He looked up at the few stars visible in the night sky. "We look for the connections between things. There are answers if we are willing to seek them."

"Maybe," Leo said.

"The wulver, that's a key to something, I know it."

Leo considered this a long time, had nothing to say. He thought of the Shadow Wulver and its counterpart, the Silver Wulver. He thought of how the Silver Wulver had guarded the sacred land where Mr. Goodman was building the Brookside Chapel. Would it think Leo was a good man, as Ezra had said? Leo recalled the crushing sound of the bones in Declan's legs, and later seeing the boy on crutches, head down, mind and spirit broken. He thought of the other boys he'd terrorized. Was it a good thing he'd done with the Shadow Wulver? And what of the shoats, the way the beast had eaten several whole, slaughtering their parents? Was this what a good creature would do?

"I want to find such power," Ezra said.

"How's that?"

"The power you have. The way you can wield the Shadow Wulver. The way you can walk along country roads and city streets at night, not a care in the world, because you know that nothing can hurt you. I want that. I'd do good with it, like you're doing. The way you want to rescue the girls."

"I ain't never thought on it," Leo lied. He thought of the new pants he wore, the bright white shirt, the new leather shoes, his black hat. All these things the wulver had given him, and more. Leo did feel powerful, though sometimes guilty. Guilty for the things he'd made the wulver do. Of the anger he held still, toward so many, his bloodlust insatiable, like the wulver's.

"Do you ever fear you'll lose this power?" Ezra asked.

"No," Leo lied again. "I figure he's always been there and will always be." Leo thought about telling Ezra about how the pillar of smoke had come to him, and his dead brother Jacob, but decided against it.

"I saw a dog turn on its owner once," Ezra said. "The owner got too close to its food. And even though he always fed the dog, it bit his hand. Drew blood."

"What did the owner do?"

"He took a stick. Well, a club, really. Beat the dog down. Till it bled. Said it never turned on him again."

After hours of watching the Alchemist, with no sign of Wake, Leo and Ezra went to Aunt Lila's. It was early morning, but there were a couple of lights on in the upstairs bedrooms.

They went around back and knocked on the door.

"Leo," Aunt Lila said. She looked Ezra up and down. "Least you didn't bring a girl this time."

She stepped out onto the porch and gathered her robe up around her neck. She had on no makeup and looked like she'd been sleeping. The gray streak in her black hair seemed lighter now.

"What've you heard?" Leo asked.

"Will you not let this go?" Aunt Lila asked.

"I won't let it go. I'll get answers from you, or I'll find Wake myself, hang him by his ankles to get him to talk."

Aunt Lila looked past Leo down the street.

"This ain't your fight. You boys will get yourselves killed."

"Whether it was or not before," Leo said, "it's my fight now. I can't bear to think of Camille and the other girls hurting."

"If they're still alive," Aunt Lila said.

"If?"

"You don't know what these people are capable of Leo. They burnt crosses in my front yard. I have one or two brave— brave or stupid—straggler customers that still come around. That's it. They've mostly shut us down. The girls and me, we're gonna starve to death in this house if I can keep up the taxes. You know what that filthy bastard said to me? Said if I wanted to, I could go back into production. Production, Leo. Like a woman is a machine. He said I wasn't too old yet, for a certain kinda man." She brought her hand to her mouth as if she'd said too much.

Leo put his hand on her arm. "You can tell me Aunt Lila. I need you to tell me. If I keep poking around the way I'm doing, I'm going to find out one way or the other. But if I find out the hard way, it could be bad. They'll know I'm coming. They're liable to run. Liable to hide the girls."

"Or kill them," Aunt Lila said.

Leo nodded.

"Mulwin Rock," she said.

"Mulwin?"

"That's where the girls are. That's what's said, anyway."

184

"Where is that?"

"North of Altamont, right ma'am?" Ezra said.

Aunt Lila looked at Ezra. "Yes, northeast. Maybe an hour out of town, to get to the base of the mountain."

"Mulwin Rock," Leo smiled. "What else?"

"They're kept at the very top of the mountain. All the way up. You take the Mud Road, they call it."

"Mulwin Rock, Mud Road," Ezra repeated.

"That's right. The girls are slaves. They aren't working, they aren't kept like they were here. Terrible things, Leo. What I've heard."

"We'll get them, Aunt Lila, don't you worry. We'll bring them back. Camille and Maude will be back in your parlor dancing before you know it."

"Leo, these men would just as soon gut you as look at you." She raised her eyes at Ezra. "And your little friend here."

"I know," Leo said. "Don't worry."

"The girl, what was her name? Lily?"

"Lilyfax," Leo said.

"They'll just put her into the trade. Don't you dare take her up there."

Leo winced. He and Ezra looked at each other. He remembered his promise to take Lilyfax with him. Of course, Aunt Lila didn't know about the Shadow Wulver.

"They call it the Temple."

"Why would they call it that?" Ezra asked. "After a place of worship?"

Aunt Lila adjusted the hem of her robe, pulling at her bare knees. "Maybe 'cause it sounds better than what it is," she said, looking at Ezra. "These men worship something different, something dark and twisted."

"You're sure?" Leo asked.

"I'd bet my ass on it," Aunt Lila said. "They've taken dozens of girls. Just the ones I know about. Some they talk into coming, but some, the ones that said no, they wanted them bad enough, they took them anyway. And not just working girls, neither. Grabbed some off the street, some off old country roads, only pretty and poor ones is what's said." Aunt Lila turned her back to them. "Have you ever looked into a man's eyes, Leo, and seen pure evil? Rot at the core. To the bone."

Leo didn't answer. Didn't know how to answer. He thought of the cold cobalt eyes of the Shadow Wulver.

"The kind that tell you everything. The kind that show their true intent, no matter what the smile says. No matter what the hands do. The eyes tell." She turned to face them. "Eyes that tell the violence of the ugliest heart, even while the lips lie and drip sweetness."

"Mr. Wake," Leo said.

She tugged an errant wisp of hair behind her ear. "You think about this business. How long I've been at it. I seen all kinds. I've seen everything. Men that come here, lonely as abandoned dogs. Just want a kind word, really, don't know any other way to get it. Men that want to replace their mamas, men that want to replace the girl that got away. All kinds of men. Some come in here, and I can tell just by looking at them that they're dangerous. They're here because they got hate in their hearts. They want to own something, if just for a minute. Be in control for just a while. All their darkness, all that ugliness. But none of them ever scared me like Wake done." She shuddered. "But there's more to it. Powerful men, he's got them all around him now. Sheriffs and mayors. Senators and judges. The Klan. They're all beholden to him somehow. And at the Temple, no ladies like me to keep men in check, to lay out rules. They're going to want to protect what he's giving them. There's a million secrets in that Temple. A million dark secrets up Mulwin Rock."

On the trip home from Altamont, Leo's mind raced. Part of him wanted to follow the North star, to sprint toward Mulwin Rock now, to fight through the hours it would take to get up the Mud Road. But there were things to do, things to prepare, before the journey could begin. He had a delivery of medicine for Goldfish. He needed to have a come-to-Jesus meeting with Hank about watching over Mama. Then there was the matter of gathering provisions. He'd grab some things at the house, some things at Wilson's. How many days would it take to find the Mud Road, to get up Mulwin Rock? And once they got there, they'd need a plan for getting the girls out without any of them getting harmed in the fight.

"I want to come with you," Ezra said.

"How good are you with a map?" Leo asked.

Chapter 24

A week before Christmas, they set out from the valley toward the Mud Road, toward Mulwin Rock, to find the Temple and the missing girls. Under a large maple tree just past Wilson's Trading Post, they opened their packs and inventoried their provisions. Leo had brought small tins of fish, dried beans that could be cooked over a campfire, some grits and crackers. He also brought a small pot to boil the coffee that Lilyfax brought.

"You got that map?" Leo asked Ezra.

"Got one from Wilson's this morning," Ezra answered. "I already found Mulwin Mountain, but there's no sign of a Mud Road anywhere. The place is isolated, all right, there aren't many roads or anything near it."

"A great place to go if you don't want to be found," Lilyfax said.

Leo held up the fishing tackle brought by Lilyfax. "Your old man won't miss this?" he asked.

"Can't remember the last time he went fishing."

They had enough food to last several days, and with the tackle they could catch fish from streams as they climbed the mountain. The wind lashed around them. It was a cold day, and though the sky was clear, a gray haze fell over everything. Ezra flipped up his coat collar and Leo pulled his hat down on his head, lest it fly away.

"What about you?" Leo asked Lilyfax. "Your daddy, is he going to come looking for you?"

"He thinks I'm off toward Barnardsville to help with my cousin's baby." She turned toward Ezra. "What about your granny? She won't miss you?"

"Told her my uncle was taking me hunting."

"That'd make Leo your uncle now," Lilyfax teased.

Leo figured it would take a few days to get up the mountain, maybe a day to rescue the girls. A couple days to journey home. They ought to be back by Christmas morning. How wonderful, he thought, to return Camille and Maude to

188

Aunt Lila's in time for them to help her trim the tree and sip hot chocolate by the fire. If times were too hard, he'd go pick out a tree for them and bring the cocoa himself.

"What about you, Mister Leo," Lilyfax asked.

"My mama won't even know I'm gone," he said. "And I got Hank's word he'd watch over her."

"Reckon you could get that boy to do just about anything right about now," Lilyfax said, smiling. "He ain't ever worked this hard in his whole life."

"I wouldn't cross the wulver," Ezra said.

"We just got one stop to make on the way out," Leo said. "We got to go by the widow's. I need to see about Goldfish."

When they arrived at the widow's, she was on the front porch in her rocking chair. She did not see them approach as she was engrossed in a conversation with Old Warne. He stood beside her, a mail sack on his shoulder.

"It's so nice of you to come by to visit. I don't have many folks to talk to nowadays," the widow was saying.

Warne seemed hurried, as if he were looking for a break in the conversation to make an escape. "I come every day, remember: rain or shine."

"Yes, you do," the widow said, "and you do it well."

Old Warne smiled when he saw Leo, "Well, looks like you got company, I best be getting on, a lot more stops to make."

The widow leaned out from her chair to watch Warne walk across the porch. She waved Leo and the others to the side so she could see the man's progress.

"If I was thirty years younger, and if that man was single," she said to no one in particular.

Warne smiled back at her uncomfortably, as if he'd heard. Lilyfax laughed, the sound of which broke the widow's fixation.

"Well, hello, young lady," she said to Lilyfax. To Leo, she said, "Hi there," struggling to her feet, cane in hand. She snuck a glance at Old Warne in the yard before turning back to Leo.

She said, "Come here and let me hug your neck."

She held Leo a moment too long, before reaching to hug Lilyfax. Over Lilyfax's shoulder, she spied Ezra. "I don't know this boy," she said, releasing the girl.

Before Leo could make a proper introduction, Ezra stepped toward the widow, extending his hand. "My name is Ezra."

The widow stared at him, not shaking his hand. "Who are your people, boy?"

"I live with my granny, other side of Wilson's."

"That right?" the widow said. "Who's your granny?" She looked Ezra up and down, her face brimming with suspicion.

Leo stepped between her and Ezra. "He's a friend of mine, ma'am. I come by to see Goldfish. How is she?"

The widow's hard eyes never left Ezra. She let her body slide slowly back into her rocking chair. "She's taken a turn for the worse, Leo, I'm sorry to say."

A knot formed in Leo's stomach. "I thought she was getting better."

"She gets better, she gets worse. It's bad this time though, Leo. I fear for her."

"I thought all the medicine I was bringing was doing her good."

"We need the good Lord to heal her, Leo. That's the only thing can help her now."

"I know," Leo said.

"I can't pray like I used to," the widow said.

"What do you mean?"

"It's like a shroud has fallen over everything," she gestured with her hand in a wide arc, out in front of her. "I see it now, on the earth." She looked at Leo. "I see it in your face. Like the whole world has gone dark."

"Maybe it's just 'cause it's winter," Lilyfax said.

"It's more than that," said the widow. "I can't see things like usual, clear like. My visions I mean. Like the good Lord can't get through to me. Like there's too many clouds 'tween me and him."

"They'll come back to you," Leo said. Then, "I'll go see the Alchemist. Things are different now, I've got money, I been working."

"Been hunting boar, I hear."

Leo eased his shoulders back. "Yes, ma'am."

"Tell me something, Leo," she said. "Were you hungry that night?"

"Hungry?"

"Yes, hungry."

"I don't know what you mean."

"Something took bites out of them boars, according to what Mrs. Johnson told. Just big bites of them, raw."

"Must've been after I killed them."

"That right?" said the widow. She glared at Leo, her eyes narrowing. "That's really something."

Leo shuffled from one foot to the other. He turned his back to the widow.

"Leo—" she said.

"I got to go see about Goldfish," Leo said, opening the door.

"Come on child," the widow said, turning to Lilyfax. "Let's me and you put some coffee on. And you," she pointed at Ezra with her middle finger, "you can wait here on the porch." Ezra shrugged.

In the bedroom, Leo bent down to pick up two small socks on the floor. They were barely as big as his hand. He turned them right-side out, fingering a hole in the heel of one.

"I kicked them off, 'cause I was hot," Goldfish said.

Goldfish lay on her back, smiling at him. Her gold hair played over the cream pillow beneath her head. It looked dull, lacking its former brilliance.

"It's so good to see my Goldfish," Leo said.

"I ain't no fish," Goldfish said, "I'm just a girl."

"Oh, but you are a little Goldfish," Leo said. "My Goldfish."

"Uh uh," she said, shaking her head.

Leo took a bunch of her long hair and held it in front of her face. "See?" he said. "Definitely a Goldfish."

She giggled.

"I missed you, big brother," she said, her voice cracking.

"I missed you too. How're you feeling?"

The corners of her mouth drooped. She crossed her arms.

"I tried to get better," she said. "I tried, but then I got sick again."

"I know," Leo said, sitting by her on the bed. "It's okay." He placed a hand against her fevered cheek.

Her eyes were shiny with tears. Leo stared into them, losing all equilibrium, as if he would fall into them and drown at the very edge of the world, at the edge of everything.

When he pulled away, he saw him. For a moment, on the bed, his dead brother Jacob was there, snuggled up against her. Leo jumped, backing across the room.

"Where're you going?" Goldfish asked. "You just got here. I never get to see you no more."

Leo stared at Jacob, who smiled, putting his arm around the girl. Jacob's smile stretched unnaturally wide across his thin face, the tips of his lips reaching his ears. Then Jacob slid under the covers, a lump moving beside the girl. Then the lump disappeared, the bed flat. Leo patted the bed where the lump had been, then sat, resting the palm of his hand against the girl's foot.

Goldfish's frown returned. "One of the church ladies, I heard her talking."

"You did? What did she say?"

"She was saying how I might go on to see Jesus. Like Jacob done."

Leo felt the air freeze around him. He squeezed her foot. "No," he said, "no."

"She said it," Goldfish said. "I heard it." Her smile returned, "What if I get to see Jesus before you do? Wouldn't that be something, Leo?"

"No," he said. "You're just a girl. You can't."

"But Jacob did," she said. "Before all the rest of us, and he was even littler than I am now."

"No," Leo said. He buried his face in the pillow beside her, their heads touching. He fought to keep her from hearing his sobbing.

After a while, he pulled away. Tears rolled on her cheeks, but she just kept smiling.

"I got to go away for a while Goldfish," he said.

"But. But – you just got here!" she whined.

"I know, but I'm going to bring you some medicine. Even better medicine this time."

"I'm tired of this bed, Leo. I need you to stay with me," she wrapped her hand around his index finger. "You got to tell me jokes and read me stories, like you done before."

"I have to go, see, because a friend of mine is in trouble."

"In trouble?"

"She's gone missing," Leo said.

"A girl?"

"Yes," Leo said.

"What's her name?"

"Camille."

"Camille," she said. "I like that name."

"She's in trouble. I've got to find her."

"She pretty?"

"Yes, Goldfish. But not nearly as pretty as you."

The girl beamed.

"Okay," she said. "But after you find her, you'll come back? You promise?"

"I promise," Leo said.

When they returned to the road, the three of them walked for a long time without speaking. Lilyfax and Ezra seemed to sense that Leo needed the quiet. He thought of the Shadow Wulver, of the power it had given him. He thought of how it could crush bones and terrify men to the core. He thought of how it could run through the forest, smashing the trees, leaping over wide creeks to thunder over everything. He thought of how it made him money, helped him get revenge, do everything – everything except save his little Goldfish. No matter how much power it gave him, he could not keep Goldfish from dying. All the medicines in the world, all the prayers, all of them added up to a big fat nothing. The girl looked worse than ever. Leo pictured the small wooden coffin that would need to be built for her, identical in size and shape to the one they'd used to lay Jacob to rest. Leo balled his fists.

Why would God take her the way he'd taken Jacob? Why did either of them need to die? For a moment he doubted the resolve he'd had that morning, upon leaving the house. What was the point of climbing a mountain to rescue girls he barely knew, if his only sister lay dying back home? He thought briefly of returning to her side, of holding her through her chills, through every fevered night. He should be there with her as she left this world, he thought, if she has to go. But then he thought, what good could he do her? He thought of summoning all the best doctors in Altamont, of making enough money with the Shadow Wulver to hire them all, to bring them to the widow's, one-by-one to save his sister. That's what he'd do, he decided, as soon as he freed Camille and the other girls from the Temple.

"Leo, you okay?" Lilyfax asked, putting her hand on his shoulder.

He looked at her, was about to speak, when Ezra interrupted.

"There's somebody coming."

Leo looked to see Mr. Goodman approaching.

"It's okay," Leo said. "I know him."

"Leo!" Mr. Goodman said, "I'd be lying if I didn't say this was a nice surprise."

"Mr. Goodman," Leo answered. "It's good to see you too."

"Who are your friends?"

"This is Lilyfax," Leo said. Before Leo could introduce Ezra, the boy stepped up and stuck out his hand. "I'm Ezra." He ever becomes a priest for real, Leo thought, he'll already have that part down pat.

"Lilyfax," Mr. Goodman said. "Ezra." He shook each of their hands in turn.

After greeting them, Mr. Goodman sniffed the air. He studied the sky to the west. "They're saying snow is coming. From over Tennessee way."

"A little snow won't hurt nothing," Leo said. He looked from Ezra to Lilyfax.

"Not a little snow. A big snow, Leo," Mr. Goodman said. "They're saying it's a big storm. One of the biggest we've had in years."

"I don't think it will bother us on the road," Leo said, immediately regretting his words.

"Road?" Mr. Goodman asked. "You're going on a trip, with this storm coming?" He eyed the packs they each had slumped over their shoulders.

"Well not a trip, exactly."

Mr. Goodman worked his fingers through his red beard. A bunch of freckles clustered in the creases between his eyes as he grimaced. "Where y'all headed?"

"We got to find one of our friends is all," Lilyfax said. She smiled at Mr. Goodman, her dimples on display, as if she knew they would ease the man's mind. Her own kind of magic.

"Yes, we just have to go pick her up," Leo said.

Mr. Goodman looked at each of them in turn. "Do you need help, Leo? I've got the Model A."

Leo thought of how the Silver Wulver had looked out for Mr. Goodman. He thought of how he planned to use the Shadow Wulver to free the girls. He did not want to share any of these things with the man.

"No," he said. "That's all right, we'll be just fine."

Mr. Goodman seemed to be weighing things, as if he might push back.

"I'd like to do something with you three, then."

"What's that?" Leo said.

"I'd like to pray for you."

"Right here?" Leo looked around. "Right here in the road?"

"Right here in the road," Mr. Goodman said, raising his hands. "Would that be all right?"

Leo didn't know what to say.

"I'd like that," Ezra said.

"Me too," said Lilyfax.

"After we get back from getting our friend," Ezra said, "I'd like to talk to you sometime about what you believe, about your faith in God. Would that be okay?"

"That'd be just fine," Mr. Goodman said. "Leo can show you where my church is, where you can find me."

"You're a preacher?" Ezra asked.

"No," Mr. Goodman said. "Church builder." Mr. Goodman put one hand on Leo's shoulder, the other on Lilyfax's. To each of them he said, "Put your hands on Ezra's shoulders, let's make a circle."

As Mr. Goodman prayed, Leo let his eyes wander over the landscape around them. He half expected a car to come down the road, to see the crazy sight of the four of them standing there.

When he looked off in the woods to his right, shadows clustered in the trees. The cool blue eyes of the Shadow Wulver formed in the gloaming, the outline of its head beginning to find its shape. Across the road, in the woods opposite, a flash of light caught Leo's eye. There, in the trees, was the Silver Wulver, its body shimmering like the surface of a lake, something like lightning where the face should be.

Leo's attention was drawn back to Mr. Goodman's prayer when the man squeezed his shoulder so hard it hurt. Goodman was still praying, but his eyes were open, glaring at Leo. For a moment, Leo wanted to run to the Silver Wulver, to leave the darkness and power of the Shadow Wulver behind. He wanted to tell Mr. Goodman about it all, to confess everything, every dark thought, every sin. He wanted to let go of the darkness, the fear of his sister dying, his shadowed memories of Jacob.

"He hears us always, he sees us always," Mr. Goodman said, gripping Leo's shoulder once more.

"Sir?" Leo said. He looked at Lilyfax and Ezra, whose eyes were open. Leo had not heard the man say amen.

"God will watch over you wherever you go," Mr. Goodman said. He was smiling, his eyes warm. "Never forget that, Leo."

The three of them continued down the road. Mr. Goodman called after them, "Remember to be kind to strangers along the road Leo!" Leo wheeled around to wave. "You may entertain angels," Goodman said.

Leo stared into the woods where the Silver Wulver had stood. It was gone. In the woods opposite, the Shadow Wulver remained, patiently awaiting Leo's command.

Chapter 25

The Mud Road lived up to its name. They reached the base of Mulwin Rock by late afternoon the next day, dusk beginning its slow crawl through the trees. Ezra stepped out of his shoe, a socked foot dipping into the cool mud. Leo and Lilyfax laughed, though aware of the mud in their own shoes.

"My papaw used to always say he was wore to a nub after a long day," Lilyfax said. "I don't think I ever knew quite what he meant. Until now."

They found a relatively dry patch of high ground just off the road, and Leo set about building a fire. Ezra and Lilyfax piled up sticks and leaves, as Leo worked the flint. Soon they were gathered around a tall campfire, warming their cold bodies. Lilyfax extended a stick out over the flames, her mud-drenched socks drooping from it.

"I hope Mr. Goodman was wrong about the snowstorm," Ezra said.

"I believe we can make it up the mountain in a day," Leo said. "We made good time. Any luck and we'll catch sight of the Temple this time tomorrow."

"I hope you're right," Lilyfax said. "And the mud ain't this deep all the way up."

"If it snows, there'll be more," Ezra said.

"Look at the moon," Leo said. It was about a quarter full, resting upside down. "If it were on its back we'd have to worry."

"That always true?" Ezra asked.

"Seems like," Leo said.

The world grew still, the sizzle of the fire the only sound.

"Ezra, how about opening one of those tins of fish," Leo said.

Ezra took the tin out of Leo's pack and stared at it.

"They's a key in my pack," Leo said.

Ezra dug through the pack until he found the key. He tried to point it at the can from different angles, not knowing how to make it work. Lilyfax reached over and took the tin from him, expertly working the key to open the can. Soon their fingers were shiny from the salty fish.

"I'm usually not one for fish," Ezra said. "But this hits the spot."

"Sure does," said Lilyfax. She turned to Ezra. "Your granny don't ever fry fish up on Sundays?"

"No."

"What do you do with it then?" Lilyfax asked.

"With what?"

"The fish you catch," Lilyfax said. "You do go fishing, right?"

Ezra looked at her, eyebrows flexed. "I don't really go fishing."

Lilyfax looked at Leo, and back to Ezra. "What does your granny like to cook?"

"All kinds of things. I guess her favorite thing to do is to roast a chicken."

"That right?" Lilyfax asked. "She cooks up a whole chicken for just you and her?"

Ezra nodded.

"Seems kind of wasteful, for just the two of you," Leo said.

"That's what I was thinking; expensive too," Lilyfax said.

"My granny eats a lot," Ezra said, his voice earnest, as if he were trying to convince himself.

"What's her name?" Lilyfax asked. "Your granny."

Ezra stirred the dirt near his feet with a stick.

"Who are your people?" Leo asked.

Ezra stared at each of them, then back to the dirt.

"Was there some reason you didn't want to tell the widow?" Leo asked.

"Her name is Bell."

"That ain't what we mean, and you know it," Leo said. "What's her last name?"

Ezra said nothing.

"I think Ezra has a secret," Lilyfax said.

Ezra looked to the trees above him for help, as if answers rested in the branches.

"Ezra," Leo said. "Look here."

Ezra looked up.

"We're all friends here. You came to my aid when Declan had me on the ground in the barn. I won't forget that. Way I figure it, I owe you. Whatever it is, you can tell us. We won't think nothing bad about it. But we brought you into our world here, on this trip, and it don't seem right of you to not level with us. Hell, you know my daddy's in prison. Now, how bad could your story be?"

"That's right," Lilyfax said. "And my mama, we ain't seen her for years. She run off with another man. Least that's what my daddy says."

"I remember," Ezra said. "Being with my mother. I remember her smell. We were at the lake."

Leo and Lilyfax traded looks.

"We were at the lake, and I remember it was warm. Maybe July. The sun was shining. The sky was bluer than any day I can ever remember since. Impossibly blue. And Mother, she had me in the water. And I was on my back, floating, Mother had her hands under me. If I started to sink, she'd ease me back up. The water was warm, like a bath. And I was at peace there, with her. Someplace – a moment I never wanted to let go of. I don't know how old I was, three or four?"

"That's beautiful," Lilyfax said.

"And Mother, she would hum to me, out loud. And my head was underwater, but I could still hear her humming. Sometimes, if I close my eyes, I can hear her humming to me, just like that, through the water. And the tunes she hummed. She made them all up. I asked her. Some people walk around humming songs they heard at church, hymns, or maybe nursery rhymes. But she said she made hers up. She said that one day she'd find a piano and put them all down to music for me. But she never did."

"What did she look like?" Lilyfax asked.

"She had long brown hair. Always wore it to one side, in a braid. Blue eyes. She was beautiful. So beautiful. I can still see the lake reflected in those eyes."

"Why don't you live with her?" Leo asked.

"It's like I can go there with her, anytime," Ezra said. "Just by closing my eyes and letting go of everything else. Do you know what I mean?"

"Yes," Lilyfax said. "I think I do."

Ezra took the stick he'd been holding and threw it on the fire. "That's the only memory I have of her. The only one. I try so hard to think if there are others, if there's anything else. But nothing ever comes."

Leo studied the boy's face.

"I kept wondering," Ezra said, "all through my childhood, if there was some way to get back to her. To get back to that lake. I kept looking for ways."

"So, you live with your granny now?" Lilyfax asked. "Your mama's dead?"

"I don't know," Ezra said. "She could be alive, but if she is, she's never come looking for me."

"I'm sorry," Lilyfax said. She put her hand on Ezra's. "But you have that day at the lake. It's always with you."

"I lied before," Ezra said. "I'm sorry, I don't know why I did, but I didn't want to tell you."

"Tell us what?" Leo asked.

"I don't live with my granny. I don't even have a granny. I mean I have one, everybody does, but I don't know her. I never knew her. Or any of my people."

"Where do you live then?" Lilyfax said.

"I didn't want to tell you. I'm sorry." Ezra rubbed his eyes.

"Ezra, it's okay," Lilyfax said. "You can tell us. Whatever it is."

Ezra let his hands drop. "I live at the Elijah House. The orphanage. The one on Exeter Road. You know it?"

"Both your parents are dead?" Leo asked. Leo pictured the Elijah House in his mind. It was a huge old farmhouse surrounded by acres of fields on all sides, with barns and cows on the grounds. People said the orphans did most of the work, so as to earn their keep.

"I don't know," Ezra said. "I don't know if they're dead, or they just left me because they didn't want me."

"Maybe they were too poor to tend to you," Lilyfax said. "I'm sure it wasn't about them not wanting you."

"Maybe," Ezra said. "But I'm sorry I lied. When I made some friends in the valley, friends outside Elijah House, I mean, I didn't want them to look at me like I was some poor orphan kid they needed to pity. I just wanted them to look at me like I was any other kid, you know?"

"I know about not wanting to be judged," Leo said. "Feels like that's all I've thought about my whole life. People looked down their noses at us wherever we went. Whether it was Wilson's, the clerks afraid we would steal 'cause we looked like we had no money, or those old ugly church women, staring at the ragged dress my mama had to wear ever Sunday."

"Everybody back in Tennessee," Lilyfax said, "knew my mama ran off with some other man. That's why Daddy brought us here. He was tired of all the whispering they would do. Said they'd talk about how he couldn't keep a woman satisfied, so she had to go off and find her a new man. Me and my sister? Just the daughters of some whore. If we stayed there, they'd just think we'd grow up to be the same."

"It ain't your fault," Leo said. "Preachers go on about the sins of the father. But I ain't nothing like my old man, and you ain't nothing like your mama."

"Well, I'm a little like her, but not the bad things," she said.

"How's that?" Leo asked.

"Well, you know how Daddy is always trying to get me to wear dresses, and be proper like? That's because Mama

202

always wore pants, and she smoked. She'd go outside and climb a tree she took a notion. Daddy sees me in her when I'm wearing some overalls or acting a tomboy. He can't stand it."

"Ahh," Leo said.

"Also, she had the widow's peak," Lilyfax lifted the hair from her forehead to show the point that formed beneath.

"You know some superstitions say that is a sign of evil?" Ezra said.

Lilyfax looked at Leo. "Ezra and the widow need to spend some time together." Then, "my daddy ain't been right since Mama run off. They's womenfolk at church, single women, and widows that try to catch his eye. But he just walks on, head down, like he don't see them. I asked him about it one time. I asked him about if he'd ever consider re-marrying. He said love starts off like a star, flashing bright, but eventually turns off cold and disappears like a winter fog."

"It sure got cold between my folks," Leo said. "Daddy running to liquor and Aunt Lila's, Mama home taking care of young'uns, losing her mind." Leo stared at Lilyfax. He could never imagine his feelings for her fading. But did she feel the same? Could she love him?

"She did what womenfolk are always expected to do, your mama. That's why it was so hard for everybody to take when my mama run off. Men are supposed to do the running."

"I don't know if my mother ran or if my father did," Ezra said. "I don't know if they were killed off. Got consumption? I just don't know anything."

"That must be hard," Leo said.

"Yeah," Lilyfax said. "But you've got us now."

"But the folks at the Elijah House," Leo said. "They gonna come looking for you? Or will you lose your spot? Will you still have a bed if you stay gone a week?"

"Surely they won't do that," Lilyfax said.

"I'll get in trouble, but it will probably just mean more chores." Ezra's eyes fell to his lap. "I understand if you're mad at me."

"No," Leo said. "We ain't mad. You only told that lie because you know how people act when they hear you don't have parents. I know a little about that, I ain't had a daddy for some time."

"Yeah," Lilyfax said. "We don't judge you."

"I won't lie to you all again," Ezra said. "I swear."

"Let's swear on it," Leo said, standing. "Both of you, come here, put your hands on top of mine."

Ezra and Lilyfax came over, each placing a hand on top of Leo's. Then Leo stacked his other hand on, and they followed. "We're in this together," Leo said, "no matter what."

Ezra smiled. Leo was happy the boy had told them the truth, hadn't held back. He was about to say so when he heard a low rumbling noise, off in the distance. When he looked at the others, he could tell they heard it too.

Leo walked toward the road. After a moment, he recognized the sound. Horses.

"Quick," Leo said, "the fire!"

The three of them kicked dirt over the flames, and Leo took the lid off his canteen to dump water on what remained. The embers sizzled in loud protest. Off in the distance, a yellow glow emerged in the night. The horseback riders were carrying torches.

"Behind the trees," Lilyfax said, leading the way.

Each rider wore a white robe, with the white pointed hoods of the Klan. Eyes were cut out for the men to see, and some had openings for their mouths. Some of the horses had hoods as well. Many of the men carried banners with words Leo could not see to read, while others carried crosses. The fog of the huffing horses clouded the air around the men and as they marched the horses through the mud, it flew up around them, giant chunks of mud landing on the backs of their white robes. There were maybe two dozen of them. Two near the trees were speaking and Leo could just make out their conversation.

"How much further to that black church?"

"An hour, more or less. Only it ain't just blacks up here."

"How's that?"

"Race mixers. They's whites that goes to that same church, right alongside the black folk."

"Oh. That's worse."

"Like rats."

"Lower than rats."

When the riders passed, Leo stepped out to watch their progress on the switchbacks up the Mud Road. They resembled an orange and white snake, twisting up the mountain.

"Cowards," Lilyfax said. "Only cowards hide their faces."

"I don't know why they can't just leave people alone," Ezra said. "What's wrong with them?"

"Let's get the fire started back," Leo said. "And try to get some sleep. We got a lot of ground to cover tomorrow."

Chapter 26

The next morning, they woke to a gentle warm rain and gray clouds overhead.

"So much for Mr. Goodman's storm," Lilyfax said.

After eating canned meat and brown beans cooked over the fire, they set out again on the Mud Road, in muck thick from the rain and horse piles left by the Klan.

They walked all day, making slow, hobbled progress. The sky grew darker as the day wore on, and Leo began to think of the sun as some foreign thing, something that no longer belonged in the world of the living. He thought of the widow, of how she said a shadow had fallen over everything. In the late afternoon, the temperature dropped quickly, and the morning's tranquil showers bore into a harsh cold rain.

After a while, Ezra said, "we're going to have to stop someplace and get warm."

"Yes," Leo said. "But there's no way we can keep a fire going in this rain. We need to find shelter. Let's get off the road and look for an old shed or barn." He wiped the cold rain from his eyes. "A dry patch where the trees are thick. Anything."

Leo led the way into the woods along a creek bank. His bones ached and Lilyfax was breathing heavily, moving in slow motion.

"Come on you two," he said.

"I can't feel my fingers," Lilyfax said.

Ezra blew hot air into his hands, a cold fog forming around his head.

"We got to keep moving, or we'll freeze to death," Leo said.

He tried to push the cold from his mind, to walk harder, faster, to show the way.

"Too bad the big bad wolf can't build a fire," Lilyfax said.

Leo felt a million miles from the Shadow Wulver. He tried to think of any way the wulver could help.

"Leo!" Ezra said suddenly. "Behind that rock, I saw someone."

Sure enough, someone was hiding behind a large boulder along the creek bank. Leo thought of the Shadow Wulver, of bringing it forth in his fear.

"Hey, you there," Leo called out. He tried to steady his voice. "We don't mean to be trespassing. We're just travelers on the road is all. Looking for a place to get out of the rain." His heart was lifted by the possibility of being led to a cabin and a warm fire.

A black boy sprinted from the boulder to a nearby tree. There, he leaned out to look at them. He was about Leo's height, though his face looked younger. His hair was cut short, and he wore overalls and thick soled boots.

"Do you know who owns this land?" Leo asked.

The black boy peered from around the tree, seeming to consider Leo's question.

"Hey," Lilyfax said, her teeth chattering. "My name is Lilyfax. This is Ezra and Leo."

"Mattis," the boy said.

"Mattis," Lilyfax said. "It's nice to meet you."

"You trying to get in out of the rain?" Mattis asked.

"Yes," said Lilyfax, "can you help us?"

"I know a place. Good and dry too," Mattis said.

"Will you take us?" Lilyfax asked.

"Come on," Mattis said. He stepped from the tree and gestured for them to follow. "The place where the rocks come together," Mattis yelled over his shoulder. "Good and dry."

The trail narrowed along the bank, snaking between the trees. Leo was reluctant, following someone they barely knew, but pushed on, fighting his fatigue.

Mattis expertly navigated the thickets, leaning under some branches, stepping over others. It was so cold that when Leo's shirt touched his skin, it felt as if he'd been stabbed by a thousand icicles.

They crossed a small ridge and large boulders came into view. Mattis guided them through an opening in a vast rock formation. Inside, the rocks curved up over them, forming a cave. The ground was dry, with only a few drops of water trickling down the rock walls. The space at the center formed a circle, maybe ten feet wide.

Mattis said, "Dry as a bone. We can build a fire. Top is open over yonder for the smoke."

Ezra sat down hard on the earth, and it echoed as if hollow.

"Ain't no use to sit down just yet," Leo said. "We're gonna need to get a fire going."

They gathered kindling and piled it in the center. Mattis sat cross-legged and stacked the wood into a pyramid. He was rubbing two sticks together when Leo offered his flint. Leo added dry pine needles he'd fetched from the mouth of the cave. It took a moment, but soon there was a spark, and the pine needles caught.

"We get it hot enough, we can even put wet logs on," Mattis said.

Soon the fire was tall and warm, and the four had stacked enough firewood against the wall to keep the fire going all night. They draped their jackets on the rocks to dry. Outside, the rain kept on. From time to time a single drop would gather on the ceiling of the cave before falling on someone's head or sizzling into the fire.

"Mattis, you saved us, sure as the world," Leo said.

Mattis lifted his chin.

"Are you from Mulwin Rock?" Ezra asked.

"I'm from down east before," Mattis answered. "Been here going on a year."

"What brought you?"

"Me and my mama and brother run from the sharecropping work down there. Man that owned the land, he hit my mama one day. My brother too when he took up for her. Mama said she'd had enough. We come to Altamont but couldn't find no work on account of how hard times are. Kept coming north till we found a piece of land here."

"Seems like a nice place," Ezra said. "Except the Mud Road."

"Mama said we had to keep coming north till we found land that nobody wanted. Land that no white people wanted anyway."

Leo thought of the Klan riding up the mountain. What they'd said about a church full of race mixers. He started to bring up the riders to Mattis but held his tongue.

"Mama said we'd come up here, live like the Indians do. Hunt and fish. Grow some crops. Live off the land."

"A good honest living," Leo said.

"You live close by?" Lilyfax asked.

"Just around the mountain."

"Why were you over this way?" Leo asked.

"Looking for a friend of mine that's gone missing is all," Mattis said.

Lilyfax met Leo's eyes.

They stood with their backs to the fire, feeling the heat through their wet clothes. When it got too hot, they faced the fire, laughing and smiling. Mattis let down his guard and smiled too. He had bright white teeth, perfectly straight up top, crooked on the bottom.

Leo woke to see the fire dying. It took a moment for him to realize where he was, to shed the view of the world he'd held in his nightmares. In his dreams, Mama had shapeshifted into the Shadow Wulver, biting into Leo's side, before setting his bed aflame with him in it. Leo sat back on his heels. To his left, Lilyfax slept on her side, her knees pulled up to her chest. Ezra slept on his back, arms crossed over his chest like a man in a coffin. Mattis lay on his side, eyes open.

"You seen a haint," Mattis said.

"Do what?" Leo asked.

"A haint. A spirit. You seen something."

"Just a bad dream is all." Leo took a stick and stirred the coals awake.

"I had bad dreams too. Maybe it's something about this cave," Mattis said.

Leo looked at him, held his hands out to the fire. "What did you dream about?"

"Seen my uncle. He died last year. He come to me and started talking."

"What did he say?"

"He was trying to tell me something," Mattis said. "But he was talking funny. I couldn't understand him none."

A chill feathered over Leo's back. "What else?"

"It was like the angel of death floating by. It was a dream, but it was happening in this cave. I seen you, right where you was laying. And the others. They was all asleep. And my uncle. He floated up over the fire. And then he changed into something else. Just a bunch of dark ugly clouds."

"What did it look like? The cloud thing?" Leo asked, his heart lurching.

"Just a man made up of shadows. He didn't have no face," Mattis said.

Leo stood and paced the circle.

"What is it, Leo?" Mattis asked. "It was just a dream. A haint."

"Did you see a wulver – a wolf-like thing – did a wolf come to you in your dream?"

"No. Just my uncle talking funny, then the dark angel. Well devil maybe. Just a devil hiding under all them shadows."

"The pillar of smoke," Leo said.

"It seemed so real, too," Mattis said. "He walked right through here, right into the fire."

"Into the fire?"

"When he walked through the fire, the flames turned a different color, they wasn't orange like they are now."

"What color?"

Mattis stared into Leo's eyes. "The flames, they turned black as night. The orange disappeared. They was only black and blue."

Chapter 27 – Wake

Wake walked among the ancient trees in the courtyard behind the Temple. When he exited the building, Goat stood, eyes asking, Shall I come? *Wake waved his hand, as if to say,* I want to be alone. *Only, outside in the cold rain with which snow began to mix, Wake wasn't alone.*

All day he'd felt it. The struggle welling inside him. Something he couldn't cast off, no matter how hard he tried. The war wasn't just within him though, was it? It boiled within the very earth itself. It was below the earth's surface, down where the roots of the trees hold firm to rock.

At the edge of the woods, the snow winning in its battle with the rain, he sensed it there, just beyond the shadows.

I know you're there, *he said.* Show yourself.

The spirit arced between two trees, shadows layering upon shadows.

The boy thinks you're some trinket, some trifle to do his bidding. A toy for petty grievances.

At this, the woods growled at him, and she was there: his mother, between the trees.

Mother? *Wake said. But he knew it wasn't her. It never was what it pretended to be.* I know you, *Wake said.*

Now the beast showed its face. The long snout of some hideous reptile, on the body of a vast blue bear. It took a step toward him.

Hate is a jealous lover, *Wake said.* The boy doesn't have enough hate in him to keep your eye. Not for long. We both know this to be true.

The beast growled low and deep, the enormous trees trembling to the root. It spoke to him in his mind:

Another travels now with him -

One most angry, one most grim.

How quickly your affections flee, *said Wake.* Almost I feel sorry for the boy. *Wake looked at the palm of his hand, where a blue flame formed.* In those days, before I knew the power within. Of the storms I can bring without you.

At this the beast roared, showing its teeth. Its form spread like tentacles in the trees, snaking around the limbs above. There, high in the trees, Wake saw the face of his mother return. She tilted her head to the side. My boy, *she said.* My boy.

If you were truly here, Mother, *said Wake,* I'd climb up and tear out your throat with my teeth.

His mother laughed now, mouth open, displaying a thousand dark pointed teeth, each pricked like the tip of a sharpened pencil. Come, *she said,* try.

Wake turned and walked up the hill toward the Temple. Behind him, the cloud dissipated, the blue smoke receding, his mother laughing after him. When he reached the Temple, still shaking, he grabbed Goat by the shoulders.

In the morning we head down the mountain. We'll kill the boy and take that beautiful girl. Those dimples, exquisite. She'll fetch a pretty price.

Chapter 28

When Leo and the others emerged from the cave the next morning, they discovered the icy rain had turned to snow overnight. About four inches blanketed the earth, a bright white painting each limb and treetop. Snow continued to fall with a slow steady rhythm, the sky a soft gray, full of clouds.

"Where y'all headed?" Mattis asked.

"We mean to go on up the mountain," Leo said. "So, we need to get back on the road." He did not want to mention the Temple or the girls. Mattis was good people, but the fewer people aware of their mission, the better. Leo shot Ezra and Lilyfax a look as if to say, *that's all he needs to know.*

"I'll be with you part of the way," Mattis said.

"Maybe you can help us keep the road in all this snow," Ezra said.

"I can keep the road," Leo said.

The snow bore down on them in all directions. This wasn't a storm where one could say it's coming in from the west, or up from the south. Instead, Leo could gain no sense of which way the wind blew. At times it pushed at their backs, at others it lapped at their faces. The ground beneath the snow had hardened with the overnight temperature drop, the mud now only a memory.

"Up there," Lilyfax said, pointing. "Something's burning."

Although the air was thick with falling snow, a mass of smoke rose above the trees.

"Brushfire?" Ezra asked.

"I don't think so," Mattis said. "Not in this weather."

"Maybe a chimney fire," Leo said.

After they worked through a few curves in the road, the land leveled off. To their right, they saw the smoke's origin.

"Crosses?" Ezra said. "What the—?"

In the front yard of a white clapboard church, there stood three wooden crosses which had recently been aflame. They smoldered, the snow sizzling as it struck them. They were about ten feet in height, spaced as many feet apart. The church itself was tall and narrow, with rows of rounded windows on each side and a sharp roof line. There was a cross on the steeple, as expected, but there were also crosses on each corner of the roof, each the same size.

Leo thought this must be the "mixed church" the Klan riders spoke of.

Mattis walked to the center cross and stood studying it, hands on hips. He kicked the center of the cross until the cross bar fell to the snow, gray mist rising as it rolled. Ezra stepped forward, striking the second cross with his heel. This one didn't break apart; instead, the entire cross fell over on its side.

Leo and Lilyfax looked at each other. They kicked the third cross until it crumbled into coals.

There was a sign in the yard of the church, the name obscured by the accumulating snow. Beneath the name Leo made out the words *Founded 1818*. Beyond the church, there was a large graveyard, with vast oaks bordering each side.

"What kind of church is this?" Ezra asked Mattis.

Lilyfax rolled her eyes. "Is that really important right now?" she said.

Mattis didn't answer. Instead, he held his hands over the smoldering wood, as if to warm them. He shook his head slowly.

Leo stared down the road. "Be careful, Mattis, they're still around."

"They're always around," Mattis said.

Leo nodded.

"I have to go find our pastor. Be careful on the road," Mattis said.

In front of the church, they said their goodbyes. Lilyfax hugged Mattis, Leo and Ezra each shook his hand. He jogged around the side of the church and disappeared.

The wind whipped around them as they made their way back to the road. Lilyfax looked over her shoulder. "Can we come back on the way down the mountain? Check on Mattis and the church?"

"I'd like that," Ezra said.

"Yes," Leo said.

They walked a few minutes in silence when Ezra said, "I'd like to talk to that preacher too. Maybe black churches know things about God white churches don't."

Leo wondered if the boy would ever take a break in his insatiable thirst for theological knowledge.

"Might not be a good time," Leo said. "The Klan is burning crosses in their front yard. Might not want to talk doctrine right now."

"Some other time then," Ezra said. "I just have to learn all I can."

Leo shook his head.

By midday, they were trudging through thirteen to fourteen inches of snow, the clouds above showing no sign of breaking. Mr. Goodman had been right. In the swirl of snow there were moments Leo started to doubt his sense of direction, yet he did not let on. A few times Lilyfax asked, "Are we still on the road?" And Leo answered, "Yes," though he could not be certain.

"Do you think the crosses were a warning?" Ezra asked.

"It was against the black people at that church," Leo said, "and the white people that worship with them."

"I meant because we are on our way to the Temple," Ezra said.

"They don't know we're coming," Leo said, "or what we bring with us. Besides, I don't know the Klan has anything to do with the Temple."

Leo reached out to take Lilyfax's hand. She did not pull away. His body warmed instantly when they touched. With each passing moment, he fought the urge to pull her to him, to hold her tight. To warm her from the bite of the cold. This pull, this desire to be close to her strengthened each day and there were moments Leo regretted bringing Ezra on the journey. Each time he showed Lilyfax affection, he felt Ezra's gaze. He felt it now and turned to find Ezra staring at their hands. Leo did not like the boy seeing their closeness, knowing what passed between them. What's more, he had come to loathe the boy's own eyes on Lilyfax.

After a while, even the heat of Lilyfax's hands could not warm him, and a deep ache settled in his blood. The snow had slowed, but the temperature dropped further. Below their feet, the snow hardened. They'd walked for several hours. Surely they were not far from the Temple? Leo thought of Camille and Maude. Would they make it in time? Were the girls still alive?

"There! There's something up ahead," Lilyfax said. "Off to the left."

Leo struggled to see, but then made out the structure.

"It's the church," Ezra said. "Mattis's church! We've been walking in circles."

An ache spread over Leo's heart. At this rate they'd never reach the Temple. Some rescue this was turning out to be.

"It's getting colder by the minute," Lilyfax said.

"The church," Ezra said. "There's no place else."

Leo didn't want to intrude on the church. He also did not want to be inside, should the Klan return. But their options were limited. "Just until the storm dies down," he said.

They were approaching the church when the door opened. An enormous man stepped out. He wore a wooden booger mask. The huge nose of the mask was curved downward, its eyes deep and dark. The man came down the stairs, taking off the mask to let it drop in the snow. It was hard to make out the details of his face at first, but then the wrinkles rippling over his skin were visible, like cracks in dry mud.

It was Goat.

Leo let go of Lilyfax's hand and was surprised to realize his first instinct was to run. But then he remembered the Shadow Wulver. He took a few steps toward the church.

Behind Goat, Mr. Wake emerged. He too had a wooden booger mask but kept his on at first. He wore a blue top hat and a coat trimmed with black fur. He was remarkably dry and unsullied, given the weather.

Lilyfax sucked her teeth. To Ezra and Lilyfax, Leo said, "Stay back. Behind me."

Leo walked toward the man called Goat, his hands at his side. He thought of the black eye on Aunt Lila, the way Goat had thrown the woman on the street outside the Raven Thicket. He thought of Camille and Maude, pictured them in chains. He conjured every image he could to stoke his anger. That of the Shadow Wulver crushing Goat's head.

In the distance the Shadow Wulver growled, and the trees creaked behind them. Goat looked into the woods beyond and bared his teeth, snarling.

"Your days of stealing girls are over," Leo said.

A rush of anger took hold in his face and neck. He saw the world through the eyes of the Shadow Wulver, cascading in shades of blue. The wulver raced through the woods, its shoulders striking the trees, the snow-covered earth thundering beneath its enormous paws.

Goat approached Leo as the Shadow Wulver tore through the tree line. It bounded toward the huge man, head down. Leo looked from Goat to Wake. Neither man seemed afraid. Goat stood, back straight, loyally in front of Wake as if there were no other place on earth he belonged, no place he'd rather be. Goat pulled a long club from his coat. He held it out wide as the wulver approached. He set his jaw, his teeth audibly grinding.

When the wulver pounced, Goat swung the club, almost making contact. The Shadow Wulver lifted its head to avoid the club, then dove to catch the man by the arm. It shook Goat, the bones in his arm twisting and cracking. Goat never made a sound as the wulver jerked, even when he was thrown in the air the way the boar had been, landing hard in the snow at least twenty feet away.

The wulver turned its attention to Wake, who walked toward the beast, dropping his head as he came. His eyes darkened.

"Will you break me too, Leo? With your magic wolf?" said Wake.

"Yes," Leo said.

Leo focused all his energy on Wake, all his anger. He saw a vein in the man's skull, at the temple. He thought of the wulver's fangs severing the vein. Severing all Wake's veins. Of his blood staining the snow.

"Are you angry enough?" Wake asked.

"Yes," Leo said.

Wake turned from Leo to the wulver, opening his palms in front of him. There, a blue flame grew from his hands as the wulver bore down.

"Do you have enough hate?" Wake said. His voice was loud but even.

"Yes," Leo said.

In Wake's palms, the flames circled, found form. At last, Wake held a flaming blue bird. Its wings fluttered. As the wulver prepared to pounce, Wake released it into the air. It flew up, toward the wulver, rising quickly, above its head.

The wulver watched the blue bird's flight, reaching for it, its enormous jaws slamming together with a crunch that echoed around the mountains. The blue bird flew higher, out of its reach, and the wulver turned from Wake to give chase.

"No!" Leo said. He closed his eyes, focused on seeing the world through the Shadow Wulver, trying to keep the connection. He saw nothing. His head empty. The wulver raced after the blue bird of flame and disappeared into the forest. Periodically the snap of its jaws bellowed around them, along with the crashing of the trees.

"What will you do now?" Wake asked, his hands gripping his jacket lapels. Leo stared at him. No words came to him.

Goat trudged slowly through the snow to stand beside Wake. His broken arm hung limp.

To Goat, Wake said, "Get the girl." Goat pushed past Leo toward Lilyfax.

Leo tried again to reach the wulver. Nothing. He turned to find Lilyfax and Ezra frozen in place, a quiet shock spread over their faces. Leo's entire body shook now, as he knew, somewhere deep inside him that the wulver was gone. For good. Fear seized him. They had no defense. There was nothing.

Leo yelled to them. "Run! Hide!"

Snapped to reality, Ezra and Lilyfax made for the woods opposite where the wulver had entered. Goat ran after them, still holding his lame arm.

Leo thought to follow when he heard Wake's footsteps in the snow.

"You could do it," Wake said. "You don't need the wulver."

Leo faced him.

"You could grab a man, yourself. Hold him still. Open his throat with your own teeth. You could do it." Wake unwound a long scarf from his neck and let it fall to the snow. He pulled the fur collar down with his hands, exposing his bare throat. "Come," he said. "Come do it for yourself."

Leo looked around them, scouring the ground for something—anything—to use as a weapon. He stared at Wake's neck, saw the man's jugular, blood pumping. Could he bite this man's throat open? He remembered his pocketknife then, reached for it.

Wake let his eyes drop to where Leo's hand worked inside his pocket. "To overcome your own fear. That's all that's left," Wake said. He released his collar. "Pity," he said.

Leo was still thinking about the pocketknife, about the distance to Wake, when something caught his eye in the woods beyond. There, shadows rose and fell between two

220

trees. Leo stared into the darkness. A familiar shape emerged, the outline of a boy.

Wake followed Leo's eyes into the trees. He grinned.

"What do you see, boy? What do you see in the trees?" Wake asked.

Jacob stood between the trees. He whispered to Leo in the unknown tongue. His lips drooped into a large, unnatural frown. His downturned mouth covered half his demonic face, stretching over his pale cheeks. Goosebumps pricked Leo's skin.

"Tell me. What is it? Who do you see in the trees, boy?"

"Jacob," Leo said.

"Who is Jacob?"

"My brother."

"He's dead, yes?"

Leo looked at Wake. "Yes," he said.

Wake smiled as if a wonderful secret passed between them. "Always my mother comes," he said. "Always it tempts me with her beautiful dead face."

Leo looked at Wake, then back to the woods. Jacob folded in on himself, absorbed by the shadows which grew between the trees until the pillar of smoke came forth. It descended, floating slowly over the snow. It took the shape of a man, formed from the inky darkness. There was no face, only the stretching of the shadow's limbs, extending, like the horrible unfurling legs of some giant black spider.

"What is it?" Leo asked Wake. "The pillar of smoke? Why does it come to me?"

"It came to you because you were weak and full of hate. It feeds on your hate."

"What is it? The devil?"

"I don't know how to call it in your language," Wake said. "At home we call it the *dag tyven*. How do you say? The thief of all light."

"I eat the day and steal the light," Leo muttered.

"Yes," said Wake. "Yes. The thief of the daylight."

221

"The day thief," Leo said.

"Yes. The more hate burns in your heart, the more the darkness comes."

"It left me," Leo said. "I can't control it anymore. Why?"

"You finally met a man with even more hate in his heart."

Leo looked at Wake. The man's face was dark and covered in shadow.

"What comes next?" Leo asked.

"Now it comes to kill you. Try to face your death with dignity," Wake said. He put his hand on Leo's shoulder for a moment then walked away, leaving Leo to face the pillar alone. Wake gathered two horses from the side of the church.

Leo looked to the woods, planned to run in the same direction Lilyfax and Ezra had been chased by Goat, when his body left the earth. He floated up, kicking his feet. The pillar of smoke twisted around him.

"Put me down!" Leo said.

You smell like your father, the pillar snarled. *You smell like his sins.*

"No," Leo said.

I am darkness, and I am night,

I come to eat your dreams and steal the light.

At the edge of the woods Goat emerged, Lilyfax slung over his shoulder. She kicked her feet and struck Goat's back with her fists. Behind them, Ezra was throwing snowballs and sticks at Goat. He kicked at Goat's legs and back. His kicks, and Lilyfax's fists didn't slow the giant man, who trudged steadily along. Across the field, Wake brought the horses.

Another figure emerged from the tree line. It was Mattis, dragging a shovel behind him.

I'll eat them all, the pillar hissed.

Mattis ran now, toward Goat, but Goat did not see him, his eyes on Wake and the horses. He took the shovel into his hands and swung the flat blade, catching Goat square in the face. Goat fell on his back. Lilyfax leapt forward and ran back toward the woods. Mattis struck the man again with the flat

222

face of the shovel, then followed the others. For a moment, Wake seemed to consider chasing them, but instead he circled Goat before helping the man up, to lay across the second horse.

That's when the light came – a bright white blast that warmed Leo's skin like sunlight. It came from the church. The Silver Wulver emerged beside the structure. Its movements were liquid and smooth, like water moving between rocks in a stream. The Silver Wulver paced in front of the church, baring its teeth.

Leo came gliding slowly down to the earth, as the pillar pivoted toward the Silver Wulver. The shadows of the pillar jerked and twisted with staccato abruptness until it spread out on the ground, emerging as the Shadow Wulver, on all fours. The Shadow Wulver stirred the snow, staring at the Silver Wulver.

Wake kicked his horse and he and Goat disappeared. From the woods, Lilyfax, Mattis and Ezra returned. They ran toward the church, and Leo did the same.

"What's happening?" Ezra said.

"I'm not sure," Leo said.

"There's two of them." Ezra said. "Just like the ancient tales say."

When they reached the church, Leo turned to see the Shadow Wulver retreat toward the woods. The Silver Wulver tread slowly along the side of the church and into the graveyard around back, the snow glowing like crystals under its paws. Leo stepped off the porch, intending to follow it.

"No," Mattis said, taking Leo by the arm. "Don't go back there."

"Why not?" Leo asked.

"Old folks say it's sacred ground. They call it the Shouting Grounds. Man can't go back there, 'less he's visiting the dead. Or wants to be one with them."

In the tree line opposite, the Shadow Wulver backed into the darkness its blue eyes fading into the shadows.

Part III

... a stone, a leaf, an unfound door;
of a stone, a leaf, a door.
And of all the forgotten faces.
—Thomas Wolfe

Chapter 29

The church sanctuary was long and narrow. Once Mattis had ushered them inside, he'd set about building a coal fire in a fireplace at the far end of the church, to the right of the altar. When the fire was going, he disappeared for several minutes, returning with mounds of black sack cloth for them to use as bedding.

"You saved my life," Lilyfax said to Mattis, taking the sackcloth from him to spread out on the floor near the fireplace.

"For the second time," Leo said. He slumped down on one of the wooden church pews. He couldn't think straight. He closed his eyes tight, tried to connect to the Shadow Wulver. There was nothing. He felt nothing.

"I seen them men coming down the mountain," Mattis said. "I knew they was up to no good."

"Looks just like a white church," Ezra said, spinning in the center aisle.

There were narrow stain glass windows lining each side of the sanctuary, an attendance board mounted up behind the pulpit, whitewashed walls.

"What'd you expect?" Lilyfax asked.

"I don't know, but I want to come back here when the weather is good. I want to hear the preacher. He is black, right?" he asked Mattis.

"Yes, but white people come to this church too," Mattis said. "It ain't just black folk."

"I haven't ever heard a black preacher before," Ezra said.

"Can you just shut the hell up?" Leo said. Ezra's incessant *seeking* was wearing thin. Everything about religion was fascinating to Ezra, who would have poked and prodded the church like a scientist if he thought it would reveal its secrets.

Ezra seemed not to hear him. He bounded up to the pulpit and opened the text.

"I got to go see about my mama," Mattis said. "I don't like her by herself in this weather."

"Go on," Lilyfax said. "We'll be fine here." She stepped forward and put a hand on his arm.

Leo stood and extended his hand. "I don't know how to thank you."

Mattis hugged him instead. "You'd do it for me," he said.

After Mattis left, they warmed themselves by the fire.

"I love the smell of coal burning," Ezra said. "We use it at the home in some of the rooms."

"I prefer the smell of wood," Lilyfax said.

Leo closed his eyes again, tried to find the Shadow Wulver. When he opened them, both Lilyfax and Ezra were staring.

"What happened out there?" Ezra asked.

"How the hell should I know," Leo said.

"It's your wulver," Ezra said.

"*My* wulver?" Leo said.

"Isn't it?"

Leo stood and paced to the back of the church. He examined the double doors, there was no lock. "He made it turn on me. Wake."

"How could he do that?" Lilyfax asked.

"Said he had more hate in him than me. I couldn't get mad enough to bring it back. To get it to stop chasing that goddamned blue bird."

Leo looked around the sanctuary. His eyes rested on an American flag. He took the flagpole and ran it through the handles of the door so it couldn't be opened from the outside.

"Why're you doing that?" Lilyfax asked.

"There's no lock on the door," he said.

"What are we gonna do now?" Lilyfax asked.

"About what?"

"About the Temple. About rescuing the girls."

Leo scowled. "And how the hell will we do that? We don't have the wulver. Did you see the size of that prune-faced

226

bastard? Wake, too." Leo's skin prickled at the thought of Wake's dark face, the way the man had talked him through the vision of Jacob.

"God knows how many men are at the Temple," Ezra said.

"So just like that?" Lilyfax rose from her place on the floor in front of the fireplace. She walked down the center aisle. She looked from Leo to Ezra and back again. "Just like that? We're giving up on the women up there?"

"Who's going to fight all those men? Me and Ezra?" Leo looked her up and down. "And you?"

"I'd rather die than leave them up there," she said, crossing her arms. "I can't believe you want to give up. And do what? Go back to the valley? Knowing they're up there? Thinking about that every day, while we just go about our lives?"

"She's right," Ezra said.

Leo cut his eyes at the boy. "What are you going to do, quote scripture to them in Latin?" To Lilyfax, he said, "Do you think the *Little Priest* can fight them off for us? And how many grown men can you take down with a tobacco stake? These people ain't like Declan, a bunch of petty schoolyard bullies. They're monsters. You seen Aunt Lila's face."

"What about Camille?" Lilyfax asked. "And Maude? These are people. Human beings. You want to leave them to die up there?"

Leo sat down on the closest pew, dropped his head into his hands.

"I need to go home and see about Goldfish," he said.

"Go home to watch her lay in bed?" Lilyfax said. "How *brave*."

"Maybe you'll get the wulver back," Ezra said.

"No," Leo said. "It's gone. I don't know how I know, but I know."

"What about the Silver Wulver?" Lilyfax said. "Can we use it?"

"I don't think they're pawns," Leo said. "Maybe I never did control it. I say we let the weather break, and head back down the mountain."

"I won't go," Lilyfax said. "I can't stand the thought of them up there. That could be me up there."

"We can't fix this world," Leo said. "The Klan is up here burning crosses in front of churches 'cause they hate the people inside. The church we're sitting in. Meanness goes on in the world, goes on everywhere. We supposed to fight the Klan too?"

Lilyfax sat down in the pew opposite.

"You're a coward," she said.

"Take that back," Leo said, standing. He stared at her, his eyes burning.

Leo couldn't tell her what he'd seen, what haunted him. He shuddered when he thought of it. Of Wake taking her prisoner. He'd seen Lilyfax bound in his dreams, vines wrapped around her feet and arms. How could he take her further up the mountain, risk her being taken like the others? Wake would kill Leo and Ezra but keep Lilyfax alive for things much worse than death. Wake knew they were on their way to the Temple. They would be walking into a trap.

"I'll go by myself," Lilyfax said. She stuck out her chest. "I don't need either of you."

"We don't have to decide tonight," Ezra said. "But we'll have to do something soon."

"How do you mean?" Lilyfax asked.

Ezra held up a single tin of fish. "Because we're out of food after this."

The next morning, Leo set out before the others were awake. He took his tackle, meant to return to the stream near the rocks they'd sheltered at with Mattis. The surface of the creek was frozen so Leo cracked it with his heel. He dropped his bait into the water. He never got a bite and the ice quickly returned, trapping his hook. He tried to break it to free the hook, and his entire foot plunged into the icy water. He thought his toes would freeze off before he could get back to the church to warm them. On the way back from the creek, Leo stared into the woods around him, craning his neck to see if the Shadow Wulver would present itself, or if Jacob would come to him again in the trees. He saw nothing, but found little comfort in this.

For three days they waited in the church for the weather to break, and while the snow did slow, it never stopped. The temperature dropped even lower. Frost splintered across the church windows, forming first at the edges, then covering them entirely. There was plenty of coal in a box near the fireplace, but hunger took its toll. By the evening of the third day, it consumed Leo's every thought, aching deep in his bones, the familiar feeling he'd had so many times back in the valley.

Ezra stopped opining on the deep questions of philosophy and the meaning of life, choosing instead to stare at the ceiling for hours on end, humming hymns just loud enough for Leo to catch the basic outline of the melody. Lilyfax grew weak, struggling to stand when she took trips to the outhouse at the side of the church. After one such trip she collapsed near where Leo lay on the floor.

"I seen a man out in the Shouting Grounds," she said. Her voice was just above a whisper.

"In the graveyard?" Leo asked.

"Had a red beard. A big staff."

"Like Goodman? You're seeing things." Leo said.

"You should unlock the church door," she said. "Might could've been him. What if he needs shelter?" She closed her eyes. Leo put an arm over her, but Lilyfax twisted away. Out of the corner of his eye, he felt Ezra's stare. He hated the way the boy always watched, took in everything. He wished he'd never brought Ezra along, thought of leaving him in the church when they went out. If only he and Lilyfax had the strength to sneak down the mountain while Ezra slept.

Leo said, "I'll go back out and try to catch some fish again tomorrow."

"I keep thinking about how I heard that cock crow," Lilyfax said.

"What?"

"When we were on our way to the cave with Mattis. There was a rooster."

"Are you sure?"

"Yes," she said. "Three times it crowed."

"Where there's chickens, there's eggs," Ezra said from across the room. Leo didn't acknowledge him.

To Lilyfax, he whispered, "I'll go for the chickens at first light. I'll bring you an egg. I promise."

She didn't answer. Lilyfax slept.

Chapter 30

Leo woke at first light, the red and green glare of the stained-glass windows in his eyes. As he'd fallen asleep, the warmth from Lilyfax had been a comfort and he'd basked in the way his body felt at the places they touched. Now he realized her body was cold against his, as if he lay against marble. He sat up on one elbow. The fog of her breath was the only sign of life. He kissed her forehead and was astonished at how clammy her skin had grown. Something was wrong. She needed some food, fast.

He eased away, careful not to stir her. When he stood, he saw Ezra was awake.

"I'll go with you," Ezra said. "Maybe we can find those chickens?"

"I need you to stay with her. Get a big fire going. Her skin feels like ice."

"But she has to eat today."

"I know, I'll find something if it kills me." Leo knew he would too. He'd search for the chickens, but if they didn't materialize, he'd go door to door if he had to, beg for some rice, a mess of beans. Anything.

Ezra stood.

"You'll get a big fire going," Leo said. "Melt plenty of snow. Keep her drinking water."

"I will," Ezra said.

Leo headed for the door.

"Wait," Ezra said. "It's gotten colder out." He gathered up a piece of the black sackcloth and wrapped it around Leo's body, neck, and head. "This will keep you warm." Leo dipped his head at the boy.

Outside, the hard snow crunched under foot. Brooding gray clouds formed in the sky, the sun a faint ring behind them. *Come sun*, thought Leo. *Melt this snow and show me the way.* A gust of wind replied, working the hood of his makeshift cloak off. Leo grabbed the fabric at his neck to pull it back over his head. He made his way off the road toward the creek and rock formation where Mattis had helped them find shelter.

Every so often Leo stopped and listened. Each time he heard only the wind, but as he approached the creek he heard it—the sound of a rooster in the distance. Hope flooded his limbs. He pictured Lilyfax in the church, the color returning to her cheeks once he'd cooked her breakfast. He found a log to cross the creek and sprinted up the hill.

Leo moved along the edge of the farm, just inside the tree line. He spotted a small house, a barn, and eventually the chicken coop. He looked for a dog but saw none. The only sign of life was chimney smoke, which snaked up in a funnel above the house.

Leo ran to a tree near the chicken coop, studied the house and barn. There was a lone cow milling about the entrance.

When he reached the coop, the hens clucked indignantly. He turned the wooden block on the door and opened it. He fished under the hens for their eggs. A fat red hen pecked at his hand, drawing blood.

"Move, you bitch," he said.

Finally, he found a cluster of eggs, and placed them carefully in his pockets. When all was said and done, he had six eggs. He closed the door and turned the block, sprinting back to the tree. Six eggs! Enough for he, Ezra, and Lilyfax to have two apiece. But Leo's mind turned then to the fat hen. He'd felt the weight of her on his arm. She had full breasts and legs. He pictured her over a spit, chicken fat dripping deliciously into the fire. He licked his lips. *Just one chicken.* What was the harm in that? Leo looked around the tree to the farmhouse and barn. There was no one. He ran back to the coop.

When he returned, a skinny rooster protested by pecking his shins. Leo turned the block and scooped out the hen, holding her by her legs.

"You there!" someone yelled behind him. Leo spun to see the farmer standing outside the barn, about a thousand feet away. "You get away from them chickens, you black bastard!"

Leo thought of the black sack cloth. He calculated the distance to the tree line.

"I'll shoot you right where you stand," the farmer yelled.

Leo looked again. The man had no rifle, no gun. Leo took off for the trees.

He heard the man yelling after him, and the hen kept doubling on herself to peck him. Once he was in the woods, Leo took her by the neck and wrung hard. She fell still. He kept on through the woods, stopping periodically to listen for the farmer. When he heard nothing, he relaxed.

He'd almost made it to the road to the church, when he saw the shadows dance between two trees. As he came on, he saw his brother Jacob there. Jacob grinned sideways somehow, one side of his lips turned up, the other twisting down like the curl of a snake. He whispered to Leo in the unknown tongue before the pillar behind him began to twist and jerk.

Did you think you could run from me?

I, who crash the wind and shake the tree?

The Shadow Wulver emerged with a loud crow that shook the branches above. Leo looked around the beast to the road on the other side. He would run, giving the wulver a wide berth. Once he hit the road, Leo thought he'd be safe. He was so close to bringing his bounty to Lilyfax.

The Shadow Wulver began to laugh. It reached down with its paws, gripping its own rib cage. There was a loud crack as the Shadow Wulver broke open the bone there and spread its chest wide, as if opening some menacing dark cloak. It held its chest open. In the darkness of the beast's open ribs, a pair of cobalt blue eyes emerged. Then another. Then more.

A face drew forth. There was a stripe of white fur across its head; it was the wild boar from the night Leo and the Shadow Wulver had hunted for old man Johnson. To its side, the old sow emerged, then three more boars. They looked exactly as they had on the night of the hunt, only their jaws were longer, wolf-like, with canine teeth alongside their tusks, now larger and sharper.

The Shadow Wulver cackled as Stripe took a step forward.

Leo ran.

He made it through the trees, the boar on his heels. As he stepped onto the road, there was a tug at his sleeve. One of them had the hen's head in its mouth. *No,* Leo thought, *you're not taking my prize.* Leo yanked the chicken and the head popped off into the boar's mouth. Blood sprayed over Leo's face and neck. The undead boar crunched the chicken head in its canine teeth, continuing to run alongside him. Stripe flanked him, drawing closer. Up ahead, the church came into view.

Leo burst through the double doors, slamming them behind him. He ran down the center aisle and collapsed.

"Leo!" Lilyfax said. When he looked up, she screamed, seeing his face covered with blood.

Leo bent over, panting.

"What are those?" Ezra asked, looking out of the rear window of the church.

Leo peered out beside him. "Boar hogs. The wild boars I killed with the Shadow Wulver. They're back."

"The dead ones?" Lilyfax said.

"Undead boars," Ezra said. "Zombies."

"Yes," Leo said. He turned from the window and fished the eggs from his pockets. He presented them to Lilyfax.

"Oh my stars!" Lilyfax whispered.

Ezra walked over and took one from her hands. Then he looked nervously to the back of the church. "Can they come in here?"

"No," Leo said. "This is sacred ground."

Lilyfax took the eggs to the front of the church to fry over the coals. Leo slipped out on the back porch of the church and began to pluck the chicken. He scanned the Shouting Grounds for signs of the Silver Wulver but found none.

Chapter 31

Leo sat back against the wall near the altar, rubbing his overstuffed belly.

"I ain't eat this much in my whole life," Lilyfax said, rolling onto her side.

"We ate the whole thing!" Ezra said.

"There's a little left," said Leo, "And bones for broth near on a week."

The thick smell of roasted chicken settled over the sanctuary, savory, and intoxicating. The meat had been perfect, the hen living up to the promise of her thick body. Leo stood and felt wobbly on his feet for a moment, as if his brain couldn't process the sudden richness of protein and animal fat. He ambled to the window and looked out. The glass was iced over. He blew against it and rubbed his sleeve over the surface. The five boars stood watch, in the same position as when he'd come in. Stripe, spotting Leo, stirred the snow with his front hooves.

"Look! They're leaving," Lilyfax said, looking out the window. Sure enough the boars ducked back into the shadows of the trees. Peering down the road, Leo saw nothing. Then came the sound of horses trudging through the snow.

"It's the Klan," Lilyfax said. "Reckon they've come back to burn more crosses out front?"

The first riders cleared the church, and Leo moved the flagpole to open the double doors. The Klan passed as if the church weren't there, though a week ago it had been the center of their focus. In the daylight, their robes appeared yellow and dingy against the crisp white of the snow. Some of the men grimaced as they rode by, their teeth showing beneath their hoods, as if something about their purpose vexed them too much to keep their lips closed. At the back of the procession, beside a man in a red robe, there was a black boy tied up on a horse. It was Mattis.

"Look," Lilyfax said.

"I see him," Leo said.

Ezra started toward the stairs.

Leo placed his palm on Ezra's chest. "Wait," he said.

When the last rider passed, the snow was riddled with horse piles. Leo heard someone talking. Two women came out of the woods and made their way along the road, stepping carefully around the horse droppings. They turned into the churchyard, their movements brisk and efficient.

"You see that?" said a black woman, a red bonnet on her head.

"I seen it, but why?" Another woman spoke. She wasn't black, but she had the features of a black woman. In fact, she was neither black nor white, bearing splotches of both on her hands and face. Leo had never seen a woman—anyone—with skin like hers. She was beautiful.

"They'll lynch him sure as the world," the first woman said.

"We got to do something. Tell somebody."

The women noticed Leo and the others on the stoop of the church. They frowned as they approached, staring down the road. The first woman held up her hand as if to end the conversation.

"You must be our guests," said the first woman. "I'm Martha," she said, holding her arms out to Leo for a hug.

"Martha," Leo said. "Nice to meet you. I'm Leo. This here is Lilyfax and Ezra."

"Ezra, Lilyfax—what a name, praise God," said Martha. "This is Josie."

The woman named Josie dipped her head. Both of the women were carrying large sacks. A loaf of fresh bread protruded from one. The women entered the sanctuary. The smell of roasted chicken accosted Leo as he turned in behind them. It hit the women too.

"*Chicken*," Josie said.

"Uh huh," Martha said, cutting her eyes at Leo.

"We heard there was some folk stranded here in the storm, might be hungry," Josie said. "We done some baking, and the other womenfolk too."

Ezra approached Josie, eyes wide. He held his hand out as if to touch her. "Your skin," he stammered.

Lilyfax stepped between them.

"Everything different ain't for you to paw on." She crossed her arms.

Josie smiled. "It's okay, I get that all the time. God painted me up different all right. Used to hate it. Now I love it. Love what God gives us, we should."

Martha unloaded the bags at the front of the sanctuary. She set a couple of loafs on the pew, along with a crock of butter and a jar of jam. "What in the world are you three doing on the road in this storm, anyways?"

"Looking for a friend," Leo said.

"That right?" Martha asked.

"Oh my stars," Lilyfax said. "What heaven in these bags!" She ran her fingertips over the bread, letting them rest on the tip of a long loaf.

"That boy," Leo said, "the boy they had roped up. What did he do?"

Josie clucked her tongue. "What did he do? Does he need to have done something?"

"They *say* he stole a chicken," Martha said. She walked over and looked into the pot at the remaining chicken bones. She scowled.

"Don't mean he done it," Josie said. "He don't have to have done nothing. Just be black on this mountain is all. That's enough."

"What will they do to him?" Ezra asked. He seemed to stare at a patch of white skin on her neck surrounded by a sea of darker skin.

"They liable to kill him. Just a beating, if he's lucky." Martha crossed her arms. She set her eyes on Leo. She was sturdier than Josie, with wide shoulders and large eyes.

Leo couldn't bear her gaze. He looked away.

"Stole a chicken?" Lilyfax asked. She glanced at the pot.

"From a farmer across the creek," Martha answered. Her eyes never left Leo.

Leo felt sick. He sat on the closest pew.

"What if he didn't do it?" Lilyfax asked.

"Do you think they care?" Josie asked. "They looking for a reason. They got one."

"Mattis wouldn't do that, unless he was hungry," Ezra said.

The women stared at him, their mouths open.

"Mattis - you know Mattis?" Martha asked.

Leo glared at Ezra. There was no end to the trouble caused by that boy's mouth.

Ezra looked startled. "Well, we don't really know him."

"How'd you know his name?" Martha asked.

"We met him," Leo said. "He helped us."

"Of course he did," Josie said. "Just like that boy to help strangers out on the road. Whether it's good for him or not."

"Did he steal that chicken?" Martha asked.

"I don't know," Leo said. "He might have. People are hungry in this storm."

"And yet, there's a chicken right here, praise God," Martha said. She motioned to the pot. "What's left of one anyway."

"We just found that," Leo said.

"You just found it," Josie said, shaking her head. She took a step toward Leo. "Did Mattis steal it for you? Was he trying to help you out 'cause you were hungry? You can tell us."

"No, ma'am," Leo said. He held his head in his hands. "No, ma'am he didn't. I don't know nothing about any of this."

"What're we going to do?" Lilyfax said.

Leo's stomach torqued. He could have gotten away with just the eggs. He could have fed everyone. But he'd been greedy. He'd gone back for the red hen. The farmer had seen the black cloth, thought it was a black boy that stole from him.

How could the farmer think that? Maybe the old bastard was half blind.

Ezra was connecting the same dots. "The sack cloth."

"What?" Martha asked.

Leo couldn't talk. Everything rushed up into his throat, the whole world. He leapt to his feet and ran out of the church where he threw up the chicken in the hard snow. After he'd emptied his insides, he kept heaving. It was everything, everything inside him. It all came up.

When he returned to the sanctuary, Martha was sitting cross legged on the front pew. She shook her head. "If you know Mattis ain't done this, y'all got to do something. They'll lynch that boy. They're itching to do it. They might be doing it right now."

"No," Lilyfax said.

"Our people, the people of this church. They get wind of it, they'll get their rifles and go out to take things into their own hands," Martha said. "Everybody round here knows Mattis."

"They do that," Josie said, "and men in hoods will swarm every rock on this mountain, burn our church to the ground, every house and lean-to, every barn and outhouse, burn us out."

"I know," Martha said. "Make it worse, but what can people do?"

Martha stood and she and Josie gathered their things. In the middle of the sanctuary, she met Leo. She placed a hand on his arm.

"I don't know why y'all here, what you're looking for, but I hope you find it and get home safely, praise God." Her face grew stern. "But you got to go help him first. Y'all are white kids. They might listen to you. You said he helped you before, I pray you help him now."

"God have mercy on him," Josie prayed.

"Have mercy on our Mattis," Martha repeated.

Leo looked at the colors that twisted on Josie's hands. Such a simple thing, really, he thought. Just a simple thing that can change so much.

Chapter 32

When the women left, Leo could no longer bear to be indoors. He grabbed his coat, the black hat, and went out. Mattis had warned him not to go behind the church into the graveyard, a place he'd called the Shouting Grounds. But Leo went back there anyway. Maybe the Silver Wulver would be there, Leo thought. Maybe the Silver Wulver would tear him limb for limb for being on sacred ground since he wasn't visiting his dead. Maybe the Silver Wulver would smell the evil of the Shadow Wulver on his skin. Feel it in his heart. But something had to give. Leo pictured Mattis on the back of the horse led by the man in the red robes. Leo had never seen a lynching, but he'd heard about what the Klan did to black people, stringing them up to hang in the trees for the most minor offenses, sometimes for no offense at all.

If the Klan did that to Mattis now, using the stolen chicken as an excuse, it was Leo's fault. So if the Silver Wulver was going to eat him, Leo decided, he had better do it. If God was going to smite him down in the middle of this sacred place, have Leo's insides eaten by worms the way he did his enemies in the Old Testament, Leo decided, *let Him come.*

When he got to the center of the graveyard, there were small stone markers in neat rows that seemed to go on for a mile. Old stately trees lined both sides of the graveyard, running parallel with the road. Leo wanted something to happen. No, he needed something to happen, good or bad. He talked to the sky, hands raised. Or maybe praying.

"I don't know why the shadows come to me. I don't know why the wulver did what I said. But for the first time in my life, I got my way. I had my way. I didn't have to walk with my head down like my mama and daddy. And you know what? I liked it. But if you're listening, Lord, I need your help. A way to help that Mattis boy get free. He didn't do nothing. You know it was me that stole the chicken. I only done it because we were starved. I didn't know what else to do. I didn't have no meanness in me about it."

Leo stood still. He spun around in the center of the Shouting Grounds, arms outstretched. He saw no sign of the Silver Wulver, or anything else. There was no bolt of lightning from God. There were no answers. Leo grew desperate and began to shout at the sky.

"Are you listening? Do you hear me? Will you help me?"

Then Leo had no words. There was nothing left to say. He held his hands as high as he could, as if he would reach up into the heavens and find something there, find a kind of light to open up in all this darkness. He moaned from someplace deep within him. His whole body moaned.

Around Leo, the wind began to stir. First the tree branches swayed, then gusts pushed the trees to bend. The wind rushed through the Shouting Grounds and Leo could barely stand. Some of the gravestones were pushed onto their sides. A small concrete angel hurled through the air, and Leo dodged, the statue whizzing just overhead. The gales grew more violent, and Leo began to yell into the wind.

Leo heard another voice. At the edge of the Shouting Grounds, he saw Lilyfax. She raised her hands toward the sky and screamed like Leo as she walked toward him.

"Go back," Leo said.

If she heard him, she didn't acknowledge it. She struggled against the wind but came on.

Leo braced his body, but still he was pushed around in the snow. He looked for any sign of the Silver Wulver and its face of lightning, but there was only the wind, and Lilyfax, who gripped a large tombstone. Leo's black hat was blown from his head. It bounced along the ground and disappeared.

He stepped forward, meaning to get to her, to pull her away from the Shouting Grounds, when his body was lifted into the air. At first, he thought it was just the power of the breeze, but then he was a foot off the ground, then three, then ten. He feared being thrown into the trees but then a strange calm came over him. A warmth washed over his skin like he'd had the night he first saw the Silver Wulver and the crystal rabbits. Ahead of him, Lilyfax rose up into the air. At first, he couldn't see her clearly, but then he was able to make out her smile as they floated up through the trees, then above them.

While the storm continued below, the sky above them fell quiet as they rose. The world seemed to slow and tilt as they ascended through the dark clouds above the mountain. The sky opened, the brilliant sun beyond the darkness warming their skin. Lilyfax and Leo floated near each other, circling. She smiled and held out her hands. They came together, and Leo took her hands in his own and pulled her close. He wrapped his arms and legs around her, and she buried her face in his neck. When he pulled away, her eyes were shiny with tears, his own vision blurry. Above the dark clouds, in the sunlight, Leo had again the feeling of having known Lilyfax before he was born, before man, before the earth was made. He pulled her close and she rested her cheek against his. They twirled gently there, together.

Their bodies soared above the clouds at a great speed, but Leo never felt uneasy. It was as if he'd been born to walk in the sky, born to leave the ugliness of earth behind. Their love was ancient, yes, but enduring too, somehow, something that would continue long after their time on earth. It would pass down through the leaves of the trees, through generations, floating on the humming hymns of those who would come after, in the very blood of their descendants down through the ages.

When they stopped hugging, they floated gently apart, still holding hands.

"Are there such beautiful things?" she asked.

"Yes," he said.

Lilyfax looked around them.

"Is it God?" Leo asked.

"It's Love," she said, and he knew she was right. Her dimples shimmered in the sunshine like the surface of a lake catching dawn's first light.

They spun gently, weightlessly. They descended gradually, then, through the blue sky, their feet entering the dark clouds below. When they cleared the clouds, they saw the Shouting Grounds below them. To the east, up the mountain, they saw the Temple, the ancient trees around it aglow in sinister ember. To the west, they saw a burning cross in a field, the Klan marching through the woods, Mattis walking there, his hands bound behind him.

"We have to go, Leo," Lilyfax said.

"I know."

"We have to get Mattis," she said.

"I know."

"And after that," she said, "we have to go to the Temple."

"Yes," he said.

"We have to save the girls," she said. "Even if we rescue them one at a time."

"Even if it kills me," he said.

"Yes," she said. "There are things worse than dying. Things like being in a cage."

"We can shut the Temple down," he said. "Take out one man at a time as they crawl out from under their rocks."

"That's right," she said, "you saw what Mattis did to that old Goat with just a shovel. We can hide in the forest and pick them off one by one."

They floated toward the earth, the windstorm having subsided below them. At the edge of the tree line, near the road, stood Ezra. He had not crossed over to the Shouting Grounds. His eyes were cold and gray, his arms crossed. Leo studied the boy, but quickly let it go.

In this new world, there was no more running, no more denying what they were put here to do. They would let nothing stop them. For a moment, Leo saw a vision of his own death, and resigned himself to it. But Leo had seen the other side now. Should they not make it down the mountain, he knew he and Lilyfax would meet again in the clouds. Above the ugly earth, above everything.

When their feet hit the earth, they embraced there. Lilyfax cried into his shoulder as if she too had seen their dark future, but knew it wasn't the end.

They trekked up the Mud Road in the late afternoon. The snowfall returned, and the trees groaned around them, their rustling in the wind, sloughing off sheets of heavy snow. Somewhere in the distance a branch struck the earth. In the top of a tree, a black squirrel worked an acorn in its teeth.

They saw smoke in the distance and left the road.

Deep in the woods they found the horses of the Klansman tied to trees. In a clearing beyond, the men were gathered. They'd set a crooked cross afire there. Mattis was tied to another cross, his arms bound behind it.

A large man stood in the center, fists raised. He yelled slogans which the other men chanted back at him. He went on about the evil of jews and black people and homosexuals and men who lay with the beasts of the field. Something about the man's voice struck Leo. It was familiar somehow, the way he curled his words, the way he moved his arms up and down. But the man's voice was off, as if he changed it for this specific audience. He wore patches on his robe that the others did not have. When his sleeve slid up, Leo saw it. There on his wrist, the blue snowflake.

Could it be? Wormley?

"Look!" Lilyfax said. "Behind Mattis."

"It's a red fox," Ezra said. Leo and Lilyfax exchanged looks.

The fox crouched behind where Mattis was seated, its head bobbing.

"It's biting through the ropes," Lilyfax said.

246

One of the Klansman seemed to have noticed. He fished beneath his robes and produced a pistol. He walked toward Mattis, raising the gun.

"He's going to kill it," Ezra said.

"We have to do something," Lilyfax said.

Soon the man would be so close he couldn't miss.

To Ezra and Lilyfax, Leo said, "Go set their horses free in the woods. Turn them away and set them off back toward the road."

"What'll you do?" Lilyfax asked.

"I'll think of something," Leo said. "Go now."

Soon came the sound of the horses galloping away through the woods, their feet heavy in the snow. Some of the Klansman heard them too.

"They got our horses," said a man with a thick country accent.

"Who?" another asked.

The man with the gun stopped his approach and faced the woods.

"They want to interfere with God's work," Wormley yelled. "Don't let them do it!"

Several of the men ran toward the woods as a wind kicked up in the trees. It tore through the tree limbs and through the clearing. The hoods of the Klansman were blown off their heads, and they were pushed around in the snow as if they were on skates.

Someone grabbed Leo's arms and pulled them behind his back.

"I got me one," a man yelled and pushed Leo out into the field.

"You," Wormley said. He made his way toward them, fighting the tempest.

"Good Christian men?" Leo said, lifting his chin. "Hiding behind hoods so the world can't see what you really are?"

"Give me my watch," Wormley said, before slipping on the snow onto his back. He was pushed along the ground by the wind, arms and legs flailing. He struggled on his back like a turtle. Eventually he worked over onto his side, then to all fours. He crawled toward Leo, his jaw set, then found his feet.

Suddenly the man gripping Leo's arms let go. Leo spun to discover a tree had fallen, a mammoth limb cracking the man's skull open. A thick stream of blood stained the snow beneath him. The man was still for moment, his eyes rolling up, before he fell face first into the snow.

Wormley was still coming.

Leo ran to meet him, fists balled.

"Come here boy," Wormley said, "I'll kill you now, send you on to hell where you belong."

The gusts swirled around them, catching in Wormley's filthy Klan robe, filling it like a sail. He was pushed back, away from Leo toward the tree line opposite. There he fell to his stomach. Around him trees begin to fall, one just barely missing his head. Wormley stood and shook his fists at Leo before lumbering off through the woods.

Lilyfax and Ezra stood with Mattis at the edge of the field. There was no sign of the red fox.

When Leo joined them, Mattis bent toward him, resting his forehead against Leo's.

"I knew you'd come," Mattis said.

Leo didn't answer. The shame of his initial indifference hung around his neck like a millstone.

Lilyfax and Ezra joined them. They stood like this for a long time, arms around each other.

"God was in the wind," Ezra said. To Leo, he said, "Can you conjure the wind now, Leo? The way you once conjured the wulver?"

"No," Leo said. "That wasn't me."

Around them limbs cracked in the wind. In the distance, a horse whinnied.

Chapter 33 - Maude

Goat, he was in the room when we got there. Sat in a chair by the window, his arm in a sling. He looked tired. Him and Mr. Wake talked some, and I didn't know what to do, so I just sat down on the bed. I couldn't hear much, just Wake saying what a good and faithful servant Goat was, how brave he'd been to stand up to the beast – whatever that meant. I took it that I was to be some kind of reward for Goat, and this didn't surprise me none. I'd seen the way Goat looked at me, the way he seemed to marvel at my red hair when he didn't think nobody was looking. Wake saw it too. I know that figured into it.

Wake left and I was terrified. The girls all talked about what Goat's hands could do, but I'd seen it up close. He beat a man to death 'cause Wake told him to, 'cause that man left marks on a girl's neck. Wake didn't want nobody to bruise his girls, 'cept him. Goat beat the face off that man. I don't mean it was bloody, I don't mean it was a mess; I mean there was no face left. So, I knew what Goat could do. The thought of what he might want to do to me behind closed doors shook me down deep. Wake just offering me to him, like some kind of sacrifice.

We sat quiet for a long time. Him in that chair, me on the edge of the bed. He didn't say nothing, didn't even look at me. I was afraid he might get angry if I didn't talk, didn't do what was expected of me.

How'd you hurt your arm? *I asked. The girls had said something bit him. Wake mentioned a beast. Was it a bear? Something else? They said his bones had been twisted, his arm wrung like a dishcloth.*

I fell down off a horse is all, *he said.*

That must've hurt, *I said, meaning the bite, letting him think I meant the horse fall.*

It got real quiet then, and I worried about that. I knew from experience you had to watch the quiet ones. A quiet man was like a powder keg. You had to be careful how you handled them.

You know, *I said,* you can sit on the bed. You don't have to sit all the way over there. *I tried to make my voice light. Tried to make it sound like it did when I flirted with a man.*

He shook his head, still looking at the floor.

You ain't got to do nothing.

But I wouldn't mind, *I lied.*

When he run a finger through the deep wrinkles on his forehead the tip disappeared. I needed to keep him talking.

How'd you get that name, Goat?

Mama give it to me, *he said.*

What's your last name? *I knew his last name. I'd heard some of the other men – the guards – say it. All the girls laughed about it when I told them.* Lamb. *Lamb was his last name. His name was Goat Lamb, if in fact his given name really was Goat. If that was really the name his mama gave him.*

Smith, *he said.*

Goat Smith, *I said.* That really your name?

Just a plain name, is all.

Oh, I don't know, *I said,* Nothing plain about the name Goat.

That's when he raised his eyes, looked at me for the first time. I tried to smile.

There was a kind of brutal innocence to him. He looked like he might grab a woman up, have his way right in the field if it struck him. Just out of some kind of animal instinct, not because he wanted to hurt her. That was Wake's territory. Goat might just pounce, do his business, not realize he was breaking things.

I looked away, out the stain glass window. The snow still came down. I'd never seen this much snow. All day long for days. When I looked back, he was staring at me. I tried again to smile.

You can keep them clothes on, *he said, looking back to his feet.*

I wouldn't mind, *I said.*

No, *he said. I felt sorry for him then, knowing his whole life women had shunned him because he was so ugly, that the men had just walked on him. Still he went on, one foot in front of the other, the way an old farm beast will go until it falls over dead, or the master comes out to shoot it.*

No, *I said.* Honest.

He started to stand, but froze, as if changing his mind.

My heart jumped. I was afraid he was considering it, of what he might want after all.

He scratched his leg, and when his pants rode up, I seen there was white all over them, like they'd been dipped in calamine.

Reckon, *he said,* I could sit by you on that bed?

What could I say? Sure, *I said* Come sit by me. *I patted the bed with my hand.*

He trudged over, holding his limp arm. Never made eye contact, and he didn't let his eyes rest on my body neither.

He sat on the bed, and it sagged from his weight. There was no fat on him, he was just solid, like he was made up of twisted pine knot. He sat way on the other end, like he was afraid of me, afraid of being too close.

We sat that way for a while.

Your hair, *he said.*

You like it?

'Minds me of strawberries.

Do you want to touch it? *I said. It came out before I had time to think on it, before my mind could register just how bad of an idea it was to encourage him. But the truth was, he was already close enough. If he wanted to break me, he could.*

He slid down the bed, reached up behind me, ran his thick fingers through my hair. His breath slowed then, like it calmed him.

Then he put his head down on my lap. He didn't grab or squeeze me, just crossed his arms against his chest. He closed his eyes then, and all the air just went out of him, like he'd never been able to let go like this, to just be.

Mama never let me, *he said.*

Let you what? *I asked, but he never answered.*

Goat slept.

We stayed like that for a long time, and I tried not to stir, 'cause I didn't want to wake him. His eyes never fluttered, like he was at

251

peace. His head was so heavy on my lap, like a big creek rock. His long legs stretched out on the floor, and he just sighed like a baby. I thought, maybe he is just a big baby after all. One that can crush a man's skull.

Chapter 34

It was Lilyfax who spotted the trail that ran off Mud Road and into a thick cluster of close leaning trees.

"I can't hardly breathe in here," she said, as they made their way around the curves of the narrow trail. "But this is the way." She looked at Leo. The two of them had not discussed how they'd seen the Temple from their vantage point in the clouds the day before.

"They's horse tracks," Mattis said, leaning down to examine them in the snow. "Fresh, too."

Mattis had asked to come on the journey to the Temple after they had escaped the Klan in the woods.

"Black girls have been took too," he'd said. "From right here on Mulwin Rock. Three or four I know of. Girl named Vey I was close to."

At first Leo had hesitated, not wanting to involve another person, but Mattis had saved the trio twice, once by finding them refuge in the freezing rain, and then by taking a shovel to Goat's face. Without the Shadow Wulver, they could use all the help they could get.

"You got your shovel?" Leo asked, bringing a smile to Mattis's face. "We're gonna have to bring that big Goat down for good this time."

Lilyfax grimaced. "I never want to see that ugly face up close again."

Along the trail, they talked strategy. Lilyfax repeated her idea of picking off the visitors to the Temple one by one. Ezra suggested they find a way to sneak into the Temple and rescue the girls directly.

"What if we burn them out?" Mattis asked. "Set the place afire?"

"They'll scatter like rats," Lilyfax said, "and leave the girls to burn up."

"She's right. The kind of men who'd steal girls don't seem like the type that are going to step in to rescue them, things go south," Leo said.

"That's right," Ezra said. "It'll be every creep for himself."

Behind them they heard horses approaching.

"The Klan?" Lilyfax asked.

"Up the bank!" Leo said. They scrambled up, slipping on the frozen snow. Mattis took a stick and wiped away as many of their footprints as he could before taking his place with them in a twist of magnolia trees. Soon the riders came into view. There were two men on horseback, each wearing wooden booger masks with exaggerated features. One had sharp pointed eyebrows, the other a dark frown.

"Why in the hell do they have to be up here on this mountain, instead of in town, where we can just pull up in a goddamned car is beyond me," Eyebrows said.

"Ain't a place open in town for us now," said Frown.

"Wake is eccentric, but this is ridiculous," Eyebrows said.

"Wait till you see what he has here. It'll be worth it, Senator, I promise you."

"It had better be."

"I've never seen anything like it," Frown said, "Not in Europe, not in the big cities. The most beautiful women. All kinds."

"One thing about it," Eyebrows said, "Nobody here to see who's coming and going, no flash of photographers trying to make a name."

"We're almost there. You'll get your fill: wine, women, and song."

"Lead on, good man."

When the men passed, they scrambled back down the bank to the trail.

"Senator," Lilyfax hissed.

"Only the best of society," Leo said.

"Wake has so much power," Ezra said. "It's amazing, really."

Leo stared Ezra down. "You talk about him like you like him. Like you admire what he's doing here."

"Oh no," Ezra said. "I don't like anything about what he's doing at the Temple. I can't understand why anybody would kidnap girls, hold them against their will. But his power. The way he held the blue flame in his hands. The way he has everyone following him, doing what he says. Isn't it something?"

"Maybe power is the problem," Lilyfax said. "Menfolk can't seem to handle it."

Leo flushed. He pictured Aunt Lila's bruised face. "We're gonna get these girls down off this mountain. I don't care if the president himself comes calling."

The late afternoon sky cast orange through the trees like campfire embers.

"Why men have to wear masks?" Mattis asked. "If it ain't hoods, it's those wooden ones. Never seen so many people trying to hide their faces."

"If you got things to hide," Ezra said.

"Let's keep moving," Lilyfax said, leading the way up the trail. Mattis looked from Ezra to Leo, smiled, fell in behind her.

Dusk wore on through the trees when the Temple came into view. It was an enormous rock structure lurching on the edge of the mountain's face. The front of the Temple jutted angrily over the cliff side, and in back an elaborate courtyard was surrounded by rows of mammoth trees. Each side of the Temple bore elaborate stonework, though there were no windows. There were two towers on either end of the structure. On the path leading to the courtyard there was a sign. On the sign there was a large blue snowflake, the edges of the snowflake wrapped in thorny vines resembling barbed wire. Leo's throat tightened. Now that he saw the size of the building, thought about what might be inside, he was terrified. Deep down, to his core.

"What do we do now?" Mattis asked.

"We wait till nightfall," Leo said, trying to keep his voice level. "Then we get into that courtyard. See what we can find."

They took up a position in a cluster of trees where they could watch.

"Who's hungry?" Lilyfax said. From her pack she pulled a large piece of bread prepared by the church women. She broke the bread into four pieces and passed them out. They drizzled honey over the bread before taking a bite.

"Can't nobody bake like church women," Leo said.

"Especially Miss Josie," Mattis said. "Lord God."

As they ate, another man came up the trail on horseback. He, too, wore a booger mask. He stabled his horse in a large barn out beyond the courtyard and entered the Temple.

At nightfall, they crept through the courtyard. Though it was cloudy, a sliver of moon lit the path. They hid when a man came out to light large brass gas lanterns mounted high along the walls. The light from the lamps flickered over the faces of gargoyles that appeared in the rock walls. Once the man disappeared inside, they moved closer.

The trees were even larger than they'd seemed at a distance. Some were as wide as a hay roll. All of them had black leaves but they weren't dead. The trees were very much alive and seemed sinister somehow.

"What—What is that?" Lilyfax asked.

"What?" Ezra asked.

"Over there," she said.

Leo followed her line of sight to a tree at the edge of the courtyard.

"Looks like a statue," Mattis said.

There was a girl in the tree, a soft amber glow behind her, highlighting her silhouette. Leo approached the tree. Her hands were over her head as if she were dancing. One knee was placed gracefully akimbo, her painted toe pointing down.

Leo put his hand against the tree. Something like ice bound her there.

Behind him, Lilyfax inhaled sharply. "Oh God," she whispered.

Leo almost jumped when he saw it. Another girl in a different tree.

Leo spun. There were women and girls in all of the trees. In one, a girl had her arm stretched out in front of her, another had her legs crossed. One had her hands on her hips, one leg pushed out wide. Her face bore a hint of sadness, as if she'd tried to smile but couldn't find her way to it.

"They're so beautiful," Ezra said.

In a large tree in the center of the courtyard Leo saw a familiar face. He ran to her. The same ember glow lit behind her body. She stood with her arms outstretched, her head hanging to one side. Her legs long beneath her, coming together at her feet, one foot placed gracefully over the other. Her blonde hair was up, a few delicate wisps falling over her face. It was her. Camille.

"This is no statue," Leo said.

Camille's eyes were open, and Leo marveled at how young she looked. She'd seemed so grown at Aunt Lila's, but here, in the moonlight, she seemed child-like. His heart wrenched within him.

"She's beautiful," Lilyfax said beside him.

"Camille," Leo said. "We have to get her down from there."

Just then they heard men approaching from the Temple. Their torches cast long shadows through the courtyard.

"Run," Mattis said. "Hide!"

The four of them hid in a thicket. The voices of the men became clear as they drew closer.

"We have many beautiful things from which to choose." The thickness of the voice floated on the air, the words burdened by the heaviness of the man's tongue. Mr. Wake. "Stroll through our courtyard, just as one might enjoy an immaculate garden, see our lovely fauna in bloom. Pick that which you desire, Senator, and she shall be yours."

The senator sucked his teeth. "My God, there's so many of them! And so, so beautiful."

"Yes," said Wake, "They are the most beautiful in all the world. They are treasures, each. Notice the perfect flush to the cheeks, the magical allure of their eyes. Call to you, they do, like sirens upon the deep."

Neither man wore a mask now, but a group of masked men hovered around them, with exaggerated fangs and bulging eyes. They moved from tree to tree, lingering before each girl as if examining works of art.

"So many," the senator repeated. "And so young."

"However young you prefer."

"I want them all," said the Senator.

"Yes, of course. But one must choose. Isn't that the way of life? Our enchanted girls remain in the trees until they are selected. And after they are enjoyed, back again they must return."

The senator stopped in front of an ancient Oak. He stared at the girl there. She had bronze skin and a slender frame. Her eyes sparkled in the light of the torches.

Mattis took a step forward. "That's her," he said. "That's Vey. She's from on the mountain, from right here."

Leo placed a hand on his shoulder. "Wait. We'll get her, but there's too many of them right now."

"This one," the senator said. "I've never had a black before. Look at her, she's striking!"

Mattis ground his teeth.

"Excellent choice," said Wake. "I will take her down for you. But eat slowly. A woman is a precious fruit to be tasted, savored. Rush not."

Mr. Wake reached for the tree and rested both palms against it. After a moment, there was a spark of light and the girl fell out into his arms, the magical ice disappearing. For a moment Vey was still, then she began to kick and squirm.

"Let me go!" Vey yelled.

"Sometimes the most beautiful art," said Wake, "can be the hardest to behold." He handed the girl to a third man who threw her over his shoulder. The man's other arm was in a sling. Though he wore a booger mask, Leo recognized the loping gait. It was Goat.

"Maude," Wake called.

The red-headed girl emerged from the shadows. She stepped forward and dipped her head. She wore a purple dress trimmed in gold. "Yes, Mr. Wake?" Leo tensed at the sight of her.

"Prepare the Indigo Room for our guest, and make sure the girl is ready, yes?"

"Of course," said Maude. Then she, Goat, and Vey walked toward the vast blue wooden doors of the Temple.

The senator watched after Vey as if she might float away, out of his reach.

The men moved away, the light from their torches dimming.

Leo and the others met at the tree holding Camille.

"We have to get her out. We have to get them all out," Lilyfax said. "Now."

"Yes," Leo said. He examined the tree, running his hands over the clear ice-like matter that covered her body. He hit it with his fists, which stung so hard he held them out and shook them, his knuckles cracked and bleeding.

"Try this," Ezra said, producing a large stick he'd retrieved from the woods.

Leo took the stick and swung it hard against the tree. The stick splintered across the tree.

"Let me try," Mattis said. He pulled a hatchet from his pack. He stood in front of the tree and held the handle with both hands. He swung it hard at the ice, and when it struck there were sparks, but the blade just glanced off. He tried several times. There was no sign where the blade had struck it, no crack or mark of any kind.

"How do we get through?" Ezra asked.

"Let me try," Lilyfax said.

"If we can't make a mark," Leo said, waving his hand. "There ain't nothing you can do."

Lilyfax walked toward the tree anyway, when the light of a coming torch flickered through the trees.

"Someone's coming," Leo said.

Leo stopped at the edge of the courtyard to see a lone figure moving through the trees. The man wore a booger mask with a huge downturned nose. He wore a black coat and pants over his long narrow frame. He paused in front of a tree, rubbing his hands over the ice. He took off his mask. It was the Alchemist. He took a liquid and poured it down the face of the tree.

Leo took a step forward. Behind him, Lilyfax tugged at his shirt. "Come on."

Leo lingered for a moment, watching the Alchemist. The man tapped at the frozen ice that held the girl in the tree. He poured more liquid over the surface and blue smoke rose into the night. He turned away slowly and returned to the Temple.

When they made it back to the trail, Ezra said: "It's cold. What will we do for the night?"

"The barn," said Mattis. "Let's shelter in the loft."

In the barn, they gathered hay over their bodies to keep warm. Lilyfax bedded down next to Leo and he took her hand as she rested her head on his shoulder. Leo thought about the Temple, the look of fear in the eyes of the girls in the trees. He knew Mattis's heart was heavy with the thought of Vey in the temple with the senator. He thought of Lilyfax trapped in the trees, then his mother, then tiny Goldfish. He heard Wake's voice in his head as he slipped under. He saw Jacob's face turning in his nightmares, the twist of the Shadow Wulver coming to life. Wake's whisper on the night breeze:

What do you see, boy? Tell me.

Chapter 35

The next morning and into the afternoon, they watched the Temple. Four men left around noon, and more arrived on horseback. They sat as still as possible as the horses were brought to the barn stables beneath them. Leo watched the men through the cracks in the floor; all wore wooden masks and had white skin. Lilyfax tore off small pieces of bread for them to eat as the day wore on, each sprinkled with drops of honey.

In the late afternoon, a large figure came into the barn. It was Goat. He wore no mask, his arm up in a black sling. Leo's throat tightened as he stepped beneath them. Leo motioned for the others to be still. Goat poured feed out for the horses and then went to each stable to shovel shit. He stopped often to pet the horses. He rubbed their backs and bellies. He smiled at the animals, the deep trenches of his crinkled face extending, giving him the appearance of a bemused ghoul. He was even more frightening when he smiled.

After a while a portly man came to the barn. His mask was perfectly rounded, mimicking the shape of his body.

To Goat, he said, "prepare the fatted calf for the feast. Need you to prep it."

Goat looked pained. "We got that old bull. Plenty good eating. Been giving him nothing but corn."

"No, he says it has to be the calf, on account of it being the Odin feast. He has declared it."

"Ask Wake about the bull," Goat said.

"He has declared it." The portly man ducked out the door.

Goat led a plump calf out of one of the back stalls. The calf was red and white, bearing a bright white spot the shape of a sickle on her chest. Goat prepared a pulley over one of the barn's beams. In the loft, Lilyfax squeezed Leo's arm. Cows were her favorite animal.

Goat took the calf and raised it up by its hind legs. The calf cried out and the other animals in the barn panted and shifted in their stalls. A cow, perhaps the calf's mother, kicked her stall door, groaning.

Goat leaned into the calf and whispered something in its ear. He slit its throat and the calf's cries shifted to a muffled gurgle as blood filled a bucket he kicked in place beneath. Leo looked at Lilyfax, her eyes full of tears.

Below, there was a ruckus as a wild dog crept through the door of the barn, growling. Goat looked at the thin dog, its brown straggly hair standing up on its back. He turned from the dog and ran a curved knife into the belly of the calf, letting its guts fall to the barn floor. The dog approached, mouth watering.

Goat licked blood from the curved blade, eyeing the dog. The dog came on slowly, its hunger perhaps overwhelming the natural fear it should have of the big man. It bared its teeth, though several were missing. It rushed forward and grabbed at the intestines on the barn floor. It backed away slowly, the entrails in its teeth. Goat stepped on the pile to prevent the dog from pulling them out the door. Goat bent at the waist and growled at the dog, baring his own jagged teeth.

The dog snarled back, unwilling to release its prize. Goat grabbed the intestines and pulled the dog toward him, the two of them in a bloody tug of war. When the dog realized he was losing, it let go of the intestines and lunged at Goat. It bit hard into the man's leg. Goat offered no reaction. Slowly, he pulled his lame arm from the sling, and taking both hands, he grabbed the dog by the jaws. He took them and pried them off his leg, then yanked them open, violently breaking the dog's jaw. The dog stepped back, its bottom jaw flopping down, yelping in pain. Goat brought the curved blade down into the top of the dog's head, ending its suffering. Then Goat jerked, looking up at the ceiling of the barn as if he'd heard something there. Leo rolled away from the crack, heart hammering. Mattis and Ezra held their hands over their mouths in terror.

Lilyfax had her eyes squeezed closed, her hands on her own neck. When Leo had the courage to look back through the crack, Goat was cutting the meat from the calf and placing the pieces neatly in a wheelbarrow. He took some of the blood and spread it under his eyes.

By dusk the barn floor beneath the loft was clean, the bucket of blood and the dog's carcass all removed by workers from the Temple.

"Gonna take more than a shovel to get that man down for good," Mattis said.

"We have to get what we came for without being seen," Leo said.

"I wonder," Ezra said. "Mattis mentioned burning the Temple down. But we were afraid of hurting the girls. But if the girls are all outside in the trees—"

"I thought about that," Lilyfax said. "But how many women are inside on any given night? They'll be a dozen or more. We can't risk hurting them."

"A distraction," Leo said. "What we need is a distraction. What if we set the animals free tonight? Set the barn on fire?"

"We still don't know how to get the girls out of the trees though," Ezra said.

"Yes," Leo said. "But if the men all come out to see about the barn, maybe we could get into the Temple and at least get those girls out. Then we could set the Temple on fire."

"While they're distracted by the barn fire," Mattis said. "That could do all right."

"Wait," Lilyfax said. "So let me get this straight: we set the animals free, burn the barn. The men, hopefully, come out to see what's going on at the barn, and we go into the Temple and get the girls who are inside. We get them out, then we set the Temple on fire? That it?"

"Yes," said Leo.

"What about the girls in the trees?" Lilyfax asked.

"Well," Leo said. "If the Temple is gone, and the barn too, the men have no shelter. They'll have to head down the mountain."

"And they won't want to leave the girls behind," Ezra said. "They'll set the girls free and they'll march them down the mountain."

"That will give us a chance to try to pick them off one at a time, maybe," Mattis said.

Lilyfax said, "This just might work."

As nightfall took over, they set about their work. They released all of the barn animals into the forest. Leo and Mattis built a small fire using Leo's flint. They each lit a stick with the fire, and went through the barn, lighting the hay. Afterward, they stood at the edge of the courtyard, well away from the path to the barn, watching the flames rise.

The courtyard behind the Temple was soon illuminated by a dozen torches as the men poured out of the Temple and made their way to the barn. Among them, Goat and Wake.

"Now," Lilyfax said. They crept along the perimeter of the courtyard toward the rear entrance. They were standing in front of the huge oak double doors, when they were flung open from inside. There in the doorway stood Reverend Wormley. Behind him, there were rich wood-lined walls with the heads of wild animals mounted: elk, and bear, wolves, and foxes. Wormley stepped out, one hand punching his open palm.

"It's always you."

Leo backed up into the courtyard, Wormley following, leaving the doors unguarded. Behind Wormley, Mattis and Lilyfax slipped inside. Leo felt his hands shake and he balled his fists to make them stop.

"Almost didn't recognize you, Reverend, without that Klan hood."

"Tonight, Leo, you'll meet your maker."

Leo backed along the edge of the Temple, around the rock side, leading Wormley toward the cliff. Ezra moved behind the big man, slipping from tree to tree.

"Wake says your magic wulver has abandoned you. What will you do now? No one to call down from the woods to save you?"

"I don't need the wulver to handle you."

Wormley laughed. He rubbed his enormous hands on his pants legs. "That right? You know I'm going to break you." He squinted his eyes. "You're as worthless as your daddy, crawling up this mountain just to die. This is all so much bigger than you, boy."

The light from the gas lanterns at the edge of the Temple were fading, and Leo gingerly stepped backward, knowing the ledge was coming soon. He felt for it with the heel of his shoe and for a moment he had a sense of vertigo, thinking about what lay behind him. *If I can just get him a little closer,* he thought. Behind Wormley, Ezra dug around in the snow. He pulled up a big rock and staggered as he slid it up his legs to his belly.

"Give me my watch, boy," Wormley said, "and I'll let you go. I'll say I couldn't catch you."

Leo reached into his pocket, fished out the watch. He twirled it around his finger clockwise, then let it unwind in the opposite direction. His hands began to shake so hard he couldn't spin the watch. Wormley stared at his hands.

"You scared, boy? You should be," Wormley said. He licked his lips. "I get scared, I say the Lord's prayer. You know it?"

Leo shivered. Behind Wormley, Ezra approached with the rock.

"Our father, who art in heaven. Hallowed be thy name. Thy kingdom come, thy will be done, on earth as it is in heaven," Wormley said.

Behind the preacher, Ezra lifted the rock over his head. His arms quaked under its weight.

"Give us this day our daily bread. And forgive us our trespasses, as we—"

There was a loud thwack as the rock struck the back of Wormley's head. The big man fell to his knees. He raised both of his hands and felt the back of his head. When he brought them down, they were covered with blood. Behind Wormley, Ezra struggled to lift the rock once more, his breathing labored. His face was pale.

"And Samson said," Wormley started, "with the jawbone of an ass, heaps upon heaps, I have slain a thousand men."

"No—" Leo started, watching Ezra.

The rock came down again, and Wormley slid face first into the snow, a gray pink showing beneath his slicked back hair.

Ezra stood over Wormley breathing hard. His mouth moved, but Leo could only hear his own heart in his throat. He took a step toward Wormley.

Wormley struggled up to his knees, blood running down his forehead into his eyes. He looked skyward and lifted his hands.

"Of the cloven hoof," he said, "of the bruised head, of thy bruised heel."

Ezra picked up the rock again.

"Ezra, he's done," Leo said.

Ezra's face grimaced. "Look how bright the blood," Ezra whispered. "There is power in the blood." He bore an expression Leo had never seen on him before. Darkness descended over his face, his eyes alive and wild. His shiny black hair slick across his face.

For a moment, Leo almost felt sorry for the preacher, but then he thought of those fat hands on his mama's flesh. Wormley kept his eyes on the sky, blinking as they filled with blood.

"Of the split tail," Wormley said.

Ezra let the rock drop the final time.

Wormley groaned, flat on his stomach.

Chapter 36

In the courtyard, they found Mattis and Lilyfax standing with five girls they'd gathered from the Temple. One was Vey, the black girl that had been chosen by the senator the night before. She clutched a quilt up around her body, her feet bare in the snow.

"Did you get them all?" Leo asked.

Before Lilyfax could answer, the courtyard swarmed with men carrying torches. Lilyfax took a step to the side, as if to run, then froze, realizing there was no place to go. Leo spun around. There were men everywhere. They were surrounded, the four of them, their backs touching.

The oak doors of the Temple opened, and more men emerged. One was the Alchemist.

Leo stared at him. "I trusted you," he said.

The Alchemist smirked and dipped his chin.

"Master Leo," he said.

He then looked over Leo's shoulder where the men parted for Wake. Wake wore a black suit with a blue tie, his eyes as black as the fabric of his suit. When he approached, Wake motioned with his head, and each of the girls that had been rescued was grabbed up by one of the men. When they came for Vey, she ran, dropping the quilt in the snow. To Goat, Wake said, "Chase that down." Goat glared at Mattis, perhaps remembering the boy and his shovel, before ambling through the darkness after her. When Goat cleared the crowd, he took off with a nimble sprint that belied his enormous size.

To Leo, Wake said, "Thank you for bringing me what I've coveted for so long." He winked and walked past Leo to Lilyfax. He took her face in a black-gloved hand. "My little nymph, what grand luck to have you here with me at last." He turned to Leo, lifting his chin. "And here you are, my dear, the only thing missing is a big red bow."

"No," Leo said.

When Wake turned again to Lilyfax, she spit in his face. He smiled, striking her with the back of his hand. He hit her so hard she fell on her back. Leo lunged forward but was held back by two of Wake's men. Lilyfax stood up again to face Wake, blood welling at the corner of her mouth. The outline of a bruise bloomed jagged along her cheek.

"Take her," Wake said, and two men hooked their hands through her arms, lifting her from the ground.

"Maude," Wake said, and the red headed woman came forward. "Prepare her straightaway. A most violent guest travels even now for the Temple." Wake glared at Leo. "She is to be his. Let us break all the wildness from her."

Maude bowed her head but caught Leo's eye before she turned and went into the Temple. There was something about the look she gave him, as if her eyes meant to say something. Something Leo couldn't understand.

"What of you three?" Wake said, circling the boys.

"Foxes in the henhouse," the Alchemist said.

"I'm going to free these girls," Leo said. "Mark my word." His voice rattled. Too high to be threatening.

"Free the girls?" Wake laughed. "Tell me, can you free even yourself? And freedom? You speak of freedom for them? Freedom to what world? Tell me, if you can, where on this God forsaken earth is a woman as treasured as here in my garden?" Wake raised his arms, and when he did so, the orange ember glow brightened in all of the trees around them, highlighting the faces and bodies of the women. Wake spun slowly, hands in the air.

"Treasured?" Leo said. "This is a prison."

"You're a monster," Mattis said.

Wake approached Mattis, placing a gloved hand against his face. He pulled a large bowie knife from his belt. He let the blade rest against Mattis's cheek. "You've no idea." He stepped back and smiled, his eyes growing even darker. "Take them."

The double doors opened to the great hall Leo had glimpsed before. Gas lamps flickered along the walls, and a girl with a short flapper dress carried drinks to a group of men gathered by a vast fireplace. While the other three walls of the Temple had no windows, there were great windows facing out over the edge of the mountain. Paintings of nude women covered the walls alongside the mounted beasts.

They descended a winding staircase, down a hall to a dark room. There, guards pushed them into small iron cages. These appeared to be animal cages, such that each boy could only position himself on all fours, with no room to stand or even stretch out. They could only lay on their sides if they balled their knees to their chests.

After several hours a woman came into the room. She wore a gray mask, bearing horns that curved like those of bison. She had on a long dark green dress that swished when she walked. She glided through the room and knelt on her knees in front of Leo and the others. She sat there quietly for a moment, looking at each of them through the mask.

"It's Christmas Eve," she whispered. "Did you know that?"

"No," Leo said.

"Don't imagine you thought you'd spend Christmas here, in a cage, you poor things."

"Imagine not," Leo said.

"I remember you," she said. "Hi, *Little Pony*. I told you I was the ticket, boy."

It was Maude.

She took off her mask, her auburn curls falling over her shoulders. Her hair was longer now than when Leo first met her at Aunt Lila's.

"And what a brave little pony you've turned out to be," she said. "Brave or stupid. I can't tell."

"Can you help us get out of here?" Leo asked.

Maude looked over her shoulder, then back to the boys.

"Look what I have for you," she opened a small basket. It was full of chocolate candies.

"I don't care about all that right now," Leo said. "We have to get Lilyfax. There's no telling what they'll do to her."

"Take it," she said. "You'll need your strength." She held the basket up to the bars.

Leo took a piece. Maude slid across the floor on her knees and handed pieces to Mattis and Ezra.

"Thank you," they said.

"Merry Christmas," she said.

"You have to help us," Leo said. "I know you don't want to be here. I know you ain't part of this."

Maude smiled. She pursed her lips.

"Tomorrow is a big feast. We've been planning something for a long time. A way to bring it all down. And then here you are."

"We?" Leo asked. "Who?"

"The Odin Yule. That's what Wake calls it."

"Calls what?" Ezra asked.

"The big feast tomorrow. He calls it Odin Yule. Lets the Christian guests think it's for Christmas. He'll make a show of it. Have that preacher Wormley say a few words. Let them think he's in on it. He'll let them have God, they pay high enough price for the girls."

"Umm," Leo said. "Wormley's dead."

Maude smiled. "That so?" Her face grew serious. "Tomorrow night when the feast is started, and the men are drunk, he'll come for you. Everything is in motion."

"Who will come for us?" Leo asked.

Maude didn't say. She smiled instead.

"What about the girls?" Leo asked. "What about Lilyfax?"

"I know how to free the women," Maude said. "It's funny. Wake said it one day, and I didn't know what he meant. Said it like a riddle. The answer was right there."

"What is the answer?" Ezra asked.

"Takes a woman to do it. A man can't do it, can't free a woman. Men know only of binding things."

With that, she stood and placed her mask back on. She headed for the door.

"Wait," Leo said, "How will we know it's the right man who's come for us?"

"That's easy," she said. "If he's the right one, he won't kill you."

Chapter 37 – Lilyfax

They took me to a room, laid a red dress on the bed, told me to put it on. Reckon they didn't know who they were talking to. I wasn't putting on that dress, no way. Only my daddy can get me to do that. Wake came in the room. Had that old Goat tie my hands up over my head, looped up to the ceiling some way. I felt like that calf he'd killed. That red-headed girl, she came and undressed me. She put the red dress on me, buttoned it up, slow-like. When she was done, Wake took the dungarees I was wearing, threw them in the fireplace.

That's better, *he said. Then he sent the others away.*

He sat in a chair and lit his pipe. The smoke was thick, the tobacco smelled like berries.

He started talking, looking far off. I had to wear a kind of uniform when I left my room. Mother had crisp white shirts for me, high collars, so hard the starch. So scratchy. I had to wear those and short pants. People in America don't wear them, but they broke just below the knee, and I wore them until I was almost twelve. Shiny hard shoes that hurt my feet. Always I had to look perfect. My hair too. Mother gave me a hard part I hated. Slicked my hair with grease.

What will you do, *I asked him,* when all this is over? *It was like I hadn't spoken.*

He said, I hated that uniform. But I loved to walk through the parlors. So many beautiful painted girls. Everywhere. Always rushing about. Always someplace to go. I wasn't allowed to go upstairs where the girls took the men. But I'd stand at the bottom of the staircase, watch them walk, their tall heels rapping the floor.

If I saw any men, I was to stop whatever I was doing, and stand against the wall. I was never to be heard from, just to bow. There was one man. All milk and freckles. He'd come in, chest out, like he owned the place. Like all the women belonged to him, the other men far beneath him. Always he found a reason to strike my face, as if I hadn't bowed low enough, hadn't moved far enough out of his way. I learned to stay out of sight of the men. Just watch the girls. They'd kiss my cheeks and touch my face.

Why are you telling me this? *I asked. He looked at me then, astonished, as if he'd forgot I was there.*

Your red dress, it reminds me of those days, *he said.* The way the girls sat in the parlor waiting for the men to come. The excitement over who might be chosen. The dread on some of their faces. But the real work, it went on down below. Old Jewish woman, Helda, taught me to cook stews and soups and how to boil rice. The women, they got hungry. We cooked huge pots of food. Mother would say they don't have time to cook for themselves, and if they were hungry, they couldn't perform. The men wouldn't fill the coffers for hunger-weak women. We'd all starve, she'd say.

The cellar was an ugly place. I never wore my fancy starched shirts down there. There we wore rags, the same rags every day. I scrubbed the girls' underthings on a giant washboard. Miss Helda would smack the back of my head if I did it too hard. *A man don't want to look at holes when they undress a woman,* she'd say. *Get them clean boy, but don't rub holes in.* I washed their stockings and dresses, frocks, and brassieres. I loved the feel of it all on my fingers. Never got enough of it, the way it felt.

He circled me then. Put a hand on my back, held the hem of the dress in his hand, admiring it. I eyed the door, thought of Leo and the others. What would he do to them?

I never knew anything besides this life. The sweet smell of perfume on a girl, the way the blush of her cheek meant she was ready. Mother taught me to paint the girls when I got older. Slapped me when I did it wrong.

Then Wake held my face in his hands, turning it from side to side, studying me.

Start with the eyes, Mother said. Always the eyes. Work with what God gave her, she'd say. If her eyes were big, just trace them, give them just an outline. If God made a girl's eyes too small, then really work with the shading, make them look

273

bigger. Men love big eyes like yours. *He traced the outline of my eyes with his thumb. He smelled like meat, like the blood of the fatted calf.*

Once you have the eyes right, move on to the cheeks. Don't overdo it, she'd say, just give them a color that will draw the men in like bees to a flower. Then the lips, of course. *He put his fingertips on my lips, squinted his eyes, studying.* Same as the eyes. You want to make them look bigger for women that don't have nice thick lips. As for lips that were too big — mother said there was no such thing. Men wanted a woman that looked ever hungry, a mouth full of appetite.

Let me down from here and I'll show you an appetite, *I said.*

He just grinned. As I grew older, I wanted to be close to the girls, *he said.* Mother would get angry at how long it took me to paint them. I wanted to just let it all linger, them up close, my face near their faces; I could feel their breathing on my neck. Sometimes our knees would touch, their heat would become mine.

I've news for you, *I said,* they all hated you.

He was serious for a moment, then his smile returned. Maybe so, *he said,* maybe so. I know Mother did. But I hated her more. But I loved her power. She had so much—how do you say— sway over everyone. Men and women. They'd do anything for her, for what she offered. They'd bring her gold, pluck coins from the eyes of their dead ancestors. She could have run the world. If only she knew what I know.

Then he went out.

Chapter 38

The kitchen must have been close by. The sweet smell of meat roasting all day overwhelmed Leo, giving him the familiar ache of hunger he'd known so well back in the valley. Upstairs, the men gathered, their raucous laughter and excitement building. Sometime during the day, a guard appeared, wearing a wooden mask. He carried a small leather club, which he let smack the palm of his hands as he stared at the prisoners. He paced the room, letting the head of the club glance off the bars. Occasionally, he stopped and leaned down to stare into the cages at them, never speaking.

In the late afternoon, a second man appeared. He wore black cowboy boots and black pants, sporting a large silver belt buckle with a skull and crossbones. He approached the guard, his back to Leo and the others. He took off his mask. The other man grumbled, something like anger in his voice. The man in black reached up and pulled the mask off the guard.

"What in the Sam hell you doing?" the guard asked.

The man in black blew some kind of powder into the guard's face, and immediately his knees buckled. He lowered the guard to the floor slowly. When he turned, Leo saw it was the Alchemist.

"You!" Leo said.

"I am he."

"What kind of man are you," Leo said. "I gave my sister your pills and potions. And here you are." Leo's eyes fell on the snowflake tattoo on the man's wrist. "Part of this cult."

The Alchemist reached down and unfastened the lock on Ezra's cage. Ezra emerged, stretching his back.

"I kept hearing rumors about the kidnapping of women," The Alchemist said. "The way the homeless and poor, especially, were being trafficked. I did a lot of work to win the trust of Wake and the others, to put myself here among them."

He unlocked Mattis' cage and reached down to take the boy's hand.

"You're not part of it?" Leo asked.

The Alchemist unlocked Leo's cage. "Only insofar as I needed to be to get close enough to affect the escape of these women."

Leo climbed out of his cage. He was sure he would never stand straight again. He pushed a fist into the small of his back.

"How did you find the Temple?" The Alchemist asked.

"Aunt Lila gave us a clue."

"Ahh, good woman, she."

"What do we do now?" Mattis asked.

The Alchemist fetched his pack at the far side of the room. He handed each boy a booger mask. To Mattis, he said, "Please excuse this, but should we see any other men in the halls, kindly put your hands in your pockets."

Mattis looked at his black hands. "Yes, all right."

The Alchemist gagged the guard on the floor and put him into one of the cages, replacing the mask he'd removed.

"Follow me," he said to the others and led them down a dark hallway. There were knapsacks propped against the wall.

"Kindly fetch those," he said, "Only be sure not to drop them."

"Okay," said Ezra.

"No," The Alchemist said, placing a hand on Ezra's chest. "I need you to hear me. If you drop these packs, it shall be quite grave. For our very mortality." He looked them each in the eye with an expression that matched his words.

Leo swallowed hard and tightened his hand on his sack's handle. The Alchemist saw this. "Good," he said.

They went down more stairs, deep under the Temple. They walked in silence for some time before the Alchemist stopped to face them.

"Tonight, this Temple will burn. Perhaps burn is too kind a word." His S sounds were the thick Zs Leo had remembered. "An explosion of Biblical proportions. You each have in your sack orbs full of gun powder. We are going to plant them in every nook under this structure and at the appointed time, I shall set them off. This Temple will be no more."

"What about the girls, what about Lilyfax?" Leo asked.

"We have an ally in the house. I spent weeks and months. Every magic powder and elixir. Liquids. I tried everything on that enchanted ice. The answer was right in front of us the whole time, if only I had known, I could have spared so many of Wake's victims."

"What is it?" Ezra asked.

The Alchemist met Ezra's eyes. He studied Ezra for a moment but did not answer. "We haven't much time. This is the day. Most of the Temple's patrons are here for the feast. We have the chance to wipe them all out at once. The traffickers and those who partake. So many wink at Wake's evil, so long as they have access to the girls in the trees."

"Where is Lilyfax?" Leo asked. "Is she in a cage someplace?"

"No," the Alchemist said, frowning. "I'm afraid Wake has her outside."

"No!" Leo said, his eyes clouded as he pictured her in the trees.

The Alchemist placed a hand on Leo's shoulder. "Come Leo, we all have our part to play. Let us be about our business."

They placed the gunpowder orbs at even intervals along the walls, in the corners of the structure, and against each support column.

When they finished, they stood together.

"When night falls and the men are drunk in celebration, you'll meet Maude in the courtyard. I'll show you the way," the Alchemist said.

Leo nodded.

"I'll have to be under the Temple, down here, to set off the first charge. I have to make sure the entire chain fires, do you understand?"

"Yes," Leo said.

"So," the Alchemist said, pulling a brown leather notebook from inside his jacket. "I need you to take this."

"What is it?"

"It's just some notes, a few poems. Some formulas of chemistry. Nothing terribly exciting, I'm afraid, but it is precious to me."

"Why can't you bring it with you when you come out?" Leo asked.

"If I drop it in the commotion, I should be devastated. I need you to keep it for me. Keep it safe."

"All right."

"And Leo," the Alchemist said, a hint of melancholy in his eyes, "should you not find me after this is all over, I need you to give it to my sister."

"Your sister? Where—How—?"

"The widow, as you call her," the Alchemist said, "she's my sister. You'll give it to her, yes? Should the need arise?"

Leo studied the smooth leather cover of the book before putting it in his jacket pocket. "Yes."

The Alchemist nodded. He smiled at Leo, but his thoughts seemed far away, far off the mountain, away from the Temple, away from the girls in the trees.

Chapter 39

At nightfall, following the path laid out for them by the Alchemist, they emerged from a side entrance of the Temple. As they passed under the great hall, they heard men celebrating with drunken howling. Outside, the gas lanterns had already been lit, and they followed them to the courtyard. There they waited for Maude as instructed. Leo scanned the trees until finally he found her.

Lilyfax was in an enormous oak with dark bark. She wore a red dress that floated around her body, the shrug of the hem suggesting motion. Though her eyes were sad, her jaw was set. Her arms crossed in one final act of defiance before she'd been frozen. Her hair was down around her neck, rather than up in her typical ponytail. She looked beautiful, but something wasn't right. At first Leo couldn't put his finger on it. Gone was the hint of mischief, the magical draw of her eyes, the spark of her dimples. Her beauty could never shine through, no matter how much Wake painted her, no matter what fancy clothes adorned her body, as long as she was bound.

"Let's get her down from there," Maude said from behind him.

"Please," Leo said, unable to swallow. "I can't stand to see her like this."

"He said something about it once," Maude said. "About keeping us house girls away from the trees."

"What do you mean?" Ezra asked.

"Women have a power men don't."

Ezra stood close to her, studying her face.

"Women have the power to free other women," she said, smiling. She placed her hands on the tree. She closed her eyes. There was a spark of light, and the ice holding Lilyfax disappeared. She fell forward and Leo rushed to catch her.

Her eyes were wild for a moment, and she kicked her legs, before settling against him. "About time, mister," she said to Leo. She nuzzled his face.

Ezra and Mattis looked at their feet, while Maude glowed. "The pony has a girlfriend," she said slyly. "Might have known."

"How did you do that?" Ezra asked.

Maude winked at him, then turned to Lilyfax. "Now, you do what I did. Go put your hands on the trees and close your eyes. Picture them free and they'll be free. Hurry! We've got to act quickly. Get them on the trail."

Leo followed Lilyfax to the center tree, the one holding Camille. She put her hands on it and closed her eyes. Soon the enchantment fell away, and Camille slid free. She was out for a moment but sprang to life as Leo lifted her from the snow. She wrapped her arms around his neck, her legs around his waist. Leo's face warmed and he saw Lilyfax frowning over Camille's shoulder.

"Once you climb down off that boy," Lilyfax said, "you can give me a hand with the others." Camille kissed Leo's cheek, leaving dark red lip prints, before hopping down. Soon half a dozen women were free, all working to release the others.

Maude ran over to hug Camille. When she pulled away, she said, "Can you get the girls started down the mountain? There's an old lean-to about a mile down. It's got jackets, coats, hats stashed. Some blankets. Go."

Camille grabbed a group of girls and ran through the courtyard into the woods. Maude, Lilyfax and the others kept freeing girls, ushering them down the path after her.

Suddenly the world around them was lit with harsh torchlight. Shadows stretched long in the snow. Leo spun, trying to determine which way to run. Then he saw them.

It was Goat. Goat and Wake.

"What have you done?" Wake grimaced. "To my trees? To my girls?"

Maude stepped back. She was closest to the men. She turned to Lilyfax and the others. *Run,* she mouthed. Maude herself made no attempt to escape.

Leo and the others backed away. Three other men from the Temple appeared behind them, wearing booger masks, and holding torches and pitchforks. There was nowhere to hide.

To Maude, Wake said, "I brought you into my house. Warm baths and chocolates — as many as you wanted. As many fine dresses." He circled her. "And this is how you repay me? You steal my girls?"

"They're not yours," Maude said. Her voice was even, almost calm.

"Look around you," Wake growled. "All this is mine. Everything you see. The land, the Temple, the girls. Even you. Especially you."

"No," Maude said.

Wake stopped circling. He leaned in close to her face.

"Just eat your chocolates. Just sit in your hot baths. Just look pretty on a fine bed made of feathers," he said. "This is all you had to do."

Maude met his eyes. "That ain't enough."

"Let me free you then. Finally. Forever," Wake said. He pulled his large bowie knife from his jacket.

Maude looked down at the blade, then up at the sky. Wake pulled his arm back, prepared to thrust. Behind him, Goat grunted. Something like *No*. Wake looked over his shoulder, met Goat's eyes. Wake snarled, plunging the knife deep into Maude's stomach. Never taking his eyes off Goat, he pushed so hard her feet left the ground. Maude sucked in all the air she could, fighting to find it and draw it in again. Her eyelids fluttered.

Goat wailed as though the blade had pierced his own gut. He held his fists out in front of him. Wake's lip curled dryly over his teeth staring at Goat. Goat moaned, his arms tense, jaw working.

Leo stared at Maude, his stomach twisting. He remembered the way she'd stood behind Camille when they danced at Aunt Lila's. The way she'd winked, called him the

Little Pony. He ran to her and put his hand over the wound as if he could stop the blood from coming out, push it back inside her. He watched the red trickle over the snow beneath her feet.

Then Goat was loping across the earth toward Wake. His motions smooth and powerful, like a wild animal in the last seconds of a hunt, just before the strike.

Wake dropped the knife. He squared his body with Goat's.

Goat growled as he came, dropping his head. Wake tented his fingers, blue flame dancing on his fingertips. He lifted his chin, grinned. Goat caught Wake across his midsection, lifting him from the earth before they both fell hard to the ground. All the breath exited Wake's body and he coughed.

Goat picked Wake up by his coat, and threw the man over his shoulder, much the way he'd carried Lilyfax a few days before. He marched slowly toward the edge of the courtyard, toward the mountain drop off.

Wake beat Goat's back with his fists, growling. His hair shined in the torchlight as it fell across his face. He conjured forth the blue flame in both hands and thrust it onto Goat's back.

The blue flame caught on Goat's coat and whooshed loudly as it spread over him. Goat never made a sound but kept marching toward the edge. Soon the flames engulfed them both, but only Wake made noise—an otherworldly howl, more animal than man.

"*Mor*! Mother," Wake cried as they approached the drop off. "I see you! Have you gone to prepare a place for me?"

Blue flames whipped up over the men, caught by the wind that raced up the mountain's face, consuming them both. When they reached the edge of the drop off, Goat lifted Wake up over his head.

Wake screamed. "I see you, Mother. You bitch, I see you."

Goat threw Wake over the side. Wake howled as he fell, silenced only by the dull thud of his body crashing into the trees below.

Goat fell to his knees, his body consumed by blue flame, his face beginning to droop from the heat, his long wrinkles stretching like candle wax.

The big man looked toward the courtyard, craning his neck. Lilyfax stepped out of the way. Goat was looking for Maude. To glimpse her again, one last time.

They were watching Goat when they heard a wail in the forest behind them. A crescendo that shook the earth. Fear seized Leo as he looked to the trees. A beast emerged, something different now, foul and grotesque. It stood taller than a horse, its stance wide. A bear's body, tinged with blue fur, bearing a huge reptilian snout. Rows and rows of jagged black pencil-tipped teeth. The beast wailed and dropped to all fours, galloping toward where Goat sat on his knees. Goat never took his eyes off Maude, who lay in the snow, her red hair falling over her face, her eyes open, glassy. The beast picked up speed as it bore down, catching Goat in its jaws, the two of them flying over the edge of the mountain in a ball of fire.

Leo took a step toward the edge when he heard the first explosions at the Temple. In the north tower, he saw the first flames. After a few seconds, another explosion came, perhaps twenty feet down the wall. Then another, and another, rippling along the base. The Alchemist's charges were working. The three men who'd been with Wake and Goat ran into the woods, dropping their masks in the snow.

When Leo turned to the courtyard, Camille was sitting in the snow, cradling Maude in her lap while Lilyfax and the others freed the remaining girls. They streamed through the courtyard toward the trail.

Finally, there was a huge explosion and the Temple's face broke away. It slid over the edge and down the rock face of the mountain. A few men emerged, their bodies engulfed in orange flame. They screamed as they ran, eventually falling to the ground, their charred bodies hissing in the snow.

Leo waited a long time for the Alchemist. More explosions echoed around the mountains, and one of the ancient trees near the Temple caught fire, then another. Soon they were all burning. Lilyfax put her hand on his arm. "We have to go."

"But he'll come. I know it," Leo said.

"I don't think he meant to escape," Ezra said. "You saw how much gun powder, how many orbs we put along those walls. If he stayed down there to make sure they all fired like they were supposed to, there's no way he could get out."

"Why would he do that?" Leo said, "Why didn't he try?"

"It had to be done," Mattis said. "There weren't no other way. He knew that. He knew what he was doing. There just wasn't no other way."

Leo patted his pocket. The Alchemist's notebook was still there. He turned away from the Temple as the next round of explosions rocked around them.

"Come on," Lilyfax said. "Let's get down the mountain. Make for the church."

Lilyfax coaxed Camille to release Maude. Reluctantly, she let Maudes's head rest on the snow. She bent down and kissed Maude's pale cheek. They found the trail and made their way down. Leo looked over his shoulder one last time. He looked for a figure emerging from the trees, hoped to see the Alchemist. But there was nothing. No one came.

"Godspeed," Leo whispered, turning away.

Chapter 40

At first Leo thought it was the heat from the Temple fire that warmed the air around them as they began their descent. The snow softened and water dripped from the trees. The night grew warmer as if the December earth briefly shrugged away winter's clutch. When they'd gotten a good distance down the mountain, they located the lean-to shed where the Alchemist and Maude had been stashing blankets, socks and boots for the rescue they'd been planning for months. Lilyfax donned some black work boots under her red dress, wrapping a quilt over her shoulders. Camille stood at the edge of the trail. Leo followed her eyes up the mountain where the glow of the Temple fire pulsed behind the trees.

Camille's eyes dropped from the fire to her hands. They were covered in Maude's blood. So too, the front of her dress. She wiped her hands over her belly, as if she could wipe away the stains. Leo fetched and draped a green army blanket over her shoulders.

"I'm sorry," he said, feeling the inadequacy of the words, the foolishness of saying them.

"She was the best soul," Camille said.

"She was," Leo said.

"She was just good down to the core." She looked at Leo. "Why her? Why not me? Why should I make it out alive, and she's up there on the ground, her body cold as stone?"

"I don't know," Leo said.

"It's because of her we're free," Lilyfax said walking toward them.

"Yes," Camille said. She cried, her shoulders shaking. Leo and Lilyfax encircled the girl, hugging her. Her legs buckled, but they kept her upright. Camille leaned onto Lilyfax, resting her head on the girl's shoulder.

They stood this way a long time when a sound echoed through the woods. A shuffling of hooves.

"I'll be right back," Leo said. After making sure Camille was steady, Leo slipped into the trees. Three of the horses from the Temple barn circled in a small clearing. One was black, one brown, the third red and white. Leo approached, careful not to spook them. He spoke to them in a low, even voice.

"There, there. It's okay. I'm your old friend Leo."

They eyed him with suspicion but did not run.

A limb cracked underfoot. The black horse snorted and stepped back. Leo was sure they would gallop away but by some miracle they didn't. He put out his hands on the brown and red horses. They nuzzled him, the way Old Possum used to, back at the widow's. The black horse let Leo approach when he saw the others were calm. The horses had halters but no saddles. He grabbed their leads and led them back to the shed.

To Ezra and Mattis he said, "I'm going back into the woods to see if I can find the other horses. Let's get everyone down the mountain quick as we can." To Mattis he said, "Do you think we can shelter at the church till morning?"

"We can," Mattis said.

Leo returned to the woods. He found two more horses and brought them out. When he returned, Lilyfax had the red and white mare by the reins.

"She's sturdy," Lilyfax said. "We can share."

The girls on foot led the way down the mountain. Leo and Lilyfax rode behind them, with Ezra and Mattis following, each carrying a woman on the back of their horses. Mattis rode down the mountain with the girl called Vey, who was wrapped in a purple shawl, her arms around Mattis.

Leo smiled at Lilyfax's long black boots paired with the red dress. He reveled in her arms around him, the way their bodies wedged together on the back of the horse.

"Did you see the way Wake set Goat aflame?" Ezra said.

"Crazy," Lilyfax said.

"So much knowledge died with that man," Ezra said.

"Knowledge he used to hurt women," Leo said, cutting his eyes. Leo nudged the mare ahead, shutting down the conversation.

"That boy," he whispered to Lilyfax.

"He don't mean no harm," she said.

"It's like he ain't paid attention," Leo said, "to all we've seen. All we've been through. The way things can turn on you. The Shadow Wulver. The way Goat turned on Wake because he took it all too far. The way that beast finished Goat."

"Curiosity killed the cat," Lilyfax said. "Maybe they don't teach that at the Elijah House."

"Guess not," Leo said.

"I know it's been a terrible night. And my heart aches for Maude and the Alchemist. And the widow, I feel for her," Lilyfax said. "But there's a part of me that is so relieved. It's over Leo. We're going home." She squeezed her arms tighter around him.

Leo leaned back into her, resting his cheek against hers.

"And Goodman," Leo said. "I want to get home. I've been thinking about the shingles on that old roof. I wonder if Mr. Goodman's tools are still down by the little church. Reckon I could get a roof up on the house in a few weeks, keep Mama warm. Get it fixed up so Goldfish can come home."

"I'll help you. Just get me down this mountain so I can get out of this damned dress."

Leo eyed the hem of the dress against her leg. "I kind of like it."

"Shush."

"Reckon she's all right? Goldfish?" Leo asked.

"I do, Mister Leo," she said. And Leo believed her. For once, things seemed to be going their way. He thought of Goldfish, of taking her fishing when the cold broke into Spring.

Lilyfax gripped his hand.

They rode for a while in silence, when the mare suddenly drew up, throwing Leo and Lilyfax forward. Leo looked at the ground in front of them. There was nothing. There was no reason for her to have stopped. Then the mare took off running and Leo pulled her halter hard, Lilyfax's arms digging into his stomach, both of them digging their heels into the horse's sides to stay upright. The mare ran off the road and into the woods, onto a trail they hadn't seen before. This trail snaked along the edge of the mountain, and in the moonlight, they saw she was galloping only a few feet from a monstrous drop off.

"Turn her around!" Lilyfax said.

Behind them, they could hear Ezra and Mattis coming through the woods, yelling after them.

"I'm trying," Leo said. "She's gone wild."

"She's gonna throw us," Lilyfax said.

Leo leaned his body away from the drop off, pulled harder on the halter. He rested his forehead against the horse's head, trying to sooth her, afraid she'd get spooked again. The trail snaked back into the woods and narrowed. The mare slowed to a trot.

"Leo," Lilyfax said, "she'll get us lost."

"No," Leo said, "I think she's headed back to the road."

They heard Ezra calling, somewhere behind them.

"Just get the girls down the mountain," Leo yelled out. "We'll catch up."

Ezra said something Leo couldn't understand, and they could hear the dull gallop of his horse in the distance, moving away from them.

Leo stopped fighting the mare, convinced they were headed back to the road. The trail continued to narrow, and Leo struggled to see ahead, the twist of magnolia limbs growing thick around them.

"It's like it's closing in on us," Lilyfax said.

"I know," Leo said. The trees seemed to lean together, blocking the way. Leo felt queasy.

"Oh my god," Lilyfax said.

288

"What?"

"The trees. They're moving."

The twisting magnolia limbs were moving. What was a tangle of tree limbs a moment before was now a cluster of snakes. The roots of the trees emerged as the snow melted. They twisted into dark serpents, and the mare reared, dumping Leo and Lilyfax onto the wet snow.

Leo scrambled to his feet, pulling Lilyfax with him. They looked back to the magnolia branches. The snakes were gone. On the breeze came a girl's voice. A troubled humming, something familiar, something like a church hymn. Then the voice called out to him.

Leo, the voice said, *Come find me. I tried to get better.* Goldfish.

"Do you hear that?" Lilyfax asked, eyes wide.

"Yes," he said. "Stay here."

"Why?"

"It's back. Pretending to be her."

"I'm going with you."

"No," Leo said, with a little too much force. He held his hand up. "I don't want you to go."

Her eyes were defiant. "We've come too far. Seen too much, to go it alone. You don't remember what it was like to float with me in the clouds?"

She squeezed his hands.

"That we've always been together?" she said.

"It's not safe."

"Since ancient times. Ain't that what you told me?"

"Yes," Leo said. He couldn't swallow. "Yes," he said again, pulling her close.

"I go where you go," she said.

The voice called to him again.

Help me Leo. Come find me. I tried to get better. The voice trembled. Goldfish on the verge of tears.

They made their way through the woods, and it wasn't long before she appeared. She was suspended between two trees, hanging in what looked to be a spider web.

"Goldfish?"

I tried to get better.

Leo's heart sank. If Goldfish came to him in the trees, the way Jacob always had, did that mean that—did it mean his sister was dead? Gooseflesh spread over his arms and back.

"Come down from there," he said.

Then Goldfish spoke in the unknown tongue.

"What is she saying?" Lilyfax asked.

To the apparition in the trees, Leo said, "You ain't my sister."

Goldfish laughed. At first it was his sister's laugh, then her voice dropped. Then deeper. A bottomless laugh Leo knew well. He blinked and the girl in the trees was Jacob.

"You're back," Leo said.

Jacob smiled, his lips thick, like broad purple wounds. Then came the twist of the shadows behind him, grays and blacks, folding in upon themselves.

"What is it?" Lilyfax asked.

"It's coming," Leo said.

Behind them the mare snorted and stomped. The five dead boars had appeared, circled her, their eyes glowing like blue coals. The sow came in, goring the horse in her hind leg. Stripe swept her front legs, and the horse was on its back. The boars swarmed her, biting at her with their long canine teeth, goring her with their tusks. The mare whined and rolled. She quieted, the crunch of bone and tearing of meat the only sound.

The Shadow Wulver howled behind them. It stood on its hind legs, walking toward them. It wavered slightly, like a drunken man. It snarled and bared its teeth.

No day for you shall ever come,
No bird's song, nor morning drum . . .

To Lilyfax, Leo whispered "Run!"

Chapter 41

Leo and Lilyfax ran down the mountain, the melting snow and mud slick beneath their feet. Several times they fell, their knees sinking into the cold mush. Finally, they tangled together, tumbling off a steep bank, stopping when they struck a tree. The boar snorted behind them, at times right on their heels, and more than once Leo braced his body for the thrust of a tusk into his back. Yet somehow, they stayed ahead. The Shadow Wulver howled in the distance. Leo knew it could catch them if it wanted: he'd seen how fast it could move. Maybe it was toying with them. Or maybe it wanted them to die in the misshapen, elongated jaws of the boars.

When they reached the road, they turned down hill.

"Where can we hide?" Lilyfax said, panting.

"There's nowhere, not until we get to the church."

"Should we climb?" She pointed at an oak with her chin.

Leo had seen the way the Shadow Wulver could knock down trees as it sprinted through the woods. If they were in a tree, they'd be easy prey.

"No, let's keep moving," he said.

He heard the snorting of the boars, but when he faced the road, he saw nothing. Then a pair of cobalt blue eyes appeared in the dark of the trees, then another. The boars were flanking them. Leo ran so hard his lungs burned.

"Up ahead!" Lilyfax yelled, her thick boots clomping the snow. "The church is just around the bend!"

The curve in the road looked familiar, but Leo wasn't sure.

When they cleared the curve, Leo was heartened to see she was right. The church was there. Ahead, the striped boar stepped out into the road, blocking their path. They slid in the slush as they tried to slow. Behind them, the other boars approached, heads slung low. The sow emerged from the trees to stand beside Stripe. Under the moonlight and away from the shadows, their elongated snouts were more clearly defined, rows of sharp canines between their tusks. Stripe took a step toward them. He huffed, his breath a cloud before his snout.

To their left was the graveyard and Shouting Grounds of Mattis's church, to the right was the forest.

"The Shouting Grounds," Lilyfax said. "Sacred ground — they can't enter."

Before he could answer, she had Leo by the hand pulling him across the road. They ran toward the tree line at the edge of the graveyard. Stripe gave chase, veering off the road. The boars behind them came on then, the night echoing the sound of the galloping undead.

They'd almost reached the tree line bordering the Shouting Grounds when Stripe and the sow cut them off. Something was on the road where they'd stood moments before. Something or someone.

"Hey," a man yelled. "Come up here! You old toads," he taunted the boars. "Come pick on someone your own size!" Leo recognized the voice but couldn't place it.

"It's the man I saw before, the man with the red beard!" Lilyfax said.

"Mr. Goodman," Leo said, his mouth falling open.

The boars behind them headed toward the road, toward Mr. Goodman. Stripe and the sow headed for the road as well, but when Leo and Lilyfax continued running toward the Shouting Grounds, Stripe turned back. The demon boar was so close its breath echoed in Leo's ears. Leo held Lilyfax's hand as tight as he could, fearing the beast might grab her and pull her away into the darkness.

They were steps from the trees, steps from freedom, when the tusk ripped into his side. Leo cried out and fell, tumbling with the beast along the ground. Stripe came for Leo's leg, catching the denim of his pants in its teeth. Leo tried to pull away but the boar held firm. Lilyfax grabbed Leo's arms and pulled him toward the Shouting Grounds.

"Go," Leo said. "Cross over!"

"You go where I go," she said. She was in a tug of war with Stripe, her feet slipping in the slush before she found her footing, pulling Leo forward, the boar's hooves plowing deep grooves into the soft earth. Leo struck the boar's broad head with his fists, but it had no effect. Finally, Lilyfax gained the upper hand, stepping through the trees onto the sacred ground of the graveyard, pulling Leo's shoulders through. She and Stripe continued their struggle, until finally Leo was past the trees.

Stripe stepped past the trees, his dog-like snout still gripping Leo's pant leg. Then the boar cried out, lifting its hooves as they sizzled in the snow as if burnt from some unseen source of heat. Finally, it let go and backed away.

"It worked!" Lilyfax said.

Leo wanted to answer, but his side burned, as if someone held a hot coal against his skin. He couldn't speak. She helped him to his feet and together they limped to the back of the church and up the stairs. Inside the sanctuary, Lilyfax eased Leo back on the first pew. Ezra, and Mattis rushed over.

"What happened?" Ezra asked.

Leo grunted in reply. He couldn't form words at first. Then he thought about the undead boars outside, heard the groan of the Shadow Wulver in the distance. "Is the door locked?" he asked.

"We don't lock the door," Mattis said. "It's God's house. Not ours."

Leo struggled to his feet.

"Wait Leo," Lilyfax said. "What're you doing?"

He limped to the back of the church, found the flagpole, struggled to place it in the door. He hobbled back to the pews and fell in beside one of the women from the Temple. She slid down to give him room.

"You heard Mattis," Ezra said. "We shouldn't lock it."

"Leave it be," Leo said. Then his side seized so violently he bent over to vomit in the floor between his feet. He then lay back on the pew, the room spinning before his vision narrowed, the world fading into darkness.

Leo woke to the sound of someone banging on the church doors. Ezra and Mattis were at the back of the church looking out, debating whether to open the door.

"No," Leo said. "You know what hunts us."

"What if it's Mr. Goodman?" Lilyfax asked. Leo had forgotten about Mr. Goodman when they'd come into the church, the excruciating pain having consumed his thoughts. He struggled to his feet and headed to the back of the church.

"Is it him?" he asked.

"There's a man on the stoop," Mattis said.

"I can't see his face," Ezra said.

Leo jerked the flagpole through the door handles and pulled open the door.

Mr. Goodman was on the front porch. He made eye contact with Leo, whispered, "Fret not, Leo. Goldfish lives."

Mr. Goodman took a step forward when the striped boar leapt across the porch, knocking him to the ground. Then the sow emerged, her eyes like blue flame, followed by the other undead boars. They leapt on Mr. Goodman, biting at him, their long canine jaws snapping.

Leo stepped out, but Ezra held him back.

Then something red shone through the herd, and one of the boars was thrown back onto the ground. Under the boars, emerging from them, was the red fox. There was no sign of Mr. Goodman.

"Mr. Goodman?" Lilyfax said.

"We have to help him," Ezra said.

The red fox was at least five times his normal size when he shrugged off the last boar. It bit into one of them, tearing open its flesh. The boar shrieked and ran away into the night. Then the red fox grabbed another, besting it as well.

The fox had thrown off three of the boars when Leo saw something out in the road. It was the familiar twist of cloud, forming a pillar as it floated along. This time it did not dance between the trees, nor did it tempt him with his brother Jacob. It grew in the moonlight, swelling, its surface undulating with black and blue streaks. Then the head of the Shadow Wulver pushed through as if it were behind some dark shroud.

"Mr. Goodman," Leo yelled. "Quick! The wulver is coming."

Lilyfax and the others yelled and waved at the red fox.

The red fox turned toward Leo, the gold flecks of its eyes gleaming in the lamp light. As it stared, Stripe caught it in the side, gnarled tusks sinking deep. At that moment, Leo felt a deep pain in his own side where he'd been gored. He doubled over, the world spinning.

The Shadow Wulver pushed through the pillar now, floating along the air before touching down on the road. It galloped toward the church yard, leaping through the air to catch the red fox in its teeth. The horrible crack of bone. The Shadow Wulver shook its head violently before letting the fox drop. It fell limp, its eyes losing their light.

"No," Lilyfax yelled.

Ezra and the others were yelling at the wulver when Stripe came slowly up the stairs toward them. They backed into the church.

"He can't come in here," Ezra said. "It's sacred ground."

Mattis closed the double doors, and they were working to bar them with the flagpole when Stripe rammed the door. The boys were thrown to the floor as the doors banged open against the walls.

The sow joined Stripe, and they marched into the church, down the center aisle.

The girls from the Temple screamed and ran toward the altar.

Leo looked to Camille. "Take them out back, the doors behind the pulpit. Get them out of here."

Camille, Vey, and the other girls ran out of the church, Leo and the others hoping to follow, but when Leo looked back, all the boars were in the church. Stripe and the sow had Lilyfax and Ezra cornered on one side, Leo and Mattis pinned by the other two opposite.

The Shadow Wulver howled. Its enormous head emerged through the door, and it crept through the church, the red fox in its jaws. The monsters had crossed over, there was nothing to stop them.

"How're they in here?" Ezra said. "I thought they couldn't come in. Even Satan has to follow the rules."

"I don't know," Leo said. Stripe moved closer to Lilyfax.

The Shadow Wulver slunk through the church. It let the red fox drop and lifted its head. It roared so loudly the church windows shattered, raining shards of red, green, and green over everything.

Then the Shadow Wulver crept toward Lilyfax.

Mine the girl shall ever be,
No prison cell of ancient tree.

The striped boar dipped its head and backed away from the girl. The Shadow Wulver cackled, lowering its body, positioned to strike.

There was fear in her eyes, a redness to her cheeks from the cold. For a moment, Leo was up with her again, racing through the air above the earth. He felt her cheek against his own, the warm of her skin when she lay on his shoulder. He remembered her face from the days before the world began, when they knew each other before men walked the earth.

"Stop!" he yelled. He stepped toward the wulver.

The Shadow Wulver tensed its shoulders, faced Leo.

"I'm the one you want," he said. "Take me."

"No Leo," Lilyfax said.

The Shadow Wulver squared its body with Leo. The deep cackling laughter came in waves, running through them, rattling Leo's very spine. It spoke to Leo in his mind.

The gift of death you'd have me give?

The gift of death, to let her live?

"You'll have to kill us both," Leo said. He walked toward the Shadow Wulver. Suddenly a gust of wind rushed through the sanctuary, but it didn't come from outside. The wind whipped at their clothes, running circles through the pews. The Shadow Wulver's eyes darted around the sanctuary as it snarled. Hymnals and Bibles were blown through the church in a twist of wind, and Leo ducked to avoid being struck. At the center of the church, near the altar, a burst of white cloud formed. Then the head of the Silver Wulver emerged, its face of lightning so bright they all had to look away. As its body formed, the pews in the church were knocked on their sides. The Silver Wulver dropped its head. It threw off so much light the church was as bright as a spring morning, and just as warm. It continued to grow as it moved along. It stood on its hind legs, its head raking the high ceiling of the church.

The Silver Wulver paused at the body of the red fox. It scooped the fox up with a paw and pulled it to its chest. The fox disappeared into the body of the wulver. It then dropped to all fours and faced the Shadow Wulver. The Shadow Wulver did not back down, baring its fangs, cobalt eyes ablaze. They roared at each other, shaking the walls of the church.

The Silver Wulver leapt over the Shadow to the back of the church where it grabbed the striped boar by the spine. Its jaws clamped down pulverizing the boar's bones with a sickening crack, the light leaving its eyes. The Silver Wulver then took up the sow and did the same, hurling its carcass across the floor. The three other boars ran out of the church into the forming dawn.

The Silver Wulver then turned on the Shadow Wulver. It raised its head skyward and howled, but what came out was more of a roar, like the rush of a storm through the mountains, the shaking of an earthquake.

The Silver Wulver pounced on the Shadow, pushing it around the church, the pews slamming into the walls, splintering. They twisted in a thrash and blur, until at last the

Silver Wulver emerged, the Shadow Wulver's neck held fast in its teeth. The Shadow Wulver whined like an angry barn cat as it was pulled through the church. The Silver Wulver stood up on its hind legs, dragging the Shadow Wulver along by the nape of its neck.

The Silver Wulver dragged the Shadow Wulver out of the church and through the graveyard onto the Shouting Grounds. Leo and the others followed. Blue flame flashed where the Shadow Wulver's body touched the sacred ground, its cries growing louder, more desperate.

The Silver Wulver dropped the Shadow Wulver in the melting snow at the center of the Shouting Grounds, and an enormous blue flame rose around the beast. The Shadow Wulver twisted and jerked into a cloud of shadow, then back again. It did this over and over, once emerging with a blue bear's body, and the long reptilian snout of the beast that had taken Goat over the edge.

Above, the trees began to shake. They were full of black and blue butterflies. They swarmed over the beast, filling the pink morning sky. They covered the Shadow Wulver, swallowing its body in a huge mound. Finally, the Shadow Wulver fell silent. One of the butterflies on its body flickered silver. Then another. Soon there were thousands of silver butterflies covering the earth. They ascended into the trees. Once they were all off the ground, nothing remained there.

Leo looked for the Silver Wulver, but it was gone. Then Leo's legs weakened, his side burning with a bright pain that worked through his body. He fell to his knees, Lilyfax's arms around him.

Chapter 42

March 1932

He'd forgotten the way it looked, the sunlight, the way it moved slowly over the earth, gently pushing its way behind the mountains, wrapping around the trunks of trees, crowding the thin shadows that held on briefly before disappearing. Leo had also forgotten the way it felt, the sun's rays on his skin, a feeling that hadn't just disappeared because of the change of seasons. It had become something foreign and unfamiliar in the days of the Shadow Wulver, and of Wake and the Temple. But now Leo opened his palms to feel it, took off his jacket to let it warm his arms and back. He wanted to lay down in the grass and let it move through him, seep into every pore.

Beside him, Lilyfax held up her chin, the sun pinking her cheeks, just the hint of her dimples showing through. The two of them walked along the road to the widow's and Lilyfax reached over to hold his hand, interlacing her fingers with his. For months, after the battle of the wulvers in the church, they'd struggled. Moving through the world, they looked ever over their shoulders, always expecting something to emerge from the shadows. Eventually they stopped watching, craning their necks, bracing themselves for what evil that might come. Nightmares jerked Leo awake many a night, but eventually they began to subside. They became less skittish, more convinced that maybe, just maybe, it was over. Each sunrise brought a bit more peace, a bit less fear.

"I've always known you," she said.

"I know."

"Since ancient times," she said.

Leo didn't answer. It was all too much for words, for it was everything. It was in the trees and leaves that rattled in the wind, the warmth of sunlight and the smell of pine and green moss.

When they entered the last curve in the road before the widow's, Lilyfax stopped walking. They faced each other. She looked as if she might speak. Instead, she smiled, wide this time, her dimples sparking. Leo put a hand to her neck and pulled her close. They kissed, the sun warming their cheeks and necks.

When the house came into view, the widow was on her rocking chair. When she saw them, she waved. They let go of each other's hands.

"Well, hello there, strangers."

"Hi," Lilyfax said.

They sat in chairs on either side of her. For a moment, the three of them stared at the green mountains, a cloud floating lazily between two peaks.

"Funny how fast spring has sprung up this year," the widow said. "It came on quick when the sun returned."

"Yes," Leo said.

"I've had enough cold to last a lifetime," Lilyfax said.

They sat for a moment in silence.

"I brought it," Leo said at last to the widow. "If you're sure you're ready?"

"I prayed on it a long time," the widow said. "I couldn't consider it when you first came down the mountain. But now I'm ready."

Leo took the leather-bound book from his knapsack. It was the book the Alchemist had given him.

The widow rubbed her fingertips over the leather as if it were a precious text. She opened it and flipped through the pages. Leo and Lilyfax peered over her shoulders.

There were handwritten notes on the pages, alongside funny drawings and diagrams of objects Leo did not recognize.

"What are them marks?" Lilyfax asked.

"They're formulas, I reckon," said the widow. "I seen them in some of my science books, ones like these."

The widow flattened the pages out with her palms.

"I can't believe what he done for those girls," the widow said.

"He's the reason they're alive now, him and Maude," Leo said. "That we're all alive."

"I felt like I didn't know him, we got older," the widow said. "I hate I turned him away. I didn't understand what he'd become. I had a lot of fear about so many things."

"He knew that," Leo said.

"Did he?" the widow asked. "I heard things. You know how people talk. That he'd gone over to the devil. That crowd he ran with, how he was selling them potions and hard liquor."

Leo and Lilyfax met eyes.

"I don't agree with all he done, but he was a good man, in the end, wasn't he?" the widow said.

"Yes, he was," Leo said.

Tears glazed her cheeks. One bubbled over one of the pages. The page had all kinds of shapes and letters drawn on it. The title of the page read, *An Elixir for Sleeping.*

On the page opposite, there was a poem.

Leo read the poem aloud, in a near-whisper:

> *let the sunlight wake you*
> *forget to wind your clocks*
> *let time pour out like molasses*
> *like honey and butter on your plate*
> *mixing like ninny made*
> *biscuits in the morning,*
> *cornbread in the skillet by night.*

"I never knew he wrote poems," said the widow.

Before Leo could answer, he heard footsteps on the porch.

"Leo!" A girl's voice.

Goldfish sprinted over and hugged Leo's neck. Leo kissed the top of her head. She smelled like spring rain.

"We still a goin'?" she asked. "You promised!"

"Of course we are," Leo said. Goldfish pulled away, and bounced on her toes, back and forth from one foot to the other, like a honeybee bopping between flowers.

"Yay!" Goldfish said. She twirled, her head tilted back like a ballerina's.

"Where is your brother taking you?" the widow asked the girl.

"It's a very special surprise," Leo said. "For a very special girl."

"Come on Leo, come see the knitting I done. The widow taught me how to do it."

The widow beamed. Leo and Lilyfax followed the girl inside.

Leo and Lilyfax held hands as they walked the trail known as Dog Leg Gap. Goldfish skipped along ahead of them, darting in and out of the trees.

"Did you get the walls painted at the chapel?" Lilyfax asked.

"Believe it or not Hank helped me," Leo said.

"That's two weeks in a row now. What's gotten into that boy?"

In addition to helping Leo in his duties as caretaker for the Brookside Chapel, Hank had also helped Leo and Mattis replace the curling wood shingles on top of the family's house.

"Ever since Mama got that job at Wilson's, he's been a lot more agreeable," Leo said.

"He's afraid you'll pull out the big bad wolf is all," Lilyfax said. "Reckon that changes a boy."

"Reckon?" Leo said. "I tell you what. Mattis is something with woodwork."

"What about Ezra?"

"Ain't heard from him. Went by the Elijah House, he wouldn't come out. Sent somebody out to tell me he was studying."

Lilyfax thought about this for a moment. "Y'all going down east tomorrow?" she asked.

"They are," Leo said. He rubbed the edge of the tickets in his pocket. Train tickets he'd bought so his family could go see Daddy in the pen. He had contemplated going himself, but he wasn't ready.

"I'm glad they're doing that," Lilyfax said.

"Me too."

"How much further, Leo?" Goldfish asked. There was still a scratch in her voice. Noticeable, but nothing like before. She glowed in the sunlight, Leo thought. Her skin grew more tan as the days grew long.

"You see that opening down there, in the trees?"

"That it?"

"Go down that a way."

The grass in the field beyond the thicket was lush and green. It was as soft as bird feathers underfoot; Leo and Lilyfax kicked off their shoes following Goldfish's lead. The three of them made their way to the center of the clearing and sat down. That's when Leo felt the sting in his side. It was only when he moved certain ways that it returned, a pain he forgot completely until such moments.

"Do you think Mama will like it?" Goldfish asked.

"The shawl?" Lilyfax asked.

Goldfish had been using the knitting skills the widow had taught her to make a shawl for Mama to wear to church.

"Oh, she's bound to love it," Leo said. "I like how you put purple in there."

Goldfish smiled.

A slight breeze moved over them, and Leo stared up through the canopy to glimpse the sky awash in blue. A new kind of calm rested his bones, a sense that he, Lilyfax, and his family had found their way in the world, that things were finally set right.

Goldfish closed her eyes. Her eyelids perfectly still, so different from the nights when she lay in the bed fevered and sick, her lids squeezed too tight, her eyes fitfully darting beneath them. Now the girl was as still as a painting, the soft rising of her chest and the gentle twitch of her hair the only moving things. Lilyfax too closed her eyes.

Leo closed his own eyes, and rested his head back, face skyward. He listened to the forest. Its energy weaved through the grass around him, washed over him in waves. He heard the rustling around them and knew they were there.

"Bunnies!" Goldfish said.

When he opened his eyes a crystal rabbit nuzzled the girl's leg. There were dozens of them.

"There's so many," Lilyfax said.

Leo watched as they petted the magical rabbits. Some bounded back and forth between the girls. Leo rested his hand on one near his leg. It was cool, as if frost glazed its fur.

"You knew they'd be here?" Lilyfax asked.

"I didn't," he said. "I hoped."

"I ain't ever seen nothin' so beautiful," Goldfish said.

"You know," Leo said, "I bet they're thinking the same thing about you."

Goldfish stood and walked through the clearing, the crystal rabbits following her. She twirled, arms outstretched, hands skyward.

Epilogue - Ezra

The other boys in the library were too loud, as usual, interrupting Ezra's sacred calligraphy practice. He couldn't understand why they came to the library to cut up. Why not go outside, why not walk one of the empty hallways, visit the atrium? Why did they come here? Was it just to torture him?

He cut them a look, eyes low, glaring. They fell quiet, at least for a moment, turning back to their books. He thought of Wormley, of how the man's brains had been pink and red. Pictured opening the skulls of each boy, one by one, just the same. Only he'd use his hands to pry them open, he didn't need a rock.

What Ezra longed for was a library all his own. How could one study the great philosophers, the deep religious thinkers with so many people chattering about? How could the answers be found when one couldn't even find a quiet place to think?

He held the quill in his hand. He dipped it carefully in the ink and laid the edge of the tip against the white paper.

That's when it came again. The ringing. Something like a headache, but worse. Much worse. Ezra dropped the quill and pushed his fingers into his temples. He squeezed as hard as he could.

Over his shoulders, the boys whispered. There he goes again. What's wrong with the Little Priest?

Ezra jerked his chair from under the table and stood up, spilling the black ink over the pages. It ran over the table, and down one of the legs to the hardwood floor.

He bumped into a few boys as he exited the library and turned to walk down the stairs to the boiler room. In the basement there were no people. A place he could think. He could contemplate all he'd learned, all he'd read. Down here, he could ponder what great men had to say about the world, of man's place in it. He could run things through his mind again and again, like the sound of the woman who had moaned in the unknown tongue before walking across hot coals when he'd gone again to see the Gelders. Or the things Wake had said about his magic. These moments he re-lived to look for meaning, to look for truth. He was a seeker, always would be. Maybe this was the answer? What he'd always been seeking?

Then the whisper of his mother's voice, words he couldn't understand. He was back in the lake, his ears beneath the warm water. She had something to tell him. He closed his eyes and focused. What is it, mother?

Then his head was full of whispers, just a mass of them, swirling over every thought in his head. He tried to push them back, but they wouldn't go.

Let me in, *it said.* I'm coming anyway.

No, *he said.* No!

His mother's face in the darkness atop the boiler, her eyes just catching the red light. She whispered:

I am the darkness, and I am night

I'll eat your dreams and steal the light - -

Ezra opened his eyes then. It came over him, the wailing. It was both within him and without him. It was everywhere at once. He welcomed it. Leaned into it. Stretched out his limbs to receive it.

No more running.

No more hiding.

Ezra held out his hand and studied the flame forming there in his palm; admired the black and red swirling.

Acknowledgements

There are more people I could thank than space allows, for helping this book find its way into the world. Thanks to Casey for being my first, most brilliant reader and for indulging the midnight poet. I want to thank my ancestors, especially Christina and Leonard Clark, whose beautiful Appalachian voices touch these pages. Thanks to Cowboy Jamboree Press and Adam Van Winkle for editorial insights and believing in this book. Thanks to Ivy Pochoda for looking at early drafts and encouraging a new novelist to keep going. Thanks to Eric Nelson for reading the earliest pages and providing feedback. Thanks to my FAB4 critique partners: Laura Platas-Scott, Christine Schott, and Becky Cartwright. Thanks to all the faculty at the Converse MFA program, but especially Marlin Barton, Leslie Pietzryk, and Bob Olmstead who spent the most time with this book and these characters. I want to thank early readers Barry Dickson, Meagan Lucas, Shawn Cross, Jeff Frisbee, Joey Dorin, and John MacIlroy for your generous time and thoughtful feedback. A very special thank you to Susan River Madison for helping me craft a stronger voice for my female characters. A special shoutout to the Threaderati for supporting The Monk and for your ruttish ways; see you in twenty-five years. Thanks to the folks who took the time to read and offer blurbs for this book, and all you do for the writing community.

Support authors by taking the time to review their books! Please review *Where Dark Things Grow* on Amazon and Goodreads. Ask your local library and indie bookstore to put it on their shelves and get to know your booksellers!

About the Author

Andrew K. Clark is a novelist & poet from the Western North Carolina mountains, where his people settled before The Revolutionary War. His poetry collection, *Jesus in the Trailer*, was published by Main Street Rag Press. His work has appeared in *The American Journal of Poetry*, UCLA's *Out of Anonymity*, *Appalachian Review*, *Rappahannock Review*, *The Wrath Bearing Tree*, and many others. He received his MFA from Converse College. Connect with him and read more of his work at andrewkclark.com.

Made in the USA
Columbia, SC
26 August 2024

40725750R00186